The Gods of Narzus Trilogy
Book One

When The Gods Play Games

The Gods of Narzus Trilogy
Book One

When The Gods Play Games

Keftra Zink

Contact Info: kefirazinkauthor@gmail.com

ISBN: 979-8-9928400-2-5

Table of Contents

Dedication

For all the people
Who were told
Your magic is too weak
For you to be a badass.

Spoiler, you are a badass.

Author Note and Trigger Warning

If you are related to me, either stop here, set the book down, and walk away or get really cool about some stuff really quickly. I'm only going to say this once and it's on you if you don't listen. I will look you straight in the eye, at the next family function, knowing you know exactly what freaky, weird stuff is in my head. Again, I love you, but not every book is for every reader.

Okay, for everyone else and the family brave enough to continue, here's my warnings. There is **swearing** in the book. Fuck and shit are these guys favorite words. There's **sex** too. Multiple guys, one girl and they all love each other a bunch and show it, in detail, on page, a lot. There are also references to **past child abuse** and **SA**, (all remembrances, discussed in depth on page, but nothing any of the main people did). There are on page significant **panic attacks** based on the SA, and they go deep, intense, and scary. Also, there is **homophobia**, and an intense emotional reaction to **sexual self-discovery**. These issues are huge to the story and cannot be skimmed over and still understand the plot.

Other issues in this book include:
- Forced violence and fighting
- Blood
- Murder and death
- Forced proximity
- Issues with alcohol
- Governmental overreach and abuse with talk of a superior race
- Magical poisoning for forced control

I think you get it. This book is challenging on a lot of issues. Reader be warned and as always, I care about your mental health more than I do readership. If you have any specific triggers that you would like spoilers on, please feel free to reach out to me on social media/email and I will willingly tell you as much or as little as you want to determine if you will feel comfortable reading this book.

As a final note, no matter what the current clues people are using to determine if an author used AI for their book, I did not. Nothing in this book was done with AI. It was written with my own blood, sweat, tears, sleepless nights and grueling days. Do not feed into the witch hunts for AI generative art. And do not feed this work into generative AI by using an AI checker (because that's what you are actually doing when you use those, giving the work to AI so that it can be used for plagiarism rather than protecting from it).

And family be warned, if you read this, I will ask you about it right in front of my mother with zero shame.

Love, Kefira Zink

Note from the Council of the Gods Games Realms-wide

The following is a recreation of the true events of the Three Hundred and Seventy-Fifth Gods Games, in the city of the gods, Veirveil, on the continent of Nazus. The records have been obtained by audio and video recordings taken from the games themselves, with assistance of Drila, Nazus goddess of games and trials, the current Gods Games officiant. As is required by the official rules of the Gods Games, the record has been written from the perspective of the leading human witch and poetic license has been taken to fill in any details unknown and unknowable for the most accurate creation of the required Manual of the Gods Games record.

In following of the regulations of the creation of Manuals of the Gods Games, this record will be translated into all known languages for available access by all gods and humans after passing their twenty-fourth birthday and, in the case of the humans, a blue blood test. In an effort to allow the greatest understanding by the largest number of readers, all scientific information, including names of animals, foods, plants, medicines, magical workings, etc. will be translated to something of a similar nature known by the realm to which the translation will be sent. Original transcripts in their original language are available by request with proof of the linguistical understanding of requesting persons. Any such requests are to be sent to the officiating council of the gods from which the record originates. The Council of the Gods Games Realms-wide is not responsible for any mistranslations, misrepresentations, or errors within these records.

Gods Games Score Board

This scoreboard can be used to keep track of the witch players and their gods position within the games. The witch is listed first with their god(s) second and the pantheon or suspected mantle of the god listed afterwards in the parentheses.

Suggested use:

Fill in the blank space for each game with the team's total points followed by their current standings. I. E. Under Game 1, Amanda & Tholdir: write 10 points (1st place)

Suggested Pronunciation Guide:

Amanda: ah-MAHN-duh
Aretha: ah-REE-thah
Asteria: ah-STEER-ee-uh
Bokysus: bahk-EE-suhs
Damek: dam-EHKH
Drila: DREE-lah
Esnir: es-NEER
Iella: ai-EHL-ah
Isis: EYE-sis
Jinx: JEENKSS
Leander: lee-AHN-dur
Nazus: NAH-suhs
Raven: RAY-vuhn
Saffron: sahf-ROHN
Tholdir: tohl-DEER
Uesis: OO-ehs-ees
Velmos: VEL-mohs
Veirveil: VER-veal
Wren: REHN
Ydum: EE-duhm
Zodum: zoh-DUHM

Cave Trial Arrival & Room Designation	Game 1 (Sept 6) Nature	Game 2 (Sept 13) Weather	Game 3 (Sept 20) Protection	Game 4 (Sept 27) Life & Death	Game 5 (Oct 4) Animalism	Game 6 (Oct 11) Strength & Combat	Game 7 (Oct 18) Intellect	Game 8 (Oct 25) Senses	Game 9 (Nov 1) Creation	Game 10 (Nov 8) Wild Card
1st: Amanda & Tholdir (Flames)										
2nd: Isis & Esnir (War)										
3rd: Aretha & Zodum (Charity)										
4th: Damek & Iella (Chance)										
5th: Saffron & Velmos (Sky)										
6th: Asteria & Wilros (Messages)										
7th: Leander & Bokysus (Mockery)										
8th: Jinx & Byder (Hunt), Ydum (Nature), & Anarus (Obsurity)										
9th: Wren & Kutar (Storms)										
10th: Raven & Uesis (Music)										

Chapter One

I HAVE THE WORST birthday in the world. I've known this since I was old enough to understand pretty much, well, anything. Oh, don't get me wrong. My birthdays have never been bad. My parents always made them as nice as possible, with parties and friends and treats and all that other stuff you do for your children to make them feel special.

My parents have always been very good about birthdays especially because it's the one day of the year that they could devote all of their attention to just one of their children without feeling like they were slighting the others. I mean, with eight of us, it did get really hard growing up to get any real quality personal time with Mom and Dad no matter how much they tried. So, birthdays have always been extra special because we always knew, barring a tragedy, that this one day a year is our chance to get them both all to ourselves.

Except this one. Everyone, on their twenty-fourth birthday, on that exact day at the exact time of their birth, must report to the testing center. No excuses, no delays, no exemptions. You must be tested on that day and that day only. I remember when Ganna, my third oldest sister, turned twenty-four. She was so sick. The healer demanded there was no way she could report to the testing center. Her fever was so high she was delirious and she could not stop shivering.

But no. She had to go. My father had wrapped her in blankets and carried her across the village to the testing center. Luckily, there hadn't been a line and so they didn't have to wait in the freezing bitter cold for her turn. She got tested, and Dad immediately scooped her back up and walked back to the healer's house, where she spent two more weeks fighting the pneumonia my parents swear she got by being forced to go outside.

So, yeah. No exceptions. I don't mind that I have to go to the testing center on my birthday. I don't mind that it's going to take time out of the one day that

I should be able to do anything and everything I want. The problem is that it's September fifth. Today is September fifth and that's the day the games begin.

Most parents purposely try to have their children in the early winter for this exact reason. The evening of September fifth is the best birthday, when it's too late and the carriage has already left for this year. When you go to the testing center and get tested, if the results mean you have to go to the games, you have an entire year to prepare. But because when the child will be born exactly is too unpredictable, most parents shoot for something closer to November or December. The beginning of the year, after the winter solstice, is even good. Anything is better than August or early September, where you only get days or weeks to prepare. Fall equinox to spring equinox, that's the goal.

For the most part, a little birth control in your morning coffee or tea works well to make that happen how you plan. Queen Anne's lace when you don't want babies. Red clover when you do. It is almost foolproof. Almost.

My parents got it right for seven of us. Dahlia was born in November. Samantha was born in January. Ganna was born in December. Shearah was born in October. Myrna was born in March. Ophelia was born in February. Catarina was born in April. They thought Catarina would be the worst one with only four and a half months to prepare if she was chosen. But then, one oops. One 'I thought we were done. Seven daughters is everyone's dream prefect family, why would we want another one?' And then, welcome to the world... me. Early in the morning on September fifth. On the day the games begin, in time for the carriage. The time between my test and going to the games is mere minutes. I won't even have time to tell my parents if the test comes back blue. Not that I think it will. It didn't for any of my sisters.

There's no line for me just like there was no line for Ganna. For Ganna, it was just luck. For me, as I said, it's because no one would plan to have a child this time of year. So, when I walk up to the testing center at six-forty am on the dot, the exact time of my birth twenty-four years ago, the man at the testing center door is bleary eyed and yawning. He hasn't had to do any work for several weeks.

The testing center is not the nicest building in the village, but it is one of the better constructed ones. Of course, it is. The gods don't want their testing equipment broken or marred by the mud and dirt that permeates every other building in the village. So, this building has a solid door rather than the wood sheets pressed together that everyone else has as a door. It's also built out of stone and mortar with a real slate roof supported with wood beams. Most homes are constructed with mud and daub and just a thatch roof that has to be replaced often. The only other building this nice is the High Priest's house, but it would have to be since that's where the gods and other high priests will go if they visit us. Not that they ever really do. We are too backwater for that.

The testing center is a cold building though, with no feeling in it. The healer's hut is nicer, in my opinion. Mud and daub with a thatch roof, like the rest of us, but always with a cheery fire in the fireplace and the spicy scent of the herbs and tinctures the healer needs to conduct her work floats around so much you can smell it from outside the hut. Plus, Granny Helen is the sweetest woman and going to her for anything, even if it's not really a physical health issues but just something on your mind, always makes you feel better. She's as much the village therapist as she is the village healer. If her hut is the heart of our village, the testing center is the cold blade at its neck.

"Jinx Bloodmorrow?" The sleepy man at the door asks, as if anyone else would be standing at this door in September.

"Yes." I tell him. Along with the worst birthday, my parents thought it would be hilarious to give me a silly name. I love my parents, but who the fuck names their kid Jinx? I guess they knew what my life would be long before I was born.

The man barely looks up, his speech memorized by now. He turns his eyes quickly back down to the book in his hands. "Go inside, wash your hands at the basin provided, then prick your finger with the provided test kit, and allow at least one but no more than three drops of blood to fall onto the provided litmus paper. If you put too much blood on the strip, you will be forced to redo the test with another finger. So, unless you want more than one poke, do it right the first time. I will be right behind you to verify the results."

I nod once and walk through the door. The inside of the building is as sterile as the outside. The whole place is only the one room. Four walls. The door opens into the center of the east wall. On the south wall, a basin stand, that could not be plainer if they tried, waits for me. The plain, unfinished wood of the stand holds a bowl that is a plain white glazed clay, the whiteness turning almost gray from time, a matching graying from age pitcher sits below the bowl and a threadbare white towel is draped on the towel rack on the side of the stand. There's a bar of coarse white soap sitting in the bowl. I take the pitcher and wet my hands with the frigid water, then suds up the soap scrubbing my hands, making sure to clean the dirt under my nails from helping my mother plant autumnal flowers in the raised beds in front of our home yesterday. Then I use the cold water to rinse them and scrub them dry with the towel.

Turning from the basin, I see a long, rectangular table along the north wall. It's empty right now, but I guess that the table is where they store the testing kits needed for the next year. The testing center will get a new shipment of them tomorrow, once the games officially start and are closed for the year, meaning anyone tested after this morning will not have to join the games until next year.

In the middle of the room is three more tables, round this time. During the months when there are the most birthdays, these tables can be full of people taking their test. Shearah said that when she took her test, she had to wait over twenty minutes past her birth time and every spot at every table was taken and there was still a line out the door of people waiting. That would be expected for an October birthday though. Now, the tables are empty except the one lone test sitting on the table closest to me. The test for me.

I walk over to the table and look at the test kit. There's a small white box, made out of a material I don't recognize, with a hole on one side and a rectangular slip of purple paper sitting on a scrap piece of regular writing paper with my name on it. The whole setup is smaller than my palm, but controls the rest of my life. I'm trying really hard not to panic, but my breathing gets faster anyway.

"Any day this year would be good." The sleepy man says from behind me. He's leaning back against another of the round tables, still reading the book in his hands as if it's absolutely fascinating. Which, to be honest, it probably is much more interesting than watching me take my test. He has seen hundreds of these and probably is frustrated that he actually has to work today.

At his urging, I pick up the white box and slide my first finger on my left hand into the hole. As soon as my finger reaches the end of the hole, there is a small click and a sharp bite on the pad of my finger. It doesn't hurt much but I jump at it anyway.

I pull my finger out and see a small drop of blood welling up from where the box bit me. I move my finger over to the purple strip of paper and squeeze my bleeding finger between my middle finger and my thumb to force two drops of blood onto it. The man said one to three drops so I do exactly two, going for the middle ground. They plop perfectly onto the center of the strip and start soaking in as I put my finger in my mouth, sucking on it to assuage the slight pain from the prick.

Red, turn red, I think in my head. For the longest moments, nothing happens. But then the red of my blood fades into the paper and all I can see is the purple it was. I stare at the paper, waiting. If it turns red, I am not fit for the games. Red and I go home, back to my mom and dad and Catarina and Orphelia. My other sisters live elsewhere in the village now, so it's just the five of us and the house is too quiet, but I want to go back there more than I ever have in my entire life.

The paper is still purple. Why is the paper still purple? I've never actually seen the testing before so I don't know if it's supposed to take this long for the paper to change colors. I keep watching. Red goes home, blue goes to the games. That's all I have ever heard the results can be. But the paper is still purple. And still purple. And still purple.

I look up at the sleepy man who was still reading as I did the test. He isn't reading anymore. He doesn't look sleepy anymore either. In fact, he looks confused. I don't think it's supposed to take this long.

"I watched two drops fall, why isn't it…" The man's voice trails off. He's watching the paper as closely as I am. In fact, he's leaning over the table, his eyes mere inches from the strip of paper, close enough his breath his making the litmus strip flutter slightly. He doesn't touch it but seems to be examining it as closely as he can, looking for any changes.

Then, slowly, as we watch, the small strip of paper starts to change. I see a small smear of red start to spread up from the middle of the paper to the top edge and I let out the breath I'd been holding. But then, before I can draw in another, blue starts to spread from the middle of the paper to the bottom edge.

"No." The no longer sleepy man says. "That can't happen." He shakes his head as I stare at him.

"What does that mean?" I stammer. "It's both. How is it both?"

He shakes his head and purses his lips. "Defective. It must be defective."

4

The man wanders away, his steps quick as he goes to the table where the test kits should have been if there had been anymore for this year. He grabs a tiny bottle I didn't even notice was on the table and comes back to me.

Defective. That makes sense. I nod to myself. It happens. Defective tests happen. The paper got wet or was made wrong. That's all. The man pulls out another tiny strip of purple litmus paper from the bottle of extra strips and sets it down on the writing paper. He removes the defective test strip and sets it to the side.

"Use a different finger." The man tells me as he hands me back the white box. I use my first finger on my right hand this time and repeat the test. Two drops, square in the middle of the strip and we wait, both of us holding our breath this time.

The paper stays purple. And stays purple. The man furrows his brow.

"Not again." He says under his breath. But, just like before, red finally starts crawling from the middle of the test strip to the top and blue crawls from the middle to the bottom. "Shit."

The man moves the second test strip and puts down yet another one. "Another finger." This time I only let one drop of blood fall from my second finger on my left hand. The strip stays purple for a really long time, then red on top and blue on the bottom.

The man sets out another strip. "Again!" His voice no longer calm. I can hear the confusion in it. Three drops from the second finger on my right hand. Purple for way too long, then top red, bottom blue.

"What's happening?" I finally ask. "Why is the test doing that?"

The man shakes his head, setting out another strip. He isn't even moving the used ones away now. "I don't know." Ring finger on my left hand. Purple for too long. Red and blue. "Fuck." His voice is barely audible. When he sets out another strip, he doesn't even have to tell me. Ring finger on my right hand. Purple then red and blue. Another strip. Pinky on my left hand. Purple, then red and blue. Another strip. Pinky on my right hand. Purple, then red and blue. Another strip, left thumb. Purple, then red and blue. Another strip, right thumb. Purple, then red and blue.

When he sets down another strip, his eyebrows furrowed and his forehead slightly sweaty, I don't do anything. "I'm out of fingers."

He looks up at me, then back down at the ten red and blue tests strips. "Shit. Shit." The man starts to walk away. "Stay here." He calls over his shoulder to me as he leaves the testing center through the front door.

I wait, watching those paper strips. One of them will change, right? At this point, I think I would even be okay if one of them changed to all the way blue. Do I want to go to the games? Crap no. But anything would be better than this. It's my birthday, for crying out loud. I don't need this today. "Just give me an answer. Any answer. Red or blue. Pick one."

I don't even realize I'm talking out loud to the paper until the man returns with the High Priest and Granny Helen. He brings them over to the table and shows them both the test strips. "Each one was done properly. We tried different fingers and different amounts of blood. But this has been the result every time."

High Priest Reuben Breedlove stares at the paper strips, his face as confused as the testing center worker's is. "Ten times. It can't be a defect in the strips?"

The man shakes his head. "I've used replacements from this bottle before and they worked fine. There was no visible damage to the kit when I opened it."

"And she's pure?" High Priest Breedlove asks.

Granny Helen answers this time, chuckling. "Seven sisters that all came back red. Unless her mother cuckholded her father after that many years, I would say it's a safe bet."

I look between the two men and Granny, wondering what they are talking about. What do they mean pure?

"Seven sisters?" High Priest Breedlove looks at me as if he's just noticing me here. "You're the youngest Bloodmorrow girl. I doubt it was a cuckhold, but get the mother anyway. I want to hear it from her." He stands with his hands on his hips as the testing center man starts walking away, but the High Priest speaks again, stopping him. "Just the mother. We need her to be honest and, with those two, she won't be in front of the father." The testing center man nods and leaves again.

"What's happening, High Priest?" I finally ask. I've never actually spoken to the High Priest directly before. I never had any plans to, except for saying two words during my hand fasting ceremony, if I ever found someone to marry, that is. If my test was red. Now, I've said four words to him, twice what I ever thought I would, and none of them were "I do."

He doesn't answer me and, when I look over at the healer, Granny Helen just shrugs and smiles at me. If she understands, she isn't telling me either. All three of us just stand, waiting, the two of them staring at my tests strips and I stare at them.

The man comes back with my mother finally. High Priest Breedlove stops Mom at the door. Parents are not supposed to come into the testing center. From the door, she can't see my test strips on the table. She looks as confused as I feel.

"What's going on, High Priest?" Mom asks.

"Avalon, I need a straight, honest answer." The High Priest points at me. "Is there any chance at all that this girl is not Maddox's child?"

Mom's face goes pale. "What's wrong with her test?" That isn't the no I expected. I expected Mom to be affronted by the accusation and defiantly deny that my father could be anyone other than my father.

The High Priest takes in a deep breath. "Answer the question, Avalon."

"Maddox is her father. I swear, he is."

The High Priest speaks very slowly and carefully. "Are you one hundred percent sure? Is there even a sliver of doubt at all? Even the most outside chance Maddox is not her father? If you say he may not be, it never has to leave this room. None of us will tell Maddox."

"I swear he is." My mom shakes her head. "I've never been with anyone else. Never."

"Will you take Eecret?" Granny Helen asks. "Would you answer again under the truth leaf?"

My mother nods her head vehemently, one of her hands going to clutch her chest, fear flooding her face. "Yes. There has never been anyone else."

The testing center man, the High Priest and the healer all look at each other.

"What do we do?" The testing center man asks finally.

High Priest Breedlove pinches the bridge of his nose with one hand and rubs his shoulder with the other. "Blue goes, red stays. That's the rules. If there was more time, I could ask, but we are running too late as it is. Put her results, all of them, on the paper and send her to the carriage. If the carriage driver takes her, he takes her. If not, then we know."

Granny Helen nods along, agreeing. "Let the gods decide if half blue means she is fit for the games or not."

My mom, still standing at the door, cries out. "Half blue? What do you mean half blue? How can her test be half blue? I swear, Maddox is her father! I swear it. She can't be half anything!"

High Priest Breedlove marches over and grabs my mom by her elbow roughly, steering her back out the door. "Say nothing about this, Avalon Bloodmorrow. Go back to your home and wait. If Jinx returns home, you just assume her test was red. If she doesn't, well, do you really want those questions if you tell people her test was only half anything?"

The High Priest continues manhandling my mother out of the testing center. I turn to the healer and the man. "What does it mean? Why are you asking about my dad? What's happening?" Suddenly, the panic about having to go to the games is the least of my worries. Could my dad not be my dad?

"The only time tests don't come out right is if the person is not purely witch or god, but something else. If they aren't actually magical at all." The man tells me. "It doesn't normally fail like this," he gestures at my ten tests strips, "but by turning muddy. This? I don't know, the best guess that we have is your father isn't all human, which can't be true if you have the same father as your sisters, since their tests were normal and red."

The only ones in the games are either full gods or full human witches. That I have always known. But children between the gods and humans are so rare, almost no one ever thinks about that. The only time humans and gods ever interact is the games. So, matings of course don't happen that often. And when they do? It's usually big news and everyone knows that child is a hybrid long before it's born. We've never had one in our village that I know of. In the bigger villages, it happens, I guess. Enough for stories about it to trickle down here and fairytales to be written about a god falling in love with a human. Always with a male god saving some poor, desperate female human from her fates, but there are enough of them that children will daydream about it and want to hear the stories over and over as their favorites told around the fires on the long winter's solstice nights. Stories like that are told more here than stories about the games are.

While I think about this, the man is using a tacky substance to glue all ten strips to the writing paper with my name on it. When it's dry, he hands it to me. I look from him to the healer again. "So, I'm going to the games now?"

The man shrugs. "Follow me. The carriage driver will decide. Give your results to him." He starts to walk out the door. The High Priest and my mother are both gone by the time I follow the man out of the door. I follow him around to the back of the building where a horse-drawn carriage waits. A man in all black clothes is sitting in the driver's seat, holding the reigns of a horse. The horse is beautiful, speckled white and brown, and the carriage looks elegant. Made out of some material that gleams in the sunlight, the black paint almost acts like a mirror, reflecting back a warped version of my confused and terrified face as I stand next to it to hand the driver my test results.

The driver looks at my results then looks past me to the testing center man who is standing behind me. "Pure?"

"Yes." The testing center man says.

The driver shrugs and jerks a thumb behind him. "Well, get in then."

I look back at the testing center man, who nods. I go over to the carriage and open the door. A small step drops down as I do and I use it to climb in to the carriage. Once inside, I shut the door and the carriage immediately lurches forward, moving through the mud of the village roads.

I'm going to the games. I have to go to the games. I never really thought I would have to go to the games, but now I am. My tests were inconclusive, but I'm going to the city of the gods and going to be in the games anyway. Crap.

Once the carriage is moving, I tell myself that I cannot freak out. I don't have time to freak out. The ride to the city of the gods will take a few hours at least, I think, and I need to use that time wisely. Most people get months to prepare themselves but I don't. I need to be ready for this and I need to be ready now.

Part of my mind tries to say that I'm not going to actually have to participate in the games, that when we get there and the driver gives whoever runs the games my test results, they'll claim I'm ineligible and send me back home. This is just a short deviation in my life, everything will go back to normal by tomorrow.

But then I realize that it's not a good thing if that happens either. By this point, everyone in the village will know, or at least think they know, that my test results said I am to go to the games. If I return home so quickly, it will cause questions. Questions that apparently might make people believe my dad isn't really my dad. Everyone will want to know why I'm back so quickly and the only thing I could tell them is that the test was wrong. Something that never happens. They won't believe me and I really, really don't want to deal with that confusion.

Being in the games would be better than that mess, I think. So, time to strategize. Not that I actually have any way to strategize. That would require knowing anything at all about the games and I don't. Not really. Greenbriar, my village, has not sent anyone to the games in so long that I don't even know who the last person we sent was. Mom claimed once that someone went to the games when her mother was little, but they never came back so there were no stories from them to learn what the games actually are. Because no one comes back from the games ever. And our village is too small for the gods to ever come to visit, so we can't get information that way either.

All I know is the basics that we learned in school. Twenty people participate in the games every year. Ten humans and ten gods. All of them are twenty-four years old. All of them must be healthy and educated. That's why the gods provide every town with a school as well as the testing center, and help fund the village healer's work. The school in our village is in the basement of the High Priest's house and had all the basic subjects. Math, reading, writing, science, history, gods and goddess comprehension, and the magical arts. The gods, our god comprehension teacher told my class once, take basically the same classes, except instead of gods and goddess comprehension, they take witch comprehension, and instead of magical arts, they take powers and control. Which the first one makes sense. The gods don't need a comprehension class about themselves and neither do we.

The second, though, never did make sense to me. What's the difference between witch magic and god powers? No one ever really answered that in a way I could understand. Sure, they told me often things like, "It's the difference between the roots and the leaves," or "it's about the start and the finish." Yeah, didn't clear anything up for me, really. But I stopped asking and just pretended I understood what they meant after they brought my parents in for a conference with my comprehension teacher and the High Priest in fifth grade to talk about my "lack of understanding."

I still managed to get good grades in almost everything anyway, so I have always just guessed that the real answer is that there isn't any actual difference. Except the gods trying to make themselves feel better and more superior to witches. Since I've never even seen an actual god, much less met one, I've never been able to figure out if there really is any true difference beyond the ones I think the gods want us to believe there is.

Well, I'm about to meet at least ten gods, so I guess I will get the real answers soon. Beyond that, the difference between them and us is that they are obviously much richer than we are. Or at least the ones who sent this carriage are because, damn. The outside of the carriage was that shiny black that made it look luxurious, but the inside is so much more. There are two black benches inside the carriage, one at the front and one at the back, facing each other. I run my hands on the soft, plush velvet bench stuffed with lots of padding. I thought the ride would be uncomfortable when the carriage first started because of how much it rocked and bounced over the muddy road, but the padding is so thick that, other than the obvious movement of turns, I can't actually feel any of the bumps now that we have moved to the harder packed roads that run between the villages.

The rest of the inside of the carriage is red, also velvet but not so plush and padded. The floor of the carriage is even red, the only marring of it the mud my own feet brought in. There's a window, an actual glass window, in the doors on either side of the carriage, covered with a sheer white, really white, fabric. I've been pulling that fabric aside every once in a while, as we travel to see where we are. Not that I could tell since I've never been outside of Greenbriar. But it's nice to at least tell if we are still in the woods, like the ones that surround Greenbriar, or have we moved to some other type of place. We did cross a cobblestone bridge over a river once. That was interesting, but other than that, all I've seen is more trees and more trees.

I make myself think more about what I know about the games. Ten gods, ten witches, all healthy, all educated. All the witches have to have blue tests strips. All the gods have to have red ones. I have no idea what the colors signify, but that tells me that whatever they mean, the gods need to be the opposite of us witches. Or maybe more like us? I think about that for a moment. That's possible. Most human witches get a red test result and can't go to the games. So, a red test from a god may indicate they are more like us than they should be.

If that's the case, then what's the point of the games? I realize I don't even know that. Why are there games at all? Why do the gods make us participate in them? And why only the witches? There are, I learned in school, other humans in the world. Humans that are not witches. They don't live in the same villages as us, or even on the continent of Nazus. They live somewhere else. Far across the seas, the non-witch humans left the continent a long, long time ago and stopped associating with anything dealing with magic. They purposefully left of their own accord because they wanted free of the magic of the witches and the powers of the gods, or so we were taught. But when they did live here, only the witch humans had to test for the games, and the non-witch humans didn't. So, the ability to do magic must be something important to the games.

Not that magic is very strong with the witches anymore. Granny Helen has magic, a whole lot of it. So, does the High Priest. Others in the village do too. My father has some. Mom too, but none of my sisters or I have shown a lot of promise with magic. Yes, I'm a witch, descendant of a long line of witches. My parents both have magic and I have enough that I was included in the magical arts classes at school and can use the stuff in a witch's kit.

Not like Sarah Goodacre. She was in Myrna's year, and never developed any magic ability at all. She had to go into a study hall instead of magical arts class with everyone else. It was embarrassing and shameful. Myrna had been Sarah's best friend until sixth grade when they finally stopped trying to get her magic to develop. Myrna dropped Sarah like a hot potato when they did that, but Myrna is a bit of a snob. I don't know if I would have necessarily dropped my best friend like that, but it definitely was not a good time for Sarah. She didn't even have to test on her twenty-fourth birthday, but was treated like a non-witch human instead and got to forego it.

There was a lot of hope for Catarina, as the seventh daughter of the family. Seven is a powerful number and women always tend to carry more magic than men do, which is why my parents were so happy that they had seven daughters. Most families don't try for that many children even if it's considered a powerful number because you still need to feed and house that many kids if you have them, and I know how much work it took my parents to take care of all of us. Not many families want that much of a burden.

My parents never made us feel like burdens though, and pretty much everyone in town seemed to have the attitude that if any family was going to actually have seven daughters, it would be Maddox and Avalon Bloodmorrow. Those two were so in love, everyone knew they were a love match instead of arranged. That's probably why the High Priest and the healer were so easily convinced Mom wasn't lying about who my dad is. Even now, my parents are the gushiest couple in the village. It was embarrassing when I was younger, but now I think it's cute. Even my one sister who is married isn't so mushy about it in public as Mom and Dad, and she's only been married for a few years by comparison, still in the honeymoon phase, kind of.

I sit back in the carriage. My mind keeps wandering. If I had any clue what was coming, I would know what I should be planning for. But I don't. I don't have a clue. All I know is that it seems like we have been traveling forever, and I didn't even get breakfast this morning. I had to be at the testing center too early. I usually don't wake up until seven or eight, and my stomach doesn't wake up until even later. Coffee is all I can manage that early, but needing to be at the testing center before seven meant I didn't even get that. I look out the window again and, judging by the placement of the sun in the sky, it's probably noon.

I'm definitely hungry. And I have to pee. Another thing I didn't get to do before leaving. I wonder if I knock on the front of the carriage if the driver will hear me. I give it a try and within seconds, the carriage is pulling over to the side of the road. I feel the carriage sway as the driver gets down and comes to open the door.

"What'cha need?" The driver asks gruffly.

"I need to pee." I try not to blush. It's a natural thing and I am not a child. But I don't know this man.

The driver pulls the door wider and gestures for me to step out. I do and find that the woods I saw out of the one left window are not on the right side. There are farm fields on the right side. I cross the road to head into the trees for privacy and hear the driver call out to be quick about it. Luckily, I'm used to using the washroom in the woods, and my rough, gray homespun cloth dress is loose enough but not too long, so I don't have to worry about ruining it squatting in the mud.

Once I'm done, I go back to the carriage. The driver stops me before I get in. "There's some water in that black box underneath the bench. No soap, but at least you can clean your hands somewhat."

"Thank you." I say as I reach for the box and pull it out. I hadn't even looked under the bench I was sitting on. When I open the box, I see there's not only a canteen of water, but also some sandwiches and dried fruit and nut mix in there. Food and water. I've been hungry for no reason.

"How much longer do you think it will be?" I ask the driver as I dump a little water over my hands and rub them together as an attempt at cleaning them.

"Another couple of hours. Games open at sundown, we'll be there on time if we don't need to stop too often." The driver gives me a pointed look as I take a drink of water. Don't drink it all and need a bunch of washroom breaks, he's telling me. I get the message and cut off my drinking to climb back in the carriage.

"By all means, then," I say, climbing back into the carriage, "let's get moving."

The driver doesn't respond, just shuts the carriage door and I feel it tilt as he climbs back up to the driver's seat. The carriage lurches again and we're back on the road.

The games start at sundown. Well, if it's starting so late, and my day already started so early, I should probably try to rest some so I'm as refreshed as I can be for whatever is going to happen. I eat a sandwich, nut paste and strawberry jelly, then a handful of the dried fruits. I don't recognize all of the fruit, since it's a luxury we can't always afford. I avoid the ones I don't know, something green and another one that's orange, and stick to the banana chips and raisins I know, taking only a few more sips of water before putting it all in the box and back under the bench. Then I curl up on the bench and try to rest, doing my best to use my magic and meditation to calm myself faster. Peace, I think as I close my eyes. Give me peace.

Chapter Two

THE CARRIAGE BUMPS, JOSTLES, then stops. I must have actually fallen asleep because we are definitely not in the woods anymore. When I look out the window, we seem to be in some sort of large tunnel. There's plenty of light and I can see the rough stone walls easily. The driver opens the door to the carriage and I step out. The floor is sandy, with so many footprints that they overlap each other.

I look to my left and see we are actually in the entrance of a cave. I can see the mouth of the cave just behind the carriage. Beyond that is just white and blue light, like I am looking at the sky with clouds in it. As I watch, the edges of the light are changing colors, turning slightly pink as if sunset is happening. I turn to the right and see that the cave goes down into darkness. There are torches in brackets along the wall in front of me, creating the light I can see by.

I walk around to the front of the carriage, following the driver, and see him handing my test results to a woman with long black hair and a very white face. Too white skin to be natural. As I watch her look at my results, I realize she must be a god. The touches of pink at her cheekbones look like perfectly done tinted cream rather than natural. Her eyebrows, arched in question at my results, are far too perfectly straight to be real and set over perfectly oval black eyes with lashes so dark and thick I can see them from across the cave. Her clothes, a red flowy dress, are impeccable and made of a shimmery fabric I have never seen before paired with perfectly matching strappy sandals.

Definitely a god. She is just all over too perfect. She looks like she was carved from stone. And she is definitely not happy with my test results. Her mouth pulls down in a frown, wrinkling her unnaturally smooth skin. She looks over at me and crooks her finger, gesturing for me to come over to her.

"Pure?" She asks me the moment I am close enough.

I nod, still not sure what that means other than questioning if either of my parents is a god. "That's what my parents say."

Her eyes narrow and she huffs. "Blue is blue. Good luck with this."

When I don't answer or move, she huffs again. "You are not going to be here long. Not with a result like this, but get over with the others. Blue is blue. You have to compete even if we know you will fail."

Blue is blue. I guess they only require there to be some pure blue on the test for me to be in the games. But somehow, the fact that there is also red there means I'm good enough to play but not good enough to think I will play well. I move to go past the god to where she indicates, and see that there are a lot more than ten people, all human I think, standing around waiting. I try to count, but as soon as I have joined them, the carriage is moving, backing out of the cave, and with it gone, the people start shifting and dispersing around in the bigger space. I can't count while they all keep moving.

What I can tell is that there are a lot of them, too many, and they all look different. There are only a handful of men, with the majority being women. They all have much nicer clothes than me too. I look down at my simple gray dress and bare feet. I didn't even put on shoes this morning since it wasn't cold. I didn't even think about it. Usually, we only wear shoes in the winter when we need to protect our feet from the ice, snow and cold. Shoes are too expensive to buy and too hard to make to wear them all the time and keep wearing them out so fast.

I look at the ground. Everyone else is wearing shoes and none of them look homemade. Crap. These people all come from much nicer places. They probably actually have real schools and teachers. While they all look different from one another, different hair, skin, builds, all of that, it's very clear that they are all the same in one very important way. All the other humans in the games are from wealthy places, places that probably know a lot about the games and what's going to happen. My test results make it clear I already have one disadvantage and the way I look tells me that I have another.

I thought there are only supposed to be ten humans in the game. That's what I've always heard. That's what everyone says. Ten humans, ten gods. But if that's true, why are there, twenty, twenty-five, thirty-two, thirty-six, I finally get an accurate count. Why are there thirty-six humans in this cave? Are they not all part of the games? And if not, who are the extra people?

The goddess clears this all up for me rather quickly. "Now that the last carriage has arrived, we can begin." As she speaks, everyone in the cave turns to listen intently. "Tonight is not the official start of the games, but just a trial to pick teams. There will be ten teams of gods and humans. How many people will be on your team depends on the results of this trial. The idea is that you have a team that works well together. Most of the time, teams will be one male and one female, but exceptions happen. There are no real rules for how the teams are constructed, as long as the rules of the cave trial are followed. If you follow the rules, you will end up with the team you should. If the trial ends and you don't have a team," the goddess points her unnatural eyes right at me, "then you are not worthy of being in the games and will be eliminated."

Well, that sounds ominous. I try not to focus on the word eliminated, while the goddess keeps explaining the trial. "Within the cave behind me are many places to hide. Your job is to use the magic your testing on your birthday deemed you have enough of to do all of the required games. Use that magic, and your knowledge, to hide, and hide well. You may not hide in groups. Wherever you choose to go, you must not be visible to any other humans.

"The gods who are participating in the games will attempt to find you. I know it sounds counterintuitive but the better you hide, the more likely you are to be found by your rightful teammate. Not actually attempting to hide, or not using magic to hide you, will count as not following the rules and will eliminate you from the games. It will also eliminate any god who thought they found you as a teammate, and trust me, they will not be happy when they find out you got them eliminated by breaking the rules. So, hide well. You will have twenty minutes before the gods come after you. Your time starts now."

The goddess moves to the side of the cave entrance and every one of the thirty-six of us scurry off down into the dark cave tunnel. Hide well using magic and knowledge. Well, crap. Happy birthday. Had I had more time to know that I would be coming here, someone may have been able to work with me on magic. At least, more than those stupid magical arts classes. How to hide using magic is not exactly something we were taught. That class, every year, mostly focused on meditating to be able to focus and find your magic, on plants, stones, crystals, and other natural sources of magic, and on creating protection circles and healing salves. What should go into a witch's kit and how to use everything from one. I can meditate pretty well, like I did in the carriage to help myself relax to go to sleep, and know a lot about protection and the plants for salves, but I am not really confident I have enough magic for more than something like that. Maybe that's why my test was all messed up. I have magic but just crappy magic.

I keep moving down the tunnels as I think. At this point I am trying to focus on finding a good hiding spot. But my mind keeps worrying over the magic part. The tunnel splits and then splits again as we move down. At every juncture, some people go one way and other people go the other. I put myself at the back of the pack. That way, when the group splits at a fork in the path, I can follow the smaller group. If the idea is to be away from the other humans as much as possible, then I will go wherever everyone else isn't.

Eventually, there are only ten of us in this group, then five, then just me and another girl. At the next fork in the path, she goes left so I go right. Now, to look for a good hiding spot. I slow down and examine the cave as I walk. There are still torches just often enough that I can see where I'm going, but they are infrequent enough to create pockets of shadowy corners at turns and junctures. There are also stalactites and stalagmites in the cave that make the path move or are grouped next to the walls of the cave that help with making dark hiding spots.

I come to a spot in the trail where three paths converge. The three paths come together to create a rather larger, round, open spot. I stand in the center and look around. There are torches in each of the three paths, but none within the round open spot, making flickering shadows jump all along the walls. I look up and notice that there, just about a foot above my head, one of the cave walls is depressed in a way that makes a shelf that might be big enough for me to curl up in. There are also some small stalactites hanging in front of the shelf, keeping it even further in the shadows.

Best place to hide if there ever was one, if I can get up there. I go over and jump up. My fingers just graze the edge of the shelf. I jump again, having the feel of its height now. My fingers grab the shelf and I brace my feet on the cave wall, then shimmy and pull until I'm high enough to slide the top of my body onto the rock shelf. Once I'm that far, it's just a matter of flipping onto my side and pulling my legs up and I'm well and truly hidden.

I shift until I'm as comfortable as I can get. The shelf is too short for me to sit up and only just barely wide enough to fit me curled in a ball. I slide one of my arms under my head as a pillow and focus on the next part of hiding. Now, I have to figure out how to hide with my magic.

But the problem is I don't think I have great magic. The goddess at the beginning said that our tests showed we have enough magic to do this, but my test was a mess. So, does that mean maybe I actually don't? Magic couldn't be the only deciding factor on the test, though, because Dad, Mom, the High Priest, and Granny Helen never came to the games and they all definitely have good magic. So, maybe my magic is fine and something else made my tests wonky.

I need to figure out how to use my magic to hide, then. Maybe the meditating magic would be good enough, because I definitely am not finding any plants in a cave to work with. Crystals, maybe, but that would mean leaving my perfect hiding spot. If only I had a witch's kit with me, I would have at least a few magical items to work with. But I don't, and none of the other humans had anything with them either. Meaning they probably aren't allowed anyway. So, meditation and hope it is. I close my eyes.

Peace, give me peace. My mind settles and I feel my breathing slow. I don't want to fall asleep, just hide. So, I focus hard on the idea of being hidden. I have always thought that the calming feeling I get when I meditate might actually be my magic working, but if it is, I'm not sure if focusing on anything else like this will actually make my magic do that thing. I've never tried to do it this way. But it's the best hope I have.

Continuing to focus on the idea of peace and staying hidden, I open my eyes again. I have no idea how long it's been or how long we have until this trial is over. No one seems to be coming though. Did I hide too well? Or not well enough? No, I need to focus. Peace and hidden. My teammate will come if I am supposed to have one.

After long enough for my leg muscles to feel cramped, I see movement in the tunnel right in front of me. I can't see down the other two tunnels that connect to this juncture from my position, but there's definitely someone coming down that one. I can't see much since the last torch in that tunnel is behind them, but there is definitely some shadowy figure coming down there. I hear other noises too, making me believe that whoever is coming isn't alone.

There's movement and talking directly below me. "Aw, fuck. You here too?" One voice asks.

"Yeah. You moving on, or staying here?" Another asks.

"I dunno. Give me a minute."

There's a shuffling sound then soft swearing comes from one of the tunnels from the first voice. The second voice calls out to the swearing first one. "What?"

"Ani." The first voice responds, closer again.

"Aw, shit. You too?"

"Well, don't look so pleased to see me." That's a new voice.

"We each come from one of the three tunnels and we all end up here? Where they all come together. Gotta be someone here." I'm losing the ability to tell which voice is which, so I just listen.

"But that would mean we're all on the same team."

"Yeah. Three on one? Not sure the games do that."

"We should check that the sense doesn't go past this spot. Just because you all came from there, doesn't mean that you didn't walk right by someone."

"Then check the other tunnels, Ydum, if you want. Just because you suck at sensing things doesn't mean the rest of us do. I can tell where I'm being led and it's here."

"Fuck, man. Don't be an ass. I'm just trying to help. The games don't do three. At least one of us is wrong."

"Orrrr... you are an idiot and think the training manuals tell you everything."

"Ani, come on, man. Don't start out this way. If we end up on the same team..."

"Listen, I don't even want to fucking be here. I'll be any way I want."

"We all know you don't want to be here, Ani. Blame your parents, not us. Oh wait..."

"Fuck off, man."

"Yeah, low blow, Ydum."

"Hey, just call 'em like I see 'em."

"Fuck you!" I hear scuffling and it sounds like a punch lands and one of them groan. Should I do something? Am I supposed to reveal myself now? That goddess in the red dress did not explain this part well. And there are three of them. She said most teams are one male and one female, but these males just argued about that, so. Shit, I have no idea what's going on.

"Um, guys. Stop fighting for a second."

"What?"

"You split my lip, bastard!"

"Ydum! Shut up a second!"

"Yeah, Ydum, shut up... Wait, what is that?"

"You feel it too?"

"Yeah, man. What is that?"

"It's gotta be our human."

"What the fuck? That feels weird."

"That is the strangest fucking thing ever." That's the one they are calling Ydum. I can tell because he's mumbling around a swollen lip.

"Where is it coming from?"

"The ceiling. It's coming from the ceiling, but how?"

"Guys, step back. Look at the walls from the other side of the circle. There are little spaces up there. Could a human fit in there?"

"How would a human even get up there unless they are crazy tall?"

I see someone walking along the walls of the circular space. They are looking up towards where I am, but they are still too shadowed for me to make out anything about them. They come directly across the circle from me and stop.

"Well, hello. How'd you get up there?" He has to be speaking to me. Two other shadowy figures come and stand right next to him.

One of them laughs. "That's fucking great. A perfect hiding spot."

Ydum, with the split and swollen lip adds, "Well at least you're smart. We know that much."

"You can come down now."

Okay. I slide my legs over the edge and try to lower myself down the same way I got up. But somehow, while getting up was no problem, getting down is a lot more difficult. I have to just let go while my legs are dangling an unknown height above the ground. It can't be far though, right? I let go and the fall is farther than I thought. My cheek scrapes the wall and I land badly, my right ankle twisting under me, making my butt hit the ground painfully. "Fuck."

"Aw, shit. Did our human just break herself before the games even start?"

"Ani!" Not Ydum yells. "Don't be a jackass."

Hands are helping me stand up. Once I am on my feet, my ankle hurts a little, but I know I just rolled it weird, not actually hurt it. I pull out of the hands and step back, brushing the sand from the ground off my dress.

"Where are your shoes?" I look up and find myself staring at three males. The one who asked about my shoes is the same one that helped me up. He's tall, broad, and tan. Dark hair flows down his back to just below his shoulder blades, and his dark eyes are twinkling like he likes to smile a lot. He's wearing a simple cloth sleeveless shirt in dark green and black leather pants. They are simple but definitely nicer than anything I've ever seen before. One of his arms looks like it has faint lines banding around the wrist. A tattoo maybe?

Ydum, recognizable because of the split and swollen lip bottom lip, is much paler than the one who helped me up. Not as pale as that goddess in the red dress, but a normal looking pale. His eyes are vibrant green and his hair is blonde, cut shorter but still long enough so I can tell it is curly. His clothes are also simple, brown soft cotton pants and a blue long-sleeved tunic, both definitely of very fine construction.

The third, Ani I assume since he is neither hurt nor the one who helped me, is very dark. Everything about him is dark, skin, eyes, hair, clothes, well what clothes he's wearing. He only has on tight black pants. His chest is bare and I can see shadows on his chest that makes me think he also has tattoos, although I can't quite make them out since he's still standing in shadows. His black, I think it's black, hair is braided down to the small of his back. His eyes are a mystery since I can't see most of his face through the shadows he's hiding in.

"Um, shoes?" The one who helped me up repeats.

Ani, I think, groans. "Aw, don't tell me she's mute or something."

"Not mute." I say. "Just stunned. I did just fall on my ass in front of three gods. You could give me a second to compose myself, Ani."

The male I think is Ani steps close to me very quickly. Faster than I think he should be able to move across the space. "Do not call me that, human. My name is Anarus, and you will respect it."

I don't let him intimidate me, even if he's very close, staring down at me almost menacingly. "Sorry. It's not like you politely introduced yourselves or anything. I mean, I'm only guessing your names from the fighting I overheard you do before bothering to actually look for me. My name's Jinx, thanks ever so for asking."

Anarus's mouth falls open. "You're shitting me. Your name is Jinx?" He turns to the other two, pointing at me. "Our human is named Jinx. There are three of us and our human is named Jinx. We are so fucked."

The one who helped me up pushes Anarus out of the way and comes back to stand next to me. "Don't be a dick, Anarus. I'm Byder. Split lip there is Ydum." He hikes a thumb toward the blond haired one, as I had guessed. His tone is nice, but insistent. "One more time, where are your shoes?"

I look down at my feet, then at all six of theirs. They all have very nice, well used, black boots of very solid construction. Boots far nicer than anyone in my village would ever have. Probably nicer than even the High Priest would have. "I don't have any."

"Did you lose them?" Ydum asks, curiously.

"Never had any." I clasp my hands in front of me and try to keep my chin up, refusing to be ashamed. "Too poor. Shoes are only for winter."

"Aw, fuck." Anarus mutters, but Byder doesn't even turn around when he flicks a hand behind him to slap Anarus in the stomach.

"Be. Nice." Byder says through gritted teeth.

"Why?" Anarus is going to piss me off, I can tell.

"Guys." Ydum stops any arguing that is about to start up again. "Tick tock? Do you really want to be out of the games because we spent too long arguing over shoes?"

"You're right, we should get moving." Byder says at the same time as Anarus says, "I really wouldn't mind that much. Our human's name is Jinx!"

I roll my eyes at Anarus so hard it hurts and let out a long, exasperated sigh. He raises an eyebrow at me, tilting his head to one side. I hold his gaze and raise both my eyebrows. I will not let him intimidate me. Anarus's mouth quirks just a little, like he might actually smile, but it vanishes as quickly as it appears.

Byder takes one of my hands into his and pulls me past Anarus. His grip is too tight for me to pull away from, not so tight as to hurt, but tighter than I'm comfortable with. "Fine. It's all fine. Let's just get back to the mouth of the cave." He starts walking up one of the tunnels, still pulling me along. I glance back and the other two are following, Anarus slightly begrudgingly and muttering to himself, his arms crossed over his chest.

We say nothing as we walk. At the mouth of the cave, the goddess in the red dress is waiting with a piece of paper on a board. There are several other groups standing around the mouth of the cave.

"Eighth." Ydum says as we walk over to the goddess. "Could be worse."

"Would be better if you two wouldn't have decided to duke it out in the middle of the hunt." Byder grumbles. Clearer and louder, he tells the goddess in red our names. "Ydum, nature god, Byder, hunt god, and Anarus, obscurity god, with human Jinx."

Obscurity god? That explains why Anarus still looks like he's in the shadows even though the mouth of the cave is well-lit.

"All three of you?" The goddess in red looks surprised. "With her?"

"Is there a problem, Drila?" Anarus drawls darkly.

"No. No. Just, are you sure all three of you? You found her together, right?"

"We know how this works, Drila." Byder says confidently. "We were all three together. It was very evident she is the human for all of us."

"Alright." Drila elongates the word like it's actually not all right, and she's not happy. "Never thought Ydum would be a poor bet, but here we are."

"Why would we be a poor bet as a team?" Ydum furrows his brow. "Three gods, three strong powers, and a human, albeit one with no shoes. What can be so bad?"

Drila smirks at me. "Well, I guess I should tell you so you can choose to opt out if you want. That human's tests were, well they're odd."

"How odd?" Anarus pushes past Byder to stand next to the goddess.

"Repeated ten times, each time half pure blue, half pure red. If you would like to forfeit now, I'll just need your signature here." Drila holds out the paper to Anarus, but he just turns to look at me.

"Named Jinx, no shoes, and a fucked up blood test?" Anarus is about to say something else, but the other gods in the groups already waiting start chuckling, not even trying to hide it. Anarus whips his head to look at them. "What the fuck is your problem?"

"Dude." One of the other gods, a male with blond hair, bare chested like Anarus and with far too many packed muscles for them to actually be worth anything in the real world, is still laughing. "A human named Jinx and Anarus on a team together? A team that has three? Oh man, you're dead in the water before you even leave the cave."

Anarus looks like he's going to lunge at the male, but Byder grabs Anarus and pulls him back. "And what do you have that's so great, Boinkus? Your human looks like she's about to pass out in fear. At least ours is standing tall and strong, bare feet and all."

"Don't call me Boinkus!" The male rages, surging forward. "My name is Bokysus, and you know it." Apparently, gods have a thing about their names. Really touchy about them.

Drila steps between Bokysus and Anarus, her hands up to push back on both males' chests. "Gentlemen, tempers, please. Save it for the games."

"We won't forfeit." Anarus spits. "And we'll win."

Byder takes my hand again and pulls me to stand in the line of teams in our eighth spot place as another group, one human and one god, comes out of the tunnel. Anarus and Ydum stand behind Byder and me.

"Well, this is fun." I say sarcastically, low enough that only my teammates can hear me.

"Oh, it gets better. Just wait." Ydum whispers, just as sarcastically.

We don't talk anymore as we wait for the last groups to come up. The ninth group that had just came up, checks in with Drila, and then we have to wait for the tenth and last group for a bit. Also, only one god and one human. I look down the line as they check in.

"Hey, guys. We're the only group with more than two." I say quietly. "Is that good for us, or not?"

"Could go either way." Byder says. Helpful, I think. Really helpful. I'm really beginning to wish I had more than a couple of minutes and a carriage ride to prepare to come here. I'm going to have to let my teammates know how woefully unprepared I am, and soon, I think. All the other humans don't seem at all confused about everything happening. Either my village was not taught right about these games, or everyone else got a briefing I didn't after they tested blue for the games. Either way, my disadvantages are starting to pile up and I think these guys, especially Anarus, are going to really regret not forfeiting.

With the last team checked in, Drila talks to all of us, but most of what she says seems like she's narrating to someone not here. "The games are closed to participants now. Anyone not already checked in has failed the teambuilding trial and are now eliminated from the games. We have twenty-two participants this year, ten humans and twelve gods. The teams will now be sent to their dorms for the night. Congratulations, to our final teams, for making it into the games. And good luck. We will see you in the morning for the first game in the Gods Games."

Drila snaps her fingers and everything goes black for a second. Almost like I blinked without meaning to. When my eyes open again, we are in a foyer in a building. A very wealthy person's foyer. The foyer is a large, open, square area with three full walls and one wall bisected by a hallway. The two walls on the right and left each have two windows, paintings in between the windows on both sides. The wall behind us is blank except sconces that light the whole foyer brightly, and the one in front of us is the one with the hallway. There's carpet on the floor, the whole floor, wall to wall. It's cream with a pattern of swirling flower buds. The walls aren't wood, or stone, but something else. Something smooth and painted the same cream as the carpet. The paintings are of random scenes. They are nature scenes, but just bland paintings, not like someone made them with love and care but just basic. One is a picture of the sea. Not a stormy sea, or a cliff over the sea, but just a plain beach with basic water coming in small waves onto the sand.

The carpet goes down the hallway that has ten doors, five on each side. There are flickering sconces on the wall between each door, making the entire hallway as bright as daylight even though there are no windows and more paintings, one between each door and the next. The doors are even better wood doors than the testing center has. They gleam as if they have been polished often. There is a small gold plaque on each door with a number on it, with the odd numbers on the left and even numbers on the right.

Byder is still holding my hand. He pulls me along the hallway to the door with an eight on it. Of course, we were the eighth team to arrive at the mouth of the cave. The door handle is also gold and has a key in it with another small piece of gold with an eight on it. Byder turns the key, opens the door, and leads me inside.

The inside of the room is just as opulent, if not more, than the hallway. The carpet continues in the room, as do the cream walls and the sconces on the walls. There are two couches sitting in an L shape. Two leather couches. Real leather. The short part of the L shape is made by a couch pushed against the far lefthand wall and the long part of the L is made by a couch sitting far enough away from the far wall to allow people to walk behind it. On the same wall as the door to the dorm, facing the couch set away from the wall, is a stone fireplace that is currently empty, but has wood stacked neatly on the hearth next to it.

A round wood table sits off to the right side of the room with two wood chairs and a pendulum light hanging over it, flickering in a way that makes me think it's gas lit or something. Directly in front of the door is a large open area. On the wall beyond the table, open area, and couches are three doors. Byder lets go of my hand and shuts the main door after Ydum and Anarus have come inside the room.

I wander to one of the doors, the one on the far right, behind the table, and open it. Behind that door is a bedroom with one very large bed, more carpet, smooth walls and lights that are off right now, one window on the far wall and a dresser. I move from that door to the one on the far left, behind the couches, and see a bedroom that mirrors the first one. Then, I open the door in the middle, past the open area. It's a washroom. Toilet, an area closed in by clear glass, and a sink basin. All inside. I wander into the washroom, not even bothering to turn on any of the lights, and fiddle with a knob at the sink basin. Damn, indoor plumbing. I put my hand under the running water and it starts to get hot.

"No shit." I mutter. "Hot water."

"Never seen indoor plumbing before?" Ydum is leaning against the doorframe, his arms crossed over his chest. He isn't being snarky, more like curious. In the dim light of the washroom, I notice out of the corner of my eye that there's something odd about his skin. I don't look, assuming it's rude to gawk at whatever is different about him, but keep my eyes down on the sink.

"I've seen it. The High Priest has indoor plumbing, but not that gets hot all on its own." I tell him. I look up and realize there's a mirror right above the sink basin. One look at myself and suddenly I'm blushing, hard. I didn't realize how grimy I am. I glance back towards Ydum and the other two beyond him in the sitting area. They are all pristine, their clothes still perfect even after walking through the cave. My brown hair doesn't look dirty, but it's a mess, fly aways coming off my braid down to the middle of my back everywhere. My face doesn't have any streaks on it or anything, just a small scrape from the cave wall on my right cheek, but it still seems gritty compared to them and their flawless skin.

Even Anarus, with his ever-present shadowiness, and Ydum, with the whatever is odd about his skin, look far too perfect to be real. Or I guess, to be human. And I look not. Not perfect, not clean. Crap, I don't even have a change of clothes with me and I'm pretty sure I don't smell great. I was sweating climbing into that hidden shelf in the cave. I will not even look at my feet. They are bad, I know. I got mud on the inside of the carriage, so they probably look filthy.

"I think I'm going to…" I start to say, but I stop. I don't know how to fill a bath here. There's no tub anywhere I can see. I look around for a moment then look back at Ydum. Or really, the floor in front of him. He smiles slightly and walks into the washroom.

"You want a shower?" He offers, walking over to the glass walls. He opens a glass door in the wall, and reaches in to twist knobs that look similar to the ones on the basin. Water starts pouring from a spicket on the wall. "Red is hot, blue is cold. Turn the knobs until it's just right for you before getting in the water. The hot can get hot enough to burn if you're not careful." He shuts the water off again, then walks over to the sink basin I'm standing in front of. I keep my eyes on the floor and force myself not to stare at him. Crouching down, he opens a cabinet below the wash basin and pulls out several bottles and a large fluffy towel. "Thought this would be here." The bottles are soaps.

Ydum walks casually back to the door. "Let me know if you need help with anything else." He leaves, pulling the door shut behind him. I hear murmuring coming from the other side of the door. I try to ignore it and go back to the glass box. The shower, Ydum had called it. I turn the knob with the red line on it and the water pours out again. Quickly, it's steaming hot. I turn the blue-lined one until the water cools down enough for me to stand it on my hand. It's still hotter than any water I have ever bathed in, and, after I strip out of my dirty clothes, I grab the soaps and step into the stream. Oh, gods. I drop the bottles on the floor. That is freaking good. The hot water feels good on my skin and muscles. I just stand under the water for a long time. Eventually, I convince myself to actually wash and get out.

Now clean, I shut off the shower and dry off with the fluffy towel. Then my other problem comes back to me. No clean clothes. After a moment of hesitation, I wrap the large towel around me. With the top at my armpits, the towel is long enough that it almost hits my knees. If I'm going to be staying here for the games, these males and I will probably see a lot of each other, in various states of undressed, and I will not start out shy and embarrassed. Making sure I'm at least covered appropriately, I open the washroom door.

"Hey, guys, you wouldn't happen to have something I can borrow to wear for now, would you?" Three male heads whip to look at me. The look on their faces tells me they were not expecting to see me rather very naked and only covered by a towel, but they are not unhappy about the sight.

Surprisingly, Anarus is the first to move. He jumps off the couch he was lounging on and moves to rummage around in something on the floor at the end of the couch away from me, where the two couches form the corner of the L. I can't see what he's doing, but when he stands up, he has black fabric balled up in his hand. He walks over to the washroom door and hands me the fabric.

"I'm tall enough, it'll probably do well." Anarus mumbles. "Just until your bags get here."

"I won't have any bags." I tell him.

Anarus furrows his eyebrows. "No bags? You didn't bring anything?"

23

I shake my head. "Went straight from my test to here this morning. No time to pack, and never knew I would need to."

Byder leans over the back of the couch he's sitting on, twisting his head back to look at me. "Wait, you take the test on your twenty-fourth birthday, not today. Why did you wait so long?"

I smile just a little. "It is my twenty-fourth birthday today."

"Aw, fuck." Anarus moans again, but I shut the door while he keeps talking. "That means you never..." His voice is cut off by the door. Yeah, that means I never. Never got told what to expect, never packed clothes or a witch's kit for this, never knew what the fuck is going on. Never anything I will need, apparently. Sorry, I don't tell them. Because I'm not sorry. They're the gods, their people made these rules, not us.

I put on Anarus's shirt and it does drape down almost to my knees, covering almost everything the towel did. It's something at least. I mop up the water I got all over the floor with the towel, finger comb through my hair then braid it, and fold my dirty clothes and leave them sitting on the counter in the washroom. I head out of the washroom and join the males in the sitting room, sitting carefully to maintain my modesty. The males all track my movement, their conversation halted momentarily.

Fortunately, there's a small throw blanket on the back of the couch. As I curl up, I use the blanket to cover my legs. The three gods watch me. Anarus still looks like he's half in shadows even though the room is bright. "Can you turn those shadows off, or is that like a permanent thing?" I ask him.

I hear Byder suppress a laugh under a cough, but ignore him. Anarus growls. "Yes, I can turn them off, as you so kindly said, but it's harder when I'm highly annoyed or pissed. Does it bother you, little hex, that you can't look at me?"

I have a feeling that this male will make me roll my eyes so often, I'll strain a muscle or something. I choose to use his own words against him. "My name is Jinx, and you will respect it." After Byder suppresses another laugh, I add. "Or if you really feel the need to tease me about it, try to come up with something creative. Unless you aren't intelligent enough to. I mean, hex? Really? The other kids at school got bored of that one when we were six."

Ydum is laughing with Byder now. But Byder is really trying to pull himself together and be serious. "Okay, okay. Guys, we have a lot to figure out here. Jinx, have you eaten?"

I shake my head no. "Not since the sandwich in the carriage earlier this morning."

"Get food." Byder says, a little too much like a command. I look over at the small table and see that someone must have delivered food while I was in the shower. I ignore the part of my brain that revolts against following a god's command, because I'm hungry, and wander over. There's so much food. So, so much food. It's more food than my parents would make for dinner when all eight of us were still living at home. Ground chicken and beef and pork, a pot with noodles and another with red sauce, and another with white. A plate loaded with cheese covered bread and garlic butter. Spaghetti. The Gods Games is feeding us spaghetti for dinner. Somehow, I expected something more luxurious.

I make a plate with white sauce and ground beef and swipe a piece of the bread, then settle back onto the couch to eat. I'm sitting on the couch that's angled to the side of the fireplace. In the corner created between the two couches, where Anarus had fidgeted to get the shirt, I see there are several suitcases and bags. Their clothes and things they packed to come here. Ydum is sitting on the other end of the couch I am on, closer to the fireplace. Byder and Anarus are on the other couch, with Anarus closer to me.

"So, there are several issues we need to figure out." Byder starts as soon as I start eating. "One, Jinx has no clothes or anything. Two, Jinx has no idea what is going on because she didn't get any of the manuals about the games." So, there are lessons I'm missing. "And three, these rooms aren't set up for four players."

"What do you mean not set up for four players?" I ask before eating a piece of garlic bread. I'm ripping the soft center of the bread out and leaving the hard crust. Anarus is eyeing me do this, one eyebrow cocked up.

When I've eaten all the soft parts and set the crusty edge to the side, Anarus swipes the hard crust and starts eating it. "Did you not notice the two beds? I mean, unless you are down with sharing, someone is sleeping on the couch."

"I can sleep on the couch." I shrug. They actually feel pretty comfortable. More comfortable than my bed at home. "Or I can share. Those beds look huge, and I shared a much smaller one with at least two of my sisters growing up."

"At least two sisters?" Ydum asks. He's behind me, the way I'm angled to look towards Byder, and I don't turn to look at him. Not sure what I saw with his skin in the dim bathroom, but I don't want my first conversation with these gods to end up with me staring at him if it's some sort of deformity or injury or something he's self-conscious about. So, I just try not to look at all for now.

I nod. "Youngest of eight girls. Two bedroom house. You do the math."

"Eight?!" Byder sputters. "Your parents had eight kids and didn't know better than to not get pregnant in January?"

"I wasn't exactly planned." I point at him with my fork. "It's not like birth control is totally foolproof."

All three males bob their heads as if that makes sense. "There is a big difference between sharing a bed with your sisters and sharing one with one of us, Jinx." Byder gestures at the three of them. "I mean, which one of us do you want in your bed?"

My mouth goes dry at the purposeful double entendre. Yeah, I did not think that statement through. "Couch." I manage to croak out. "I can sleep on the couch."

"The human needs better sleep than the rest of us." Anarus grumbles. "She doesn't need any more reasons to suck. I'll sleep on the damn couch."

"Why are you assuming I'm the one that will suck? And why are you talking about me like I'm not right here? Maybe you'll be the one that is the weak link, Ani." I purposefully use his nickname. I don't know why this male rankles me so much but he does. Wait, yes I do know. Because he's an ass. "I mean, I had that awesome hiding spot and you can't even keep yourself fully visible in a brightly lit room."

Anarus's nostrils flare slightly, the only indication he's mad, but then the shadows clinging to him drop, almost completely disappearing, and I see him, all of him, for the first time. His hair is black, jet black, thick and coarse. His dark brown skin is just as perfect and flawless as all the other gods I've seen, but tattooed like I thought. His chest is nearly covered with a scene in shades of gray of a wolf baying at the moon. There are tattoos on his arms as well. One arm has a sleeve from shoulder to wrist with black symbols surrounded with barbed wire and angular patterned lines. The other arm has more symbols wrapped in flowers. The flowers are all in full color, the only color in any of the tattoos.

Anarus is strong. I can tell. He is layered in muscles over his bare chest and stomach. Not a rippled six pack that is only attainable if you spend hours working out every day and keep yourself slightly dehydrated like that Boink god who laughed in the cave was, but the real muscles of pure strength that make you look built, solid, tense.

Looking at his face, I realize he's also the only one who is not clean shaven. He has a short mustache above his upper lip that connects to a goatee on his chin. It's well maintained and cropped close, but thick and full enough that I know it's intentional rather than he just forgot to shave. His eyes are not actually black, but a very dark golden amber color with black lines through them and his eyebrows are thick, dark black and curved over his eyes in a way that makes him look like he is perpetually skeptical. His lips are full and soft. Well, they would look soft if he wasn't almost scowling.

I shift my gaze, realizing I'm staring, and actually look at Byder and Ydum. Byder looks like I thought in the cave. Same realistic muscular look, although I can't tell as much since he's actually wearing a shirt, but his shoulders are much broader than Anarus's and his thighs are straining the fabric of his pants. He's probably an inch or so taller than Anarus, who is maybe six feet tall. He looks tanned, like he spends a lot of time outside in the sun. His dark brown hair is streaked with tiny bits of lighter brown, his eyes matching his hair with dark honey color shot through with gold. He has thrown his hair up in a quick, messy bun at the crown of his head.

His right arm has several thin lines tattooed on it. Starting at the wrist, the thin lines each create a perfect circle around his arm, with a small space, less than a finger's width between each one. None of the circles touch each other and they are all just plain black lines. One of them, I notice, is a little red, as if the line was just tattooed.

Ydum, I realize, is not just pale, but that problem with his skin is actually that it has a slight green tint. Not like he feels ill, but rather than the pink tint my skin has, his is green. His blond hair is more of strawberry blonde color. And those eyes? Emeralds. Glittering emeralds inside narrow eyes that look like he's wearing kohl, but I can tell he isn't. That is natural. His split lip looks like it already healed. He's not as built as the other two. His frame is slighter, narrow but still emanates the idea of strength. Just because his shoulders aren't as broad and his arms are not as thick as the other two, I hold no illusions that he's less powerful. I notice his right wrist peeking out from beneath the long sleeves of his top and see a hint of something fully green there, like maybe he has tattoos too. He's the tallest of them all, probably six and a half feet tall.

All three of them are perfect. Too perfect to be real. Gorgeous even, I'll admit. All three of them are perfectly, mouth-wateringly beautiful. If someone were to ask me what would make a male beautiful in my mind, I would point to the three of them as the perfect examples. Even though they all three look completely different than each other, it's like they were each made perfectly. Perfectly for me. To be mine.

Looking at them stirs something in me. Not just the normal feelings you get when you look at someone who's attractive, but something else. Something I've never felt before. Like there's static in the air. Like little static shocks are crawling up and down my arms. Like I need to touch them. There's a taut line between me and each of them. One that wants me to draw closer to them. A panic I haven't felt in quite a long time, I've kept pushed down and asleep, lifts its head in my mind and mentally I rear back, away from that taut line. But I don't want to pull back from it and now I'm confused.

Yeah, no. I'm definitely the weak link here. All of my sisters are considered beauties, with hair ranging from golden blond to dark brown, their eyes going from clear blue to dark blue like Mom, with only Ophelia having golden brown eyes like Dad. They all have sweet, prefect heart-shaped faces, full pouty lips, slight and curvy bodies, the works.

Me? Not so much. The unplanned kid got the leftover genes. I'm not short for a human female, but I'm several inches shorter than Anarus and probably an entire foot shorter than Ydum. My light brown hair goes to my waist when braided, and my eyes are just mud brown. I know I'm not ugly, just kind of average. Not slight, but thicker, my curves hidden a little more. Less hourglass, more athletic as my mom calls it. Not that I necessarily have the athleticism to go with the athletic shaped body. I'm no slouch, but I'm not winning any sports awards either.

The three males are all watching me appraise them, as if maybe they are appraising me too. As if maybe they noticed that taut line and are unsure if they want to pull away from it. Or maybe they know they do because that's not how people look at me, not how they think about me. I look away, focusing on the plate of almost untouched spaghetti in my lap and force myself to eat.

Byder clears his throat. "We'll take turns sleeping on the couch, Anarus. I don't mind sharing the bed with either of you. Jinx will get the other one alone. As far as clothes and whatnot, we'll figure something out. Ydum, did you bring extras? You look closest to Jinx's size without the collars and waistbands being so wide they just fall off. Too long is more manageable than too wide."

Ydum nods and goes over to grab his bag from between the couches and starts sorting through it. "They really will be long on you, but these should work." He tosses me two shirt and pants.

Anarus grumbles and grabs his bag. "Here." He tosses a pair of boots at me and a handful of socks. "Good thing I brought two pairs."

I set my plate aside and try on the boots. They mostly fit. I take them back off and stuff the toes of the boots with a pair of socks and try them again. "Perfect."

"Huh." Ydum watched me stuff the socks in the boots, curious. "Humans are creative."

I shrug. "I'm used to hand-me-downs that don't quite fit right."

"Hand-me-downs?" Byder repeats.

"Yeah, you know. Your older siblings' clothes that they outgrow so your parents give them to you." I offer. All three of them stare at me blankly. I sigh and slump in my seat. "That's right. The gods are all rich. You've probably never worn anything that wasn't brand new."

"I know what the fuck hand-me-downs are." Anarus mutters, looking away from everyone.

"You would." Ydum snorts, retaking his seat behind me. "Seeing as you—" Anarus lets out a soft snarl, cutting Ydum off. This is the second time Ydum as alluded to Anarus not being exactly the same as the rest of them. I would ask, but Anarus does not seem like he's feeling very 'let's share our life stories' friendly right now.

Byder, taking command again, speaks loudly over Ydum's cackling and Anarus's growling. "We'll sort out the rest of the clothes issue later, but for now, at least you have something, Jinx. Now, the games. What do you know?"

I swallow the bite of spaghetti I had just taken, coughing slightly as the lump moves down my throat. "Apparently, not much. I know it's witches and gods and no one else. I know the gods set it up and make us participate, get tested at twenty-four. All of us are twenty-four. Blue goes, red doesn't for humans. I thought it was always ten witches, ten gods, but that's obviously wrong. Other than that," I shrug again. "Not much."

"Anarus isn't twenty-four." Ydum tells me. When I look at him questioningly, he explains. "Anarus is only twenty-one. They made his go into the games early because—" Anarus snarls again and Ydum shuts up quickly.

"No." I turn to Anarus, crossing my arms over my chest and giving him my most scathing stare, the one Mom does when she already knows what we did wrong, she's just waiting for us to admit it. "If you're going to call me a problem because of all the stuff different about me, then I should know all the issues with you. We're teammates now, and winning the games matters for me as much as it does for you. I don't know what happens if we lose, but I did not like the way that goddess in the red dress said we would be eliminated. So, tell me. Why are you here three years early, Anarus?"

Anarus sucks in his cheeks and looks away. Byder answers for him. "Because they didn't have another foster placement for him. Gods should live with their parents until they go to the games, but our world is not exactly set up for orphans. Anarus is the only orphan god I've ever heard of. They decided he'd go to the games and if he passes, he gets to just be crowned early. If not, well, it won't matter."

So much information in that, I'm not sure what to focus on first. So, I say it all. "You said passes, not wins. And crowned? What do you mean by that? Why won't it matter if he doesn't pass?" I stop there. I have questions about the whole orphan part, but not the time and Anarus's story to tell, if he wants to, not mine to demand.

Ydum speaks as if he's reciting from a textbook. "All gods participate in the games. You would have learned this if you had been given the time. Witches test, we don't." That's not what I was told. Again, more information I was told wrong. "Well, we do but it's different. Not like you, but an assessment done at birth and a record kept for later. It's more of a check of what pantheon we might belong to. Anyway, the games are winnable, technically. But that matters for the witches more than it does the gods. For the gods, passing each game proves our ability to handle the mantle of godhood, being crowned it's called. Winning is fun, but not necessary. If we pass each game, our godhood, our powers, are unlocked, and we become a full part of the pantheon our powers call to. If not, we become nothing more than powerless witches, forced out of the city of the gods and made to live with the humans."

"And what happens for the humans if we win, or at least pass each game?"

"You get to live in the city of the gods and become immortal." Ydum's tone is very blank, almost purposely devoid of any emotion. The way he says that sounds like there's more to it than that, but he doesn't want to say it.

"And if we don't?" They don't answer me. None of them are even looking at me. All three gods look anywhere but at me. "Tell me. What happens to me if we fail a game?"

Ydum speaks so softly I almost can't hear him. "The humans that fail a game usually don't survive."

"We die?" I'm shouting. I know I'm shouting, but I don't care. "The gods either get to live in a city or don't, but the humans get to die? For what? What's the fucking point of the games that it's worth us dying over?" I stand up, my dinner forgotten. I clench my fists as I tremble in anger. They're killing us for their stupid games?

Anarus shoots up, standing so close to me I can feel his breath on my cheeks. "We die too! Gods die in the games just as much as witches do! Do not fucking blame us for this system. We aren't the ones who made it up and we have no choice but to participate. At least you have a chance. Your blood could have been red and you wouldn't have to come here. We get no choice. None! From birth, we know that we get exactly twenty-four years, then we die, become mortal, or survive these games." Anarus turns away from me, raking his hands over his face.

"Or we're supposed to get twenty-four years." Anarus laughs bitterly, still not looking at me. I'm not sure he's even really talking to me anymore. "But no one wants the fucking god with shadows he can't control, so they just decide to throw me to the wolves and hope I die. Or really, to a fucking human named Jinx with a birthday that means she learned nothing!" He turns back to me quickly, his anger and shadows barely held in check. "Welcome to life sucks, little human. You aren't the only one whose got something to complain about."

There's a very big part of me that wants to comfort Anarus. His anger makes sense now. He's too young. They, whoever they are that control these games, expect him to die in the games so they don't have to deal with him anymore. He's an orphan that's unwanted. My life might not have been great, being poor and living in that village, bad shit happening to me sometimes, but at least through it all, I always knew my parents would love me, my sisters too in their own way. Who did Anarus have? Probably no one. I reach out my hand and place it comfortingly on his arm, right over a rose on his bicep. There's a weird sensation as my hand moves through his swirling shadows. It feels cold before I actually touch his warm skin.

"Then, tell me what I need to know." I say softly, ignoring the odd sensation that I feel touching him. The cold feeling disappeared as soon as I made contact with his skin. This sensation is something else, almost like I am wearing wool socks on a rug in winter. "If they expect both of us to fail, to die, to make life easier for them, tell me what I need to know to not die, so we can make them all fuck off."

Anarus looks down at my hand on his bicep, then at my face. He looks confused, as if no one has ever touched him before. Or at least, never touched him kindly. He swallows hard, then pulls away, going over to the table with the food on it.

"The games are supposed to save us." Byder watches Anarus closely.

Ydum isn't watching Anarus but me. He is speaking in that academic tone again. "The bloodlines of the gods are too polluted. We are all too closely related, having come from just a handful of original gods. The point of the games is to find a compatible witch to mate with. Witches that survive all the games are suitable. Witches that don't," he shrugs, "aren't. That's why the first test was what it was, and ends in mostly teams of one male and one female. A mating pair. But sometimes, the teams are... different. Like us."

I am teamed with three males. The games expect us to become mating pairs and I'm teamed up with three males. Do they expect? My heart starts racing as memories flood me. Memories I have worked really hard to push away and never think about. Memories that are part of why I can meditate on peace so well. Will they? Shit. No. This is a fucking mating game. What will the games be if it is a fucking mating game? I can't breathe.

"Jinx? You okay?" Ydum stands up, coming over to me. He is too close. Too fucking close.

"No." I barely force the word out as I step away from him. I can't breathe.

"What's wrong with her?" Ydum is still too close, stepping closer as I move away. Byder is standing now too. He puts a hand on my arm.

"Don't touch me!" I scream, pulling my arms around my middle protectively. "Don't fucking touch me!"

"Shit." Anarus pushes both Ydum and Byder away. "She's having a panic attack. Don't touch her." He turns to look at me, an arm's length away. "No one will touch you, Jinx, but I need you to look at me. Look at me." I try to look at him, but I can't see him. All I can see is the three of them. The other three. The ones who made it hard to breathe.

Anarus speaks softer. "Look at me, Jinx. Whatever is in your head isn't real. They aren't here. Look at me. Who am I?"

"Jacob." Part of me knows I'm saying the wrong name, but my mind won't let me see anything else. I can't breathe. I suck in hard but nothing reaches my lungs. I can't breathe. He's crushing me, they all are. I can't breathe.

"Jacob isn't here. He isn't hurting you, Jinx." Anarus's voice is soft, too deep. It's wrong. It's not the voice that it should be for the weight on my chest. "Take in a breath and look at me. Who am I?" I close my eyes and force my lungs to accept the air I am trying to drag in. It's the wrong voice, so I should be able to breathe. "Good girl. Now breathe out and open your eyes. Who am I?"

I exhale, opening my eyes, finally seeing the god that's in front of me. "Anarus."

"Good. Take another breath." I do as I'm told. "Let it out." Anarus holds out his hand but doesn't touch me. "Take my hand." I breathe out and put my hand in his. "What do you feel?"

"Cold shadows and warm skin."

"Does Jacob have shadows?"

"No."

"Then, is he here?"

"No."

"You good now?"

I nod, lying. The panic is still there but I don't want them to know that. Anarus was barely even speaking to me and now he is talking me through my panic? While I appreciate his help, I don't think he did it just to be nice. I don't want to owe these gods anything. I barely know them. Anarus doesn't resist when I pull my hand away but he's watching me like he knows the lie.

"What the fuck was that? Who's Jacob?" Ydum asks from the couch. He and Byder both must have sat back down after Anarus pushed them away from me.

Anarus responds before I can, growling as he stalks over to the couch, leaning down to get in Ydum's face. "You don't ask that, Ydum. Leave her alone about it." He turns back to me. "You don't have to answer him, Jinx. Your pain is yours. You don't have to share it with anyone. Sit down."

I keep following Anarus's directions even though I can breathe again, mostly. I sit down where I was on the couch, and Ydum scoots over to make sure there is plenty of space between us. Anarus hands me the blanket that had fallen off my lap when I stood so suddenly and retakes his spot on the couch. I take my time settling it on my lap, looking down, embarrassed now that my panic is ebbing.

"If this is all about finding mates, will the games make us?" I swallow hard. I don't want to say it, but I have to ask. "Will they make us do things?"

"No." Anarus tells me firmly. "The games focus on different types of powers. Magic for the witches. No one will touch you, at least not in that way, unless you ask us to. The game makers hope that it will happen, that the paired up god and human will become entangled and want to be romantic, but nothing beyond the close quarters forces it or even pushes for it."

I stutter a sigh of relief. "Why are you suddenly being nice, Anarus?"

His mouth twitches slightly. "I'm not." Something dark crosses his face and it isn't just his shadows. "I may not like you, little human, and may think we are fucked with you as our teammate, but I would never want you worried we would do something like that. We're gods, but we aren't assholes."

"Well," Ydum tries for levity, "the rest of us aren't assholes. Ani, on the other hand, yeah, you're usually an asshole. Just not in that way."

The glare from me, Anarus, and Byder makes Ydum shut up again. I look over at Anarus surreptitiously. He may actually be younger than the rest of us, but somehow, he feels older. Like his twenty-one years have been harder than our twenty-four each combined. Which would probably be right for an orphan. Orphans have a hard life among the humans but we at least try to take care of them. I can't even begin to imagine what life would be like to be parentless among a people who are immortal. When your kind shouldn't be able to die unless they are purposely killed, having dead parents probably isn't something their system is set up to deal with.

"The games." Ydum attempts yet again to pull us back on topic, sounding like a textbook again. "Each of the ten games are designed to test a different facet of power and magic, and how a witch and god work together. How each game exactly works changes year to year, but the skills needed are the same. Nature and plant lore first, then weather. Third is protection, fourth is life and death. Fifth is animalism and sixth is strength and combat. Seventh and eighth are intellect and senses respectively. The ninth is creation and the last one is always the wild card."

He tries to decide on who is best for each game, explaining their powers at least a little to me. "The first game and seventh should be easy for me since I'm a nature god and pretty smart. I may do well in the ninth too, depending on exactly what it is. The fifth and eighth Byder should be able to handle being a hunt god. Ani's got the fourth, life and death, easy. Maybe the protection one too. That leaves the second one, weather, the sixth, combat, and the wild card. You any good with weather magic, Jinx?"

I shake my head. "We only ever worked on meditation to control our magic and knowing things like how to use plants and crystals in our magical arts classes. If they would have taught me more once my test went kind of blue, I don't know, but they never did before the twenty-fourth birthday."

"Fuuuuccckkkk." Anarus is back to being a jerk.

"Did you at least take, I don't know, a basic gym class or something to learn how to fight?" Byder asks, being kind in a way Anarus isn't.

I bite my lip and shake my head no again.

"We. Are. So. Screwed." Anarus leans back and lets his head hang over the back of the couch to stare at the ceiling. "Should have forfeited when I had the chance."

"Don't count us out yet." Ydum leans forward, resting his elbows on his knees. "Jinx may not be well trained, but there are three of us, and between us, we cover a lot of the basics. None of the other teams are as well balanced. And there are only two of them. The god is going to have to carry a lot of the load, even if their human is better prepared. Depending on the rules of each game, we may get breaks to rest while they don't. That could be a big factor in winning."

"Breaks?" I ask.

"Not for you, unfortunately, Jinx." Ydum shakes his head. "Every game requires at least one human and one god. Sometimes, the rules say all the gods on a team must compete if there are multiple gods in a team, but sometimes the game rules say it can only be one. We'll be told before the game begins what the rules are. We get a week between each game to prepare, except the team set-up and the first game. Today's trial and tomorrow's official start of the games. But they don't tell us exactly what the game will be, beyond the subject we already know, until just before it starts. We'll have to plan for each one like it might be all of us or only one of us with you in the game."

"And that could work in our favor or against it." I nod, understanding. "If we plan for a game with all of us, or one or another, and then find out it can only be one of you, we could be screwed. But if we can have more, we could maybe be better off than a team who doesn't have so many options to work with."

"Exactly." Ydum confirms. "There was one year that a lot of the teams were multiples and the games made them draw lotteries for which god participated when only one was allowed. It really bit a bunch of teams in the ass when they did that. Like the nature god sometimes lost out of being in the games that could use a nature god, and instead the team was forced to do the game with a chance god. It was a mess. There were only two teams left by the wild card and a lot of strong gods and powerful witches died that year."

"How many usually die in the games?" Again, don't want to know but I have to know.

"Witches? About half." Byder tells me honestly. "Gods? Only two or three, sometimes. Sometimes more but never none."

"Usually, about five or six teams make it to the wild card." Ydum adds. "When a team finishes the game, whatever that means exactly in that game, they move on to the next round, no matter if they come in first or last. Every finished game gets you points, but points are bad. A hundred points is a perfect score, meaning your team came in first for every game. One thousand points is the worst possible score, but never happens because even finishing in last place is better than not finishing at all. Like we said, teams that don't finish, usually the human dies trying. Sometimes the god does. If either dies during the game, the whole team is eliminated, even if it's a group like us and only one of the gods is in that game or only one dies."

Byder takes over again. Anarus seems to have gone back to sulking on his corner of the couch, scratching his facial hair absentmindedly. "For the witches, passing all the games without winning just gives you the right to live in the city of the gods and immortality. Winning actually comes with rewards. I'm not totally sure what all the winning witch gets because, well, I didn't really pay attention to that part since it didn't matter to me, to be honest. The god gets crowned with their mantle as long as they pass all ten tests, and winning is just a kind of, well," he stammers and looks away, like he's hiding something, "bragging rights?"

"So, my motivation in this game is survival, while yours is bragging rights?" That's ridiculously skewed in favor of the gods, I think. But what did I expect?

"No." Anarus finally chimes in. "Ours is survival too. We can die in the games as much as you, but some would think that is preferable to the other option if we don't manage to complete all the games. If we fail even one game, we are denied our mantle. We are made mortal, cut off from everything and everyone we know, forced to live a mortal life, forced to die slowly and painfully in a way our bodies are not meant to. It hurts a fucking lot. More than dying hurts for an actual human. Our bodies fight it the entire time because it's not supposed to be able to get sick or die like that. Most gods who fail a game but don't die in it choose to end their own lives rather than stick it out for sixty odd years in horrible pain. If you die in these games, we won't just die too, we will be tortured for the rest of our lives."

"Why?" It's all I can think of to say.

Ydum answers me, straining to be kind about it. "Because if we can't even keep one human alive, then we don't deserve to be gods. It's our punishment for letting our human die."

"What if we fail a game, but I don't die? What if one of you does? Or none of us do, but we still fail? What about all the ones today that didn't find teams or get back with them in time?"

"They all died. Or will soon." Byder is not as kind as Ydum was, but carries a straightforward tone. Not quite Ydum's textbook one, but close. "Gods who haven't taken their mantle yet are not quite immortal. We need food and water, air, whatever, like the humans do, just not as much. The people who didn't find teams will be in that cave, searching for a teammate they will never find until they die from starvation or dehydration. The ones who did find their teammates, but came too late, will just find an empty mouth to the cave and no way out, forced to just wait for their death."

"There were thirty-six of us. Only ten witches found teams. That means twenty-six people are dead and the games haven't even started." I pick at a non-existent piece of fuzz on the blanket on my lap.

"And there were twenty-three gods." Byder tells me. He is looking at me in a way that makes me think he expects me to say something about the human lives being more important, and is ready to argue about it. "Only twelve of us made it on a team."

"So, thirty-seven people died for a stupid competition just today. How many have died over the course of all the games?" None of the gods answer me. They probably don't know either.

"To answer your other question, I really don't know that it's possible for us to fail a game without one of us dying." Ydum changes the topic. "As far as I know, it has never happened."

That is not exactly helpful. But not all of their answers have been. I'm not sure how much they actually know, how much those manuals taught them. "Do you get to watch the games or something in the city of the gods? The way that goddess in red was talking at the end of the trial today, it seemed like she was talking to an audience rather than us."

Byder and Ydum both shake their heads. "The manuals have transcripts of the games." Ydum says. "Drila was speaking to the auditory recording, which will be transcribed after the games are done."

"How many games have there been?" My head is doing mental math.

Thirty-seven deaths before the games even begin, half the humans usually die and maybe two or three gods do as well in the games. That is about forty-four or -five deaths for each year, if this first trial was average.

"We got the transcripts for the last fifty, but I don't know the full number." Ydum says.

"Three hundred and seventy-five." Anarus says quietly, not looking at anyone. "This is the three hundred and seventy-fifth games."

Quick math makes me disgusted. "That's like, rough estimate, fifteen thousand people, humans and gods, that have died since the games started."

"Sixteen thousand, eight hundred, and eighty-six." Anarus recites. "So far."

Byder swears. "Fuck. How do you know that?"

Anarus looks at him. "Ydum isn't the only one who read the manuals. I'm too young to be here, but I'm not stupid."

None of us say anything for a long time, the weight of that number silencing us.

Eventually, Byder stands, pulling out the hir tie and running his hand through his hair. "We should get some sleep. It's already late and the first game tomorrow will start early." He grabs his bags and walks toward the room on the left of the washroom.

Ydum grabs his bags and follows Byder. "If you snore, man, I'm gonna punch you."

I stand up too, handing the blanket over my lap to Anarus. When the other two are behind the closed door of their bedroom, and I am gathering up the clothes Ydum gave me, Anarus stops me with a look. "You gonna be good tonight?"

I freeze. "What do you mean?"

Anarus scratches the side of his head, absentmindedly. He looks away as if ashamed. "When I have a, well, when I freak out like that, sometimes I have nightmares afterwards. Just, should I maybe be prepared for that or something? You gonna be good or?"

I lick my lips. That's an admission of something from him. Anarus has demons like I do. "I should be fine. I mean, I get bad dreams sometimes, but I can handle it if I do."

Anarus only nods. Neither of us want to admit being that type of weak. I leave the sitting room with the clothes the others gave me clutched in my arms, trying really hard not to run. I close the bedroom door behind me and start concentrating really hard on peace. Please, please, give me peace.

Chapter Three

I DID NOT DREAM. Thank the gods. Well, no. The gods are here, so I guess not thank the gods. But I do wake up to hearing the gods. Ydum and Byder seem awfully cheery in the sitting room. I can hear them laughing from here. I groan and force myself to sit up. Ydum's clothes work fairly well, a little long and I have to roll up the long sleeves of the blue shirt I put on almost halfway so my hands are actually outside the sleeves and a third of the pant legs are tucked into the boots from Anarus, but they at least cover everything and aren't falling off me.

I open the door and step out into the sitting room, where Ydum greets me with a smile. "Those clothes worked out great, it looks like."

I only grumble "coffee?" and glare in response. My sister Samantha is a morning person, like Ydum seems to be. She learned quickly to never speak to me before I have had at least one cup of coffee.

"Sheesh, someone get that girl coffee before she murders us." Byder pulls his hair up into a messy bun. "She's almost as bad as you, Anarus."

Anarus walks over to me from the table, coffee in hand. He's almost completely in shadows as he hands me the mug. "Bite me, Byder."

As I sit down on the couch, taking up my same spot from last night, the others do the same. All three of them are wearing clothes similar to last night, just different colors. Byer's pants are still brown leather, and Anarus is actually wearing a shirt this time.

Ydum opens his mouth to say something, but I hold up one finger at him, and take a sip of the coffee. "Do not speak until this cup is empty if you want to live."

Ydum bends over me to look in my mug, then shrugs, smiling. He looks at

Byder, waggling his eyebrows. "Two against two? And they need coffee to function? We could take them."

Byder shakes a finger, also laughing. "Ah, yes, but you forget to factor in the not-a-morning-person rage. While we are pleasant, they have undeserved hatred to tap into before the coffee makes their brains functional. It's like wrestling a bear instead of a god, or human in Jinx's case."

"What do you think the odds are then?" Ydum rubs his chin as if he's actually considering this academically. "The morning hostility power bonus versus lack of caffeine deficit? Does it equalize out or do they actually have an advantage over us rational morning people?"

"Hmm." Byder rubs his chin as well. "Not sure. Shall we experiment with this?"

Anarus and I both growl at the same time. "Shut up."

Ydum's eyes pop comically wide. "Probably better we don't, friend. I have a feeling they could actually do some real damage."

"Shut. Up." I say again, popping my lips on the p before taking another sip of the coffee that's actually really good.

Ydum pantomimes sealing his lips while Byder pokes the inside of his cheek with his tongue and smiles. I roll my eyes, landing them on Anarus who has his eyes closed as he holds his mug up to his face, inhaling the steam from the coffee as if he's unwilling to waste even that part of its effect. His shadows are simmering down as he takes another sip. At least the effect of the caffeine is visible on him. They'll know it's safe to talk to him when they can actually see his whole face. Me, they'll have to just guess.

They guess wrong. Anarus starts talking before I'm ready. I really want to tell him to shut up for five more minutes but I don't know how long we have before the games officially start, so I stay silent and drink more coffee. "First game."

"Obviously, if given a choice, I should be the god in it." Ydum rests his hands lightly on his knees. "Then, Byder if we only get two."

"Obviously." Anarus drawls. "Jinx? Any good skills with nature and plants?"

I twist my mouth, thinking, before taking another sip then answering. "I didn't do too bad in herbology lessons. Poisons and preventions either. I didn't actually fail gardening and plant care, only came close, if that makes it any better."

"It does not." Anarus sips his coffee again, not hiding his brooding mood.

I throw out my free hand, exasperated. "What the fuck do you want me to say? Without knowing what I'll need to know, I don't know how to tell you if I know it or not."

"I say we go with the assumption that Jinx knows nothing and build from there." Anarus is pissing me off again. I swear he's doing it on purpose.

"Bite me." I mutter, but I'm cut off by a tone sounding. I have no idea where it sounded from but it just reverberates through the air.

"That's time." Ydum slaps his knees and stands. "Well, I guess we'll find out the first game soon enough." The others stand with him and start moving to the door. I drain the rest of my coffee, as does Anarus, and we head out of the dorm. Byder uses the key that was in the door last night to lock our door and we head down the hallway to the foyer we popped into before. The other teams join us.

Drila is wearing a blue dress today, just as shimmery, with matching strappy flat sandals. I try not to scowl at her shoes. She gets a ton of sandals that would do nothing practical, ones to match all of her outfits, but I have to wear shoes made scraps of leather that barely protect me from the cold? I shake my head and push these thoughts away. Not the time or place. I need to listen to what she's saying if I don't want to die, apparently.

"Is that everyone? Okay. Well, welcome officially to the Gods Games." Drila smiles way too much. "First game. Defend your base. The human must plan, the god magically creates and both can act. Jinx, you can have all your gods present and acting, but only one can create for you and you must plan. You have to defend your chosen base from not only attacks on your teammates but being invaded at all using only natural elements. The humans will pick the bases by standing in front of the painting that represents the land they want. You will have five minutes to strategize before we begin selection in order of ranking. Since none of you have points yet, we will rank by order that reached the mouth of the cave. The human will have ten seconds to move to the painting once it is their turn or be forced to accept the one closest to them when the time runs out." Meaning we go eighth. Crap. "Your planning time starts now."

Ydum immediately turns to me. "We need a base with lots of plants. Or something like that."

"I didn't actually pay attention to the paintings on the walls yesterday." I admit. "One is the sea, I know that. But I have no idea the other options."

Byder thinks out loud. "The sea wouldn't be good, would it Ydum? Doable but not great."

"Forest, sea, desert, plains, snow. There are two of each. Two paintings are in the foyer with us and eight in the hallway between each room door." Anarus says. Does he notice everything? "Snow or desert is the worst, meaning we will probably get one of them since seven will be claimed before us."

"Which do you prefer, Ydum?" I ask.

"Fuck. Both suck." Ydum taps a finger on his leg, staring at the ground. "Snow, go for snow if none of the others are available. At least there will be plants under it."

I turn to Anarus. "Where are the snow pictures?"

"By door five and door nine." He really does see everything.

"What else?" I ask all of them.

"Oleander." Ydum tells me. "Remember oleander. Oak, ivy, sumac, the poisons still work in the cold. Winter hellebore. Anything with thorns. Most of the evergreens. Think about crafting, not just the plants themselves being dangerous, but weapons we can make out of them. We don't know what we're defending against. Ingestion doesn't probably matter. Inhalation is good. If we can start a fire, but protect ourselves from the smoke, that would be great." Ydum stops talking, crossing his arms over his chest, thinking.

Byder rips the hair tie out of his hair, half of the messy bun having already fallen out of it. He quickly pulls the hair up to contain it again. "Don't second guess yourself, Jinx. That's a big thing. We don't know how long we'll have before whatever attacks. You have to tell Ydum what to do. Just spit it out, as fast as you think of it. Even if you think it may be a dumb idea, just say it. Anything is better than nothing because you panicked."

"Do not stop talking." Anarus stares at me, holding my eyes with his, serious and no longer showing any anger or frustration. "No matter what else is going on, keep feeding Ydum instructions. Byder and I will defend you both, so you can instruct and he can make, but you have to give us things to defend with."

I turn to Ydum. "How fast can you make something if I ask for it? Like if I ask for an evergreen tree, how long will it take to have a full, mature tree in front of me?"

"A few seconds to a few minutes, depending on what it is and how specific you are." Ydum replies. "Be very, very specific, Jinx. As specific as you can, as fast as you can."

I nod and take a deep breath. "Oleander, hellebore, evergreens, the three poisons. Oleander, hellebore, evergreens, the three poisons." I keep repeating the plants Ydum told me about to memorize them.

"That's time." Drila draws our attention back to her while I keep repeating what Ydum told me in my head, as well as which pictures to go for. Drila is still smiling. I do not like that smile. It seems very disingenuous. "When I say the human's name, they will have ten seconds to stand by a portrait. If the gods could all come stand by me, please?" Drila moves to the back wall, away from the hallway of doors, and all twelve gods line up along the wall as well. It's the only wall without any paintings on it. "Now, humans, line up in front of your gods." We all move in front of our teammates. I stand in front of Ydum, with Byder on one side of him and Anarus on the other. I feel a hand rest gently on my shoulder.

"You got this." Byder whispers. It's his hand on my shoulder. I roll my shoulders, but he either doesn't notice or thinks I'm just trying to relieve tension.

Drila clears her throat. "Up first. Amanda." A short girl with dark brown hair in two braids down her back darts to a picture in the foyer of the forest. Smart. She stops and Drila immediately calls the next one. "Isis." A tall blonde runs down the hallway to a picture I can't see. "Aretha." A small female with chin length black curls also goes down the hallway. "Damek." An incredibly tall male with very blond ringlets that hang to his chin and bounce as he moves scoots quickly to the picture of the sea I saw last night. "Saffron." A girl with straw yellow hair in a long braid like mine runs down the hallway almost to the end.

"Both forests and seas gone." Anarus whispers. How can he tell? He must have memorized where each painting in the hallway is and can guess by how far down it each human went.

Drila is still calling out names. "Asteria." A very tiny brunette darts to the closest picture in the hallway.

"Must have chosen that desert because it's close and she's not fast." Ydum murmurs.

"Leander." I don't see where she goes because I am bracing to run. Door five or nine.

"Jinx." I take off, ignoring everything else and run to door five. It's painting of a fucking avalanche. No. I move to door nine and stop. I look at the picture. There are trees in that snow. I shrug. I'm out of time, so we're stuck with it. I hear Drila call out, "Wren," then a moment later, "Raven," and we're done.

"Gods, join your humans." Drila says and my three gods join me.

"Fuck, good job not going to five." Ydum sighs and glares at Anarus.

Anarus just shrugs. "I didn't know it was my job to know everything. The human figured it out."

"At least you didn't trip like that Leander girl." Byder chuckles, crossing his arms over his chest and shaking his head. "They got the last desert because she tripped over her own feet."

I didn't even notice that she fell, I was so focused on my own turn. "Crap. Did I miss something better?"

"Nah. A plains picture one more door down, but honestly, I'm good with this one. Plains can have a lot of clay soil sometimes. Byder told you to be decisive and not second guess yourself, and you did that." I think Ydum is just trying to make me feel better.

Drila speaks again. We stop talking and listen. "Your first game begins... Now!" The world blinks again and suddenly I'm in a copse of evergreen trees in the woods, a foot of snow on the ground around my feet. Ydum, Byder and Anarus all look at me. I take in the scene quickly and start rambling.

"More evergreens, just like these ones." I say, thinking defensively. "In a circle around us. Fill in all the gaps until we can't see through them."

Ydum is doing something with his hands and trees start sprouting up as he moves around the circle. They grow quickly, but are spindly, their branches short and not very well covered with needles. "The soil has to be able to support what I am growing, Jinx."

"Should have told me that before." I mutter. We all whip our heads to the north as we hear a crashing sound. "Oleander. A circle of it inside the circle of trees."

"Good." Byder tells me as Ydum complies. "Weapons, Jinx. Think weapons."

Weapons. I bite my lip. Water is nature. "Balls of ice. A fuck-ton of them, the size of my palm."

"How many is a fuck-ton?" Ydum yells as Anarus says, "Fucking smart. Shit."

"Start with twenty." I guess as something crashes through something else in the west.

A pile of ice balls forms between Byder and Anarus. They each pick up one as I think again. "Poison ivy, poison sumac, and poison oak, weaved through the trees like netting."

"Keep going." Ydum says as he weaves vines through the trees. He's starting to sweat. The crashing sound to the north is getting closer.

"Hellebore, around the outside of the circle of trees." That covers all the plants Ydum told me about. I turn to Byder and Anarus. I'm not sure if I'm supposed to direct them as well. Drila said only one god can create for me, and that I have to plan, but I'm not sure if that means Anarus and Byder can do things without me telling them the plan to do it. I err on the side of caution and toss out directions to them as well. "Guys, grab a vine and prep it as a whip."

Byder grins. "You got this, Jinx." He does what I say, as does Anarus, breaking off enough of the vines Ydum made to have a serviceable whip. Byder makes a second one for me and hands it to me. Anarus makes one for Ydum but he keeps it in his hand as Ydum is still making Hellebore plants.

Ydum looks pale and is sweating profusely despite the cold. He just made a lot of plants really fast. "Ydum, stop. Rest." I don't want him to overdo it. He stops like I said, heaving. He bends over to put his hands on his knees as he crouches down.

"Thank you." Ydum gasps out.

"You have to tell me if you need breaks, guys." I admonish them. "I don't know your limits." I turn around in a circle, thinking. Weapons. Defenses. It would really help if I knew what was crashing through the trees, making all that noise. "Do any of you have good eyesight?"

Byder nods. "What do you need?"

Something booms to the west. "What is making the noise? Can you look?"

"How?" Byder points around the circle.

Oh yeah. I made Ydum basically seal us in the copse. Good defensively but it was a mistake that now screws our ability to prepare. "Um…"

Anarus clears his throat and I look at him. He twirls his fingers and shadows dance around the tips.

"Can you, maybe, lift Byder with your shadows so he can see over the trees, or something?" I ask him.

"Or something." Anarus rolls his eyes. Shadows start blooming out of his hand, filling the air. But after only a second, Anarus yelps and all the shadows disappear. "Or something is not a clear enough direction apparently." He gasps, bending over and clutching his hands to his middle.

I dash to his side. "Shit. Are you okay?" I pull Anarus's hands to me and see that his fingertips are blistered. He pulls them away from me.

"All good." But I can tell Anarus is lying. His voice is strained, and he's paler than Ydum.

"Not all good, Anarus. Don't lie." I'm interrupted by another crashing sound.

Anarus looks at me. Hard. "Jinx. Do something."

I turn my head to look at Byder, to tell him to climb a tree, but Anarus grabs my chin and turns me back to face him. "Jinx, it will take too long. Tell me."

I bite my lip then say, "Byder. Can you…"

"Jinx, do what Anarus says. Be decisive." Byder walks up to stand next to me. "There's no time. If he says he can, let him."

Fine. I huff. "Anarus, can you look and see what is coming over the trees with your shadows?"

"There you go." Anarus attempts a smile, but he's in too much pain. Shadows shoot from his fingertips to the treetops as he groans and swears.

"Fuck. Three yetis. Fuck." The shadows retract and Anarus shakes his hands.

Yetis. "We are going to need a shit ton more ice balls." I mutter.

"What's the difference between a fuck ton and a shit ton?" Ydum asks.

"About a hundred?" I'm being sarcastic but Ydum starts crafting anyway. "Throw in some long icicles too? Thick as my arm, long as them too? They'll make good spears."

"What else, Jinx?" Byder encourages me. "Think. What else?"

Nature, we can only use nature. What can we do to fight off three yetis? "Rocks are nature, right?"

Ydum nods at me as he crafts four ice spears, one for each of us. "I would say so. I can sense them. What are you thinking, Jinx?"

"Are there any really large boulders nearby? Ones where we could play a little bowling for yetis?"

Ydum thinks for a moment, his head cocked to the side. The ground rumbles, then a loud thumping that reverberates the ground starts in the east. Something thumps hard once to the east, again more to the west, then a third time even further west. We hear a loud howl, and the thumps continue to the west, getting softer and more frequent, then there is only a crashing sound of trees falling, then nothing.

Ydum smiles tiredly. "There are only two yetis now."

"Sweet viciousness." Anarus looks at me, impressed.

I place a hand on Ydum's shoulder. "Could you do that again?" One look and I know the answer is no. Ydum is spent. "Never mind. Sit, rest."

"Sorry, Jinx." Ydum says as he collapses into the snow.

I cross my arms over my chest and shift my weight to one hip and tap my other foot. "Don't apologize. You did," I wave around one hand, "all of this and took out a yeti all by yourself. It's our turn now."

The crashing through the trees we ignored while Ydum went bowling is much louder and closer, coming from the north side of the circle. I take one of the icicle spears in one hand and a whip in the other. Anarus holds two icicle spears, and Byder has the last icicle spear and an ice ball. Anarus and Byder position themselves between the trees and me, facing north, with the pile of ice balls between them. I put myself between them and Ydum sitting in the middle of the circle. And we wait.

A group of trees directly in front of us start to shake and a roar comes through them. Anarus thrusts one of the spears through the moving trees over and over again as he yells until he hits something solid and is rewarded with a higher pitch roar. He yanks back on the icicle spear and it comes back bloody.

Byder starts throwing ice balls through the hole in the vines Anarus's spear just came out of. He and Anarus take turns, Byder throws an ice ball then Anarus stabs, as the trees shake and move and roar. When his ice spear breaks, Anarus switches off to the other one without missing a beat.

A second roar comes from a few feet over. A hand comes through the trees, white fur on rather human looking fingers, and I dash over. I wrap the vine around it several times, pulling as hard as I can to force the hand, and the attached large forearm covered with a dense, white fur, to come through more. I can see the outline of an enormous body through the trees and vines. I shove my spear towards the figure while holding the vine-wrapped hand taut.

The hand jerks as my spear makes contact with a hard body and the vine I'm holding snaps. I fall back onto my bottom in the snow with a yelp, almost dropping my now bloody ice spear as I fumble to catch myself. Byder looks over, "Jinx!"

"I'm fine!" I tell him. "Just slipped."

Byder sees the hand with the vine wrapped around it disappearing back through the trees and moves to that yeti, leaving Anarus still stabbing through the trees at the first one. Half of his hair has fallen out of the bun and he roughly shoves it out of his eyes as he grabs for the vine.

"Shit!" Anarus hollers as his second ice spear snaps as he stabs through the trees again, making him stumble forward into the tree in front of him. I tossed my spear to him quickly and he snatches it right out of the air. He quickly rights himself and starts stabbing blindly. It snaps too.

I move over to the pile of ice balls and start feeding them to Anarus. When Byder's ice spear snaps, I start handing him ice balls too. Both males are whipping the ice balls through the holes the yetis made in the tree-vine nets Ydum made as our protection. Byder is having an easier time hitting his yeti since he was able to recapture its hand by the trailing vine wrapped around it. That yeti can't dodge as easily. Anarus is having to just throw and hope.

There is a high-pitched squeal and Byder's vine goes taut. He lets go of it. "Two down. One to go." He shifts to help Anarus.

"We're almost out of ice balls, guys." I tell them.

Behind me, Ydum calls out, "Jinx!" I look back and see he has two sticks holding a pile of oleander leaves. He gives me a pointed look as he pulls his shirt over his mouth and nose.

"Ydum, set the oleander on fire to use the smoke on the yeti." I tell him, knowing what he wanted. "Anarus, Byder, cover your mouths and noses."

Anarus and Byder pull their shirts over their faces as I do, then we all step back from the hole in the trees. I didn't see how he made the fire that quickly, but Ydum steps forward and shoves the sticks with burning oleander flowers on it through the hole. My eyes burn as the smoke goes past me. There is one cough from the yeti on the other side of the trees, and the world pops.

We are back in the foyer. Ydum, who had been leaning on the trees to shove his arm all the way through the hole, falls over, bashing his face on the floor. When he gets up, I notice he split his lip open again. Anarus snickers at him. Our hands, Ydum's that had been holding the burning oleander and Byder's, Anarus's and mine that had been holding ice balls, are all empty. Our clothes are all wet from instantly melting snow for only a second, then dry faster than Ydum stood back up.

We look around at each other, and each let out a sigh. We finished the first game. There are six other people in the foyer, mostly all sitting on the floor, leaning against the walls and looking as worn out as I feel.

"Fourth. We're fourth." I say. I had been kneeling in the snow to grab ice balls so I just collapse where I am. _____

"Forty-five points to Jinx's team." Drila says blandly.

"Forty-five?" Ydum cries out. "Why forty-five?"

"Five point penalty for a broken rule." Drila tells him. "Or something is definitely not an instruction."

Well, fuck. Ydum looks like he is going to argue, but I cut him off. "It's not a bad start." I say, looking at Ydum. I groan and get up off the floor. I pull Ydum by the arm over to where Anarus and Byder are sitting next to each other, against the wall. I plop down on the other side of Anarus and Ydum sits down on my other side. I pull one of Anarus's hands into mine and examine his fingers. They are still red and blistered. Keeping my voice low, I ask him. "Does it hurt a lot?"

He shakes his head. "No. Should heal soon. I think they stopped me from healing in the game, otherwise they would be fine already."

"I'm sorry." I say. "I should have listened better."

Anarus contradicts me. "I should have known better than to think or something was good enough to do whatever I wanted."

"Yeah, Jinx, you did great. Ice spears? Freaking genius." Byder smiles at me broadly and reaches around Anarus to pat my leg.

"Ice spears?" One of the male gods from the other group asks. He's shorter than Anarus, I think, but very built, his body almost a square. His hair is shaved short and he has dark gray eyes. Like all the other gods, he has perfectly flawless tan skin. He's beautiful, like all the gods are, but he's not beautiful like my gods are.

Ydum nods, beaming. "Against yetis in the snow."

"Damn." The male god whistles. "And I thought Isis's seaweed net against sharks was good."

"Hey," the female next to him, Isis I assume, the tall blonde who's very thin and pale, and has bright blue eyes, slaps him playfully. "Those nets got us first place."

The god grunts softly at the play slap, and holds his hands up in surrender. "I never said they weren't a great idea. Just saying, ice spears against a yeti? Pretty smart."

I look down at my lap to hide my smile and realize I'm still holding Anarus's hand in mine. The blisters are healing now. I let go and Anarus pulls his hand back. I tell myself I am not going to look at him even though I can feel him looking at me. Instead, I close my eyes and lean my head back on the wall. It's a good thing we have a whole week before the next game. I feel like I could sleep for three days of it.

From what they said, Isis and her god came in first. I wonder what place the others came in. I think the other two humans are the ones who ran when Drila said the names Aretha and Asteria, but I'm not totally sure. "How do we keep track of the ranking?" I ask my team.

Ydum and Byder just shrug. Anarus says nothing. None of us know. Oh well, I think, either they'll tell us or they won't and we can just focus on surviving. This game didn't feel that hard but it was the first one. My guess is they'll get harder from here.

We aren't the only team given extra points for breaking a rule. As the other teams trickle in, it's interesting to see how they look. Whatever they were doing and whatever they had in their hands as they completed the game disappears around them. Apparently, the game is completed by defeating three enemies, some real like Isis's sharks, some not like our yetis.

Amanda, the girl with two braids, who is about my height and has dark brown eyes and skin, and her god, a very ruddy looking male with bright red hair and blue eyes, pop into the foyer, sweaty and covered in dirt. There is a scratch running down her cheek, but they both are already sitting down. "Freaking wolves!" Amanda cries out as soon as she realizes she's back in the foyer. "Three freaking wolves and your first idea is to throw a stick at them like they are dogs playing fetch?" She stomps over to the wall, sits down and crosses her arms over her chest angrily. When her god comes over to sit next to her, she points to the other side of the room. "No. I got bit by a freaking wolf because you threw a damn stick at it. You go sit over there!"

Her god teammate does as instructed, moving to sit on the opposite side of the room, muttering, "You didn't get bit, just scratched."

I lick my lips trying to hide my laughter. "Could be worse, right?" Ydum whispers. "At least none of us tried to throw a stick at a yeti." I clap my hand over my mouth as Byder looks down, shaking his head. I can even feel Anarus's shoulders next to me shaking as he tries not to laugh.

Sixth place is taken by Damek and his goddess, the only female god in the game. Damek is very tall, like I thought, and he has broad shoulders like Byder but a narrow waist like Ydum and his eyes are even more blue than Isis. His goddess has perfect porcelain skin whiter and more devoid of any color than even Drila. Her straight, perfectly blonde hair is loose and hanging to her waist and her eyes are as green as Ydum's. She's so pretty, she almost hurts to look at. They are both soaking wet, but dry instantly like we did, and are lying on the floor, their arms and legs twirling as if they had just been swimming. Drila announces that they get an extra five points for Damek crafting rather than his goddess.

"Worth it." Damek smiles. At the interested looks from the rest of us, he explains. "Three octopi. I fashioned a lasso from seaweed and lassoed two of them together, so they killed each other instead of us."

Seventh place is taken by Asteria and her god. I was wrong that the two humans in second and third place were Aretha and Asteria. I can't remember what the other girl's name is, but one of them must not be Asteria, since Drila calls this new one Asteria. They were in the desert. I remember she was the tiny one that chose desert because it was close. Asteria isn't only tiny but looks very young too. Everyone is supposed to be twenty-four, but Anarus isn't. It makes me wonder if Asteria is actually too young, or just looks too young. One of those people who just age well, maybe? She has dark blonde hair that stops at her shoulders, light amber eyes that look terrified, and her cheeks look like she still hasn't lost all her baby fat.

Her god is about my height and has that same slight but definitely powerful look that Ydum has. His hair is short and straight, just enough light brown so his whole head is covered with hair he probably doesn't even need to comb and his eyes are a basic blue. They both look sunburned and overheated. I'm curious what they fought and how, but neither of them look like they feel like talking. They both just move out of the center of the room and collapse along a wall. I think they either pass out or fall asleep immediately.

Raven and her god are eighth. Her skin is a soft umber and her black hair is pulled into a hair tie at the crown of her head, but it looks like it would be a beautiful afro if she let it loose. Raven must have been swinging something in circles because when she pops in, she has one arm over her head and is spinning it around, her golden-brown eyes fierce. It takes her a second to realize she's back and stop. Her god is screaming loudly, but he stops as soon as he lands. He has more of an olive complexion that's complimented well by his wavy black hair and darker brown eyes on a tall, but not Ydum or Damek tall, frame.

I look at Ydum, questioningly. He whispers, "Uesis, music god. He was singing a death song, but it cut off when they came back, I'd bet." I nod, understanding.

Raven just says, "Gryphons. Three gryphon mothers with babies."

Everyone else in the foyer cringes and groans, commiserating, so I assume that's something hard. But Wren and her god pop in right behind them, both covered in snow and mid-swing of their arms. They must have gotten the avalanche. Wren is tall and graceful, like a dancer, her peaches and cream skin almost as flawless as the gods. Her eyes are a sapphire blue that glitters. Her god is a tawny male that is shorter than her with hair that is almost a shade of gold and eyes that are definitely gold.

"Ninety-five points for Wren's team. Five extra points for the injury." Drila says. I look at Wren and realize one of her fingers is almost black from frostbite.

"So glad you skipped that picture." Ydum whispers.

Drila keeps talking. "With all the teams returned now, you are all free to head back to your rooms. A board in your room will track the team standings as we move through each game. You will have six days, starting tomorrow, to prepare for the next game, which will be weather."

At that, we are apparently dismissed because everyone starts to stand and move to the hallway. I open my mouth to speak, but Byder puts a hand on my shoulder and shakes his head. "Wait." He says almost silently.

Once we are in our room, I turn and ask him. "That was only nine teams."

Byder blows out a long breath and points to a board that's now attached to the back of our door. There's a list of the names of the humans, each with a number next to it. I look at my name and see it says, "45" there. My name is also fourth on the list. The name "Leander" is at the bottom with a red line through it and no number.

"She's dead, isn't she?"

"She is or he is." Ydum tells me from where he's standing at the table, surveying what was provided to eat. It looks like tacos and drinks. I guess the gods in charge of the games decided to give us a reward for surviving because there's alcohol along with the other drinks.

"My guess?" Anarus says, collapsing on the couch in his spot and putting his arms over his face. "Him. Boinkus was an idiot."

Boinkus, the god that laughed at us in the cave. His name was actually something else, Bokus or something, I think. He said we would be dead in the water because of me and Anarus, but instead he's already out of the games in the first one, either he or his teammate now dead.

"Why?" My voice shakes with anger and my hands are clenched in fists. "Why are they dead? What killed them and why? It's not right. She just skipped over them like they didn't matter. Like Leander wasn't a person, her god too, and deserving of at least some acknowledgement for what they sacrificed for these games. These stupid games."

"Let's not focus on that." Byder says, slinging an arm around my shoulder. "Let's just focus on how we did. Fourth. Not fucking bad."

I step out from under Byder's arm, but he doesn't seem to notice as Ydum comes over and hands him a beer. "Not fucking bad? Jinx was smart enough to remember that nature includes water, frozen water, and thought to ask for ice spears! And rocks. That's better than not fucking bad!"

I smile slightly, trying to do like he said and not focus on the loss of a team I didn't even know. "And you did all that work making everything. You made the net around the trees so tight we couldn't even get out, much less anything else get in." I tell him. Ydum holds a beer out to me as I come over to the table to look at the food, but I wave him away. I don't like alcohol. More accurately, I don't like what drunk people do, so I avoid it.

The dinner, I guess it's dinnertime, is actually tacos. Really? Spaghetti yesterday and tacos today. They're really going all out here, I think sarcastically. I make a plate and then hang back by the table. Ydum and Byder are now over on the couches, drinking and eating. Anarus groans and stands.

"Don't forget someone used their shadows to see what the fuck was coming. Who was that again? Oh, right." He says as he saunters over to the table and starts making himself a plate of food.

"And you're so modest about your contributions, too." I tease, leaning against the far wall away from the couches to eat.

Anarus just looks at me. I can't figure out what he's thinking, but he doesn't touch the alcohol either and comes over to lean against the wall near me to eat. He doesn't say anything, doesn't even keep looking at me, just eats his four tacos an arm's length away from me. I nibble at my one taco and watch Byder and Ydum drink. They eventually eat their food as well, but both drink more too.

Ydum and Byder seem to really be enjoying themselves, laughing and talking about something. Byder ducks into his room quickly and comes back out with a small black bag. He holds it out to Ydum, who nods, apparently knowing what it is. Once they settle again, Byder lays his right arm on Ydum's knee while Ydum starts pulling out something from the bag. As they talk and laugh, Ydum seems to be doing something to Byder's arm.

They don't even seem to notice Anarus and I standing on the other side of the room. But, once Ydum finishes whatever he was doing to Byder's arm, they start getting louder, and I decide I'm done. I really wish I was the type of person who could just join them, but I'm not, and I feel like Anarus is staying over by me because he doesn't want me to feel alone. Although, he isn't nice like that and he hasn't said anything, so I'm not really sure his reason for staying over here.

Either way, I decide it's time for me to be out, so I go into my room and close the door. I have no idea what time it is, but I get ready for bed anyway. I strip off Anarus's boots and Ydum's pants and undo my braid then climb into the bed. I wish I had something to read because I'm not really ready to sleep, but I definitely do not want to be out there in the sitting room, so there's nothing else to do.

There's a soft knock on the door. It has to be Anarus because I can still hear the other two laughing and talking. "Yeah?"

Anarus opens the door and comes in, making sure to close the door behind him. He just moves to the wall next to the door and sits down on the floor, pulling his legs up so he can prop his elbows on his knees. "They're loud and on my bed." He offers by way of explanation.

"Why don't you make them sleep on the couches and take the bedroom?"

Anarus raises his head and just stares at me, shadows swirling in my dim room. I hadn't turned off any lights, but only one was on when I came in and I didn't turn any on either. His face, or what I can see of it, says everything. He doesn't want to have to deal with drunk gods any more than I do. And him going to the bedroom will make him have to deal with them at some point when they are probably well and truly sloshed.

I sigh. "Fuck it." I move two of the pillows to make a barrier down the middle of the bed. "You're not sleeping on the floor. Get in."

"No."

"Don't be an ass, Anarus. You can't sleep on the floor. Get in the bed."

Anarus stands up and grabs one of the pillows I made the barrier with and takes it back over by the door. He puts it down on the floor then sprawls out, his head on the pillow, his feet stretched out until they are almost under the bed. "No."

I huff at him. "Whatever."

Anarus sits back up quickly. "You don't like to be touched. You can't stand people drinking. You had a panic attack about someone named Jacob. I don't know how far he got hurting you, but I know enough to know I will not get into that bed unless you mean for me to be in your bed." Anarus disappears to the floor again.

I sit quietly for a long time. "Jacob didn't hurt me." I finally whisper.

"Someone did." Anarus softly says back. "You don't have to tell me anything."

"I never told anyone anything. You're the only one that ever noticed me acting weird."

Anarus sits back up. "Not even your parents?"

I shake my head. "How do you tell them that the High Priest's son..." I swallow. "It would have been my word versus his. No one would have believed me."

"I believe you." Anarus tells me.

"You don't know anything. You don't even know what happened. You barely know me."

"I don't need to. I know you are sitting here terrified and that doesn't happen unless something happened." I don't know how to answer that, so I don't. Eventually, Anarus lays back down again. "Go to sleep, Jinx."

So easily said, not as easily done. Meditating on peace gets me nowhere.

Chapter Four

I WAKE UP TO sunlight streaming in through cracks in the curtains over the window. Rubbing my hands over my sleep crusted eyes and yawning, a noise makes me jump. I sit up quickly and see a shadowy figure on the floor. Oh, right. Anarus fell asleep in here last night. He's still sprawled on the floor next to the door, lying on his stomach, one arm under the pillow, his other arm and both legs flailed out around him.

I'm glad he didn't take me up on the offer to sleep on the bed. He looks like he would be a bed hog, like Catarina is. Gods, she would kick me all night long until I gave up and slept on the floor.

Getting up, I snag the other set of clean clothes Ydum gave me and head to the bathroom, quietly so I don't wake Anarus. I manage to nip into the washroom without Ydum and Byder seeing me. Inside the washroom, there are four bags lying on the counter next to the sink. Each bag has one of our names on it. The bag for Ydum and Byder are full, while the bags for Anarus and me are empty. I look in the bag for Byder and find it has clothes in it, the clothes he was wearing yesterday. Ah, laundry service. Perfect. I slip back into my room, grab the clothes I came in, and stuff them, as well as what I wore yesterday into the bag and leave it next to the others.

A quick shower, that still feels so good, and I'm dressed. Ydum found the soaps and towels in a cabinet under the sink, so I start digging around to see if there's anything else I can use down there. I find a toothbrush, thank goodness, and a brush and comb. I only have the one hair tie, and don't find more under the sink, but maybe either Byder or Anarus will let me borrow some if I need it. I finish righting myself for the day then head out to the sitting room.

First stop, coffee, because murder is not on the agenda today and Byder and Ydum are far too perky and awake already. Especially for people that got drunk last night. Besides the normal breakfast fare of eggs, bacon, toast, and fruit, there are also doughnuts on the table. Every conceivable type of doughnut, and ones I never thought of before. One of my sisters works at a bakery, so I recognize the cruller and the chocolate covered with sprinkles, but what that yellow cream oozing from the side of one doughnut is, I couldn't even guess. The one with pink flecks is raspberry, maybe? I decide it's better to ignore the food I don't recognize and just pour myself a cup of wakey-wakey juice.

As I'm taking the first sip, Anarus comes out of my room. He's shirtless again. He dips into the bathroom and reemerges about half a cup of coffee later, still shirtless but with obviously clean pants on and his wet, loose hair tells me he showered too. Shaved as well, evidenced by his now smooth cheeks and tidy moustache and goatee. I pour him a cup of coffee and hand it to him, then head to my spot on the couch.

Byder and Ydum are sitting on the couches, neither wearing a shirt, but Byder in another of those leather pants again while Ydum is in white cotton ones, talking about something. I notice that a spot above the top tattoo ring halfway up Byder's right forearm is a little red. The one that was red the first night looked fine yesterday, so he must have added new ring again. That must have been what Ydum was doing to Byder's arm last night. Both stop and stare as Anarus and I come to sit on the couches. They look from each other to the two of us, then back again, not even trying to suppress grins.

"Good morning." Byder says, far too cheerfully.

"Did you two have a good night?" Ydum is definitely not asking how we slept.

I point to my cup. "Not empty yet. Shush." Ydum leans over to look in my mug, then shrugs at Byder, smiling. I close my eyes, drink my coffee, and try to ignore them giggling like little school girls.

Anarus can't ignore them. He grumbles. "I slept on the floor. You two were loud and drunk."

"We were not drunk. Just relaxed. Is that a crime?" Ydum laughs.

"You were drunk." Anarus and I say at the same time, my words more a complaint, his are an accusation.

Byder shakes his head, his hair swaying. He didn't put it up yet. "Leave them, Ydum. There's no talking to them right now."

"Oh look, a surviving brain cell." Anarus snarls. "Any chance it will replicate and you can give one to Ydum so I don't have to deal with morons today?"

Ydum ignores the comment. "You'd think Ani would be in a good mood today. But I guess even getting laid doesn't tame shadow boy."

"I did not get—" Anarus starts to grumble, but he and I both know at this point getting defensive isn't going to help. "Whatever. Think what you want. I slept on the floor because you two were being numbskulls."

I drain the last of my first cup of coffee and go for a second. With my brain somewhat firing now, I notice the hint of green I saw on Ydum's wrist yesterday is a tattoo. He has ivy tattoos covering his whole left arm to the shoulder. As I watch them, I almost swear the ivy is moving.

Ydum notices me looking. "Yeah, they can move." As a demonstration,

Ydum twists his arm, flexing it, and the ivy sprouts new leaves.

"That's so cool." I say, actually awed a little. "Do yours do that, Anarus?"

"No. Mine are just actual tattoos." Anarus tells me. "His are part of his power. I get shadows and he gets moving vine tattoos."

I look at Byder. "Not mine either." He holds out his arm. "These are ritual tattoos for a hunt god. One line for each successful hunt from birth until completion of the games. Got my first line at nine." He says this with a hint of pride, as if that's an accomplishment. "But I could get a power tattoo when I'm crowned. My dad's also a hunt god and he has a tattoo of a bloodhound on his leg that can turn its head towards prey."

I frown. "Your dad? Is your mom also a hunt god? How does that work?"

"Mom is a witch." Byder explains. "A normal witch before the games, but after so long with dad, her magic tends to be better at working with hunting animals or whatever."

Ydum nods. "Basically, the same for me. Except it's Dad who is the witch. Mom is nature like me, but different. I can work with pretty much any plants or anything nature, and what they need to exist, but Mom is really only flowers. Dad's magic is nothing like Mom's, but is rather more metallurgy. Probably how I ended up a nature that can use anything in the ground, since most metals come from the dirt. Either way, most gods nowadays have one god parent and one now immortal witch that were paired up in the games. Almost no gods are all god anymore because there is too much inbreeding and it causes issues."

"When my tests came back funky, everyone kept asking if I was pure." I tell them. "The High Priest and healer even threatened to make my mom take Eecret, but she swore up and down that my dad is my dad."

"Makes sense they would think that." Ydum stands and heads to the table to grab a doughnut. He takes a bite and there's that yellow cream inside it. "One of the things the test looks for is god genes. All the humans who come to the games can't have any ancestors who were gods. That would defeat the whole point of the games if they did. It doesn't happen often, but sometimes a god who was made mortal because they failed at the games does end up marrying and having kids with a witch or another failed god. Years later, no one even remembers that great-grandparent used to be a god."

I shake my head. "It's so weird the things we were told wrong in Greenbriar. We thought children between gods and humans was a rare thing. Like a fairytale. But now, you're saying you are all children of a god and a witch."

"Well, almost all of us." Ydum corrects me.

Anarus has been silent this whole time. I turn to look at him. His face is blank as he sips his coffee. I wait a beat and he doesn't offer anything up, so I let it go. Not my story to demand. I change the topic instead. "The next game is weather. Any clues as to what we will need to do?"

Byder shrugs but Ydum sits back on the couch and answers. "In past games, they have had to cause weather to happen, stop it from happening, protect an area from weather, lots of different things. Pretty much all we can know is you will probably have to pick a painting again, like yesterday, and what that painting is will dictate what the environment is for our game."

"Is that how it works every year?" I ask.

"Kind of." Byder gives me a once over. "You should eat too, Jinx, not just have coffee."

While I scowl at Byder trying to command me to eat again, Ydum explains in his academic voice. "Each year is different on how, but there's some sort of choosing system the human does. Last year, everyone was in cabins in the woods and it was flagpoles. The human had to take the flag off the flagpole to make a choice. The year before was a city street and everyone had their own little house, the choosing done with flowers in pots. So far, this hotel with pictures isn't too bad."

Byder chuckles. "Yeah. Could you imagine trying to choose our environment for yesterday's game based on flower colors?"

I shiver at that idea. Our snow would have probably been a white flower, but I only can guess that because I know what the choices were. Had I not known, we could have ended up anywhere with no time to plan. As it was, we only did so well because Ydum was able to feed me plant ideas before we chose the snow.

"We should look and see if the paintings have changed." I say, ignoring Byder's not quite a suggestion that I should eat. "The sooner we know the options, the more time we have to try and prep."

"Good idea." Anarus finally speaks. He stands and heads to the door. The rest of us follow.

We aren't the only one with the same idea. In the hallway, Damek and his goddess, and Saffron and her god are milling around, moving from painting to painting. Saffron was the human whose name I got wrong last night. I know from the point board in our room that her team came in third with thirty points.

I move to look at the painting across the hall, near door nine, the one I chose yesterday. It's different, no longer a snowy copse. Instead, it's just an abstract with red lines everywhere. My gods move down the hall, looking at other paintings.

"They're all abstract lines." Damek tells us. His goddess gives him a pointed look. "What? It's not like that helps them any more than it helps us, Iella."

"Five colors. Red, blue, green, yellow, and black. Two of each except black." Saffron adds.

"Any thoughts on what the colors might mean?" I ask, more to my gods than the other teams, but Saffron and her god, Damek and Iella all shrug as Byder and Ydum shake their heads. Anarus is moving from painting to painting, his brow furrowed in thought. All seven of us watch him.

"Weather." He mutters to himself. "Yellow for sunshine? Blue could be clouds, maybe. Red, lightning? Black would probably be something bad, but what would green be?"

Anarus notices us all watching him. "I'm just guessing here. Don't pin anything on what I'm saying."

"I dunno." Saffron's god steps over to look at a painting. "It sounds good to me, Anarus."

Byder puts his hands on his hips. "If you think it sounds good, Velmos, I would trust your opinion on it."

Ydum comes over and stands close to my back and tilts his head toward the god Byder called Velmos. "Sky god."

I nod. A sky god would have the best guess about a weather game. "We should…" I don't want to be rude, but if we're going to work on this, I don't want to do it in front of the other teams.

Byder gets what I'm saying. "Yeah, thanks guys. Anarus." When Anarus looks at Byder, he lifts his chin to our door. Anarus walks back over from the foyer where he had been examining a painting and we go back in our room.

"Well, that was completely unhelpful." Ydum says, flopping onto his spot as soon as the door is shut.

I grab a cruller from the table and pick at it as I sit as well, only to appease Byder who's looking from the table to me, like he's going to get upset if I don't eat soon. "How do we plan?"

"None of us are especially gifted with anything weather related." Byder grabs a doughnut with blue cream filling and stands, eating it. "I mean, I can basically smell a storm coming, but that's about it. Can't even tell you if that storm will be rain, hail, or snow."

"That's something." I disagree. "It's better than nothing. Either of you have anything better?"

Anarus shakes his head. Ydum twists his mouth to the side. "I've made lightning before, but that was on accident. I can tell how much moisture is in the air and ground. You know, is there enough for the plant I want. I can gather it together for that plant. It's how I made the ice stuff with the yetis. I just shaped the water I pulled from the air into a specific shape and let the cold air freeze it how I wanted it. Since it was so cold, most of the moisture in the air was mostly frozen already and it didn't take much for it to freeze that little bit more I wanted. I can probably do something with storms eventually, but haven't done it before to know what."

Thinking, I realize Anarus is wrong that he can't do anything weather related. "Anarus, how dark can you make it with your shadows?"

"Hm." Twirling a finger, he lets shadows out. The room visibly darkens.

"You can block light. Probably heat too because your shadows feel cold." I sigh. "That just leaves me. I got nothing, though. Really nothing. I don't think plants or crystals will help here."

"You hid with your magic." Byder finishes his doughnut, wiping the powder off on his leg, and sits down. "How did you do that?"

"Basic meditation. I didn't even really know what I was doing. I know when I concentrate, I can use my magic to make my mind peaceful so I can go to sleep. I just thought of peace like I do for that, then concentrated on being hidden."

"Show us." Ydum sits forward in his seat.

I set my half-eaten cruller next to me on the couch and stretch my neck, closing my eyes. It's hard to concentrate knowing all three of them are watching me, but I focus on peace. Give me peace. Breathe in, breathe out, peace. The peace settles over me easily.

"Woah." Ydum says softly. I open my eyes and look at him. His eyes are wide, and he points to Anarus. Anarus is asleep, his head hanging back and his mouth slightly open. Byder is watching him as well. "You made Ani fall asleep."

My concentration breaks in surprise and Anarus's head snaps up. He looks disoriented and confused. "What the fuck?"

"Jinx made you fall asleep." Byder tells him.

Ydum is excited now. "Can you do anything else? You said you meditate on peace. Can you try something else? Like anger?"

"I've never tried." I tell him but I close my eyes. Anger, give me anger. I breathe deeply. Rage. Hostility. I say words that are related to anger that I can think of in my mind and feel the beginning of a small frustration that has no point building.

"You can fucking stop now." Anarus grumbles. My eyes pop open and I look at him. My concentration broken, I see fury seeping out of his face. I look at Ydum and Byder, who are just watching, not angry looking.

"Sadness." Byder says quickly. "Sad next."

Once again, I close my eyes, focusing on my breathing and all the words for sad I can think of, letting that little slice of melancholy start to burrow into my skin. Within minutes I hear a sound and open my eyes. Anarus is fighting tears. "Why is it only me?" I drop my concentration while he scrubs at his eyes.

"Why is it only Anarus?" I echo.

The others ignore our question, I think because they don't know either. "Is it only emotions?" Ydum just moves on. "What about something physical? We need weather. Can you try rain or something?"

I look around. "Maybe we should try that in the washroom. I don't think it'll work but, just in case, do we really want to soak our sitting room?"

"Good idea." Byder stands and we all follow, tromping into the washroom. It really isn't big enough for all four of us to be in comfortably. Byder hops up to sit on the counter by the sink and starts pulling his hair into a loose ponytail. Ydum uses the toilet as a chair, and Anarus just leans against a wall.

I go inside the shower stall, leaving the glass door open, and settle myself cross-legged on the floor, leaning back on the regular wall at the back. I close my eyes and concentrate. Breathe in, breathe out, rain. I need rain. Give me rain. Nothing happens, that I can tell. Breathe in, breathe out, come on, just a little rain.

"What are you thinking about?" Byder asks.

I don't open my eyes as I answer. "Rain."

"You tell yourself that you need peace, but emotions are easy. You already know why you need to create peace when you're making it." Ydum says. "You aren't doing magic with yourself though. You're doing it with the water. Try telling the water why you need what you need instead of asking it for the weather you want."

He's right. Intentions. We've always been taught magic only works with the right intentions. The water would need to know why I want it to do what I'm asking it to. Why would I need rain? A dry ground would need rain, flowers and plants and trees would need rain. An empty cistern would need rain. A parched throat.

"Jinx." Anarus says quietly. I open my eyes and look at him. He points to the mirror above the sink. Byder twists around to look at it as I do. The mirror is fogged over. It starts to clear up immediately as my concentration breaks.

"Well, damn." Ydum swears softly. "It's a start."

For the next hour, the four of us sit in the washroom while I concentrate on trying to make it rain and the males throw out ideas of things that would need the rain. I never get any further than making the mirror fog up.

"Random idea." Byder finally says, when I have tried yet again and failed to do anything beyond fog over a mirror. "Anarus, go touch Jinx."

"Why?" Anarus is still standing against the wall, his arms hanging down and his fingers drumming on the wall.

Byder shakes his head and leaps down from the countertop he was sitting on. "Call it a hunch. You were the only one effected by Jinx's moods."

Anarus grumbles but pushes off the wall and comes into the shower stall with me. He sits on the floor next to me and whispers quietly. "Where?"

"Shoulder." Anarus places his hand lightly on my shoulder. I twist, stretching my back under his touch.

"You sure you're good?" Anarus is still speaking very quietly.

"Yeah," I tell him, "just stiff."

"Let me know if you're not anymore, okay?"

I just nod and close my eyes to concentrate and think of all the ideas we have had about things that would need the rain.

"Say it out loud to me." Anarus instructs me.

"A dry cistern, the desert, a barren field." It's harder to concentrate with Anarus's hand on my shoulder. "A dry lakebed. A rainforest."

"Jinx." Byder says my name quietly. I open my eyes and see that, not only is the mirror fogged over, but so are the glass walls of the shower stall.

Ydum runs a finger down the wall next to him and it comes away wet. "Now, we're getting somewhere."

An idea comes to my mind. "Ydum, yesterday you told me that the soil had to be able to support the plants you were growing in the snow. But you are a god. Why did you need that to create things?"

"Because the life needed something to live with." Ydum explains. When I just stare at him, he tries again. "Without my mantle, I can make the start of life, without already having a seed beforehand, but I still have to start with a seed and make it grow. But the seed needs things to grow. Water, nutrients in the soil, air, whatever. And when I'm making it grow fast, it's going to use stuff a lot faster. If I had my mantle, I could just pop things up, a fully grown tree or whatever."

"Oh!" Byder exclaims. He reaches over and turns on the sink next to him. "To make it really rain, you need water. You're a witch, not a god. It's the end, not the beginning."

Not this shit again. "My teacher always said stuff like that and it never made any sense to me."

"Gods make the things." Anarus tries to make it make sense. "Witches just use the things."

"Not helping." I grumble. "Still confused what you mean."

Ydum comes over and crouches in front of me with his hand outstretched. "Make a flower grow in my hand."

"I can't." I tell him.

He nods. "That's right, you can't. Because you have nothing to work with." Ydum clenches his fist, then opens it. There's a small bit of dirt and seeds in his hand. "Now, I've given you the start. The seeds and dirt. Now, make the end, grow a flower."

"I still can't."

"Yes, you can." Anarus says, his hand still on my shoulder. "You made me cry and get mad. Make the flower grow."

I take a deep breath and concentrate on reasons I would need a flower. All that happens is I get a headache. "It's not working and my head hurts now."

"Maybe she actually can't." Byder shuts off the sink, comes over and crouches next to Ydum. "All her other magic has been made from something already there. Anarus's moods, the fog from the already damp washroom. She thinks of needs, not things."

Ydum furrows his brow. He clenches his fist around the dirt and then opens it again. The dirt sprouts a small green stem that grows into a single rose bud. "Try to make it bloom."

I concentrate on the rosebud. "Beauty, rose hip tea, pollen for honey." I start saying things that I would need a bloomed rose flower for. Slowly, one petal of the rosebud peels open, then another. Finally, the whole tiny rosebud is open.

Ydum smiles. "You are an end magic witch, Jinx."

I shake my head, confused. "I still don't get it."

He tries to explain again. "Magic, god powers, all that, it's a spectrum. A line from start to finish. Think of it like building something. A god, a full god with their mantle in place, could make a house appear where they want it without ever going to a market to buy a single tool or hammering a nail into a piece of wood. They can just need the thing and have the thing. They will just know they need a two-bedroom house made of stone and mortar, with one washroom with running water, and poof. There it is, fully decorated and full of all the furniture they would want exactly as they want it. A god's power. They started with nothing, used nothing, and ended up with what they wanted."

Byder shifts his weight to sit all the way down. "We don't have our mantles yet, so we can't be full god powers. If we want to build that same house, we need to make the stones, mortar, whatever the base pieces are. Then, we can use our power to build the house really fast, then do the same with the decorating."

"Exactly." Ydum nods at Byder. "A beginning magic witch has to actually get the supplies and equipment, but can build that house fast with their magic, and decorate it fast, with stuff they know is available somewhere in the world, but can't just make the stuff themselves. An end magic witch, like you, can only walk through that house with a list of items available at the marketplace, and know there is a need for that thing. The sitting room needs a couch, and there are three types of couches in this specific market, so you pick one that fits the space and, poof, it appears where you want it. End magic can't build the house, because that's not what they need. They need a house to live in, so they can't make the house itself since that isn't the actual need, but can fill an already built house with all things they need to live in it."

Ydum is still holding the rose. "If I was a full mantled god, I could have made a whole fully-grown rose bush out of nothing. But I'm not, so I needed dirt and seeds and to actually make the flower grow, faster than normal, but still, it had to grow. If you were a beginning magic witch, you could have made the rose grow like I did from just the seed and dirt I provided. But you are an end magic witch. So, you couldn't make a rose just to make a rose. You had to coax a need from the rose. You needed the petals to open so you can make tea from them."

"So, what's the difference between a beginning magic witch and you three right now?" I am still confused but it feels like I am getting it a little better than my teachers ever explained it.

"The dirt and seeds." Anarus answers this time. "A beginning magic witch would need to get the dirt and seeds from somewhere. Ydum just had them because he wanted them."

I turn to Anarus. "Wait, what? Ydum got the dirt and seeds from somewhere, didn't he? Now, I'm confused again."

Ydum smiles. "That's where you're getting tripped up. No, I didn't. This dirt and seeds did not exist before I made them. Since I am not a full god yet, I can only make the base things exist when they never did before. Dirt, rose seeds, oleander seeds, whatever the most basic parts of something is. The beginning magic witch needs to actually get them from somewhere. If a beginning magic witch did what I did, there would be a small hole in the ground somewhere that is missing a handful of dirt. You couldn't do what I did because you had no need for it the dirt itself, or the seeds. You needed the petals of the flower, so you needed the whole flower. And because you are end magic, you had to have the flower already here when a beginning magic witch could have called those things to them."

"So, how does that work for you two?" I ask Anarus and Byder.

Byder answers first. "I am a hunt god. When I get my mantle, I'll be able to have whatever tools I need to hunt an animal with instantly. Need to catch a rabbit? I'll be able to just know where the rabbit trail is and catch one as they come to me, either with my hands or whatever weapon I want to use, a weapon I can make instantly. For now, I can create the string and make a perfect snare and can scent out a rabbit trail easily. I can catch a rabbit in about twenty minutes, rather than a human who has to get the string, make the snare, take it to the woods, set it up, and wait who knows how long hoping they got the spot right."

"My powers are a little more nebulous." Anarus scratches at his goatee as he explains. "Obscurity is not really something people can quantify that well. I have shadows because the root word for obscurity means darkness, or at least, that's what I think. Other than that, I can make people not notice me around, cause confusion, or make people forget about something with my shadows. What that will translate to when I get my mantle," he lifts only one shoulder in a half shrug, "not sure. There aren't any other obscurity gods I can ask. They aren't even sure what pantheon I belong to. I've been mostly making it up as I go along, just trying to do something because it might work, and either it does, and I know I can, or it doesn't and I know I can't."

I think I'm understanding. "So, you guys can conjure up any most basic parts of something you want or need, based on your powers, and just have those things to make whatever you want really fast. But I need to have a viable need for something and that thing already available, within my sight and completely made already, to be able to use it."

"Exactly!" Ydum exclaims. "It'll be something we have to play with for you. See how much of a need counts as a need and how already there and created the thing needs to be for you to use it, but we have five more days after today to try it out. For now, to make rain, you have to already have water. You haven't been able to do more than make things foggy because there's only so much moisture in the air for you to work with."

"Let's try it one more time, with the sink on to give you access to more water." Byder jumps up to turn on the sink.

I twist and stretch, then settle, Anarus's hand still on my shoulder. I close my eyes and concentrate again. It's harder because I'm tired and there's a lot of information rattling around in my mind which I push down. I take a deep breath and try anyway. "Rain. I need rain. Dry cistern. Desert. Blooming flowers. A dry river bed. I need rain."

I feel little splashes on my head and Ydum whoops loudly. I open my eyes and smile. There are fat drops of rain falling from the ceiling. Not many, and it seems more like the water is just condensing on the ceiling rather than storm clouds forming, but it's definitely rain.

I hold my hand out as a few drops fall into my palm. "It's no hurricane."

"But it is rain." Anarus removes his hand from my shoulder. "We'll keep working on it. But for now, you're exhausted. You need a break and food."

We all get up and leave the bathroom. Byder shuts off the sink before leaving, but the ceiling is still raining. I smirk as I realize one of us is going to have to clean up a lot of puddles in the bathroom. In my mind, I decide it won't be me. I cooked, one of the gods can clean.

The doughnuts that had been breakfast have been replaced with sandwiches and cut vegetables. Coffee, hot tea, and milk replaced with fruit juices and cold tea.

"Did someone come in while we were all in the bathroom?" I'm not comfortable with that idea, someone being able to just walk in our rooms at any time, even if they are probably working for the gods controlling the games.

Ydum just shakes his head. "Gods. No one came in. Drila probably just made them appear. Didn't you notice the laundry bags were gone from the bathroom?" I hadn't noticed actually. "They'll just reappear in our rooms when the clothes are clean."

"Why doesn't she just magic our clothes clean instead of making someone wash them?" I ask absentmindedly as I fill up a plate with a nut paste and strawberry jam sandwich and carrot sticks. Once I have everything I want, Byder sets his plate, with three sandwiches and cut cucumber slices on it, on top of mine in my hands. I look at him questioningly.

He just asks, "juice or tea?"

"Tea." I tell him and he pours a cup of tea and another of juice and starts walking to the couches. I follow and, once we're sitting, he takes his plate back and swaps me it for my cup of tea.

Ydum answers my initial question as he comes to sit too. For some reason, without talking about it, Anarus and Ydum have swapped spots on the couches. "Time. Energy. That's all limited. Probably some humans have jobs working in laundry for the games. They'll do it the regular way, or with a little magic if they are witches with the power to do so."

"You saw it yesterday. Ydum got really tired doing all that growing plants." Byder says around a cucumber slice in his mouth. "Mantled gods wouldn't get as tired as fast, but even they have limits. Eat, Jinx."

I start eating because I'm starving, not because Byder told me to. And tired. Once my food is gone, I curl my legs under me and scootch down so I can rest my head on the arm of the couch. "Why did you have Anarus put his hand on me in the bathroom, Byder?" My eyes are closed but I'm still listening to his answer.

"Your mood stuff affected him." Byder tells me. "You two must have some sort of bond already that Ydum and I don't. The closer a god and a witch are, emotionally or whatever, not just physically, the more they can help each other. Mom and Dad paired up in the games. Now Mom can help Dad when his energy is low, and Dad can help Mom too. But, when Mom is pissed at Dad, his abilities as a god are hampered. But then, they've been together for thirty years."

Byder is still talking but I'm tired and not really listening anymore.

I must fall asleep because I wake up, still on the couch, the blanket pulled over me. I open my eyes and look around. Anarus is still sitting on the other end of the couch, but Byder and Ydum are nowhere to be seen. "Where are Byder and Ydum?"

"In the hallway. A bunch of the different teams are out there, trying to figure out what the pictures might mean." Anarus tells me.

"Why didn't you go with them?"

Anarus just looks down at his lap. I follow his gaze and realize my feet are on his lap. "You started mumbling every time I tried to move, so I stopped."

"Oh." I move my feet to pull them off his lap, but Anarus drops one his hands down on my feet, holding them there. Instantly, I feel that static charge again. That one that makes me want him to keep touching me. He realizes what he did and immediately lifts his hand back up.

"Sorry."

"No. I'm sorry I sprawled all over you." I pull my feet back and sit up. The idea of being alone with Anarus should bother me. He's always standoffish and grumpy. But it isn't. Not at all. And the idea of him touching me is not as panic inducing as it normally is. When did I stop being annoyed by Anarus and start feeling something... else?

"I didn't mind." There are shadows moving over Anarus, but he doesn't look angry.

"What emotion are you trying to hide, Anarus?" I think, based on what he said before about how his power of obscurity works, that when his shadows are more obvious, it means he wants to be less seen.

Anarus doesn't answer, but the shadows over his face clear up. I had felt something when he touched me. Something that drew me in, something making me not want to pull away from his touch. Which is confusing considering I've only known him for two days and he's been rude and mostly hostile for all that time. But it's there, an itch under my skin that wants to be closer to him.

Anarus clears his throat, not looking at me. "I'm, um, I'm not good with touching usually. I was passed around a lot when I was younger, most of the families taking me because they were told to. Pure gods are usually not good, and I'm pure, probably. So, the families were more likely to touch me only for physical discipline, whether I actually did something to deserve it or they were just worried I would eventually. No one really ever did that hugging stuff or whatever. So, yeah. I understand the whole no touching thing. But, um, you? You, I want to, um, I don't mind so much."

I don't look at Anarus either. "When I was sixteen."

Anarus interrupts me. "You don't have to tell me shit because I told you shit, Jinx."

I glare at him for half a second then keep talking. "When I was sixteen, the High Priest's son, Jacob, invited our whole class to his seventeenth birthday party. My parents made me go because, well, it was the High Priest's son. Everyone was getting drunker and stupider the later the night went on and the adults were all gone, not caring anymore. I wanted to leave, but Jacob told me not to. He cornered me in a room, he and his friends." I've never said any of this out loud before. I'm not sure I know how. Anarus just waits patiently. "Anyway, um, Jacob never touched me, just told his friends what to do while he watched, laughing. I ran as soon as I could get free from them. So, I don't like being around people drinking. I don't like being trapped with no way out or touching. But, um, you? I don't mind so much."

Anarus just nods. "Always leave you an escape route. Got it." He waits a beat, then adds, "can I touch you now?"

As soon as the word, "yes," leaves my lips, Anarus has me by the waist, lifting me over to him. He turns me so I am facing him, kneeling on the couch, my legs straddling his lap.

"You good?" He asks roughly. He takes his hands off my waist and leaves them loose on the couch, on either side of my knees.

"Yes. You?" Anarus answers by kissing me. His lips are as soft as I thought they might be. I bring my hands up and cup his cheeks, running my nails through his scruffy facial hair. My heart races as that static energy burns and goosebumps erupt on my arms.

Behind me, the door opens and Byder and Ydum come in the sitting room. "It's not like they know more or anything, just because… Hello." They're looking at us. Without even seeing them, I know they're both looking at us.

Ydum chuckles. "Should we leave again?"

I move back over to my seat on the couch, my face aflame. Anarus glares at them. "Fuck off."

Byder is laughing too. "I think you mean fuc…"

I cut him off. "Did you guys figure anything important out?"

"We didn't." Ydum says. "But I think you guys did."

"Let. It. Go." Anarus snarls at them.

Ydum sits down on the couch, with his hands up in surrender. "Not joking. Seriously. That actually may be something. Like Byder said, the stronger a bond between a god and a witch, the better the witch's magic works. You two," Ydum clears his throat with a fake cough, "well, Jinx's magic may be able to do more than make the ceiling drip."

"Later, though." Anarus says. "I was thinking while Jinx was asleep. We have five weeks until the combat game. That one always has some heavy level fighting. If she doesn't know how to fight, we may want to start training for it now."

Byder nods and sits down with us. "That's actually a good idea, Anarus. The physical workout can strengthen your magic too, Jinx."

I'm glad to be focusing on literally anything else right now. "They always talked about knowing your body and being centered in it for meditation. I assume fighting skills would require a lot of the same knowledge."

"We make this our permanent schedule?" Ydum suggests. "Mornings are magic, afternoons are combat?"

We all agree and, immediately, Byder and Ydum are grabbing the table and chairs to move them over by the couches to make a larger clear space for working on combat skills. Byder fights his hair back into the ponytail again, almost all of it having fallen out during the course of the day. I am just about to ask why he always makes his hair tie so loose when he gruffly tells me to put my boots back on. It almost sounds like a command again, so I roll my eyes at him. But I do it anyway.

I thought that they were going to make me fight one of them but when I asked who I fight first, all three gods laughed.

"The air." Ydum tells me.

"Yourself." Byder says.

"What?" They aren't making any sense. Again.

"Do a push up." Anarus tells me. I lie down on the floor, on my stomach and put my palms down to push myself up and, immediately, Anarus stops me. "Hands are wrong, neck is wrong, feet are wrong, butt is wrong."

I grumble. "Was there anything I'm doing right?"

Ydum laughs. "You are on the floor. That's right."

I roll my eyes at him, but Byder gets down on the floor with me. "Here, Jinx. Do what I am doing. Anarus, correct her form." Byder puts himself in a plank, and I try to copy him.

Anarus touches each of my wrists gently. "Move your hands so they are under your shoulders." I move one hand, then the other. "Now, put your feet together." I do as he says. "Pull your butt up."

I turn to look at him. "What?"

"I'm gonna touch you." Anarus warns me first, then he places one hand on my stomach and another on the small of my back. "Lift up here. Make your back straight from your shoulders to your toes, on an angle to the floor."

I focus on holding my body at that angle, but as soon as he moves his hands, apparently, I do it wrong again.

"Hold this tight. Don't let yourself sink back down." Anarus puts his hand back on my stomach. I do what he says, but as soon as he lets go, I know my hips sink back down again. He puts his hand back, and I pull it back up.

"First goal." Ydum decides. "Be able to plank without Ani holding you."

My arms are already twitching. I look over at Byder. He looks like he could carry on a whole conversation while I am gritting my teeth and starting to sweat.

"Good idea to start this now, Anarus." Byder says, proving my thought right. He doesn't even sound like he's struggling. "You doing good, Jinx?"

"Mmhm." I hum through gritted teeth.

"She's shaking." Anarus tells them my lie. "Lie down." I drop to the floor with a groan.

"That's was almost a whole minute. Not bad for a first try." Byder says, jumping up.

I don't get up from the floor, but speak into the carpet. "A minute is good? Byder isn't even sweating."

"And I have been doing this since I was five." Byder chuckles. "We all have. We have nineteen years, or, well, sixteen in Anarus's case, experience over you."

"Now, for sit ups." Ydum tells me.

We continue this way for sit ups, squats, and planks on each side. For every exercise, Byder demonstrates, Ydum comments and times, and Anarus corrects my form. I feel like my arms are burning and my legs will fall off when Ydum finally says, "running."

Byder furrows his brow. "How?"

Ydum only smiles in a way that makes me scared. "Follow me." We follow him out of the dorm into the hallway. "Byder, Ani, stay in the doorway and watch. Jinx, follow me." I follow Ydum to the farthest end of the hallway between door nine and ten.

"When I say go, run to the other end of the hallway, touch the floor by the far wall, then turn and come back. Fast as you can." Ydum tells me.

I hear Byder laughing. "You're a sadist, Ydum." But it doesn't sound nearly as hard as the pushups were, so I don't understand.

I stand at the wall and wait. "Ready?" Ydum asks and I nod. "Go." I take off, running as best I can. At the end of the hall in the foyer area, I touch the floor where Ydum said, then turn and run back.

As I get closer to Ydum, he tells me, "Touch the spot on the floor where you started, then go again. Don't stop. Keep going." I do as he says, and as I make my way back down the hall towards the foyer, I see people watching from the foyer area. I ignore them and keep going.

A male I don't know calls out, "You're making your human do shuttle sprints?"

I don't hear any of my gods reply, and I can't see them because they are behind me, but they must do something to acknowledge him, because he laughs, shaking his head. "Smart."

As I make my way back to Ydum, he says stop. "I want you to watch how I run. Look at my knees, my arms, my head. Notice how I move from my hips instead of knees. I stay on my toes the entire time. My head is up, not ducked down. Notice how I turn to go back the other way. Okay?"

I nod and Ydum takes off, doing two laps like I did. When he gets back to me, he's barely winded. I hate him for that. As he ran, more doors along the hallway opened up, with gods and humans poking their heads out to see what's going on.

"You see the difference?" Ydum asks me. I nod but I'm looking down the hall at everyone watching. Ydum uses one finger under my chin to turn my head back to face him. "Hey. Ignore them, beautiful. This is about you and our team, okay? About us being the best we can. If they copy our idea, that's fine, but they get nothing from watching you run. Go again."

I take in a deep breath, and wait. Ydum tells me to go, and I run, trying to focus on all the things Ydum told me. I do two laps and when I stop, Ydum nods.

"Better." He tilts his head back to our door, where Anarus and Byder are still watching. "Too many eyes. That's good enough for now."

We go back in the room and, instead of sitting on the couch, I collapse on the floor in front of it, leaning back on it, groaning. "I hate all of you right now."

"Sore?" Byder chuckles.

"I feel sore and like I suck at everything." I know I'm whining but I don't care. "Maybe Anarus was right. The games gave me three of you because I'm too crap to do anything without extra help."

"Actually," Anarus comes over and sits on the couch next to where I'm leaning against it, "you are doing pretty well, all things considered."

I turn to look at him. "What do you mean?"

Ydum answers for him, ticking things off on his fingers. "You got exactly zero time to prepare. You were never given any of the manuals. You literally came here with just the clothes on your back and no idea what the fuck was going on. You had almost no magical training and actually no physical training."

"Yeah," Byder chimes in. "You have more right to bitch than almost anyone here, but you really haven't. You just do what we say. And you keep asking questions when you don't understand."

Anarus touches my shoulder with one finger, getting my attention. "I don't think you realize how much you did today. You went from thinking you just meditate to fall asleep better to making it rain in the bathroom just because we told you that you could."

"That's no mean feat, Jinx." Byder concludes.

I cross my arms over my chest and frown. They are making me sound like I did well and I really, really feel like I didn't. "You said I could and I just trusted you know more."

Ydum snorts. "Yeah, the three gods you met two days ago after they had a fist fight in a cave. You just trusted us. You're in the games where you can get killed and you just trusted us. Totally normal, rational behavior."

I roll my eyes. "Nothing about these games is rational. Why should I be any different?"

Chapter Five

WE DON'T TALK AFTER that. We never moved the table back, so when dinner appears, we just load up our plates from the couches and eat. Hamburgers and fried potato sticks. I swear the games are going so simple with the food. If Drila is in charge of the menu, it's like she forgot that we're all adults and not teenagers in high school. Although, the way the guys talk, it sounds like they aren't actually considered adults until after the games. I was done school at eighteen, and considered an adult. We can't get married until after we test for the games, and really no one bothers moving away from their parents or planning any kind of life until after that either, because why bother if you might end up coming here, but we're adults by all rights.

As we eat, Byder's hair is a problem. It keeps slipping out of his bun and falling in his face, annoying him.

"Who taught you to do your hair, Byder?" I ask him as he complains about it again.

He shakes his head as he eats, making more hair fall loose. "No one. I always had short hair until this year."

I give him a confused look. "Then how has this not been an issue before?"

Byder blushes so Ydum answers me. "His mom has been doing his hair for him since he decided to grow it out last year."

I hold in my laughter. "Why did you decide to grow it out?"

"Kind of a hunter god tradition thing to have long hair at the games. Like the tattoo lines. Dunno why, just is." Byder mumbles as he remakes the bun for a fourth time.

"Oh, for frack's sake." I mutter under my breath and go stand on the couch next to him. I slap at his shoulder. "Sit forward." He does as I say, and I slip behind him to sit on the top of the back of the couch. I pull the hair tie out of his hair and hold it up for him to take. Using my fingers as combs, I work a quick woven braid starting on the crown of his head.

"Thanks." Byder tells me as I get off the couch.

"My turn?" Anarus asks.

"Your hair is already braided." I turn to Ydum. "And before you even ask, yours is too short."

"Not fair." Ydum pretends to complain.

I change the topic while I sit on the couch. "You guys all seem to know a lot about each other. I don't know any of the other humans here."

"We were all in school with each other since we were little." Byder explains. "Ydum and I were in the same grade, Anarus a few years behind us obviously. But all the gods here were in me and Ydum's grade together besides him. The twenty-one gods besides Anarus that entered the games in the cave were all the gods born twenty-four years ago. All of them, from everywhere. We all live in Veirveil, so we all have known each other since we were really little."

"Humans are everywhere." I tell them. "There were at least fifty kids, I think, around my age in school, in my grade. We kind of all combined classes by the last four years of school since we were such a small group. We had more kids in my class in just my village than all the gods had for one year."

"Gods don't tend to have big families. One or two kids at most." Ydum steals a potato stick from my plate even though there are more right there on the table. He just smiles when I glare at him. "Braid my hair too. There are less and less families every year. Less and less kids."

I roll my eyes at Ydum and climb back up on the couch between him and Byder. He immediately sits forward so I can sit behind him. "It's going to look stupid. You don't have enough hair." But I try my best anyway. When I am done, it does look ridiculous, but Anarus hands me the hair tie from his braid and I do what I can to tie it off and move back to my spot on the couch.

Ydum pretends to prance into the bathroom, looks in the mirror and cries out, "I'm gorgeous!" Which makes the rest of us laugh. He comes back out and acts like he's modeling his look for us. The hair tie falls out when he tries to toss his head back and the whole thing comes undone, making us laugh even harder. Yeah, maybe we aren't as adult as I think we are. Or maybe we're just bored in a really stressful situation. Probably a little of both.

Ydum rescues the runaway hair tie, and hands it back to me. Immediately, Anarus scoots down on the floor and sits in front of me. "It's not braided anymore."

I shake my head and lean over to whisper in his ear. "Jealous?"

He turns and gives me a look, one eyebrow raised up, then slides back on the floor until he's sitting between my feet, leaning back on the couch. He pulls his long hair up so none of it is trapped behind him. I start combing it out with my fingers, since most of his braid actually stayed braided without the hair tie.

While I comb out Anarus's hair, Ydum and Byder start telling stories about the other gods. When the hair is all untangled, Anarus leans his head back and stretches out his legs so that they end up under the table in the middle of the space. He closes his eyes and soft shadows start playing around his face, but not like he's trying to hide. More like he's just too relaxed to hold them all in. It's the most relaxed I have seen him, so I keep doing what I am doing, running my fingers through his hair, not really braiding it, just sort of massaging his scalp while I play with the hair and the other two talk.

Byder tells a story as I play with Anarus's hair. "Wilros, the god with Asteria, when we were ten, he shaved off all his hair. There was a bunch of older kids that started that trend back then. But unfortunately, Wilros didn't know that he had a huge bright white skin mark under his hair, right at the top of his head. So, when he shaved it all off to look like the cool, older kids, he ended up just looking like a bird had pooped on him for three months."

"Oh, good grief." I laugh. "I bet you were all so nice about that."

Ydum flashes me a wicked smile. "Not a chance. But that wasn't as bad as when we were fifteen and Iella, the goddess with Damek, tried to use color powder to make her blond hair red."

I look at him, askance. "Color powder doesn't work on god hair. It says so right on the box."

"Yup." Ydum pops his lips on the p. "Her hair was bright pink for almost the whole year. She was called fairy lace for years because of it."

"I was in class with Iella's younger sister." Anarus says without opening his eyes. "Her sister found the leftover powder like three weeks later and used it on purpose, hoping to make her hair the same pink as Iella. Unfortunately, her dark blond and the powder did not make that same bright pink. She ended up with streaks of a muddy pink randomly throughout her hair. Her parents were livid."

The other two keep talking but I mostly stop listening when Anarus pulls on my left foot, moving it so that my leg wraps around him. He unties my boot and pulls it off, then does the same thing to my right foot, but instead of just letting my right foot go, he starts massaging it. His eyes are still closed, but I see his shadows move so that his hands and my foot in his lap are hidden.

My hands still as he moves to rubbing my left foot. Anarus tips his head back further and looks up at me, his eyes questioning me. My eyes flick over to glance at Byder and Ydum, but even if they were paying attention, between the table in the way and Anarus's shadows how they are, all they would be able to see is Anarus sitting on the floor in front of me. Not that he's doing anything crazy, just rubbing my feet, but it feels more intimate, especially with him looking at me like that.

The dinner poofs away, startling me. I hadn't seen that magic at work yet. It feels weird. But my gods don't seem fazed by it at all. Byder and Ydum just move the table back where it belongs. We hear a noise outside the room and Byder goes to investigate. When he opens the door and starts laughing, the rest of us come over to see what's funny. I poke my head out and see Isis and Amanda running up and down the hallway, like I was earlier.

"I hate you, Jinx!" Amanda calls as she sprints past. "You and your fucking gods too."

"You're welcome!" Ydum calls out to her as we all laugh.

Byder closes the door and I say, "We went from the team they thought would be out right away to the one they are all copying in two days. That's gotta be a record or something."

"Definitely a record." Byder agrees.

For the next five days, we follow the same pattern. Mornings after breakfast, once Anarus and I have had enough coffee to not start a land war, and I have ensured Byder's hair isn't going to annoy him all day, we all head into the washroom and work on creating rain. I ask on the third day if we should attempt some other type of weather, but Ydum nixes that idea.

"If it's cold enough to make snow or hail, then it'll be the same process, just a different need you focus on." He tells me. "If you can make it rain, reliably, then everything else can come from that. True storms will come from having enough water to build up clouds until they are that powerful. We really don't want to try to work with lightning inside. We saw what happened with Wren and Kutar."

Wren's god, Kutar, is actually a storm god, and they were practicing working together in their room the night before when Wren's magic went a little off and Kutar accidentally made lightning hit the carpet. There was a lot of smoke and their room got doused with water as Drila popped in fast to put out the fire. Everything they owned got soaked and they had to spend the night in the extra room that used to be Leander's while their room was fixed.

We definitely don't want to repeat that. So, for now, I stick to trying to make the ceiling rain. Two days before the next game, I can reliably make it drip fat heavy drops and twice actually get enough moisture to build up in a rising warm air that there are wispy white tendrils that look like they might be thinking of becoming clouds eventually. We realize on the last day that, if Anarus sends his cold shadows to the ceiling to make the upper air cooler than the lower air, it helps.

After practicing weather magic every day, we move the table and work on physical fitness. Everyone caught on to the using the hallway for running, so we have started delaying eating lunch to have the hallway alone. After a quick stretching session, we move right out to the hallway once the lunch food appears on the table. While everyone else eats, we run, or really, I run and Ydum instructs and the others placate me. The hallway is big enough for two of us to run side by side comfortably, so the gods have been taking turns running with me.

Ydum usually does a warm up jog with me, then I do more of the sprints he had me do the first day, only he makes them more difficult. Instead of just up to the foyer and back twice, I have to run from the ninth and tenth doors to ours, touch the floor, then turn and go back. Then, I immediately turn again without stopping and go to between the sixth and fifth and back, then between the fourth and third and back, then between the first and second and back, then to the end in the foyer, stopping to touch the floor at each spot where I turn. Then I work my way back again, going up from the first and second doors to the ninth and tenth.

Then, when I hate Ydum enough again, I race Anarus. It's just an up and back regular run of the hallway, but I never win so it's annoying. Then, I race Byder and never win. Finally, Ydum comes back and takes me through two cool down laps. On the fourth day, I complain that they are only racing me and that I have to do the most work while they just eat and watch. So, Anarus and Byder race and Ydum races Anarus when he wins. Ydum wipes the floor with him, which is funny because my money was actually on the hunt god being the best runner.

When the other teams start trickling out to use the hallway for running practice, we go back into our room and work on the exercises. Byder and Ydum do them with me, encouraging me to keep going when I want to drop, while Anarus handles making sure I keep my form. I don't know if Anarus said something about my touch issue, or ever since they caught us kissing the other two just assume things, but when I ask if they are going to switch off watching my form so Anarus can do the workouts too, Byder waves me off.

"You're comfortable with the routine as it is." Byder dismisses me. "Don't change what isn't broken."

"That's not how that saying goes. It's don't fix what isn't broken." I grumble by way of complaint as I try really hard to not let my butt sink in my plank again.

"Same thing." Byder shrugs. The fact that he can shrug while doing a plank pisses me off enough I stop bothering to complain.

After that, I eat what food one of them nabbed for me before the lunch cleans itself up. We had to play around with it for a bit, but figured out all the food and dishes in the front room, crumbs, spills, and all, get magically whisked away whenever the gods doing the magic for food distribution decide a meal is over, but what isn't in the sitting room area or on the table doesn't. So, they have to purposely set plates of lunch aside in the bedroom for me to eat later. For the rest of the afternoon, we usually just relax and try to find some way to fill the time until dinner.

On the second day, Ydum makes us keep the plates that come with lunch and dinner rather than set them back on the table after we are done eating. When we ask him why, he just smiles and taps the side of his nose like he has a secret.

The third day, he finally shows us why we kept the plates. After I finish eating and we rest a bit from working out, Ydum spreads the plates out on the floor where the table should have been. He had written numbers on small pieces of paper and sets them on the plates. The two plates closest to the couch are labelled ten, then twenty on the next two, then thirty on the next two, then the ones furthest from the couches are labelled forty. He hands us each a few balled up socks.

Ydum tells us to move out of the way, and, from standing on the couch at the point farthest from the plates, he throws his three balled up socks, one at a time, and writes his score down on a piece of paper he hung over the point board on the door to our room. "First to five hundred points wins." He explains.

"You made a freaking game!" I exclaim. "Something I might even win at."

"Yes, I made a freaking game." Ydum smiles back at me, a wicked gleam in his eyes as he saunters over to me, his hands in his pants pockets. "But you will not win it, beautiful."

But I do win. Then, I find out how competitive Ydum is because we have to play the rest of that night until he wins at least once. It takes six games of sock ball for Ydum to win, because I win three times and Byder and Anarus each win once. We now play at least three games of sock ball a night.

On the fifth night, I make Byder practice doing his own hair until he can make at least a ponytail without help. Anarus helps and Ydum makes jokes about it the whole time.

"It's probably not normal how much time all four of us spend in this washroom together." Ydum comments as we stand there, making Byder redo the ponytail for the third time to make sure he can really do it.

"What's not normal is a twenty-four-year-old male who can't do his own hair." I retort. "Do it again, Byder, and get all of the hair in it this time."

Byder groans at me. "Is this payback for the push-ups?"

"Maybe."

"Even if it is, it's fucking funny as fuck." Anarus tells him.

Now, on the sixth night, the last night before the second game, after dinner, we are all a bundle of nerves. "I want to look at the paintings again." I say and head out to the hallway. I'm not the only one with that idea. Almost all the other teams are also in the hallway looking at the paintings. It doesn't seem like anyone else has a clue what they mean either.

Anarus and I stand in front of the black one between the first and third doors. I'm looking at it as closely as I can, trying to find any details that might help.

"What if we prepped completely wrong?" I whisper.

Anarus moves his fingers ever so slightly so that they brush mine with how close together we are standing, sending that static scattering down my skin again. That's all that has happened between us in the last five days, slight, hidden touches. His hand on my shoulder as we talk. My toes on his thigh as I'm curled up on the couch. Things that could just be casual or accidental, but aren't. Touches that make my skin tingle and itch for something. A confusing something that I really want to explore.

"It is what it is." He tells me. "We did the best we could."

I tilt my head to rest it on his arm and stop with my head sideways. "Anarus." I say his name as quietly as I can. "Do not copy me right now, but wait a minute then do it."

Anarus furrows his eyebrows at me, but listens. I put my head back straight and after a minute, Anarus tips his head like I had mine. "Shit. You look at the blue and yellow ones, I'll look at the red and green."

We walk apart and I go to one of the blue paintings. I pretend to stretch my neck to each side as I stand there, pushing on my chin to deepen the stretch. Like I am just trying to crack my neck. Ydum saunters over to me, his hands in his pockets. He just raises one eyebrow at me. I walk away and find a yellow painting, and he follows me. I look at it and sigh heavily. Then, cross my left arm over my stomach and rest my right elbow on it, letting my cheek fall into my right hand, as if I am tired. Ydum pointedly does not watch me do this, but looks at the painting.

"These are giving me nothing." He says blandly.

"Me either. I'm done. This isn't helping." I walk back to the room where Anarus is already waiting with Byder.

As soon as the door is shut, Ydum asks quietly. "Okay, what was that? You were looking at the paintings all weird."

I smile. "You have to tilt your head to the side and un-layer the letters."

"Huh?" Byder looks at me, confused.

"They're not abstracts." Anarus explains. "They're sideways. Jinx figured it out."

"The letters aren't in a line, either. They are stacked on top of each other." I grab a piece of paper we had been using for sock ball and flip it over. Ydum hands me his writing tool, and I draw the black painting, then hold it up for Byder and Ydum to see. I trace the letters as I say them. "Capital R, 'A' in the bottom of the R, the smudge over the leg of the R and that leg makes the 'I', and finally the 'N' is off the leg of the R."

"No shit." Ydum takes the paper from me. "The black painting says 'rain.' Jinx, you're a genius!"

"The red ones say sleet and the green say hail." Anarus tells us.

I nod. "Yellow is snow and blue is fog."

"We want the black painting." Byder says firmly. "Everyone thinks the black one will be bad, but it's actually the easiest. We want black."

"What if only one god gets to be with me?" I ask, moving to sit on the couch. The others follow me. We actually have something to plan with.

"Ydum." Anarus says. "He's got more water to work with than any of us."

Ydum agrees. "If I can conjure up enough water to make a hundred ice balls, I can get us at least somewhere with all of those weather things since they are all water based."

"If only two, I say Anarus next." Byder adds. "His cold shadows help you make clouds, Jinx. Plus, he helps your magic more than we do."

"Alright. Ydum first, Anarus second, if I have to choose." I say. "What about the paintings? We know we want rain if we can, but we're in fourth. If Isis, Aretha, or Saffron take it, what next?"

"Snow or sleet?" Anarus offers. "I can make the air cool, but to get fog the air has to be warm while the ground is cool and we can't guarantee wherever we are will have the warm for us and hail would take a whole lot of cold air, so a whole lot of shadow, in the higher clouds."

Ydum disagrees with Anarus. "Sleet would be too easy to mess up and have only snow or only rain. So, go with plain snow if we can't get rain."

I take a deep breath. "We have an actual plan. No idea what each one means, but at least it's something to go off."

Without even really discussing it, we all go back to the washroom. When I sit on the floor, Anarus goes to sit next to me but I tell him no. "I have to do it on my own. If I can only take Ydum, I'll have to do it on my own."

Anarus doesn't move but he doesn't touch me either. I keep my eyes open and focus on the ceiling. "I need rain." I focus my concentration on one spot on the ceiling and put everything into making just that one spot rain for me.

"Hey, Byder. What you get when you cross a rabbit and a goat?" Ydum says right as the first drops of water form on the ceiling.

I glare at him. "What are you doing, Ydum?"

"Do you really think that the game is going to let you have a perfectly quiet place to sit and concentrate?" Ydum shakes his head, standing up tall. "No. It won't. You don't just have to be able to do it alone, Jinx, but when there are distractions. So, Jinx, continue. Byder, joke."

He's right. I want to be mad at him but he's right. I try to concentrate on rain as Byder says, "I don't know, Ydum. What?"

"A hare in your milk." I roll my eyes and the ceiling dries up. I take a breath and try again. It takes much more effort with Byder and Ydum tossing bad puns back and forth at each other. But the mirror eventually fogs over and the ceiling starts dripping.

"Good." Anarus says from next to me. "Keep going." Anarus spins a shadow up at the ceiling and my water starts to coalesce together.

"What goes up and down but doesn't move?" Byder asks.

"Rain." I say out loud to keep my concentration.

Byder laughs. "Good try, Jinx, but no. Stairs."

I suck in my cheeks, annoyed at him. Rain. Rain. Right on Byder. Rain. Out of nowhere, a fast sprinkle of raindrops falls right over Byder's head.

"Fuck!" Byder shouts, putting his hand over his head. Then, he stops and looks at me from his perch on the sink counter. "Wait. Did you do that on purpose?"

"Um, yes?" All three males look at me. "You annoyed me with that joke."

Byder brushes off the top of his head, sending water droplets spraying everywhere. "I'm not mad. Okay, maybe slightly miffed. Ydum's jokes were worse. But you got ticked off and made it rain right over me. Maybe calm is the wrong emotion."

"Get angry." Anarus tells me. "Jinx, get well and truly pissed."

"How?" The one time I want to be angry and I can't even think of anything to get mad about. I rub my face with my hand.

"Do not hate me later." Anarus says, then he pokes my side with his finger.

"Hey!" I twist away and glower at him. Anarus just points up at the ceiling then does it again. Anarus keeps annoying me by poking me in the side, on my shoulder, everywhere, but I just grit my teeth and stare at the ceiling. "Rain. Rain!"

The ceiling lets go. It's no longer just dripping, but absolutely raining in the washroom. All four of us are soaked. I turn to tell Anarus to stop poking me, but instead he's grabbing my face in both his hands and pulling me to him. His kiss is not soft this time but hard, insistent. My skin tingles and that feeling of static is stronger than it's ever been, all over me.

"Tell me where I can touch you, Jinx."

"Wherever you want." I wrap my arms around Anarus's neck and pull him closer to me.

"Oh, thank fuck." Anarus's hand goes under my shirt immediately and to my breast, brushing his fingers against my skin as small shocks leap from his skin to mine. He is kissing me again and, when I gasp as he brushes the rough pad of his thumb over my nipple, making it instantly pebble tightly, he takes advantage of the opening to slide his tongue to meet mine. We are sitting awkwardly on the washroom floor that's covered in rain puddles, but the ceiling has at least stopped dripping.

We both shift slightly as we explore each other's lips so that I'm more comfortably sitting on his lap, my legs wrapped around his waist. His hand moves around my back to pull me in tighter as he breaks the kiss and trails his mouth down the column of my neck. I can hardly breathe as something inside me pulls taut again, that sensation of his skin against mine making me crave him closer.

With the shift in position, I can feel all of him. His desire is evident in his hardening length, visible through his soaked pants. A sliver of panic enters my brain, driving the feeling of that taut line between the two of us from my mind. "Anarus, no." The words come out before I can think.

Immediately, his hands are gone from my breast and my back. He's as disentangled from me as he can get himself while I'm sitting on him. I'm not sure if I regret it or am relieved.

"You good?" His voice is rough, brows furrowed.

"Yeah, sorry, I just got confused, unsure for a second." I look down, feeling all sorts of uncertain about what I actually want. That itch in my skin feels desperate to go back to what we were doing. But my brain is trying to fend off panic.

"Nope. You don't apologize for feeling how you feel." He lifts me slightly by my waist so that he can slide his legs out from under me and stand up. Then, he holds out his hand to me. I use his help to stand as well. As soon as I am steady, Anarus looks down at me. "No is no, and unsure is no too."

How is it that the gruff asshole is the most respectful male I've ever met? He punched Ydum in the cave for making a joke but always asks before touching me because he knows I am uncomfortable with it.

Like he can read my mind, Anarus chuckles darkly. "It's called standards, little human."

He leaves the washroom and I follow. I realize as we do that Ydum and Byder had been in the washroom too when Anarus first kissed me. They aren't in here anymore so they must have left at some point. When we go into the sitting room, both of them are sitting on a couch, shirtless but with dry pants on. They changed. Anarus and I are still soaking wet.

I slip into my bedroom and, finding my clean laundry bag, change into the dress I wore on the first day. I want to leave the pants and shirt for tomorrow. When I come back into the sitting room, the three males are sitting on the couches, talking heatedly. I hang back by my bedroom door and listen, not wanting to interrupt them. I should just go back in my room, but then Ydum chuffs angrily. Intrigued, I eavesdrop for a minute.

"The connection is more important! If I did that, I would probably just get slugged. By you, more than likely, Ani." Ydum is saying this more forcefully than I've heard him talk about anything.

"I won't be like that." Anarus clips out. "I know the way this works. I may not like it, but I won't get in the way. The squishy, mortal human needs to be protected and the games made it all of us."

Byder laughs bitterly, slapping his knee. "Right. You won't even let us touch her." They're talking about me?

"It's not me who won't let you touch her!" Shadows are swirling around Anarus thickly, but they aren't blocking him. His anger is fully visible. "If you haven't figured that out yet, you don't deserve to touch her. But what should I expect from the two assholes who didn't even see how uncomfortable she was with you getting drunk? Whatever issues you have with the human is your problem to figure out."

Ydum turns to Byder. "Ani's right, Byder. You're the asshole that keeps trying to touch her when she's made it clear she's not comfortable."

"Don't act like you're any better, Ydum." Anarus grumbles.

Byder stands, his fists clenched at his sides. "Well, excuse the fuck out of me for not knowing what I'm doing. It's not like there was a manual for this part of the damn games."

Ydum stands and goes toe to toe with Byder. "Like you even read the fucking manuals. I swear, half the stuff you don't know was on page one!"

"Fuck off, Ydum!" Byder looks like he is about to swing on him. "I did my best. You know how hard it is for me."

Ydum pushes on Byder's shoulder with his fingers. "Using that excuse again? It's getting old, Byder. One day you are just going to have to admit that you are an idiot who couldn't be bothered to try!"

"Fuck you!" Byder pulls back his arm to actually swing and I'm done.

"Woah!" I yell out, making them all turn. "What the fuck is this?"

Byder, so angry his face radiates a fury that borders on pain, takes one look at me, drops his fist and leaves the room. He goes into the hall, slamming the door behind him so hard it vibrates and I'm surprised it doesn't break. Ydum is left standing in the middle of the sitting room and Anarus is simmering in shadows from his spot on the couch.

Ydum moves like he is going to go into his bedroom, but I step in front of him. "No. Someone is telling me what you were arguing about. We have to do a game tomorrow and we cannot be a mess like this and hope to survive. As the squishy, mortal human" I look pointedly at Anarus, who looks away, "who can die too easily, I need my gods fighting with me, not against each other."

Ydum closes his eyes and sighs deeply. When he opens his eyes again, he's much calmer. "Byder and I decided that we should change the order you choose between us if you have to choose. Ani should be your first pick. It's obvious that you guys, well, the connection is the strongest."

"And I told them to fuck off because Ydum's power works better for weather." Anarus says from the couch, still not looking at me.

I cross my arms over my chest and glare at both of them. "None of what I heard had anything to do with that. What were you really fighting about? What was that about Byder and reading the manuals?"

Ydum looks back at Anarus, who imperceptibly shakes his head. But I catch it. "Tell me."

Ydum groans. "You already know. You just haven't really thought about it enough to put the pieces together." Anarus hisses in warning. Ydum turns back to him, throwing up his arms in frustration. "Do you think it's better to let her keep being oblivious? What do you think will happen when she figures it out?"

"What? Tell me, Ydum."

Ydum groans again and looks at the floor, running a hand through his hair. "Fine. You already know what the games really are. You figured that out the first night. Most teams are one on one, but we are not. What do you think that means, Jinx? Why would the games give you three gods instead of just one?"

"Because all three of you are possible matches for me." I stop talking as Ydum slowly shakes his head.

"Not possible matches, Jinx." He tells me softly. "That's not what the games base the teams on. Not possibilities, but what the cave actually wants to happen. Some say the cave just leads you to your already existing fated bonds. So, if there are three of us, the cave wants you to..."

Shit. Fated bonds. Three of them. Is that the itch? The static? "Why?"

Ydum shrugs. "It's a magic set up so long ago. If any of the original gods remember exactly how it works, they aren't telling us. But what we do know is that the test you took makes sure you have enough magic to work with, have no god ancestors, and that you are a match for someone, for at least one of the gods in the games. That first trial, we gods can only sense the witch we're meant for. The one that, for lack of a better term, completes our power. That we are fated for. Like I explained about my parents. Mom's flower nature and Dad's magic made me a god with powers stronger because of the both of them. You matched with three gods. Your magic somehow completes our powers, all three of us. We should all complement each other's and be stronger together as a group. If we survive the games, it's assumed that your team becomes your spouse. But with four of us, it's not supposed to be you choosing between us, but choosing all of us."

I laugh sarcastically. This really is just a mating game. Fated bonds. "Do I actually have a choice then? Do any of us humans? Does Saffron or Amanda who seems to hate her god?"

"Yes." Ydum answers forcefully and quickly. "You do. The humans do, at least. Or that's what it seems like right now."

"What do you mean the humans do? Do the gods not have a choice in it?" I already learned that the gods, all the gods, have to compete in the games. Do they have even less choice about the outcome of their team pairing?

He laughs bitterly, leaning back and looking at the ceiling. Ydum is usually so relaxed and casual, unless he's talking academically, so this is a lot of emotion from him. "I mean, technically, yes, we have a choice. We can choose to accept the bond or not. It's better if we do, the games are easier if we do, but it's a choice. At least, that's what we were taught. The reality of it is that, at least for me, I knew right away. That first moment you came down out of your hiding spot in the cave. It was like being hit between the eyes with a hammer. You were it. All I wanted. All I ever would. I feel it every time we touch, like lightning on my skin. Watching you let Ani... It's almost painful to want something so much and watch someone else get it while I'm denied it."

Panic starts creeping up in me again. Not just mating games, but purposely matching us up, an actual expectation that we will mate for life. A magical fated mate bond. With three gods. The games gave me three gods who are all already convinced that I'm the one they want. They can feel that magical bond. A fated bond that says I'm the one they want for life. Every time Ydum was joking about me and Anarus, he was doing it to hide that he's jealous and hurting, not just being a jerk. Breathing is hard.

"Hey." Ydum doesn't touch me but bends down so he can meet my eyes, his tone no less serious but much softer. "Breathe, Jinx. You're okay. This is an us problem, not a you problem."

"But you all feel it. You all want." I suck in air, forcing it in my lungs.

"We want you happy and safe, Jinx." When I try to turn away, Ydum moves again to keep me looking at him instead of into nothing. "That's it. Byder and I want you safe. Anything else is our problem. Nothing has changed. No one is forcing anything on you."

I shake my head. "But the games are. They are forcing you and you will want to force me. Eventually, you will. If I say no."

"Ani?" Ydum calls him over, but continues to chase my eyes with his. "No, we won't. Never, Jinx. If you never look at me like that, if you never touch me like that, I'll be fine. It's both of our choices. And I do not want what is not freely given."

"Stand sideways, Ydum." Even with the wall behind me, Ydum moves so that they both aren't standing in front of me, but almost to the sides of me. Anarus is next to Ydum, but far enough apart from him that I know I could slip between them if I wanted. "Jinx. Who is here with you?"

"Ydum and you." I say, focusing on Anarus.

"Breathe in. Are any of Jacob's friends here?"

"No." I breathe in.

"Breathe out. Have any of us cornered you or made you do anything you didn't want?"

I breathe out. "Ydum made me run in the hallway."

Anarus tries not to laugh, and Ydum actually laughs. It breaks the spell of fear around me a little. "Not what Ani meant, but okay, fair."

I take in a deep breath and blow it out, shaking my head. I hate this place. Focus on anything else, I tell myself, not my trembling hands or shaky breath. "What was that whole thing about Byder and reading the manuals?"

Ydum answers as they both move away, back to the couches. "Byder has issues with reading. His doesn't see letters right. It's like they get twisted in his mind. He always had to have help in school. He would take tests separate from us, someone reading them aloud to him. But when it came to the classes about the games, they didn't help him anymore. The professors said that he had to pass or fail on his own merit and if his broken mind couldn't read well enough to do it then he would get the fate he deserved."

"And you made fun of him for that? For something he can't control?" I'm very not happy with Ydum now.

Ydum doesn't look at me but shrugs, muttering. "We're supposed to see it as a weakness we can't afford. The games are supposed to weed out the weak gods."

I walk over to stand directly in front of Ydum, my arms crossed over my chest, and glare. "Did you ever think that maybe one of the reasons why there are three of you is so that you can each balance out our weaknesses? Anarus is too young. You aren't nearly as physically strong as they are. Byder needs help for the reading stuff. And, me? Well, I'm a hot mess. But together, we took out three yetis and moved from eighth to fourth in one go and now people are copying us."

"Point, Jinx." Anarus says. "I'm an ass but even I wouldn't have said that about Byder."

I move to the door, heading to find Byder. "Anarus just got bumped out of the jerk of the group spot, Ydum. You've won that title by a mile."

"Hey." I hear Anarus complain as I leave, but I ignore him. Byder is sitting on the floor, leaning against the wall, in the foyer. I go to him and sit next to him. For a long time, neither of us say anything. I try to settle myself but that itchy feeling is happening with him too. That tautness that wants something. I swallow and ignore it.

"Ydum told me about your reading stuff." I say when he doesn't speak. "I should have let you punch him."

Byder sighs heavily but doesn't look up from the spot on the floor his eyes are drilling a hole into. He is absentmindedly running a finger up and down the circles around his right forearm. "I tried, baby girl. I really did. Dad helped some, but we weren't allowed to take the manuals home. He could only tell me what he remembered."

"I know you did. We have Ydum for the book smarts. You have other things to offer."

He snorts. "Like what?"

"Like helping me train to fight better. You figured out the water thing. That I needed more water in the washroom because I'm an end magic witch. That Anarus helps my magic. You held a yeti against its will with a vine to kill it. That takes a lot of strength."

Byder sighs again, but says nothing so I continue. "Like I told Ydum, I think we all have strengths and weaknesses. And our strengths balance out each other's weakness. That's why it's all three of you. Because that's how we work best." I look down at my lap and pick at my nails. "They told me about the bond thing from the cave. The reality of what the games are doing when they pair up teams."

Byder looks at me from the side of his eyes. "And you're okay with that?"

"Okay? Not so much. Ready for that? Definitely not. Understand you guys and the reason you act like you do better? Yeah. Ydum said it was like getting hit between the eyes with a hammer in the cave. He said... he said it was lightning on his skin. And maybe I might have felt that some, too. That static of it, the bond like static on my skin."

"Apt description." Byder huffs, shaking his head. "Anarus didn't get it until you touched him the first time. He thought we were being overdramatic when we were talking that first night while you were in the shower, but then you touched him and it just clicked for him. Ydum thinks it was because of his age. He's the wrong age so the games didn't work right or it just took longer for him to recognize it or something. We thought that maybe his connection to you would be weaker because of that, but instead it seems to be the strongest one."

"I think it's stronger because of life experience, not anything predetermined or the games or whatever." I sigh and toy with the end of my braid. "Both of us have been hurt before and have issues because of it. He had experience with that so he knew how to, I dunno, see the pain and how to move around it for me."

Byder actually looks at me now. "Why didn't you say anything, baby girl? Why didn't you tell us that the drinking bothered you? Or the touching?"

Sighing, I ignore the nickname I'm not sure if I like or not. One more piece of evidence of how the three of them feel already when I'm still not sure. But Byder is looking at me with something of a pained expression, like he hates the idea that he might have made me scared. Byder, who is normally so tough, with only two modes, almost commandingly dominate or stereotypically rowdy, is showing his vulnerability for the first time.

"Because I never told anyone. Because you were just two guys I didn't know having fun and who was I to stop you just because I had a bad experience once?" I don't say anything for a long time. "How much did Anarus tell you?"

"Just no drinking and no touching without permission. He didn't say why, but after your panic attack, Ydum and I aren't complete idiots. We can guess a lot. It's not our business unless you decide to make it our business."

I sigh. This is all too much, too heavy for people I have only known for a week. But tomorrow, we have to go and fight for our lives again. "Come back to the room?"

Byder nods and we go back to the room. I turn right to Ydum. "You got something to say to Byder?" I ask like he's a small child I am disciplining.

Ydum hangs his head, then looks at Byder. "Sorry, man. That thing about the reading was a low blow."

"You like to hit the low-hanging fruit, Ydum." I tell him. "I don't know what's going on with you to make you feel like you need to be that way but don't. Bullying is not something I can stand. And that's what comments like that, and getting on Anarus for not having parents, is. It's being a bully. We are not five. If you have an issue, talk about it without making others less than to make yourself feel better."

Ydum just nods.

"It's late and the next game will start early tomorrow." Anarus reminds us.

"You take the couch tonight, Ydum. Call it a punishment or time to think about what type of man you want to be. You two good with that?" I said you two, but I look at Byder for a response.

Byder nods. "Sounds fair to me. Don't really want to share with him tonight." He heads off to his room and Anarus and I do too.

At the door to my room, Anarus stops me. "Where do you want me tonight?" He's giving me a choice. My mouth goes dry and a small fire starts in me, one I really am not sure if I want to stoke or ignore. The remnants of my almost panic attack still linger.

"What if I say I want you close but not anything more?"

"On top of the blankets it is, then, little human." Anarus does exactly what he says. While I strip and throw on the now-dry shirt I had on early, Anarus only removes his boots, keeping his back turned as I change. When I get in the bed, under the blankets, he only gets on the bed, on top of the blankets. He doesn't touch me. He doesn't even say anything. But I feel his shadows move comfortingly over me, and I barely need to think on peace to fall asleep.

Chapter Six

IN THE MORNING, I wake up to Anarus sprawled across the bed and me sleeping in a ball at the edge of the bed. It feels like he kicked my back several times in the night. Like I thought, bed hog. I grumble and get up and dressed. In the sitting room, Ydum is still sleeping but Byder is up. He says nothing while I get coffee, and is smart enough to stay silent for long enough to know I have drunk most of the cup.

"Get food too." Byder tells me when he feels reasonably assured that I'm well-caffeinated. When I only grunt, he becomes more insistent. "We don't know what today will be and you need more energy than just coffee gives. Eat."

When I come back to the couch with a plate of fruit, I hold it up for his inspection. "Happy?"

"Very. If you eat it all."

"I hate you."

"You love me." Byder laughs. "You just need more coffee to remember that."

"What does Jinx need more coffee to remember?" Ydum's awake.

"That she doesn't hate me for making her eat." I notice Byder's change in words but, after last night's discussion, I'm not sure if it was intentional.

Ydum leans over to look at my coffee. "That her first cup? Brave man to tease her so early."

"Why?" I ask no one in particular. "Why did I get matched with not one but two morning people?"

"Because if it was just you and me, we'd kill each other before the games could refill the carafe." Anarus is up now too and grumbling. "Did you actually eat?"

I hold up my plate of fruit and purposely eat a strawberry. Anarus just grunts. "You don't get to be surly today, Anarus. You kick in your sleep. I think I may have a bruise."

Byder and Ydum manage not to laugh.

"You snore." Anarus says.

"I do not."

Anarus comes over to the couch with his coffee, leans over in front of me until his face is very close to mine. "You. Snore."

"Seven sisters. One bedroom." I retort. "I would know if I snore."

He flops onto the couch. "Maybe you all snore."

Byder and Ydum fail at not laughing. I just finish eating my fruit. There's no talking to Anarus right now.

Ydum changes the topic. "We still good on the plan? Anarus, then me, if Jinx has to choose. Black painting, yellow if black isn't an option?"

"I thought we said you first then Anarus." I tell him.

"That was the start of the whole fight yesterday, Jinx." Byder reminds me.

Right. I settle it. "Ydum, you're first choice because you have more water to work with if we get black. If we get yellow, Anarus first because of the cold. If we have to go with neither of those, I'll decide based on my gut instinct."

"What if you have to choose god before choosing the painting?" Byder asks.

"Gut instinct then." I walk behind the couch to stand behind Byder and check his hair. Once I'm assured it won't all slip out of his bun during the game, I go back to my coffee and think. I'm not really sure I'd be able to actually know how to choose. But I hope my mouth will know what to do when the time comes.

It ends up not being a problem. When the tone sounds and we head out to the foyer with the other teams, we find out choosing is not an issue for us. At least, not choosing which god goes with me.

Drila is too chipper, a fake chipper, even after enough coffee. Her dress is yellow this time. "Good morning. Today's game will focus on weather. Each painting represents a type of weather you will need to create for the game. Humans will choose the painting first, then I will explain the rules of the game. Same as in the first game, the humans will be called in order of ranking and will have ten seconds to choose a painting, or will have it randomly assigned if they fail to pick in time. Everyone along the wall please."

We all move into the same position as we were in for the first game, gods behind their humans. I try really hard not to stare at the black painting to not give away that it's the one we want.

Drila calls out names, but I don't pay attention to where everyone goes other than if they go to the black one. "Isis is first." She doesn't take black. Drila waits, then calls out, "Aretha." She doesn't either. "Saffron." Saffron hesitates for a second at the black painting and I hold my breath. But she moves on. I breathe a sigh of relief. As soon as Drila calls my name, I run right to the black painting without a thought. I hear murmurs from the people who haven't run yet, but Drila is already calling on Amanda. They know now that we figured something out, but not what. I can see from my spot how confused the other gods and remaining humans look about me purposely choosing black. Wren looks relieved until her god whispers something and she looks concerned again. She thought she would be stuck with black, as the supposedly worst one, and we threw off their whole plan taking it.

Once all of the paintings have been chosen, and Drila records the selections, she calls us humans back over. "Now, to find out what you chose. Red, Damek and Raven, is sleet. Green, Amanda and Isis, is hail. Yellow, Aretha and Asteria, is snow. Blue, Saffron and Wren, is fog. And finally, black is rain, Jinx."

There are a lot of murmurs and voiced complaints, people arguing with their teammates, and hasty conversation. My gods and I just wait. Drila raises her hand for silence. "Now, for the rules. This game, you will compete against one another directly. Using only the weather you chose, the human will have to attack and the god will have to defend. Isis versus Wren, Aretha versus Raven, Saffron versus Asteria. Jinx, since you have three gods and there's an uneven number of teams, one of your gods will assist you, and only assist, while the other two defend. You will also battle two teams instead of one, Damek and Amanda. Damek, Amanda, you will only be attacking Jinx's team, not each other. Jinx, which god will assist you?"

"Fuck." Anarus whispers.

"Who?" I ask.

"Go with your gut." Byder tells me.

"I need an answer, Jinx." Drila isn't giving me any time to think.

"Ydum." I spit out quickly.

Drila nods and writes it down. "Now, the goal is to cause the other team to experience your weather without being exposed to theirs. There's a time limit on this game. To pass, the human must be able to accurately create the weather, whether or not it affects the other team. You will not leave the game until you are able to do so or the time runs out and you officially fail. Ranking will be decided by who causes the other team to experience their weather first, then who accurately makes their weather. This means it's possible for you to be the last two teams to arrive, but one of you actually take first place because you made your enemy experience the weather faster than anyone else, but the other team failed to produce any weather at all and had to wait the entire time limit. Does this make sense to everyone?"

"What about us?" Amanda asks. "Two against one."

"If one of the teams against Jinx completes the full objective of making her team experience their weather, but the other hasn't yet, the team that is done will get to leave, leaving it easier for the other team to act." Drila explains.

"We are so fucked." Anarus mutters.

"What did Damek and Amanda choose?" I ask. "Did anyone catch that?"

"Damek sleet, Amanda hail." Anarus tells me.

"Sleet is hard, easy to do wrong." Ydum reminds me. "Iella is a chance goddess though. Hail will be hard for Amanda, unless she's got a lot of power. Tholdir is a flame god. Not good for making it cold."

"Humans attack, gods defend." I remind him, shaking my head. "Tholdir would only be trying to prevent us from making rain. Tholdir's power doesn't matter for us too much, but he could make it hot and dry. At least our weather isn't something he can melt, though."

Drila was talking while we were and I didn't hear what she said. When she asks if we are all ready, though, I panic that I missed something important. "Off you go. Time starts now!"

The world blinks and I find myself and my gods on a beach with the sea sprawled out in front of us. There are two islands across the water from us, and I can see Amanda and Tholdir on one and Damek and Iella on the other. The first game was in the snowy woods, when there's no snow in Nazus yet and we fought against yetis that are only mythical. Now, this game is on islands. I didn't learn much about the continent of Nazus in school, but I really don't think there are islands here. Where are the games sending us? Real places I've just never heard of or places they made with magic? I'm not sure but I'm wasting time wondering about it. Byder and Anarus are already huddled together, talking about how to make it as warm as possible so the others' weather can't work.

"Ydum." I call out. "Rain. We need a lot of rain."

He's next to me in a flash. "I don't even have to create the water. There's a ton of it in the sea." There's relief in his voice.

I sit down on the sand and focus. Rain, a lot of rain, the sand is too dry over Amanda and Damek. Far too dry. It needs to rain there.

Ydum kneels next to me. "Are you even trying, Jinx? Come on, do something!"

I glare at him. "I'm trying!" Then, I realize what he's doing. He's trying to make me angry. That's right, anger worked better than peace. "Fuck, keep going."

Ydum looks at me and nods, but I can see on his face that he hates it. I yelled at him last night for being a bully but now I need him to be one. "You sure you should be here? I mean your test was fucked. Maybe you can't do it."

Anarus and Byder are arguing. I glance over at them.

"Ignore your boy toy, Jinx." Ydum tells me. "You have a job that you're failing at."

I look back at the other two islands. There are already clouds forming in the middle of the water, but they aren't mine. Either Amanda or Damek is further into this than me. Fuck. Rain. Rain! A fuck ton of it. Come on! "Rain." I am growling. It's getting colder. Fuck.

"Shit." Ydum mutters. "I'm gonna touch you."

I nod and Ydum sits behind me, bracing my back against him.

"You good?" He asks.

"Not really. But don't move." I tell him. Rain. I need rain. I will die if it doesn't rain over Amanda and Damek. I can hear Ydum muttering under his breath. Wispy white tendrils start to form over water. I can tell they're Ydum's because they're moving away from us.

"Keep filling the clouds, Ydum."

"What do you think I am doing?" He snaps.

Move. Move to them. It needs to be over Amanda and Damek, not the sea.

I need the clouds over there. "Move, fucking clouds!" I yell louder than I meant to.

I'm shivering. The temperature has dropped considerably. Ydum moves closer as my teeth start to chatter. "Sheesh, fucking human can't even stay warm."

"Fuck off." I tell him as I lean back into his warmth. He rubs my arms with his hands. I know he's purposely being mean to make me madder so I work my magic better. Doesn't mean I like it.

"Guys, Jinx is freezing over here." Ydum yells at the other two.

I don't take my eyes off the thin wisps that are definitely starting to look like clouds. "Fucking rain! Rain!" I don't care that I'm yelling anymore. I have no idea how long we get but there are a few snowflakes falling from the sky and my clouds have not even made it to either of other team's islands yet.

"Let it rain some, Jinx." Ydum commands me, roughly. "At least then we won't be out even if it never gets to them."

I think about that, and look to one small piece of the clouds forming. "Rain. I need rain right there." Nothing happens. Why would there need to be rain over a body of water? "I need a why."

"Desalination. The water is too salty." Ydum gives me.

"The water in that spot is too salty." I push the need. "Make it rain right there." I start shaking not from the cold but from exhaustion. I've been concentrating on this without a break longer than I've ever concentrated on any one thing before. When we get back, something to work on. But for now, rain, fucker. Rain.

I see a few drops falling. Not a lot, but enough I can see them. They are nowhere near Amanda or Damek, but it's rain. I made rain. We at least will pass as long as Byder and Anarus keep the snow over us snow and nothing else. I keep pushing. More water in the clouds. Keep moving to them. Rain over them. The sand on both beaches needs rain.

There are more snowflakes swirling. It's too clean of snow to be sleet, but it's definitely snow. If Damek just figures out how to make it warmer, we're sunk.

"Jinx." Ydum points to Amanda's island. It's hailing there. They gave up trying to get the hail to us and just went for not failing.

"We need to make it warm there. How?"

Ydum shrugs. "I can't do it. Can you?"

"I can try." I close my eyes and try to focus again. Warmth, it needs to be hot, right over Amanda. "Piss me off."

Ydum moves my braid to hang over my shoulder and kisses the back of my neck. I gasp as it does not make me angry. "Fuck, beautiful." He keeps kissing my neck. The itch to my skin that I got from Anarus's touch is also there with Ydum. Fainter, but still there.

"Ydum." When I say his name, Ydum realizes that what he's doing is causing the opposite of pissing me off. "Please, um." I can't concentrate on the hail becoming rain. All I can concentrate on is his lips, warm and soft on my neck.

"Shit. That didn't work like I expected." Ydum takes a deep breath. "Sorry."

"Just. Do something else. I can't think. I hate being trapped. Can't stand it.

Make me feel trapped." I look at Amanda's island again and focus. Warmth. It needs to be warm over there.

"Don't hate me." Ydum says. Then, he wraps his arms and legs around me, locking them so I can't push them away.

I'm trapped. I can't get away from him. I start to panic. I can't breathe. Part of my mind clings to the fact that he won't harm me. That he's only doing this to help. Warmth, I need fucking warmth so Ydum will let me go. "Let me go." Warmth. "Please." I'm crying now. I'm trapped. He's only helping. Warmth. I keep my eyes on Amanda and fight to breathe.

Amanda is looking up at the sky and swearing. I can hear her yelling. Her hail has changed to rain.

"Do the other one." Ydum says but doesn't let go. "Damek. Get Damek."

I focus on the forgotten clouds over the water. Go please. Rain over Damek. It needs to rain over Damek. "Let me go." I cry again. Inside my mind, I am warring between panic at Ydum trapping me and focusing on making it rain, but on the outside, all that I can say out loud is for Ydum to please, please stop.

Rain over Damek. "Let me go." I'm trapped and can't breathe but it needs to rain. "Ydum, please let me go." The war in my brain between panic and understanding is making me shake harder. I'm raking my nails down Ydum's arms, trying to pull them off me, but at the same time, I am watching Damek's island. He's fighting to do what Amanda did and just make it sleet over him.

I drop my clouds and focus on trying to make it too warm there for sleet. He successfully got snow here, but failed to make it the perfect mix between snow and rain. I wait, and focus on my breathing, I focus on trying not to scream at Ydum to let me go, not cry and forget how to breathe. I want to give Damek time to make his snow. As soon as I see the first few flakes, I immediately push for it to be warmer near him.

It becomes a battle. My overpowering warmth and Damek's fight for a middle ground. He keeps overshooting and making it so cold it only snows. But there was rain. Only rain. For a brief moment, it's only raining. We made it rain on both islands. I let go of my concentration completely and let Damek do whatever he wants. He can make his sleet on his own island if he wants.

Ydum, seeing this, lets go of me completely. He moves back away from me. My face is a mess of tears, I'm heaving for breath and his arms are covered in scratches.

Anarus is a blur. He tackles Ydum, punching him. "What the fuck is wrong with you?" Anarus screams. "She said to let her go!" He punches Ydum again, before I can stop him.

"Anarus! He was making me angry on purpose!" I yell, running over to them. "Stop!"

A tone sounds and we blink back into the foyer. All the teams are here and it looks like most of us all popped in at the same time. Anarus is still punching Ydum, yelling. "Asshole!"

Ydum is only holding his hands in front of his face to protect himself from

Anarus's punches. Byder and I both drop onto Anarus.

"Stop, man! Look, we're back. Anarus stop!" Byder is forcing himself between the two and hauling Anarus off Ydum by his waist, his hair flying everywhere as one of Anarus's swings yanks the hair tie out. "A little help here!" A few other gods head over and help Byder hold Anarus back.

I stand in front of him. "Anarus, stop. It was on purpose. Ydum was doing it on purpose."

Anarus finally seems to take in what's going on around him. He's heaving for breath, but looking at me. "It was on purpose?"

"He was making me angry, the way you did when you poked me." I tell him. "I'm okay, Anarus."

He shrugs out of the arms holding him. "I'm fine. Let me go." The gods who came over to help walk back to their humans, muttering. Anarus just comes over to me. "You're okay?"

"I'm fine." I take his hand in mine. "I'm okay. Just, let's sit down."

Anarus nods and we find a spot on the wall to sit. Ydum goes on the far end, letting me sit between Anarus and Byder with him on the other side of Byder.

When everyone finishes settling down, Drila speaks. "Well, that was an exciting return." There are a couple of people who chuckle, but fortunately, Drila doesn't dwell on it. "Every team was able to make their weather, meaning no teams are eliminated this round. Only three were able to make their weather against the opposing team. Saffron was first making fog, giving her team ten points. Then Wren, making also fog, taking twenty points. Jinx and Ydum made rain against both their opponents, so thirty points to them. Everyone else will be ranked from fourth to ninth by how long it took to make their own weather pattern, even though it never reached their opponent. Amanda takes fourth. Isis comes in fifth. Damek is sixth. Aretha in seventh. Raven takes eighth, and Asteria comes in last."

Drila pauses for dramatic effect. "That makes the current standings Asteria and Raven tied in last place with one hundred sixty points. Damek in seventh with one hundred and twenty-five. Wren takes sixth with one hundred and fifteen points. Amanda and Aretha are tied for fourth with ninety points. Jinx's team is in third with seventy-five points. Isis is in second with sixty and Saffron takes first with forty points. The next game will be protection, and will be in one week."

We all take off back to our rooms. The moment we are back in our room with the door shut, I whirl on Anarus. "What the fuck is your problem?"

Anarus's shadows are swirling violently. "Ydum was…"

"Ydum was doing exactly what we needed him to for us to win." I yell. "Do you have absolutely no faith in me at all? No trust in them?"

"Them? No." Anarus yells back. "I don't see how you are saying that I have no faith in you from this, though."

"We'll let's see. Every time anything happens that we don't expect with these games, you complain about how fucked we are and then the moment either of the other two does something that even slightly makes me uncomfortable, you are literally jumping them to make them stop like I can't defend myself at all."

Anarus roars. "He trapped you! You said that was the worst thing. The thing that you can't stand is being trapped."

"And you know that my magic works better when I am upset." I counter, stomping around a little in my frustration. "But you never stopped to think that maybe he was doing it on purpose. Tell me, who told Ydum about that? How did he know to trap me?"

Anarus looks away from me, running his fingers over his moustache and down his goatee, licking his lips.

I nod, standing in place to stare him down. "That's right. You didn't tell them that. You told them about the alcohol and touching. So, who fucking told Ydum to trap me?"

Anarus still doesn't say anything.

"I want to hear you say it, Anarus."

"You did." Anarus finally says softly. "It must have been you."

I take a deep breath. "That's right. I did. I told Ydum to do it so I could focus. We are in third now because Ydum did exactly what I told him to. Would you have done it if I asked? Without arguing first?"

Anarus doesn't respond, just looks at me.

"You have to trust me, Anarus." I tell him, a lot calmer, running my hand through my hair. "You have to trust them if we are going to survive. I don't even care about winning. But just to survive, you will have to figure out how to trust all of us."

We are still standing right in front of the door. Anarus looks at me for a moment, his shadows churning. Then he groans and rubs his hands down his face, turns and goes back out the door to the hallway. I start after him, but Byder touches my elbow.

"Let him go." Byder says, shaking his head. "Let him work shit out in his own head."

He's right. I need to let Anarus go for now. I go to the couches instead and check on Ydum. He's sitting in his spot, leaned forward, elbows on his knees, his head hanging down. I sit next to him rather than where I usually do.

"Are you okay?"

Ydum looks up at me and he has a split lip, again, and what seems to be the beginning of a black eye, not to mention the fingernail scratches running down his arms from me. Anarus got him good. "You know I hated doing it, right? If I thought anything else would have worked," he shudders slightly, "I would have done that instead."

I chuckle lightly. "I know. You did try something else first. It just didn't work like you thought it would."

Ydum scratches the back of his neck, raising his eyebrows. "Yeah, about that. Sorry."

"What did he try?" Byder asks, coming over and sitting on the other couch since I'm in his spot.

"Well." Ydum says looking away. "Um."

I don't exactly look at Byder either. "He, well, he tried a different kind of potentially unwanted touching."

Byder looks at the both of us confused still. Then it clicks and he laughs. "You kissed her. How did we miss that you kissed her?"

"You and Anarus were busy trying to keep it warm on our island so Jinx didn't freeze to death, but not make Damek's snow turn to sleet by accident. A tall order, which, by the way, great job, no idea how you managed it." Ydum's still looking at the floor, as if he's ashamed of his actions even though he did nothing wrong.

"We made it colder, not warmer." Byder explains. "Damek had gotten clouds to us so we knew that we had no choice once he started making it do anything at all. It was easier to just make it colder with Anarus's shadows and hope you would keep Jinx warm enough or accomplish attacks on them before it got to be too much for her."

"You made the snow?" I ask, incredulously.

Byder pulls his hair back up as he answers. It's not as good as I do it, but better than it had been. At least he got it all in the hair tie this time. "Damek had already made clouds and dropped the temperature enough to get a snowy mix. We didn't have an idea of how to heat things up to make it just rain, so we went with cold and only snow. Amanda was nowhere even close to making clouds or anything near us so we were safe from her hail. It was a gut decision. You and Ydum were too busy screaming at each other to consult."

"I have a lot of stuff I did today that I have to apologize for, Jinx." Ydum hangs his head down again.

I lift his head by his chin to make him look at me. "You have nothing to apologize for at all, Ydum. You did what you needed to for us to win. I should apologize for shredding your arms."

Ydum holds his arms up, looking at them like he hadn't noticed the scratches before. His eyes start to glitter and his mouth twitches into that wicked grin he does when he's teasing. "These little love scratches? Aww, beautiful, they're nothing. I've had scratches down my back that—."

"Ydum!" I laugh despite myself. He's trying to be funny again, which is better. We would become far too serious without him always trying to lighten the mood. I look over at the table and see dinner has arrived. Lasagna. "Food."

The three of us dig in. This time, Byder collects up the proffered alcohol reward for surviving the game and tells us he will go donate it to the other teams. While he does that, I notice Ydum pull off an extra plate and set it aside for Anarus. By the time, Anarus comes back in the room, we've mostly finished eating and are just sitting around chatting about teachers we hated when we were in school. Since the gods go to school until twenty-four, they have more recent experience than I do. Not to mention that my school was so small, I basically only had one main teacher each year.

"Can I talk to you, Jinx?" Anarus asks when he comes back in the room. "Alone?"

He seems much more subdued, shadows only simmering right at the surface. I point at the plate of food. "Ydum saved you food. Eat first."

He glances at Ydum, then the plate, and his mouth twitches. But he grabs the plate and brings it over to sit on the couches. We are mixed up from our normal spots, so he has to sit on a couch with Byder and that seat is closer to Ydum than me. "Thanks for thinking of me." He tells Ydum. It's not an apology, but he's being polite so I'm not going to push it if Ydum doesn't.

"You would have done the same for me, man." Ydum says.

"No, I wouldn't have." Anarus is honest. The mood is different with Anarus back and nothing is really settled so we mostly don't talk while Anarus eats. Again, he steals the hard crust I left behind after eating the soft middle of my garlic bread instead of getting his own bread. After he finishes the food left for him, and my crust, Anarus looks at me. "Satisfied?"

"Yes."

"Now, can we talk?"

I huff and stand up, going to my room, knowing Anarus is following behind me. When I sit on the corner of the bed, he shuts the door and leans against the wall.

"You called this meeting." I tell him when he doesn't speak.

"I'm trying." Anarus drags a hand over his hair. "I don't want to say this wrong."

"Just say whatever you are thinking."

He laughs caustically. "That's the problem. If you knew the things I'm thinking, you would never talk to me again. Maybe you shouldn't. Enough for the games, to get through them. But you shouldn't talk to me. You shouldn't trust me."

"Why not, Anarus?"

He groans. "I'm not right. The things in my head, I'm not right. No one has ever trusted me with anything before but you and I'm fucking it up."

"You're not fucking it up, Anarus. Sure, you lost your temper today, and you should probably work on that, but it's understandable. You thought you were protecting me."

He starts pacing the room. Up and back, from the door to the window and back. I watch him, waiting for him to say what he wants to say. "That's not." He sighs, the tension in his body deflating for a moment before doubling back. "That was wrong, I know, but that's not what I mean. That's just a part of it. A part of the problem. You trust me and you shouldn't."

"Like I already said, why not? You haven't given me a reason not to."

Anarus goes back to leaning against the wall. "That's the point. I don't want to ever give you a reason not to. I always have thoughts, too many damn thoughts. If I lose even the tiniest bit of control, they will win and I will have betrayed you."

I snort at him. "You keep saying these thoughts you have. Anarus, we all have thoughts that we think others would be appalled by. It's usually not as bad as all that. Just tell me the thoughts you think are so devastatingly bad, that make you think I shouldn't trust you anymore, and let me tell you if there's something wrong with you."

He looks at me with something of a pained expression and his shadows simmer higher, as if he's fighting the urge to hide, and something in my mind clicks. I think I know what the thoughts are. The itchy skin. The desire that makes no sense for how little we know each other. Fuck it, I think. Fated bonds. I want him. I stand up and take a step closer to him. "I trust you, Anarus."

He presses his palms flat against the wall behind him. "You shouldn't."

My heart is racing, but I step forward again. That taut line between us when he kissed me in the washroom. The way he moved away as soon as he knew I wasn't sure what I wanted. "I trust you, Anarus."

"I am trying really hard here, Jinx." He closes his eyes.

"Do you trust me?" I ask, stepping just a little closer.

Anarus's eyes snap open, as if he thought the answer to that was a given and doesn't understand why I'm asking it. "With everything I am."

"Then, trust me." I close the gap between us and kiss him. He goes rigid for a beat, then his lips soften, letting me kiss him. He doesn't move, doesn't do anything but let it happen. I stop and, when he looks at me, the heat in his eyes is undeniable. It sends need streaking down my spine. My skin feels like it's on fire, the little shocks stronger this time. When I kiss him again, and he still doesn't move, I ask him, "Do you want this?"

"If I let myself want this, I'm going to want to take everything." He groans the last word and it sends shivers over my skin to rest as warmth in my core.

"What if I'm willing to give you everything?"

"Are you?"

"Yes." I see his resolve break just before he hauls me back against him, his lips crushing against mine. He weaves his fingers through my hair, tilting my head how he wants it to push the kiss further, his tongue tracing the inside of my mouth. That taut line I felt before snaps back into place and a part of me wonders if it's the fated bond. Anarus's hand tightens in my hair. I moan into his mouth and he echoes it back, bringing a hand up to stroke along my arm and down my back. His fingertips graze the outside of my breast through my shirt with each pass of his hand and it's all I can do not to press tighter against him.

He moves his mouth to trail kisses along my jaw up to my ear. When he bites my earlobe gently, I feel it race though me like lightning on my nerves. I touch his chest with light fingertips, caressing his muscles up to his shoulders and back down. Even through his clothes, I can feel it. That racing, burning that makes me want to touch him more.

"I want to feel your skin." I bunch up the fabric of his shirt, pulling at it.

He immediately pulls his shirt up over his head, tossing it aside. "Whatever you want, Jinx. Everything you want." He leans in to kiss my neck but I pull back, only for a moment, to give what I got. Anarus sucks his teeth when my shirt falls away. "So damn beautiful."

I start peppering kisses along his chest, following the pattern of his tattoos. I kiss the moon, then the wolf, then the trees that sit on the edge between his chest and abdomen, my fingers tracing the lines as I move. Every inch of his skin, soft and silky, a touch of coolness before my lips brush against him and I feel his warmth.

"Jinx." He growls my name, then hauls my arms up so I am looking at him again. "My turn." He trails his mouth down the column of my neck. I feel every kiss in my core as I heat up, desire making me feel a little frantic. He teases along my collarbone, one hand palming my breast, holding the weight of it as his thumb brushes back and forth across the nipple. When he trails his mouth lower and sucks a nipple into his mouth, biting gently, I cry out, my nails digging into his shoulders. He moves to the other breast, teasing it with his tongue then running his lips over it so that the hair of his goatee scratches it.

His hands move to cup my bottom, pulling me even closer, like he can't stand any space between us. I can feel all of him, his length and desire. Instead of making me panic, it makes me want more. "Anarus."

"I want everything." He trails kisses lower, down my stomach and I groan, the warmth of his mouth lighting fires everywhere.

"Then, take it. It's yours." At my words, he picks me up and carries me the few feet to the bed, laying me down with my legs hanging over the edge. His mouth follows his fingers as he skims lower until he is brushing the top of my pants.

His hands hover just above my skin, not actually touching my stomach and the anticipation is worse than the actual touch, making me clench and starts an ache in my most intimate spot "Tell me to stop." His voice is harsh, insistent and strained with want.

"Never. Anarus, touch me. Please."

He bends down, disappearing beneath the edge of the bed to take off my boots, and I just lie still, staring at the ceiling, trying to keep my heart from racing away as it gallops out of my chest. It's only seconds and he reappears, his hands pulling my pants down me slowly, like he is unwrapping a gift. I lift my hips slightly to help him.

An edge of worry passes over me as his gaze sweeps over my whole body. I fight the urge to cover myself. His hands gently pull on my knees, spreading my legs apart. "Let me look at you." When I comply, his hands move up my thighs, making me squirm. "So fucking perfect. You're fucking perfect, Jinx."

His hand moves up to my slick core and he touches me softly, exploring. I fling an arm over my face, burying a moan into it. His thumb pushes on my clit, then starts drawing small circles over it and need punches through me, making me arch my back and push harder against his hand.

"Oh, gods. Anarus. I want."

He slides a finger inside me, moving it slowly as his thumb is still tracing slow, steady circles. His other hand goes back higher, palming my breast, rolling the nipple between his fingers. "Is this what you want?"

In response, I bite my own arm to muffle another moan.

"Let me hear you, Jinx." He slides in another finger and his thumb increases the pressure, sending me spiraling. He leans over me, using his mouth where his fingers had been on my breast. He licks my nipple, making it stiffen into a taut peak. The warmth of his mouth and the pressure from his fingers moving and twisting inside me makes the desire I feel push higher. I bite my lips against another moan.

I pant out. "The others."

"Don't matter. Just me and you." He curls his fingers against my walls and

I can't hold back the cry. I strain against him, my back bowing, as he moves his fingers in and out of me. His thumb keeps pace, pushing on my clit every time his fingers sink inside me. He adds a third finger and bliss rides through my bones. Every nerve sings and the tight curling in my core explodes in rippling waves.

"Anarus!" I cry out his name and push my hips against his hand. Anarus keeps thrusting his fingers in and out of my wet heat until the ripples of pleasure calm down.

"There's my good girl." Anarus pulls his fingers back and I can't hide the whimper of complaint. He strips quickly and crawls around me to lie down on the bed. "Come here."

My bones feel liquid but I do as he says, turning around to sit on the bed next to him. His cock is hard and I try to focus on his face, but my eyes are constantly drawn back to it. He takes one of my hands in his.

"You done this before, Jinx?"

"Not consensually." A flash of something dark goes over his face at this, but it's replaced by desire quickly.

"You're in charge. You're in control." He pulls on my hand so that I move to straddle him. As I settle, sitting on his abdomen, he groans softly and wraps a hand around the back of my neck, pulling me down to kiss him. The move shifts my hips and I can feel the tip of him pushing on my clit. I wiggle my hips instinctively, drawing another groan from him.

His hands settle on my hips and he guides me to slide him inside me. There's a slight burn and stretch at first, but as I move to take him in deeper, the feeling of him filling me takes over, sending pleasure rippling through me.

"Fuck." Anarus stutters. "Fertility inhibitor. Queen Anne's lace. In the food. Just so you know."

The tiny part of my brain that's still rational is glad to hear it, but then he tilts his pelvis, driving deeper in me and rationality is something I don't have and don't care to. I wrap my hands around his shoulders and kiss along his neck as he guides my hips to move along him in a steady pace.

His shadows are cool against my hot skin and the feel of them makes the intensity of the sensations rolling through me peak higher until I am a mass of quivering pleasure. "Anarus. More. Gods, more."

His hips move in time with mine as he picks up the pace, but it's not enough. The pleasure builds, tying itself in knots low in me, but there is something just out of reach. I cry out in need and frustration. Anarus echoes it in his own moan.

"Fuck." He sits me up, then flips us so I am on my back under him. "You okay?" He groans, waiting to move until he knows I feel safe how we are. When I nod, words past my ability, he resumes thrusting in me. He pulls on one of my knees, drawing it up to his hip, allowing him to thrust deeper, and, finally, he hits that spot in me that sends me over the edge. Heat slams through me with every one of his thrusts and I arch into him, seeking more and more.

His free hand quests over me, trailing tiny bursts of cold and fire over my sensitive skin, and his lips possess mine again. He finds my breast and rolls my nipple between his thumb and finger, squeezing it slightly in time with his thrusts.

Waves of pleasure pulse through me as his tongue finds the same rhythm in my mouth and I arch again as they reach a peak. He rides me through my orgasm and I scream.

"Fuck, Jinx. I." He bites his lip on his words as he pushes deeper once more. Then his movements stall as his release overpowers him and he shudders deep inside me. At that same moment, something twists, changes. Almost like an awareness comes over me that locks my mind onto Anarus. He hovers above me and we stare at each other, saying nothing but not needing to, a deep knowledge slamming through both of us. He is mine. I am his, and he is mine. His cock twitches once, still inside me, and, instinctively, my muscles clench around him. He groans, his eyes fluttering closed. "I will never not need you, Jinx."

I reach out my hand and cup his cheek. "You have me. I trust you."

A muscle jumps in his jaw, but he smiles. Kissing me softly, he pulls out of me and the empty feeling he leaves behind aches. Anarus rolls to the side and sits up on the edge of the bed with his back to me. I watch him. His back is covered with a tattoo I never noticed. Which is weird, because the tattoo of the phases of the moon down his spine and starry sky in black and white covers the expanse of his back from shoulders to waist. I don't know how I missed it with how often he goes shirtless.

I reach out and trace a swirling pattern of stars on one shoulder blade. "Beautiful."

He glances over his shoulder at me. "Yeah, it's my favorite piece."

I catch his eyes. "Not the tattoo, you."

The startled look on his face at my words makes me move to kneel next to him. I take his face in my hands and turn him back towards me. I kiss his lips softly. "You're beautiful, Anarus." In response, he reaches out, capturing a loose hair in his fingers, curling it around one finger before he pushes it back behind my ear. He watches my face the entire time, his lips parted like there are words there that he can't make himself say. He blinks, then turns away, reaching down to the floor to grab his pants and pull them on.

He stands, finding my shirt and giving it to me. "Water. I need a drink."

I pull on the shirt, Ydum's shirt that is long enough to be a dress on me, and follow him back into the sitting room. The remnants of dinner are still on the table and Anarus pours us both a cup of juice, which we just stand by the table sipping.

"Good talk?" Ydum says from the couch. I startle, not realizing he and Byder were both still there. I look over and Ydum is smiling, mirth twinkling in his eyes. His lip is better and his eye looks like the black eye happened a few days ago rather than a few hours.

I blush, looking away again, but Anarus just clears his throat, saying, "Very," before taking another sip of his drink. He takes my hand in his and leads me to the couch to sit with them. "The next game is protection." He changes our focus.

"At least I feel like I will have something to work with on this one." I say, curling my legs under me. "Protection is something we studied heavily in magical arts classes."

Ydum nods. "This game is usually very similar every year. Protect a space against something. Some type of invader."

"Sounds a lot like the first game." I tell him.

Ydum shakes his head, disagreeing. "It's not. It's very different. The first game was about using the natural elements around us to kill whatever was attacking. This game is about using any means necessary to prevent whatever is coming from ever getting to you. The first game ended when our attackers were dead, or close enough to it to not matter. This time, we won't necessarily be able to kill whatever it is, just stop it in a way that they can't undo."

"That still sounds the same to me, or close enough." My brow furrows as I try to understand. "How is it different?"

Ydum shifts, getting more comfortable in the position I have come to recognize as how he looks when he is reciting information from a textbook. "For the protection game, the object to be defended against will not be a killable foe, and the object to be protected will not always be the god or human contestant. The goal is to create a protection the foe cannot undo, create a stalemate between the protected entity and the foe, rather than win in a fight against them. The game will be considered passed when the protection will permanently hold against any act the foe could do that would not risk the foe also harming themselves. It will be failed when the foe is able to reach the object that should be protected, the human, or the god. Any and all weapons or materials the god and human can bring with them or find within the chosen environment are allowed to be used in the game."

"Weapons?" I turn to face Byder. "Sounds like you will be the lead god this time, Byder."

Byder is looking down, running his fingers over his hunt tattoo lines. It's obvious he isn't paying attention. "Hello? Byder?" I call out. Then, I reach forward and touch his knee. "Byder?"

"Huh?" Byder looks up, a little lost, then blushes. "Sorry, I was. I was thinking."

"Those must have been some deep thoughts, man. Jinx said your name like three times." Ydum chuckles.

Byder doesn't answer him, just blushes deeper and pulls the blanket from behind him and hands it to me. I suddenly am acutely aware of what Byder was thinking and how bare I am in Ydum's shirt. I take the blanket and cover my lap and legs with it. The deeper Byder blushes, the deeper I blush, so I stop looking at him.

Ydum repeats my statement for me. "So, Jinx said that with weapons allowed, it sounds like you are the best god for the next game, Byder."

"Um, yeah, probably." Byder clears his throat, shaking his head slightly as if he's shaking away thoughts before looking back up at the rest of us. "But physical weapons are not all protection needs. My dad told me that he made the mistake of thinking he could defend Mom with just weapons, and they almost failed because of that. It took some fast thinking and luck that they were able to find things to help them in the forest area they were in to keep them from completely failing. They went from fourth to last place because they put too much stock in a hunt god's protection."

"There are a ton of protection help stuff a witch can use." I explain, but then I slump in my seat. "Unfortunately, I don't have a witch's kit with me and a lot of the things that I would have in one won't be available to just find anywhere."

"A witch's kit?" Anarus asks, shifting forward on the couch to show his interest.

I turn to face him and nod. "Yeah. Every witch home will have at least one, even in the poor areas like I live. Candles, incense, different dried and preserved herbs, stones and crystals, metals, small bags and jars, matches, and anything else needed to craft different spells quickly. The wealthier a family is, the better the kit will be stocked. Gold is hard to keep in a witch's kit when you are fighting to feed a bunch of kids, but copper's not as hard. I would bet that everyone else was told to bring a witch's kit with them, but seeing as I wasn't given time to pack anything, I don't have one."

"So, that's what that box under the kitchen sink was." Ydum playfully spreads his arms wide as he leans back. "Dad was so mad when I was little and found it. I took the stones outside and played marbles with them."

I moan, slump my head into my hands and shake it. "Oh my gods. Those stones were probably imbued with your dad's magic. You could have killed yourself making them smack into each other."

"Find a different swear, Jinx." Anarus says almost reflexively. "Without a witch's kit available, what can we do instead?"

I look back up and shrug, ignoring the comment. "Get creative? I can try to find things around our rooms to scrounge together for something of a witch's kit, if they are allowed, then we just hope to get the rest from the environment we are in."

I look around the dorm that the guys had called a hotel room. There's really not a lot I could find here to make a witch's kit from. Unless they have things hidden in their belongings, even the most basic supplies for a protection circle would be hard to find in this environment. I feel a little dismayed. I actually know something helpful for once, but can't do anything about it because of my damned birthday making me not know things. Again.

"So, we have something to focus on for the next six days." Ydum says, I think catching my mood change and trying to make me feel better. "Finding things to make Jinx a witch's kit."

I hold up a finger to make them pause, remembering what I thought in the game earlier. "Before I forget, I did have a thought in the game today. I should also practice focusing on my meditation. By the time the game was half over, I was shaking because of holding the concentration that long. Even with Ydum's backup, it was really tiring and got way too hard way too quickly."

"That's what she said." Byder and Ydum say at the same time. They look at each other and laugh, making me roll my eyes. Even Anarus laughs. Will I even not be rolling my eyes at these three?

"Anyway," I drawl out. "My point is, I need to work on expanding my time limits with the magic."

"Good idea." Anarus tells me. "The workouts will help with that, but we can't forget the mind is a muscle too."

When Ydum suggests it would be best if we all go to bed and get some good sleep after such an eventful day, I stop at Byder. "Hey, Byder. Do you... Don't you need another tattoo line? We completed a game."

Ydum and Anarus both stop their progress towards the bedrooms and listen. Byder almost looks startled by the question. "Huh? Oh, no. I didn't hunt anything this time. It's for successful hunts or kills only. If a hunt was part of the game, or a kill, then I would. But I was defensive, not offensive."

I nod, understanding now, and continue my way to bed to be fresh tomorrow to start again, planning on how to survive another game. I spare a glance back at the couches as Anarus and I head to my room. Byder didn't get up when the rest of us did, instead choosing to just sit on the couch, looking at the floor. My mouth twitches but I continue to my bedroom, where Anarus kisses me before stripping and getting into the bed. I join him and he doesn't say anything when I snuggle against him and close my eyes. He pulls me closer to wrap his arms around me and whispers "peace" into my hair as I drift off.

Chapter Seven

FIRST THING AFTER BREAKFAST in the morning, we go into the hallway to see if the paintings have changed. We aren't the only ones. Every other team is also out there, moving from painting to painting, examining them and chatting about what they think would be the best.

The painting meanings seem to be obvious. There are three identical paintings of a small cabin in the woods, two of a mud and daub building in a small village that looks similar to mine, two of a large squat brick building on a busy street, and two more of a large wood barn in a field of wheat.

I wander from painting to painting, listening to the other teams' conversations.

Aretha is standing in front of a painting of the busy street, explaining to her god how a building that big would be hard to defend with the crystals in her kit because she only has four of them.

"Which ones are they?" Wren approaches Aretha from the other side.

Aretha looks over her shoulder at Wren. "Amber."

"Do you have a black candle? I would be willing to swap for a lodestone." Wren rolls her eyes. "My mom insisted on packing my kit and she gave me six lodestones and no black candles."

"Oh, gods. That sucks." Aretha agrees. "Yeah. When we go back to our room, we can swap."

I snort and mutter. "At least you have something."

Both Wren and Aretha turn to look at me. "What do you mean?" Wren asks me.

I'm startled as I didn't actually intend for them to hear me. "Oh, I don't have anything." I shrug as if it doesn't matter. "My birthday is September fifth. I tested then was put right in the carriage to go to the cave. I didn't even have time to pack clothes, much less a witch's kit. I didn't even know witch's kits were allowed."

Wren and Aretha stare at me, their eyes going wide. "Only for game three, we were told." Wren says. "We can have a witch's kit with us but are not allowed to use it in any other game."

"Wait. You didn't have time to get anything? Not even clothes? So, whose clothes are you wearing?" Aretha gestures to my shirt and pants.

I smile and point to Ydum. "His."

"Fuck." Wren swears. "He's like a foot taller than you."

I pull one pant leg out of my boot and show them how long it is on me, chuckling. "Tell me about it."

While I tuck it back in to the boot, Aretha gets a determined look on her face. "That's bullshit. I don't care about winning enough for that bullshit. Hey! Come here, everyone!" She calls out across the foyer.

"Aretha!" I hiss. "What are you doing?"

She walks into the middle of the foyer, looks back at me, and just lifts one shoulder. "That's bullshit and not fair. I want to win, but I want to win fairly."

The other gods and humans all converge around Aretha, questioning what's going on. My gods all come over to me with curious looks. "I did not do this." I gesture to Aretha. "It's all her."

She settles herself and projects her voice over everyone's mutterings. "So, I don't know if y'all realize this, but Jinx came here with literally nothing. Apparently, her twenty-fourth birthday was September fifth, and, after she tested, they didn't even give her time to go home and get clothes."

Several people start murmuring about that being wrong but a few shrug like they don't care.

Aretha tries again. "Girls, she's wearing Ydum's clothes. Ydum's!" Aretha points at him, and he blushes, looks down and scratches the back of his neck uncomfortably. "He's a giant. If nothing else, she should be able to be comfortably dressed. I know we are competing against each other, but damn. We can be decent humans, even if the gods are assholes."

A few gods grumble at that. Some of the humans glare at their grumbly gods. I hear one tell her god, "We don't mean you. I know it's not your fault. Drila, on the other hand, her we can blame." Her god seems to agree with that.

"Alright." Aretha draws their attention again. "Wren and I also realized that our witch's kits may be lacking something or another and thought to swap with each other. I suggest we all go gather anything we think Jinx could use that we can spare and bring our kits out here. We can all sit together and swap, giving Jinx what we can to give her at least something. I'm as competitive as anyone else, but I want to win fair. Plus, we already lost too many people to this stupid game. I don't think I could live with myself if she died because they penalized her for something she couldn't control when I could have helped."

The humans all seem to nod and take off back to their rooms, their gods trailing behind them. I stand there, my mouth hanging open. My gods are all just staring at me.

Byder chuckles. "Well, Jinx. Look at you, going and uniting the humans."

I stammer. "I didn't do anything. Aretha just, she just took it upon herself to… I wasn't even saying it to them. Just whining under my breath."

Ydum puts a hand on my shoulder. "Well, you did it anyway." He looks down the hall and sees some of the humans coming back out of their rooms, things gathered in their arms. "We'll go back in the room and leave you all to it."

The three gods head back to our room and leave me standing in the middle of the foyer, shocked. As I stand there, just staring, the other humans all come out of their rooms and settle themselves on the floor. They are each pulling things out of their witch's kits and setting them out. Iella also comes out of the room with Damek, but doesn't sit, instead coming up to me.

"Here." She shoves something at me. "It's only one pair of pants, but they are probably closer to the right size than Ydum's." After I take them, she goes back to her room while Damek settles on the floor with the rest of the humans.

Damek calls out to me, smiling ruefully. "No clothes or anything for you, Jinx. Sorry. Mine would probably be worse than your god's." Everyone smiles back at him at this. Damek is taller than Ydum and about as broad in the shoulders as Byder. His clothes would be worse.

Aretha just takes the lead again after she's done sorting her witch's kit out. "Okay, why don't we put anything not from a witch's kit in a pile over here." She points to a spot by the hallway. "Clothes or whatever for Jinx. Then, we can sort our stuff from our kits into two piles. One that we don't need a trade for and one that we want to trade for. Then, we'll let Jinx go first, collecting anything you are willing to give away to make herself a kit and then the rest of us can do a swap session."

Everyone agrees and several of the females move to put items in a pile by the hallway. Once they are settled back in the circle the witches have made on the floor with their kits spread out, everyone just looks at me, waiting.

"Go ahead, Jinx." Aretha encourages me.

I blush and twist my lips. I feel awkward and like there are too many eyes on me. Damek speaks. "In the last game, I was struggling. Really struggling. Your gods were good at keeping me from being able to make sleet on your island, Jinx. Sleet's fucking hard. I saw you turn Amanda's hail to rain by making it warm, and knew you could do the same to me if I just tried to make it sleet over me to pass rather than try to win. But I tried anyway. I got snow easily. And you did just what I thought you would. You made it warm and my snow became rain without ever becoming sleet."

He turns to face the other witches. "She could have just kept it that way, too warm, and I would have failed to make sleet at all and me and Iella would be out of the games completely. Instead, she dropped her heat the minute it was enough to count as actual rain and let me make it sleet so we wouldn't fail. She could have let me die and Iella suffer, but she didn't." Looking at me again, he holds up a tiny, palm-sized mirror, then sets it in the middle of circle. "I have two and the rest of my kit is pretty good. I don't need to trade for anything. Thank you for not killing me."

Wren leans forward, placing two things in the center of the circle. "Two lodestones. It ain't much, but I have plenty."

Aretha goes next. "Black candle, red candle, and black string." She puts them in the center and turns to Wren. "Black candle for lodestone?" Wren nods and they swap.

Amanda speaks next. "I saw that with Damek. You're a decent witch, Jinx. Pearl, amber, and hazelwood sticks." She deposits the stones and a handful of thin sticks the size of a finger in the center.

Saffron looks over at Amanda. "Got any more hazelwood?" Amanda nods. Saffron holds up two cacti pads. "Trade for cactus?"

Amanda leans across the circle to Saffron, holding out more hazelwood. "Ooh, gimme, gimme." Saffron hands one pad to her and deposits the other one in the growing pile for me.

"I have an obscene amount of rosemary, basil and black pepper mixed together." Raven says. "Anyone have a jade they don't need? I have three and would love to make a four corners with it."

Isis pulls something out of her kit. She holds up five stones. "These are a loan, not a gift. I want these back." She puts four of the jade stones in the pile for me and hands the last one to Raven.

"Thanks, and of course." Raven hands Isis a small black bag and puts another one in my pile.

Still standing away from the group, in slight shock, I mumble an "of course" at Isis.

Asteria looks down at the floor. She blushes, and just sets a small roll of red string on my pile. "I don't have a lot of anything."

Damek, who is sitting next to her, leans over and looks in the tiny wood box Asteria has in front of her. He slides a small bowl made out of a seashell over to her. "Your dried plants aren't already mixed. You'll need a bowl."

Wren asks Damek, "She got a lodestone?" When Damek shakes his head, Wren tosses one at him and he puts it with the bowl.

"What about candles?" Aretha asks.

"Two of each black and white, one red." Damek tells her. He looks in Asteria's box again. "And one pink. Pink?"

Asteria blushes harder. "A red and white melted together in my bag. I just made them one candle instead of throwing it away. Pink is my favorite color."

Several people chuckle. Aretha hands a spool of black thread over. "You only have red."

Amanda leans over and hands Asteria a few sticks of hazelwood, then gasps. "Oh!" She shuffles through her large box and pulls out two tiny paper boxes. "Matchsticks. Candles and incense are useless without matches." She puts one box on my stack and hands another to Asteria.

The group dissolves as the others start talking about swaps they want to make, or showing off the box their witch's kit is in and where they got it from. We all jump when Drila pops into the foyer, still in her yellow dress from the weather game.

"What are you doing?" She asks, seemingly annoyed.

Aretha immediately takes the lead again. "Swapping witch's kit supplies and making a witch's kit for Jinx, and Asteria apparently." She says defensively.

"That's not." Drila shakes her head. "You can't do that."

Aretha stands up, her hands clasped behind her back. "Is it against the rules?"

Damek stands up as well, putting his hands in his pockets as he saunters over to stand next to Aretha. "I know it isn't. I read the manuals cover to cover. My birthday is September thirtieth. I had the time to memorize the damn things. Did Jinx even get a manual at all?"

Drila stammers, her face getting hot and flustered in a way I didn't think she could.

"Didn't think so." Damek nods. "That is against the rules. All humans are to get a copy of the manuals for the Gods Games once their test turns blue. Jinx didn't get one, so you violated the rules, not us."

"Jinx's test didn't turn blue." Drila counters.

Raven stands up next. All three of them take a few steps closer to Drila. "If her test wasn't blue enough to get a manual, then it wasn't blue enough for her to be here. You gotta make up your mind, Drila. Was it blue enough for her to be here and all the rules apply for her, or was it too red and you violated your rules just by making her participate? You can't have it both ways."

They're defending me. The other witches are defending me. And helping me. And Drila looks angry about it.

"You meant for me to fail." I say low, just above a whisper. "You purposely wanted me to fail. You were mad when I actually found teammates, then even angrier when you realized it wasn't just one but three. Why did you want me to fail, Drila?"

"End magic witches are not supposed to be powerful enough to make it into the games." She gripes, curling her fists.

"Is that why my test was wrong?" I push as I stalk closer to her. Damek, Aretha, and Raven come to stand behind me.

Drila looks from me to the witches behind me and huffs. "Yes and no. You are an end magic witch, but not fully. You are something else. Something that doesn't make sense. The test was both red and blue because you are both and neither somehow." She shifts her weight from one leg to another. "Finish your swapping and stop helping each other. It may not be explicitly against the rules but it doesn't make sense for you to help those you are competing against."

"Maybe we care more about surviving your stupid games than winning." Aretha tells her. Drila has no response to that, so she just pops away.

Damek reaches out and touches my elbow. "You good?"

"I'm sorry I got you guys in trouble." I tell the group.

"Fuck her." Aretha tosses out casually. "And fuck these games." She walks into the middle of the circle of humans and starts collecting up the donations in the pile. "I don't know that any of us have a box or anything to store all this in for you, but I'm sure one of your three gods can help with that." Aretha looks at me and winks.

Damek helps her. "Yeah, which, by the way, how are you alive? I swear, Iella is too much sometimes, and you have three to handle? It's no wonder they got into a fist fight yesterday."

"Tholdir is more likely to die because I kill him than because of these games." Amanda shakes her head. "A stick. He threw a stick at a wolf. My god is dumb."

I smile at her as she helps me collect the clothes. "They're not too bad. Honestly, I think I would go crazy with only one. They can entertain themselves and leave me alone."

Raven chuckles. "If your gods are leaving you alone, you're doing it wrong." The knowing look she tosses me as she packs up her witch's kit makes me blush.

"Well, maybe they don't leave me alone all the time." I mutter, which makes her laugh more.

"Byder is fit." She says.

I bite my lip and her eyes go wide. "Not Byder? I totally guessed you and Byder by day two."

Damek laughs as we start walking down the hall to my room. "That fight had shadow boy written all over it."

"Anarus, not shadow boy." I say defensively.

"So, you admit it?" Damek asks, then laughs again when I don't answer. "Your silence is telling, Jinx."

I just step in front of him to open my door. Byder, Ydum, and Anarus all look up as I enter, then are startled when Damek, Aretha, Raven and Amanda follow me in, everyone except Raven with their arms full of things. Raven shrugs. "I'm just following for the gossip."

Aretha dumps her armload on the table, then steers Raven back to the door. "We will leave Jinx to sort out her stuff. We can gossip later, Raven, like after dinner or something. If they aren't going to play fair and want us to all stay apart, then I think we should make coming together a routine thing. Bye!" She pushes Raven out the door in front of her and Damek and Amanda follow behind.

"What did you do, Jinx?" Ydum says through a confused smile.

"I think I started a rebellion. Well, more Aretha than me, but yeah."

"How?" Anarus asks.

I grimace. "Um, Drila kinda popped in, angry that they were all sharing stuff with me to make a witch's kit and swapping with each other and Raven, Aretha, and Damek made her admit they were purposely trying to make me fail the games because my test showed I was both a beginning and end magic witch but also neither."

"Wait." Byder stands up, and paces over to me by the table. "That was just a whole lot of information in one sentence. Drila came here? And was mad at you guys for working together?"

"Mmhm." I nod. "Damek put her in her place, though, saying we weren't violating the rules but the gods had by never giving me a manual."

"You missed the most important bit, Byder." Ydum comes over to the table and starts looking at everything there. "Jinx is both a beginning and end magic witch, according to Drila, but also neither. How is that even possible?"

"She didn't know. By the sounds of it, none of the gods know."

"Well, shit." Byder says. "That's three of us."

"Three of us what?" I ask him.

Byder points at Anarus. "Too young and too pure." He points at himself.

"Can't read right." Then, he points at me. "Messed up magic that's both instead of one or the other." He turns to Ydum. "Looks like you are the only normal one on our team."

"Well, kind of normal. A jerk, but that's more an attitude problem than something messed up." Anarus drawls.

"Anarus, be nice." I say, almost instinctively at this point. But I notice Ydum fingering the ball of red string on the table, not looking at any of us. I move closer. "Ydum?"

He holds up the string. "What color is this?" He says very quietly.

I furrow my brow. "You don't know?"

He shakes his head. "I'm colorblind. I'm a nature god and I'm colorblind."

"How did I not know that?" Byder asks. "I've known you forever."

"Mom worked really hard with me to hide it." He laughs sarcastically. "A colorblind nature god? They would have thrown me to the wolves if anyone knew."

"Fuck." Anarus stands up and comes over to the table, taking up a position on the other side of it than me, Ydum and Byder. "We are the reject team."

I was right. They want us to fail. But it's not just about me, it's all four of us. They wanted all four of us to not succeed, instead the magic in the cave gave us each other.

Ydum snorts. "At least with the rest of you, they may not like it but it's not a big deal in the real world. Even if we survive, even if we win, if anyone finds out about me, I'm a goner. You can't be a nature god and be broken like that."

I turn to Ydum. "Hey. Look at me." When he refuses, I grab his chin and force him to. "No one is touching you. Not now, not ever. You did perfect in the first game and were damn good in the second. Everything else, we will figure out."

"You don't get a choice about it, Jinx." Yum tells me. "The other nature gods will…"

"The other nature gods don't get to decide your worth." I tell him adamantly. "You're mine. I get to decide. Not them."

"I'm yours?" Ydum whispers, his eyes going wide.

"Mine." I say firmer. I don't expect it, so when Ydum leans down and kisses me, I stiffen up for a moment.

Anarus growls and Ydum jumps back. I'm prepared for another fight to break out, but Anarus only growls again, leaning over with his fingertips pressed into the table. "You ask her first."

Ydum mutters. "Sorry, man."

Anarus shakes his head, his arms crossed over his chest, jutting his chin towards me. "Not me, tell it to her."

Ydum looks at me, then looks away to the floor. "I'm sorry, Jinx."

I look at Anarus. He is completely clear of shadows. He isn't angry Ydum kissed me, just that he didn't ask first before touching me, and I'm confused. Again. I seem to be confused often when it comes to these gods.

Anarus comes around the table to talk to me. "Like you heard me say when

Ydum and Byder argued, I know how this works. The cave found a fated bond between you and all three of us. I may not like it, but that means you are going to have some type of relationship with all three of us, Jinx. What type and how much is up to you. When it comes to the others on our team, I don't get to decide what that relationship you have with them is. You and Byder decide for you and Byder. You and Ydum decide for you and Ydum. Not me, not the games. If it's physical like that, I guess we all have to get really comfortable with each other. It's your choice. The only thing I was angry about was Ydum not giving you a choice."

I look at Anarus. His shadows are calmer than I've ever seen. "You hate him."

He sighs heavily, rubbing a hand down his face. "I don't hate him. I don't like him. If it was any other situation, I wouldn't even be friends with him. But that's not hate. I lo-." He looks away then looks back. "Your choice. I am happy to follow your choice."

"What were you going to say, Anarus?"

Anarus's jaw ticks and he licks his lips. "Can I kiss you?"

"Yes." I tell him and he kisses me swiftly, hard.

"Do you want to kiss Ydum?" Anarus stares at me. I look at Ydum. That feeling comes again, the one that makes me know that, if I touch him, I'll feel that static, just like with Anarus. That taut line tugging at me. But there are three of them. I shouldn't want that same thing with all three of them. But I know it. He's mine, just like Anarus is mine. Ydum is mine. Byder is mine. And I do want them.

I feel so confused. This isn't how it's done. This isn't how relationships should be. Is it? Anarus is saying they are, that they can be and it's up to me. To me and them. When I look down, my stomach clenching, making me feel like I should say no when I don't want to, he murmurs in warning. "Jinx."

"Yes." Anarus turns me so that I am facing Ydum.

Ydum moves closer to me again. "Can I kiss you, beautiful?"

"Yes, Ydum."

Ydum smooths a flyaway hair back behind my ear and leans down to kiss me. His kiss is soft, gentle, sweet, that static and taut line softly tugging on me. He stands back up and smiles at me. "Do you want to kiss Byder?"

I look around and realize Byder moved away from the table. He's sitting on the couch, staring at the floor again. I look back between Anarus and Ydum.

"Don't think about what others will think." Ydum tells me. "Don't think about what people say is right and wrong. The cave did this for a reason, and, like Ani keeps saying, it's your choice."

I walk over to the couches and kneel in front of Byder. "Why did you come back over here?" I talk quietly so that only he can hear me. The other two are watching, I know, but I want to know what Byder is thinking.

"There were too many of us." Byder says just as quietly. "You don't like to feel trapped and there were too many of us."

"Do you want to kiss me, Byder?" I ask and he finally actually focuses on me.

"Do you want me to?"

They said not to think about what other people will think. They keep telling me to go with my gut. Well, my gut, my too itchy skin that wants to touch them all, that static, that tugging, says I do want Byder to kiss me. I stand and slide onto his lap, my fingers running through his hair. Byder brings his hand up to cup the back of my head and brings his lips almost to mine. I move the last inch to kiss him and that static ignites everywhere we are touching. It blooms stronger, more intense than it was even with Anarus, more than with Ydum.

Byder groans into my mouth, his kiss deep, sucking my bottom lip between his teeth with just the smallest amount of pressure. I gasp and Byder uses the opening to thrust his tongue in my mouth. His arm comes around my waist, turning me on his lap so that I am straddling him, and leans back so my head is over his. We both pull out each other's hair ties, my loose hair falling around both our faces while his cascades down his back. Desire arcs through me as my breasts rub against his chest and he runs his hands up and down my back, pulling me even closer.

"Shit." I hear Ydum swear. "That's hot. That shouldn't be this hot, but that's fucking hot."

Byder breaks our kiss and shifts me to sitting next to him on the couch. I know my face is flushed as I feel bothered and a little embarrassed. He clears his throat.

"We should figure out what to do with all the stuff everyone gave you before the games decide to pop lunch on top of it and ruins it." Byder manages to say, his voice mostly even.

"Yeah, looks like you have a pretty good start to a witch's kit, Jinx." Ydum says. "Not that I'm sure what all should be in one, but there's a whole lot of things you didn't have this morning, so better than nothing."

I take a deep breath, and stand up, grabbing Byder's hand and pulling him to come back to the table with me. "Actually, it's really good. I just need a box to put it all in. Or something." I start shifting the clothes out of the way so I can look at the witch's kit I collected. "The only other thing I would really want is salt."

"We can steal that from the meals they give us." Anarus says.

"Wait." Byder disappears into his room for a minute. He comes back with a wooden box about as long as his forearm and half as wide. "Would this work?"

I take it from him and examine it. It's not lined inside, but does have a metal latch. "What's it from?"

"My daggers. I took the felt holder out of it." Byder explains.

I keep examining the box, looking for any defects or issues. "Can I see them?"

"Yeah." Byder disappears into the room, then comes back with five knives with sheathes made out of leather, each one a different color, black, brown, red, blue and green. The grips are made of brass and black wood and each one has a double-edged blade.

"Sweet set." Ydum appraises.

"Have you killed anything with them?" I ask him. "Gotten blood on the blades, then put them back in this box?"

"No." Byder shakes his head. "My dad got them new as a gift to bring here. I haven't used them at all."

"That matters?" Anarus asks me.

I look up at him. "Yeah. If I want a witch's kit for protection, I don't want it stored in something that's already associated with violence."

Byder furrows his brows and combs a hand through his hair. "But they're knives. Aren't they always associated with violence?"

"Have you used every knife you've ever touched to kill something?" I ask. When they all shake their heads no, like I knew they would, I continue. "Exactly. Knives are just objects, like everything else, until you give them a purpose by using them somehow. Eating, killing, shaving, making a sacrifice, or just purely decoration. Knives can have many uses, just as a witch's kit can, or a fork, or a piece of cloth. Intention matters with witch magic."

"Just like with how your magic to make it rain worked. You needed an intention, a need for rain, not just want it." Ydum say.

"Exactly." I beam at him and he smiles, proud of himself.

Byder moves his daggers off the table. "So, that box works?"

I nod. "It should." I start shifting things into the box. For now, I'm just going to store them. Later, I know, I'm going to want to cleanse them, since they came from other people that, while nice, I don't really know and imbue them with my magic to make them mine. But for now, I just don't want lunch landing on it all.

I move everything into the bedroom, out of the way, and come back out, bringing the red string with me, an idea forming. There is a protection spell I can do well I think would be helpful. The guys are watching me. "Go sit on the couches. I want to try something I learned in magical arts class." I tell them.

They each going to their normal spots, watching me silently. I try to look confident, but I was only taught how to do this between two people, not four. As I sit next to Anarus, I'm thinking over the magic in my mind. I was taught to only have one bracelet made from one string for each person. But we are a team, it should be all of us for all of us. What should the magic be if I am getting three bracelets from three people? Giving three bracelets to three people? Add more string, I decide. One bracelet, one person is done with one string, so the second person should have two strings, the third three. At least, that sounds right to me. But what if I'm wrong and...

I shake my head. I can do this. Protection is easy. Intentions matter the most for protection. That's what the magical arts teacher said. I shrug off my doubts and take Anarus's right hand and place it on my lap. I wrap my hand around his wrist, measuring it with my fingers, then pull off enough string to match the length I need.

"What are you doing?" Ydum asks.

Anarus reaches over with his free hand and slaps the back of his head. "Didn't your dad ever teach you not to interrupt a casting witch?"

"Shit, sorry." Ydum mutters.

Byder glares at him. "Stop talking, man."

I ignore them. Rubbing my fingers down the string I pulled from the roll, I check it for defects. Finding none, I rub it between my fingers again, thinking on safety and protection. Then, I bite the string to break it off where I want it and turn back to Anarus. "Put your pinky finger against your wrist." He does and I tie the string off, still focusing on protection but using his pinky in the way to make sure the string bracelet isn't too tight, and won't become so if he gets it wet in the shower or something.

I move to sit between Byder and Ydum and take Ydum's wrist in my lap. As I work, breaking off two red strings to braid them together for his bracelet, I talk to him, keeping part of my mind focusing on protection. "This string is red for protection. Red is hot. Not like the sun, but like a fire in a fireplace. It's a warmth that makes a cold night better. It's loud and gets your attention. Blood is red. The source of life. It's a heartbeat. Love."

"Friction." Byder adds.

"Power." Anarus says.

As I tie off the braided strings on his wrist, I tell him. "Red is a warning. This will warn others that you are protected by me. That you are mine."

I turn and take Byder's wrist. They stay silent again as I work the string to make a braided loop of three strands on his wrist, knowing that we only talked for that moment for Ydum. Once Byder has his, I pull off one strands the size of my wrist, turning to Anarus. "Bite the string off there, Anarus."

He does and takes the string, holding it in his hand, waiting. I turn to Ydum and have him bite off two strings. Then, Byder bites off three. "Check the strings for any defects, focusing on protection. Ydum and Byder, braid yours together. You need to keep me safe with the string. For the bracelet to protect me when you can't."

All three males hunch over, bent on their work, concentrating hard. Anarus finishes first, since he doesn't have to braid his, and I hold my right wrist out to him. He ties the string around it like he saw me do, then lifts my wrist and kisses it gently. I move back over to the couch between Ydum and Byder. I turn to Ydum first, giving him my right wrist as well. He does the same as Anarus, tying off the string and kissing my wrist where the tie on the string landed.

When I turn to Byder, he's struggling to braid the strings. His brow is furrowed in concentration and his tongue is pressed between his lips. "Sorry, I'm trying." He mutters. Anarus gets off the couch and kneels next to him. He places his thumb on the ends of the strings, trapping them between his thumb and Byder's thigh, giving Byder tension to braid them easier. Byder looks at me, as if to ask if that's okay, and I nod. He goes back to finishing his bracelet, shaking his head occasionally as his hair falls into his face, his mouth soundlessly moving as he concentrates on protection. Then, he finally ties it around my wrist and kisses the ends like the other two.

As Anarus moves back to his seat, I tell them. "If it falls off, don't put it back on. We'll burn it and make a new one. It falls off when it's done its job and protected you from something."

"Look at our smart, little witch." Ydum says. He turns and looks at the table. "Oh, and just in time for lunch." I stand to go to the table, and Ydum stops me. "Nuh uh, little witch. You know what you have to do now."

I cock an eyebrow at him.

He smiles. "Time to run."

"I hate you." I tell him as the other two laugh.

We go through our routine for running, stretches and workout, before the gods let me eat. Then, we talk through the potential benefits and drawbacks of all the different environments in the painting options. With no idea what we will be protecting, or protecting against, it's mostly all theoretical. I feel like I have more to contribute this time, though. All three gods trust what I say about working with the witch's kit and creating defensive measures.

Right before the lunch mess pops away, Byder runs to the table and grabs the shaker full of salt and tosses it at me. "Enough? Or will we want more?"

"I'll take all the salt I can get." I tell him.

At dinner, Anarus grabs the salt first before food and hands it to me. "What about the pepper?" He asks. I think about it, knowing the herb mixture Raven gave me already has black pepper in it.

"More won't hurt anything, but we don't need it as much as the salt." I tell him.

After dinner, there's a lot of noise coming from the hallway. We open the door and see pretty much all the other teams out wandering the hallway and foyer. Aretha had been serious about us congregating to just hang out.

Several rooms have their doors open. We wander out and look around at what everyone is doing. Most of the others that have their room open have something going in on in them. Uesis and Raven have their door open and Uesis is playing a violin. Aretha and her god, that I learn is named Zodum, a charity god, also have a door open and somehow have managed to smuggle in snacks. Isis and her god Esnir, a god of war, also have their door open and Esnir is having arm wrestling competitions with people.

Ydum gets excited and sets up sock ball, leaving our door open for people to come play or watch others play. As I walk around the foyer and look at what everyone is doing, sort of fascinated that this all started just because my birthday sucks, Byder sidles up next to me.

"Just so you are aware, someone managed to save their alcohol. Several people are drinking. Just thought you'd want to know." Byder looks at me. "You're safe with us, Jinx. You know that, right?"

I take a deep breath, and let it out slowly. Then, I wind my arm through his. "I know."

I mostly shadow Byder for a while, walking with him and just listening as he talks to gods he's known his whole life. I don't fail to notice how many of the other male gods are walking around shirtless. Byder is wearing a shirt, albeit a sleeveless one, and Ydum has on a long sleeve cotton shirt, but Anarus is bare chested again. At least three gods besides mine are also shirtless. I smirk and shake my head. Are the gods allergic to clothing for some reason?

The sound of Anarus's voice raised gets my attention, especially when it's followed by Ydum being loud as well. I turn back to our room, and find both of them blocking our door. Tholdir is standing at the door facing them.

"What's the big deal?" Tholdir asks, his arms thrown wide and a cup of something sloshing a little as he moves. A small bit splashes on his bare chest, dripping over a tattoo of flames over his heart.

"Because we said so, and it's our room." Ydum crosses his arms over his chest and stands taller, blocking more of the doorway. "Like it or lump it, I don't fucking care."

"Amanda, come get your god." Anarus grumbles, shadows very close to running over him.

Amanda comes over, moving around me. "What's the problem? Tholdir, what did you do?"

"I just want to play the cool game." Tholdir gestures inside our room, the cup sloshing again to spill a little of what is definitely alcohol onto the floor.

Ydum drops his arms and balls up his fists. "And we told you no alcohol in here and you are definitely more alcohol than god right now."

Tholdir scoffs. "Everyone's drinking."

"Not everyone." Anarus grinds out.

"Tholdir." Byder's voice comes from behind me, deep and rumbling with more sense of command in it than I've heard before. I don't even have to look to know his arms are flexing with power. "Go with your witch. Now."

"Tholdir, don't ruin this." Amanda drags on her god's arm. "Come on. Their room, their rules. You can play the game tomorrow when you're sober." She makes her god follow her, heading back to their room, mouthing "sorry" as she moves past me.

My gods catch sight of me now that Tholdir isn't in the way. Ydum comes right over to me. "You good, beautiful?"

I smile at him. "I'm perfect. Amanda, on the other hand, has her hands full."

Ydum smiles back at me. "That she does. Not the sharpest guy, but he's alright usually."

The rest of the evening is actually fun, especially as I win four games of sock ball. Eventually everyone starts winding down, and we close our door and clean up. Once the room is back to how it should be, I get nervous. I kissed all three of my gods today. I don't know what their expectations are now. Anarus and I had sex but I don't know if Byder and Ydum expect the same just because.

As if he senses my unease, Byder makes a point of yawning loudly, stretching, and then slapping the leg of his black leather pants. "That's me off. Goodnight, folks." He stands, and walks to the bedroom he has been sharing with Ydum. As he passes Ydum, he playfully slaps the back of his head.

"Hey!" Ydum yelps, rubbing the back of his head. Byder gives him a look and Ydum figures out what Byder isn't saying. "Oh. Yeah, um, me too." He gets up and follows Byder.

"Smooth, man." Byder says, shaking his head.

"That was as subtle as a sledgehammer to the head." Anarus grumbles at them. He turns to me. "Where you want me, little human?"

I look at Anarus through my eyelashes. "How does inside me sound to you?"

"Fuck yes." Anarus growls.

Chapter Eight

THE NEXT MORNING, I lead my gods through helping me cleanse my witch's kit parts. We stand around the table after breakfast. "The first thing we will do is clean everything the traditional way, checking for any defects as we clean them. You first, then the space we will use to work in, then the items."

"How do we clean us?" Ydum asks.

"Well, usually with soap and water." I stare at him with as straight a face as I can manage. "I mean, Ydum, you're twenty-four. You'd think someone would have taught you how to wash your hands by now."

As Byder laughs, Ydum gets defensive. "I didn't know if we had to do something specific. If playing marbles with my dad's kit could have blown me up, I dunno, I thought maybe there would be something special with that too."

I pat his cheek, smiling a little wickedly, I know. "You're just too easy to pick on. No, nothing special about washing your own hands, except for intention. Everything has to be done with the intention you have for what you are doing in mind. Clean hands, no negative influences, that type of thing."

After we all wash our hands and the space we will use, we take wash cloths and clean all of the items physically, checking them to make sure they aren't broken or damaged. Some things, like the rosemary, basil and black pepper mix in the velvet bag from Raven, take more work than others, like the pearls from Amanda. The stones, mirror, candles, matches and Byder's box can actually just be wiped down. But the herb mix has to be taken out of the bag, and the bag cleaned out while I make sure that all the spices are what Raven said they are. It's not that I don't trust her, but bad things happen if a witch isn't careful enough.

Luckily, a hunt god can help me with this. With Byder's sense of smell, he assures me that there's nothing in the mixture other what Raven said and I can put it all back in the bag quickly. Once done, I move everything into the bedroom where there is a window and leave them in the sunshine for a while. We can't actually see out of the windows completely since there is some sort of film over them, but the filminess is thin enough that sunlight, or moonlight at night, filters through. It's enough that I think using the sunlight to magically cleanse and recharge the witch's kit items should be enough.

After we finish that, I want to work on my concentration. At first, the three gods try to be quiet, but then I remind them that being quiet or leaving won't help me. Like Ydum pointed out for the second game, I'm not always going to have perfect peace to concentrate for doing magic.

Peace has always been the thing I'm best at creating from my meditation, so I use that for my intention to work on holding the focus longer. Around me, Byder and Ydum are playing a game of sock ball. Anarus is around, doing things, but I'm not sure what. I try hard to tune them all out and focus on peace but the idea of peace amid the noise of three males being, well, males is hard. I find myself constantly distracted by what Byder and Ydum are saying or where Anarus is.

It takes me far too long to realize that the reason I am constantly distracted is because I am not being distracted at all. I like it here, oddly enough. Sure, this place is actually the games and I could die but here, in the room with these three? I am happy. I'm peaceful with these three gods. I am meditating, trying to gain what I already have, so I fail because I have already succeeded.

When I groan and slouch in my seat, cross-legged on the floor, Anarus is next to me quickly. Too quickly. What was he doing that he's by me so fast?

"What's wrong?" Anarus asks.

I sigh. "I can't focus on peace because all this chaos and noise is peaceful to me."

"You need an actual focus, not an emotional one." Anarus says thoughtfully. "Ydum?"

Ydum lopes over. "What's up?"

"Give Jinx something to actually focus on with her magic." Anarus tells him.

"Ah!" Ydum holds up his hand, like he had in the washroom, a small pile of dirt in his palm and a small closed rosebud in it. "Make it bloom."

I bend my focus on making the rosebud open using all the thoughts I had in the washroom, but nothing happens. I furrow my brow. It had come so easily then, but now I'm struggling. Rose tea. Petals for wedding decoration. Pollen for the bees and honey. Why won't you open? "Why won't it open?"

Ydum smiles. "Because I told it not to."

Byder laughs and leans against the end of the closest couch to watch. "Battle of wills. Who will win, god or witch?"

Well, that's not something I thought Ydum could do. Knowing that's what's happening now, I focus on the task. Do what I say, my need is greater than Ydum's. Open for me. I feel myself start sweating with effort after a bit, but eventually one petal shivers and starts to curl back.

Behind me, Anarus smooths my hair over one shoulder and blows gently on my neck. The sensation tickles and causes a slow warmth to build in me, distracting me. I wave a hand back at him. "Stop."

"Distractions, Jinx." Anarus is smiling wickedly, I can hear it in his voice.

I groan, frustrated. He's right. Annoyingly, he's right. Why that distraction, though? Damn him. Damn all of them because that's the exact same thing Ydum tried in the second game. Why do they all go to that distraction first? Males, I huff to myself.

I shake my hands out and try to concentrate. The rosebud petals are pulled tight again. I focus and battle Ydum to open the petals. The moment one petal starts to unfurl, Anarus kisses the spot on my neck that he had been blowing on. I growl through gritted teeth as the rosebud pulls tightly closed again.

Again and again, I get one petal to start moving and Anarus does something distracting me. Soon, I'm sweating and my hands are shaking. I'm also hot and bothered thanks to Anarus.

"I think that is a good start for today." Ydum finally says. He curls up his hand and the rosebud and dirt disappear.

I groan. "That was rather disappointing. I didn't even get one petal open."

"You call that disappointing?" Byder scoffs and points at Ydum. "Look at him."

I do actually look at Ydum. He's sweating as well and the muscles in his arms are twitching as bad as my hands are. He's as tired as I am. "Was it that hard for you to fight the natural desires of the rosebud to open?"

Ydum shakes his head. "No. It was that hard to fight you. The rosebud didn't want to open yet. It wasn't time for it to open. Keeping it closed should have been easy, Jinx. You made it hard."

"You did good, little human." Anarus whispers in my ear.

Ydum and I both collapse on the couch, both of us exhausted by our exercise, and I hear soft snoring from Ydum almost instantly. I sprawl out and Anarus sits, pulling my feet on his lap. I hear him and Byder quietly discussing the merits of a small room environment in a large building versus a whole cabin or barn for physical protections but my eyes are heavy and Anarus's hands feel good on my tired feet. I think I may have actually dozed off.

The pattern of days continues this way. Mornings are breakfast, stealing the salt, then I spend a short time organizing and imbuing my power into each object in my witch's kit. I work with Ydum on my focus and ability to concentrate on magic, always with Anarus creating distraction. This practice leaves Ydum and I both sweating and tired, so we rest, while the other two do... whatever they do.

Then we have running and physical training, leaving me sweaty and worn out again, lunch and rest again. Evenings we spend either quietly with ourselves or with small groups from the other teams. None of the evening gatherings are as big as that first one, but every night a few other teams wander their way to the foyer and settle into doing something together, whether it be just talking in someone's sitting room, playing some sort of creative game that one or another team came up with, or witches and gods demonstrating for each other what they can do. It's amazing to me to see what the other witches can do with beginning magic.

Drila had revealed that the gods running the games thought that I was both a beginning and end magic witch but also neither. But seeing what the others can do, I wonder if that's true. Wren is a master at creating fabrics, drawing flax fibers to her and weaving them. She can start with raw flax plants and have fabric to make clothing within hours. She said it's tiring and takes a lot of energy, plus the actual flax plant came from somewhere, meaning someone's farm, so she doesn't do that very often. But, when I try to mimic her ability, I can only make the already prepared fibers weave together and never am able to coax them from the plant.

The days go by too fast and before we know it, it's the day before the third game. After our physical workout, the four of us sit in the sitting room, making sure our game plan is in place.

"Obviously, if you are limited to only certain gods, Byder is first on the list." Ydum announces.

"Anarus second." Byder adds. "Not just because of the connection with Jinx, but obscurity can be protective. He can hide whatever we have to protect as a last line of defense."

Anarus and I both nod. "The paintings." I say. "I would say the barn is out. Too hard to protect something that big and there are just far too many opening, cracks between slats of wood in the walls, things like that."

"What would you want, Jinx?" Byder asks. All three gods are looking to me for this one.

"Something small." I think out loud. "Well made walls. Good windows with actual glass that can seal tight. The smaller the room we can use, the better. Honestly, our rooms here would be perfect."

Byder twists his mouth. "I agree. For defenses, small and with as few openings as possible. Honestly, I think the city apartment might actually be the best."

I look at Byder. "The squat building on the busy street? Is that an apartment?"

He nods back at me. "They look like the apartment buildings in Veirveil. Inside the one building, there are four separate homes, usually small but well-constructed and only a few entry points. We wouldn't have access to anything natural we could gather for you from outside, since it's in the city, Jinx. But at the same time, it would be easier to control and watch."

"We are third. What if Esnir and Velmos have the same idea?" Ydum scoots forward on the couch. He's the least involved this time, but seems eager to learn from us about everything. Ydum seems like he's always eager to learn. He quotes the manuals verbatim. It's kind of obvious he really is the academic of the group.

"Mud and daub hut." I say at the same time Byder says, "cabin." We look at each other for a moment, then laugh.

"Why the hut?" Byder asks.

"What I'm used to, for one. Sealed walls, for two. Windows might be drafty, but I prefer that to the walls being drafty."

Byder seems to disagree. "Most wood cabins would be air-tight. And the forest gives more access to plants you could gather, as well as other things we could make and do with nature, especially if it's all three of us. A village means other people around."

Maybe he's right. I consider this and just am not sure.

"Go with your gut, Jinx." Anarus finally says. "It's done us well so far."

The rest of the night is spent with each of us preparing what we can. Byder checks over all five of his blades. Anarus and Ydum go into the hallway to double-check there's nothing in the paintings we might have missed. I check over my witch's kit once more time, making sure each thing is as prepared as possible, comfortably settled in Byder's box, as I can make it. I add all the salt we have collected and then put it away, refusing to touch it anymore with my feelings so jittery and all over the place.

Morning comes too fast. The day of the third game starts early, with coffee and everyone quiet. All three of my gods glance up with curiosity as they see me wearing my dress from home. I chose to wear this for comfort. I have worn dresses like this my whole life, and with the goal protection and relying so much on my magic potentially, I wanted to feel like I used to. My mother made this dress for me. It's like a piece of home and comfort with me.

Byder is wearing his brown leather pants, and a sleeveless brown shirt that looks like it's made from a fur pelt. Ydum is wearing a green cotton shirt and dark gray cotton pants. Anarus is actually wearing a shirt too. I think we all did the same thing, using our clothes as a form of magical armor. The magic doesn't work like that, not really, but I don't think I'm the only one latching on to anything to feel more confident. I check Byder's hair and make sure his bun is tight while Anarus gets me a coffee.

For some reason, we all feel that this game will be harder than the last two, more dangerous somehow. None of us say it out loud, but the tense lines on all our faces and the way Byder and Ydum don't even joke with Anarus and me about our need for caffeine. Ydum just looks in my mug to see how much coffee I've drank when Byder insists I eat something too.

The tone sounds and everyone immediately heads out to the foyer. All the other humans are carrying their witch's kits with them, and several gods have weapons visible. We all go straight to the back wall and stand how we had the other times, humans in front of their gods. Drila is waiting, in a green dress this time, and her smile looks anything but friendly.

"Good morning, all." Drila's voice drips with far too much saccharine to be called pleasant. "The third game is about protection. Each team of two, one human and one god, will be required to defend themselves from a magical entity that cannot be killed. Jinx, as the only team with more than one god, which god do you choose to go with you?"

I don't even look back at them. We already knew this was possible. "Byder."

Drila gives her fake smile again. "Wonderful. Now, before we go any further, it appears many of you have brought things to this game with you. I will let you know that no items can be brought into the games with the contestants. Whether they are carried in hands or in pocket, they are not allowed. Items worn on the body as part of an outfit are the only accessories allowed. Since it seems so many of you have made this error, gods and humans alike, I will give you five minutes to discard them before we continue."

We can't take the witch's kit with us. Or Byder's knives. That conniving little wench. They changed the rules because they were mad the other humans helped me.

"Quick. We need to make everything part of your outfits." Ydum whispers harshly. I look around and see the other teams doing the same thing. No one has moved to put anything back in their rooms. Drila is examining her nails like this is all boring. I rummage through my kit and grab the black string. Easiest thing is to make the little black bag from Raven into a necklace with it. I do so quickly, throwing it over Byder's neck.

"Pockets, give me your pockets." I tell my gods.

"She said no pockets." Byder says.

I shake my head. "No. Actually give me your pockets. The fabric on your pants that makes the pocket, cut them off and give them to me."

My three gods turn the fabric of their pockets inside out and cut them off with Byder's daggers. Byder is fastest and hands me two roughly bag-shaped fabric squares. I fill one with the lodestone, pearl, and amber. Then I use the black string to wrap around the top over and over until I'm sure it's secure, and make a necklace, slipping it over my head quickly. Then, I do the same with the other one, putting the matches, hazelwood sticks, and cactus pad, in it. The pocket fabric is harder to close with larger items but I manage and sling it over Byder's head.

Ydum hands me his pockets and I make another one with the, fortunately tea sized, red and black candles, and put it over my head. His second pocket square is made into a bag for the jade stones and red string for Byder. I use Anarus's pocket square to hold the mirror and the black string, leaving enough string out to make one more pocket square necklace and slip it over my head quickly. The only thing left is the salt, and I dump as much as I can in the last pocket, tie it off and give it to Byder.

"That's everything." I tell them.

Byder holds up his knives. "I really don't want to leave these. I don't care if whatever it is can't die, it may be able to be hurt and slowed down."

I think quickly, glancing at Drila then the other witches. Most of them are abandoning the weapons. Having them might make the difference for us. But how?

An idea forms. "Give me your shirts, Ydum and Anarus." They don't even question me but hurriedly strip them off to hand to me.

I tie the two shirts together by making tiny knots along their bottom hems, laying it on the floor, spread out like a long strip of fabric. I fold the fabric by the long edge several times, then hold up my hand for Byder to give me his knives. He gives them to me and I lay them along the long line of the shirts. Then, I finish folding the shirts longways. Once this is done, I stand and hand the whole thing to Anarus to hold. He holds it carefully so that the knives won't slide out of the fabric ends.

"Block me." I tell my gods. They don't move, but look at me confused. I start untying the strings for the bodice of my dress. Suddenly, Ydum and Byder's hands are pushing me behind them and all three gods use their bodies to shield me.

"What are you doing?" Anarus seethes as the top of my dress falls away completely.

I usually don't wear any underwear at all, so aren't wearing any now. The dress is supportive enough by itself for my rather small chest, so I usually don't need breast bands. Also, I don't like them. Because I wasn't wearing one when I went to the testing center, I have none at all here. But this is an exception, so I'll wear one.

I take the knife boned breast band made by my gods' shirts from Anarus and start winding it carefully around me. I keep moving the fabric around me so that the knives settle comfortably and the knots where I tied the two shirts together sits between my breasts, where it doesn't rub on me so much.

All three gods have me blocked from anyone else's eyes, but they are all watching me do this. Once there is only a small tail left, I tuck it inside the already made layers and pull my dress back up properly, securing the ties. Now, all that's left is Byder's box and we don't actually need that.

"Humans are so creative." Ydum laughs lightly, shaking his head. He's been watching me and the other humans finding ways to make the parts of our witch's kits part of our gods' and our outfits curiously.

Drila harumphs, and taps her papers on a board in her hand. "That's time. Now, if we can all settle." She looks over at everyone. None of us actually moved to put anything away in our rooms like she told us. Several people are still rushing to figure out what to do with one item or another. Isis and Esnir are staring at a bow and quiver of arrows mournfully.

Anarus taps Esnir on his shoulder. "I'll hold onto it for you." Esnir nods gratefully and hands the weapon over.

Drila continues, ignoring all of this. "The choosing of the paintings this time will be done differently. Instead of the humans choosing directly, they will draw a random number from a bag, in order from first place to last. Each number correlates to a painting that will be your setting for the game. In the case of the two ties, the gods of the two teams will answer questions to win the right for their human to go first. First up is Saffron."

Saffron steps forward, tiny glass jars tinkling as she moves towards Drila. She had used strips of her god Velmos's shirt to tie them to her clothes like they are jewels and each jar has something, or several somethings, from her witch's kit inside them. Drila holds out a cloth bag and Saffron puts her hand inside, withdrawing a small slip of paper.

"Two." Saffron reads off the paper.

Drila nods. "The painting of the apartment here in the foyer." Saffron seems to take this in stride as she moves to stand in front of the painting. Velmos joins her there.

Isis moves forward as Drila calls her name and chooses a slip of paper out of the bag. I can't see how she made her witch's kit part of her outfit. It must be under her clothes or with her god. "Seven."

"The painting of the stone hut in the village between rooms five and seven." Drila tells her. Isis and Esnir move to the painting.

Now it's my turn. I think hard on getting the one we want. Apartment, please, make it the other apartment. I reach my hand inside the bag and pull out a slip of paper. When I look, it says five. I say that out loud and Drila smiles almost conspiratorially.

Before she even speaks, I know that we didn't get what we wanted. I know what she's going to say. The gods running these games do not want my team winning. So, when Drila announces that my number means the painting between rooms three and five, I'm not surprised. Having stared at them often enough, I know that the painting there is of the barn, the one Byder and I had agreed we wanted the least.

I squash down any ill feelings and move to the painting as if it doesn't bother me at all. As if my mind isn't roaring with the idea that the games are somehow cheating. Byder, Anarus, and Ydum follow me. Even though Anarus and Ydum can't come with Byder and me, I know they will stay with us until the last second. We are a team.

At the painting, Byder groans. He hadn't memorized the positions.

"We'll be fine." I tell him, placing a comforting hand on his arm over his hunt tattoos. "We'll figure it out. I think we can just protect a part of it. Or something. We've got this, Byder."

I'm faking my confidence and I think Byder knows it. But he nods and steels himself. While the other teams choose their paintings, Ydum and Anarus talk to us, saying all the things they want to before we are gone. We don't know if there will be time after and whatever happens with Byder and me, if we fail the game, Ydum and Anarus will fail as well. I don't know if they will know somehow what's happening with us or if they'll just have to wait, wondering.

Ydum puts a hand on my arm gently. I turn to face him. "You got this, beautiful. Trust yourself."

I stand on my tiptoes and kiss Ydum gently. "Don't antagonize Anarus while I'm gone, okay?" I smile at him. "You've reached your quota of split lips for these games."

Ydum raises one eyebrow, a playful smile on his face. "Me? Never! I will be a perfect, humble little god. I promise."

Ydum turns to Byder and says something quietly to him, while I turn to Anarus. "Don't hurt Ydum."

Anarus wraps his arms around my waist, pulling me close. "No promises from me. If he runs his mouth, I will split it again." He says gruffly before kissing me. His kiss is hard and insistent. When he leans back, his shadows are simmering.

"We'll be fine, Anarus." I cup his cheek in my hand and he leans into it.

Everything is moving too fast, and before I feel like it's actually been long enough, all the other teams have chosen their paintings. Byder and Anarus just nod at each other, as Drila talks again.

"The point of this game is protection. Each team will be responsible for creating defenses that protect both the human and the god from the magical entity. This means both physically and mentally protecting themselves and each other. You are not required to stay inside the dwelling. Use of the surrounding lands is allowed since the focus is your bodies and minds. The game will be passed when you have created a barrier, both physically and mentally, that cannot be breached by the entity without causing the surrounding area to act in any unnatural ways. The entity cannot cause something to happen, such as a wind or earthquake and cannot destroy the buildings in any way. They can, for instance, pick a lock, but cannot use magic to blast through the door. The standing of your team is decided by how quickly you are returned to the foyer, having reached a stalemate with the entity. Any questions?"

No one moves or speaks. We all knew the basics of this game from the other years, and this one seems not much different. I think Byder's weapons might be worthless, but I feel better having them.

Drila nods at the silence. "Well, then. Off you go."

The world around me blinks and Byder and I are in a barn. It's large, a rectangular area with wood slat walls. A large sliding barndoor takes up most of one wall and on the other end two small regular doors fill the same space. There's a large hayloft above us, covering half of the main floor in shadow, and a ladder to it is along the wall to my left. Tools line the walls, rusted sickles, axes, hoes, and shovels. There's a large, wooden plow near the ladder to the loft and several other large tools that look like they are probably drawn by horses scattered around. There's debris all around and the floor is dirt, with old leaves and hay strewn around. The barn looks like it was abandoned years ago. Dust motes float through the air, looking thick in the sunbeams coming in through the gaps in the walls.

I move to the center of the most open space in the barn, and kick at the dirt to clear away the debris. "Let's put everything down here, and decide what to do."

Byder and I unload our clothes, sliding off our impromptu necklaces to pile it all up in between us. I undo my dress top and pull out the shirts with the blades in them, dumping them, the shirts and the blades, in the pile.

"Should we just make a spot here to protect?" Byder asks. His eyes are darting everywhere and he's breathing in deeply. I know he's trying to use his hunt god senses to figure out what our enemy is and where it is.

"I could make a protective circle, but we would have to stay within it once I do."

Byder twists his mouth to the side, stroking his hunt tattoo lines and seeming unsure as he looks around. "If whatever it is comes inside the barn and I am stuck inside the circle, I can't do anything."

I look around again too. "Drila said we can't kill whatever it is. I don't think it will help if you physically fight it."

Byder nods. "Then protective circle it is. What do you want me to do?"

I dig through my pile, grabbing the matches and the hazelwood sticks. "First we'll clean us." I use the matches to light a hazelwood stick on fire. The moment it's trailing a small line of smoke from it, I blow out the flame gently. The embers in it will continue to burn slowly, making a cleansing smoke.

"Keep your mind on purity and protection." I tell Byder. "Calm, peace, safety, no negative influences." He nods and closes his eyes, focusing, then opens them to watch me. I bend over while circling him, allowing the smoke to touch every part of him, starting at his feet and working my way to the top of his head. I think of Byder and clean, pure safety as I move.

"Now, my turn." I tell him once I'm done and hand him the smoldering wood. He repeats my pattern, allowing the smoke to touch all of me as I think only about my mind being clear and strong, focused on protecting both our bodies and minds with pure intent and no harmful influences. I purposely think of every body part as the smoke touches that part of me, relax that muscle and trust in my own strength there.

When he finishes, I take the wood and thank it for its help, crushing the end into the dirt to put out the burning embers. Then, I scoop up the dirt I used and the piece of wood and toss them away to the other side of the barn. I would have rather dunked it in water, but needs must.

Now that we are cleansed, Byder and I can create the circle. He's still breathing deeply and his eyes are roving everywhere. There's been no sign of our enemy, but that doesn't mean they aren't here or won't be soon.

I stare at the pile of things from my haphazard witch's kit. Doubt fills me. Do I have what I need? Can I actually do this right?

What? No. I can do this. This is the easy part. My magical arts education may have been extremely basic, but I have been casting protective circles since I knew what shape a circle is. I reach into the pile and pull out the brown sheathed dagger.

I hand it to Byder. The protective circle will need to be made by both of us, include both of us, to protect both of us. I decide to give Byder the job of making parts where he can use what is familiar to him, like his daggers. "Draw a circle in the dirt. Make it large enough for us to move around in comfortably. Remember to keep your focus on protection."

Byder gives me a strange look, but does as I say. Eventually, there is a perfect circle, but it takes a few tries. Byder either made the circle too oblong or the ends don't meet the first few times. I rub the failed circles out of the dirt completely until no one could tell it had ever been done.

When the circle is drawn right, I grab the salt and fill in the shallow trough Byder made in the dirt with his blade. I move clockwise, making sure there is enough salt in each spot so that the circle of it is visibly continuous. The whole time, I worry about if there's enough salt or if I will use too much here and not have more when I need it. I fight back these worries and doubts, reminding myself that I know what I'm doing.

"What next?" Byder asks. I notice his voice. He sounds unsure and worried.

"Next, we stop and recenter." I tell him firmly. "You are doubting yourself, I can tell. So am I. We can't do that if we are going to succeed at making a good protection circle."

I move so I am close to Byder and I take his hands in mine, looking into his eyes. "We can do this. We know what we are doing, the both of us do. Do you believe that?"

Byder hesitates, then nods.

"Say it."

Byder takes in a deep breath. "We know what we are doing. We both do. I know what I am doing."

I nod. "Better?"

"A little." Byder scratches the back of his neck and looks down. Somehow, I don't believe him.

But we don't have time to waste so I continue. I have four jade stones, so I use those to make a four corners at the edge of the salt circle. I place one jade at the most northern, most eastern, most southern, then most western points of the circle, just inside the salt line. Then, I do the same with the four knives Byder hasn't used yet. I put the blade with the black sheathe, blade facing out, at the northern part, its tip just barely touching the jade stone. Then, I put the red one pointing out to the east. The blue one goes south and I falter. West should be white but I only have green. This won't work like I hoped. I'm so stupid to have not...

Wait. No, I'm not. Why did I think that? It's fine if I use green instead of white. It may not hold the same strength, but it works. I place the green blade facing west and settle my mind again. I turn to Byder. "Draw a pentagram, starting with the top point to the north. Don't disturb the salt line."

Again, Byder looks at me curiously, but does what I say. His drawing of the pentagram is smoother and works right the first time. Once he finishes, I fill in the lines with more salt. Then, I place an object at each point of the star, following the same path he drew it. At the north point, I place the pearl. Then I follow the line southeast and place the unlit red candle at the next point. Following the next line northwest, I place the amber at the point. Then I follow the star line to the east, placing the lodestone on the point. At the final point, to the southwest, I put the cactus pad.

That completed, I tell Byder to move inside the center of the pentagram with me. We sit, the pile between us. Byder's hands are clenched in fists, his fifth knife still tightly held in hand, and he keeps looking around anxiously.

"Why is nothing coming?" He finally asks. "The waiting is worse than actually doing something."

"I know." I rub my forehead. There's something we're missing and that's dangerous. If we can't figure out what's going on and why nothing's happening, we will die because we failed. I will die. If Byder can't figure out what is supposed to be coming for us, I will die. That's what the games want, for me to die. For all of us to. We are the reject team, Anarus called us. We are all broken, wrong, not wanted. The gods controlling the games would rather cheat than see us survive. We have no chance to win. We might as well give up right now.

Wait. I'm doing it again. Doubting. Giving up. Why? Why would I be so unsure and doubting. Son of a... "Byder the enemy is already here."

Byder jumps up and starts frantically looking around. "Where? Stay behind me, Jinx. I'm not great but I'll do everything I can to keep you alive."

"Byder." I call out but he's still panicking. "Byder! Look at me."

Byder turns and looks down at me, still sitting on the floor. I tap my temple with one finger. "Not here in the barn, but here in our heads. Drila said we have to protect our minds too. You are full of doubt, aren't you?"

Byder goes still. "Yes." His voice is barely a whisper.

"Whatever we're supposed to be protecting against is doing that. It's not real doubt." Byder sits back down at these words from me.

"It's so fucking strong." He looks at the dirt floor as he sits cross-legged across from me.

We need more defenses. The salt line isn't helping us enough. I don't know what it is that's attacking, but currently, we are failing to protect ourselves. I wish hard that we had Ydum and Anarus too. We aren't as strong without them.

My mind focuses again. We may not have them, but we do have something from them we can use as a placeholder. I smile and grab the discarded shirts. I carefully lay out Anarus's shirt to my right and Ydum's to my left, making a circle with them and Byder and me.

We need more. We need to cleanse our minds. Whatever it is, it's already invaded there. Smoke. I need smoke. I move things around so that the mirror is in the center of the circle of shirts and bodies. Placing the black candle on top of it, I light it, letting the candle's flame reflect up from the mirror. Then, I pour out the rosemary, basil and black pepper in a small circle around the mirror. Finally, I take most of sticks of hazelwood I have left and place as many of them as I can in a circle around us and the shirts, shoving one end into the dirt so that they stand upright within the center of the pentagram, and light them, allow them to start smoking then blow out the flames so that only an ember is left making smoke.

That done, there's not much more left I can do. I take my seat again. "Take a deep breath. Let the smoke clear your mind of whatever has invaded there, then talk to me, Byder. What are you thinking?" When he only shakes his head, I push. "Give voice to the doubts. We can't defeat them unless we know what they are."

Byder sighs deeply. "I don't know what I'm doing. I can't protect you. You should have brought Anarus, not me. He may be younger, but he's stronger with his power. My power is worthless here. I have nothing to hunt, to kill. You'll die because I don't even know what we are fighting."

"Look at the flame, Byder." I instruct him. "Breathe deeply the smoke from the hazelwood. Is any of that true?"

"Yes." Byder's voice is getting quieter and trembling. He's struggling so much that sweat is gathering along his brow.

I take a breath and reach a hand out to him. He takes it. "You can protect me. You trusted me and did everything I said even though you don't know how protection like this works."

"It took forever for me to make the circle." He contradicts me.

"Doesn't matter." I shake my head and place my hand over his that's holding the knife. "You made it eventually. Your knife, your power, is the base for our whole circle. All of this is built on your work."

"You could have done it yourself, Jinx. You don't need me. The cave was wrong to give me you." Byder won't look at me again. I feel doubts creeping into my mind. He won't be strong enough to defend himself from this, whatever this is.

I grit my teeth and force that thought away. Yes, he will. Byder is strong and not just physically. "Tell me about the cave. I hid in that hole in the wall. What did you do? What was it like for you?"

Byder breathes deeply again. His eyes close but he doesn't let go of my hand. "When we first got to the cave, all twenty-three of us were all bunched together. When Drila gave us the go ahead, we all set off, walking around the tunnels. Sometimes one of us would branch off another way, sometimes we would follow a trail and end up near other gods again."

"I felt this tug," Byder uses his free hand to touch his chest, "right here. It was so faint at first and I stopped at every split in the tunnels, trying to focus on which way made the tug stronger. When I came into that area you were hiding in, Ydum was coming from a different tunnel and stopped there, looking around. I was going to move away from him but every time I went to one of the other tunnels to continue, it was like I just couldn't move. The pull was so strong, but Ydum was there too, confused and unable to continue away either. So, I tried to go away anyway and saw Anarus coming."

He shakes his head at the memory. "All three of us there, it felt messy and chaotic. Ydum and Anarus started fighting but all I could focus on was this sense that somebody was right there and I needed to find them. It almost hurt, it ached so much. When I finally spotted you, it was like the sun breaking through the clouds after a storm. My world just felt brighter. Even before you got down. Then, you fell and the panic was overwhelming. I had to know you were okay. I had an insane need to protect you, and got worried I had already failed. I helped you up and that first touch was everything. My whole being just collapsed into that touch. I didn't want to ever let you go. I forced myself to, though, and when I looked down to see if your ankle was hurt, I saw you weren't wearing any shoes. I wanted to laugh. All I could think was this little human isn't wearing any shoes. Such a silly little human not to wear shoes. When you said you didn't have any, I had to fight the urge to strip mine off and give them to you."

Byder lets out a noise that sounds like a cross between a groan and a whimper. "They would have been far too big, I knew, but my mind didn't care. My heart didn't care. I need to not just protect you, but also provide. I feel like it's the most important thing I could ever do. I have to. It's a visceral need to protect and provide for you, baby girl. You needed shoes, you could have mine."

"Ydum said it felt like getting hit between the eyes, but Anarus had just hit him between the eyes, so I wasn't sure if he was being overdramatic." I tell him.

Byder chuckles, his eyes still closed as he focuses. "Not dramatic at all. But for me, it wasn't my head. It was my heart. I swear it stopped beating. I thought it would explode until I touched you, then it raced away and really did feel like it exploded. You were everything from that first moment. That feeling has only gotten stronger since then. The moment Anarus told us that our drinking made you uncomfortable because of some past stuff, I felt awful. I felt like a fool for not noticing how you were feeling. Then, the whole thing came out about my reading problems and I just knew you would hate me. I'm not good enough for you. You deserve someone perfect, and I'm broken."

"Byder," I start to say something but I see a shadow move behind him.

Something is sliding into the barn through a crack between two wooden slats in the wall. As I watch it, my heart feels heavy and my mind races with worry. I'm a poor witch with a horrible birthday and no idea what I'm doing. I didn't even have shoes, let alone a witch's kit. All the things the others gave me to make one are their worthless leftovers and won't work right. Byder isn't the problem here, I am. I'll never be good enough. My magic is broken. I'm broken.

The shadow creeping into the barn forms a shape. It looks like a shadow of a woman. It's all dark except the eyes. The eyes glow yellow in the barn's low light. Even though it's only shadow and glowing eyes, I can tell she's beautiful, lithe and perfect. Byder would find her so much prettier than me. She probably has better magic too. He should leave the circle and join her instead of being with me.

That thought snaps me out of the trance. "No." I say out loud. But my heart still sinks. Byder would never actually want me without the magic of the cave. He would want her, though. I should tell him to go to her. "No!" I yell louder and clutch Byder's hand tighter.

A succubus. She's a succubus. My mind figures it out even if my heart's still unconvinced. Succubi want to lure males with desire and doubt. She's targeting Byder, not me. She just wants me out of the way, not holding Byder back from her.

"I should leave." Byder says, drawing my attention back to him. "I should go and leave you with the other two. They can take care of you. You don't want me, not really."

The succubus wants Byder to leave the circle. I can't let him. "Byder, there is a succubus behind you." He starts to turn, but I stop him. "Don't look. You are her target, I think. If you look at her eyes, you'll lose yourself. Look at me, Byder. Look only at me."

Byder turns his eyes to me and I can see they are shining. He's fighting tears.

"The circle is holding, Byder. We did it well, you and I. She can't come into it, so she's fighting for you to leave it instead." I grip his hand tighter and grab for the other one. "Look at me. You found me first. You belong with us, Byder. We would be nowhere without you."

Byder doesn't look away but the tears start to fall. He shakes his head. "You don't need me. You don't want me."

I jump to the other side of the mirror and candle and take Byder's face in both my hands, forcing him to keep looking at me. Peace. Give him peace. I focus my entire will on Byder and how I feel about him. "You found me first. You figured out the water for the second game. You killed a yeti. You figured out Anarus touching me helped my magic be stronger. You always encourage me."

"You called Ydum yours." Byder is crying harder. "You are in love with Anarus and called Ydum yours. You didn't even kiss me like you did them. I'm last. Always last. Last bracelet, last kiss. You don't even like touching me."

"I'm touching you now, Byder. I'm touching you right now. Can you feel that?" I lean in and kiss him.

He pulls away harshly. "You're only doing that not to lose. You want to win and I'm weak. You have to for the game."

"I did your hair." My mind scrambles for anything to make Byder know how I feel about him. That the group of us, the four of us, would not be the same without him. That I care about him just as much as I do Anarus and Ydum. That the itchy feeling that I have begun to think is the fate bond from the cave is just as strong in me for him as it is for Anarus. "I do your hair every day and am teaching you to do it yourself. That's not for the games, is it? I have no reason to do that, Byder, other than because I care about you."

"You love Anarus." He's struggling to continue looking in my eyes.

"I've never said that to him. But I love you, Byder." And I mean it. I know I do. Right at this moment, I know I do. I've known him two weeks but I know I love him. I force my feelings for him through my magic in my hands cupping his cheeks. Every smile he has had. His teasing nature in the morning when I haven't had my coffee yet. His strength, showing me how to do each of the exercises every day. The fact that I know without a doubt that he lets me win at sock ball because he's a hunt god. His aim should be perfect every time, but he holds that power back so the game is fair for all of us.

"I love you, Byder." I repeat. I can hear the succubus hissing on the outside of our circle. Her control on him is breaking.

"I need to touch you, baby girl. I need to hold you. I need." Byder keeps his eyes on me, even when I turn to glance at the succubus as she tries to move over our salt circle. Magic flares when she tries and she jumps back, hissing again.

"Yes, Byder." I move into his lap and his arms come around me as he kisses me. The kiss is desperate and consuming. I wrap my legs around his waist and my arms around his shoulders, pulling him as close to me as I can. I deepen the kiss, tracing the inside of Byder's mouth with my tongue, and desire flares in me as I feel his cock harden between us. I'm not sure if the succubus is causing our desire or not, but I decide I don't care. Even if it is the succubus, she would want Byder's desire to be for her, not me, so I do everything I can to keep his focus on me.

That taut line that I felt with Anarus, that snapped into perfect being when I was with him, is tugging on me again. This time, it's for Byder though. The static wants me to touch him more, get closer to him, give him everything of me. I push myself closer to him, rubbing his cock inside his pants between my hips.

Byder groans. "Jinx." He moves his hands to push up on my skirt at my hips, pulling the folds of fabric from between us. I'm not wearing any underwear since I only have one pair and they are currently back in our rooms in one of the laundry bags, waiting to be cleaned. Byder moves one of his hands between my thighs and groans again when he realizes how bare I am. "Fuck."

His hand caresses then cups me between my legs and need spikes in me. "Byder, please." I reach between us and pull on the strings of his pants until they are loose enough to push down and allow his cock to be free.

He moves his hand, guiding himself to my entrance. As soon as he's properly aligned, Byder thrusts deeply in me. "Fuck. I love you, Jinx." He doesn't wait for me to adjust to the size of him filling me, immediately thrusting at an intense pace, but I don't care.

Pleasure fills me, lighting my whole body on fire. Ripping my fingers through his hair, I make it fall out of the hair tie and tangle my fingers in the silky strands. I bury my face in the crook of his shoulder, moans ripping out of me as he pushes into me in a ragged, demanding pace. I tilt my hips and match his thrusts, clinging to him. My orgasm comes so fast and so strongly, it catches me off guard. It takes away my breath and I bite down on Byder's shoulder as it crests and waves of pleasure shoot through me.

Byder is also taken over by the intensity of it all and comes quickly, right after me. The world snaps into perfect focus and I know he's mine. All mine. I'm his and he's mine and we are perfect together. That taut line grips my heart twice as tightly now. He continues to cling to me, and I to him, as our breathing returns to normal. My eyes are closed and my face still buried in his shoulder. He whispers in my ear. "I love you, Jinx."

I kiss his neck and whisper back. "I love you, Byder." Then, I notice it's very dark. And my skin feels cold. "Shadows."

Byder must have had his eyes closed too. "Anarus?"

"Hey." I hear Anarus say roughly. "So, um, don't move. I'm trying to move my shadows so that you are still covered."

My brain is struggling to fire after the intense orgasm and what I'm starting to think is the cave's fate bond snapping into place. "Anarus didn't come into the game with us. How are you in the barn and covering us with your shadows?"

Anarus gives a small laugh. "You're not in the barn anymore but the foyer."

Oh no. Oh, no no no. "How long?" I squeak.

"Since about two I love you, Jinxes ago." My face blushes at that answer.

"Tell me we came in first?" I hope.

"I covered you with my shadows quickly. I don't think anyone else saw much." Anarus said anyone else. That means besides him. Anarus saw everything. And he did not tell me that we were first back, meaning we aren't and there are more people here. "I couldn't do much for the sounds that quickly, but."

Oh, gods. My face flames into a deeper blush. How many people heard me and Byder? I was not exactly quiet.

"Okay, I think you are good to sort yourselves out." Anarus tells us and I carefully move off of Byder, who quickly tucks himself away, lacing up his pants. I shake out my skirt so it covers me well, but I can do nothing about the moisture gathering between my legs. I don't look up or anywhere but at the floor. Anarus must see we are sorted and says, "I'm going to drop my shadows now. Ydum and I will collect all the stuff on the floor, okay?"

I nod and the shadowy darkness clinging to me drops. I see that all the things from my witch's kit are surrounding us. Even the salt circle and pentagram. I smudge one of the edges of the circle, breaking it and blow out the black candle, ending the working of magic, then Byder and I step away from the center of the foyer. I am so glad that we have Anarus and Ydum to clean up for us because I don't think I could focus enough to pick everything up. Byder and I find a place along the walls to sit and hide in our embarrassment.

"Well, Jinx's team seems to have a penchant for dramatic returns from the game." Drila says as we move along the wall. I sit, curling my legs up so that I can hide my face in my knees. "They take sixth place in the third game."

Sixth place. My curiosity at who came before us gets the better of me and I glance up between my knees to look around the foyer. Saffron and Velmos are completely ignoring us, actively looking anywhere else. Aretha and Zodum are both actively looking. Aretha gives me a wink. Raven and Uesis are chatting quietly, but Raven has a shit-eating grin when she catches me looking. Damek and Iella are laughing to themselves. Asteria and Wilros look like they're trying not to laugh.

Anarus and Ydum finish cleaning everything up, leaving the salt to get cleaned later by whoever cleans this place. They come over and both drop to the floor in front of Byder and me, blocking everyone else from looking at us, which I appreciate immensely. Ydum is fighting a mischievous grin but Anarus is tense. I can see the tension in his back muscles in front of me and I instantly feel guilty as if I betrayed him.

Wren and Kutar appear in the center of the foyer, distracting everyone. Kutar is wailing, tears streaming down his face. Wren is clinging to him, desperately pleading with him to remember everything will be okay. There are objects from her witch's kit scattered around her like they had been around Byder and me. As Wren focuses on Kutar, Aretha and Damek move to start collecting her things for her. Wren leads Kutar to sit along the wall as soon as she realizes they are back, giving a small nod of thanks to Aretha and Damek.

Drila ignores all of this. "Seventh place to Wren's team."

We all watch as Wren calms her god. "I'm still right here, Kutar. I'm right here. We're back and I'm right here. It was just the wraith. I'm not hurt. I'm right here."

Kutar finally looks at Wren, and collapses against her. "I'm so sorry."

"No reason to be sorry." Wren gives a half laugh. "You're worst fear is me hurt and you not able to do anything about it. See? I knew you cared."

Kutar gives a watery laugh back. "That was," he shudders, "so bad. So real."

Everyone turns their attention back to the middle of the room, chatting quietly. They all seem so reserved, a lot of them are still pale or slightly shaky now that the distraction that was my entrance is gone. This game was rougher than either of the other ones on everyone, apparently. For a long time, nothing happens. Neither Amanda and Tholdir or Isis and Esnir come back.

Eventually, Byder leans over to whisper with me. "You okay, Jinx?"

I smile at him and nod. "You?"

"I'm fucking perfect." Byder says, his hand finding mine. I try not to look at Anarus's twitching back as I hold Byder's hand. He said he knows how this works and won't fight it. It's not like we planned to be quite so exhibitionist about it.

After what feels like forever, long enough for everyone to start shifting uncomfortably in worry, Isis and Esnir finally pop into the foyer. They are holding hands but looking around wildly, both drenched in sweat and panting hard. Esnir is bare chested and it's evident his shirt was ripped into strips to make a bandage for Isis's arm. Her bicep is wrapped in the strips of his shirt and blood is seeping through the fabric.

As soon as they realize they are in the foyer, they step out of the center to slump against the wall. Isis starts crying while Esnir is pulling her onto his lap, murmuring to her while checking her arm. He removes the bandages and a sluggishly bleeding gash that wraps around her entire arm becomes visible. We all watch as he struggles to rip the bottom hem of Isis's shirt to make another bandage and tie it tightly against the wound. We hear him mumble as he pulls her face against his, "The bleeding is slowing and we're back. You'll be fine." Esnir lets out a ragged breath of relief.

"Isis's team takes last place. Eighty-five points, five extra for the injury." Drila says as if none of this is concerning.

"Last?" The word is out before I can stop it. "Amanda and Tholdir aren't back." The knowledge that they won't ever be slams into me, making tears prickle my eyes. Drila said last. Amanda and Tholdir didn't survive the third game. My mind immediately thinks of everything I know about them. Tholdir threw a stick at a wolf. Amanda made it hail and I was able to melt it into rain to win. She gave me hazelwood. A lot of it and it helped me so much. Tholdir was an idiot at the first gathering, but he wasn't bad. Just drunk and harmless. And now they are dead. Or she is and he will be forced to suffer as a mortal. I lean against Byder and he wraps his arms around me comfortingly.

Drila seems to just ignore all of us and our mourning the loss of a friend. In her mind, we shouldn't have become friends with an opposing team. "With the third game over, the standings are now Asteria in last place with two hundred and ten points. Wren is in seventh with one hundred and eighty-five points. Sixth place is Raven with one hundred and eighty points. Damek is in fifth with one hundred and sixty-five. Fourth is Isis with one hundred and forty-five points. Third is Jinx with one hundred and thirty-five. Second is Aretha with one hundred and one place is still Saffron with eighty points."

Saffron in first, me in third, and Asteria in eighth are the only ones who didn't move positions, except that Asteria's eighth became last place with only eight teams left. "The next game will be life and death. See you in a week." Drila pops away and we all sit still for a few moments in shock before slowly, team by team, we quietly get up and straggle to our rooms.

I follow my gods into our sitting room. Everyone sits heavily in our places on the couches. My mind is split. One part of me is noticing all the tension in Anarus and the other keeps looking at the point board where Amanda's name is now scratched out with a red line.

Ydum speaks first. "Tholdir was an idiot, but a good idiot."

"He never teased me about the help I needed with my reading." Byder adds. "He even helped me once when I was struggling to figure out something in a literature class."

"Amanda gave me the hazelwood." I tell them. Byder looks up at me. He knows how much that helped us.

"That shit saved me." He explains to the other two. "Jinx lit it around the salt circle and the smell of its smoke kept me focused when nothing else did and I almost left the circle."

"What was the enemy?" Ydum asks.

"Succubus." I tell him. "It targeted Byder."

Anarus nods. "Makes sense now." His gaze turns to me, and I blush. He saw everything.

"Are you mad?" I ask softly.

Anarus does not look away. I can feel his eyes on me even when I do look away. "Not mad." He grumbles. "Definitely not mad." He captures my chin with his fingers and turns me to face him. Then slowly, he leans over and kisses me.

When he lets me go, I hear Ydum breath out a stuttered, "shit."

Even though Anarus says he isn't mad, and I believe him, I feel guilty. "Our friends are dead."

Everyone sits back on the couches again, and we don't talk. Dinner appears on the table and I force myself to eat something, and I think the others are forcing themselves to as well. Byder only eats one plateful of ravioli and Ydum doesn't even finish his first plate. No one even touches the bread with garlic butter.

When we hear a noise outside in the hallway, I assume the other teams are looking at the paintings. But when we open the door, no one seems to be paying attention to the paintings at all. Instead, they all are gathering around, the humans clumped in one loose group and the gods in another, talking. As I step into the hallway, I hear that the gods are telling stories about Tholdir. I wander over to the group of humans.

We have less to talk about since none of us knew Amanda before the Gods Games, but we try. We say what we do know and Aretha swears at the gods in charge about their lack of caring for the humans they put through this. I tell them about Anarus's math on how many people, gods and humans, have died in the three hundred and seventy-four games before this one and we all allow our anger at the gods to fester in remembrance of the human female, the human witch, sacrificed to their schemes.

No one talks about what happened in the third game, except the loss of Amanda and Tholdir. We don't discuss the upcoming forth game and, even though I'm acutely aware that the paintings have changed, we all ignore them. I glance over occasionally at my gods and see that all of them, minus Anarus, are with the other gods, talking presumably about Tholdir and remembering him in their own way.

I wander to Anarus. He's leaning against the wall near the group of gods but not a part of them. "I'm younger. I didn't know him as well." He says by way of explanation.

"You can still be sad, or mad, or whatever you want to feel." I tell him. "None of us knew Amanda at all. Heck, at this point I feel bad because none of us really even cared when it was Leander. Or the others in the cave I didn't even know the names of."

"You cared." Anarus puts an arm around my shoulder. "You were mad after the first game. You were so angry, a vicious little thing. You've spoken out, or tried to, both times Drila thought to ignore the lost team."

I keep my voice low. "Are you angry, Anarus? Really?"

He glances over at me. "Do you see shadows?" I shake my head. His shadows are closely kept to his skin. "I'm not angry about you and Byder."

"Then why were you so tense after we all sat along the wall?"

"I blocked you two with my shadows." He explains. "It hid you from everyone else, but you know I can see what my shadows see. I can't not see it, either."

"You had to watch." I sigh, understanding. Even if he isn't angry, that couldn't have been easy.

Anarus gives me a slight smile. "Yeah, and it was hard to. Not because I wanted you to stop, or I was mad it was happening but I didn't expect it to be so... so potent for me. It was, ugh. This is hard to explain. I liked it."

"Oh." That's all I can say. We stand quietly, waiting for everyone else, after that. The gods take longer to break apart than the humans, which is understandable. Tholdir was their friend and classmate, and even if he's alive, they will never see him again. Eventually, they all start drifting away and the four of us head back to our room.

Ydum looks actually upset. "Did you know him well?" I ask him in the room.

"Not really." He says. "As well as any of us. Well, not as well as Uesis. They were good friends. It's still just hard. No one liked Bokysus, being a god of mockery made it hard for us to really, so it was easy to tell ourselves he deserved his fate of becoming mortal and just ignore that he might actually be dead. And the other gods from the caves? So much happened so fast, it was easy to forget, push it down. But now? I can't. Modes was my best friend. I haven't even thought about the fact that if he isn't here, that means he's dead."

"Tell me about him?" I move to the couch and pat the seat next to me. Ydum sits down next to me and I hold his hand.

"Modes is, well was, a destiny god. His mom was one of the Fates, the original god of sadness. It was crazy for her to have a child that late. He didn't know who his dad was, just that he was a human his mom had a fling with. That's not abnormal with original gods, but there hasn't been a child of an original god in the Gods Games for so long. Not since the games began, really. Everyone just kind of assumed if Modes didn't win the games, he would be close to top tier. He loved reading about as much as I do. We quizzed each other on the manuals for months, just like it was the texts for any other class. He knew about me being colorblind. He was the only one other than my family that knew. He never told his mom though and covered for me a lot with that. There were so many times I would have been found out if it wasn't for him."

When Ydum takes a break to breathe and collect himself, Byder speaks. "Dorlios didn't leave the cave either. God of beer of all things. Do you know what it's like to have a best friend who is a god of beer when you're ten?" Byder laughs. "The trouble we would get into. The funny part is Dorlios hated the taste of alcohol. He could make the stuff just fall from his fingertips, basically, but wouldn't touch it himself. I remember the fight between his mom and my dad when I came home from his house drunk at twelve. Dad was so mad and his mom was just like, well what do you expect? We always had to hang out at my house from then on, doors open, where my parents could see us. No one ever expected much of him because of being a god of alcohol, but to not even make it out of the caves? That hurts."

I don't expect Anarus to have much in the way of friends among the gods because he's younger, so I'm surprised when he speaks next. "Kara was a victory goddess. How does a victory goddess lose out in the caves of the Gods Games? I lived with her family for almost a year. It was the longest I was anywhere. Kara wasn't awful to me. She was nice, and her parents didn't make me feel like just a burden. Her mom will be devastated. Olo is a pleasure goddess, and she always wanted a lot of kids but Kara was her only one. I don't know why she never had more, but I knew they couldn't for some reason. That's why they were so happy to take me in, at least for a while. Kara's dad was okay, but I steered clear because he distrusted my shadows so much. But Olo? She's good, and Kara didn't deserve this."

Silence envelopes us again as the emotions of the day, and exhaustion, overtake us. Ydum eventually just wanders away to bed, leaving Byder, Anarus, and me in the sitting room. I feel awkward as Anarus and Byder look at each other. Ever since the second game, Anarus has been sleeping in my bedroom with me.

Ultimately, Anarus breaks the tension first. He flips onto his back on the couch, sliding down until his feet push into my side. He pulls the blanket from the back of the couch and spreads it over himself. "Move. You're taking up space on my bed, Jinx." He says gruffly. I would think he was upset but there is not one shadow peeking out around his face.

I slap his feet playfully. "Rude." I stand and Byder stands with me. As I walk to my room, I know he's following me, but I'm not sure if he's actually coming with me or going to deviate to the room with Ydum. I'm not sure if I want to ask him to come with me, tell him not to, or just let him choose.

Anarus calls out softly from the couch. "Byder, think on peace as you stroke her hair. It helps her sleep better." Byder only nods then follows me into my room, and I let him.

Chapter Nine

IN THE MORNING, I wake up to Byder holding me tightly. He's awake and watching me. "You do actually snore." He tells me as soon as he sees my eyes open. "It's soft and kind of cute."

"Bite me." I snarl. "You treated me as your personal teddy bear, snuggling me and wouldn't let me even shift."

He laughs and I roll my eyes at him. "Coffee, before you forget you love me." He jumps out of the bed and dresses in his clothes from the day before. All his clothes are in the other room. I roll out of the bed and struggle on the clean pair of pants Iella gave me and a shirt from Asteria. The shirt is a little snug but works.

By the time I make it to the sitting room, Byder has already gone into the other room and changed into clean clothes, or well pants. Why do none of these guys like shirts? Anarus, also bare-chested again, holds out a mug for me.

"Told you." He says. I know he's talking about my snoring.

I ignore him and go to the couches. "I'm sitting with Ydum now." I say as I plop down next to him. "Both of them are mean and say I snore."

Ydum smiles at me, wrapping an arm around my shoulders before looking down into my mug to see how much coffee I've had before deciding if he's safe to tease me. "If it means you'll snuggle up with me, I'll lie through my teeth about your snoring."

I roll my eyes and moan. "Ugh. You all suck." But I don't move out of Ydum's arm. "The next game is life and death."

Ydum nods as Byder and Anarus join us. They both have food. Byder hands me a cruller, with one eyebrow raised up. I don't fight him, taking it and nibbling on it as I turn my attention back to Ydum. "This game is always different. Very different. Some years, contestants needed to kill. Some years, they had to heal.

Once, forty-five years ago, they had to resurrect and everyone almost failed. The game had to quickly course-correct for that one and the rules changed in the middle of the game to stop everyone from failing and the Gods Games being over with no winner at all."

"Who decides that?" I ask him. "Who controls the games anyway?"

Anarus answers. "The original gods. They're in charge of everything in Veirveil."

"Well, almost." Ydum corrects him. "The magic of the cave was set up for that trial and is now self-contained magic. No one can control it or change it. The cave itself is the magic now. All the gods born twenty-four years before and all the humans that got a blue result on their test enter the cave. Every god has a match somewhere within the cave, or so we are told, the cave itself deciding who that match for them is. Then, it's up to each god to follow the magical tether to their human and the human's job to hide well enough for the magic to create the tether properly. If they don't pass that initial trial, that's thought to be on them. The rest of the games after the cave is what is controlled by the original gods."

I sip my coffee and think over that. "But there are only ten teams, right? I was taught ten humans, ten gods, but I know now the gods part isn't true. Is the human part? Is it always only ten team of one human and whatever gods?"

Ydum nods. "That I know of, yeah. Last fifty games I read the manuals for, at least."

"So, no matter what, only ten humans will survive that part. How does the cave decide which ten?" I look at Anarus and Ydum, not sure which one of them may know the answer.

Ydum shrugs. "It's not the cave that decides which ten. It's the humans, and the tether they create with the gods destined for them. The ten that do that best. I honestly don't know beyond that very nebulous idea. The original gods set up the design of that magic in the caves, though. It's all their plan. Only ten humans will make it past the caves. Any number of gods can, based on how many match to each human. But it all comes down to that fated bond, the tether the human creates when they hide and the gods using that tether to find them."

Ydum shifts some, moving into his academic mode. "Take us, for instance. The magic in the cave helped you tether a bond to all three of us when you hid with your magic. You weren't hiding from us, but hiding from the gods that were the wrong gods, even if you didn't realize it. Some people believe there are infinite ways that the gods can be matched to humans, and how it works out in the end for the ten teams is up to the gods and the humans. There could have been a bunch of humans that would have worked for me and you were the one I felt the pull to the strongest, you did the magic to create the tether the best, but it could have been someone else if I thought differently or turned left instead of right."

Byder shakes his head, eating his third doughnut. "That's not what my parents taught me. They said there is only one match that's right for each god. Humans could have multiple matches, like you had three, me, Anarus, and Ydum. Any or all of us, in any combination, would have worked depending on who actually found you in what order. That's what determines the final pairings, the human deciding the god or group of gods is right, not missing anyone, and choosing to go back to the cave entrance. It's the human that makes the choices, not the gods like Ydum is saying."

"I thought it was even more narrow than that." Anarus peers down into coffee. "Most people don't believe this, but I always have thought that the cave looked for fated bonds that already existed and the human and god just have to find that bond. So, there's only one combination of gods and human possible. Even if a god were to find a hundred humans in that cave, they would be all the wrong one unless one of them was the exact right one the Fates determined was the right one way back when the human and god was born. We all three had to find you at the same time because the Fates made that our fate. But then again, they threw me in early and I still found a match, so maybe that's not right."

I don't like these thoughts. While the idea of a magic cave setting me up with three males that are supposed to be my magically bonded mates is still hard to wrap my mind around, the idea that it didn't have to be me, or them, or maybe all of them, is worse. I can't imagine anything else, anyone else, being part of our group. The idea that one of them could be with someone else almost makes me angry. I realize I am getting jealous of someone else, an unknown, potentially nonexistent or now dead someone else, when Ydum squeezes my shoulder lightly.

"Looking a little vicious there, beautiful." He chuckles. "Don't like the idea of us maybe having found anyone else, huh?"

I growl around my coffee mug. "I told you. You're mine."

"Glad to hear it." Byder says. "But if we hadn't found you, depending on how the cave actually works, you might have been growling that at three other gods than us. And, wow, now that I said it out loud, I do not like that idea either. Okay, go ahead and growl at that, Jinx."

Anarus seems a little bitter when he speaks. "Veirveil is ruled by the original gods. They are the ones in charge. They don't only control the games, and how they work after the cave, but everything in Veirveil. Twenty original gods that set everything up, and supposedly created the humans, both the witches and the ones who are not, the non-magic humans that left the continent. Everything from the testing centers to what gods and humans learn in school is all set by them. Each human community now has some control over their own systems, to some extent, as long as the rules of the gods and participation in the Gods Games is followed. They are also the ones that decided what to do with me, the orphan god when gods are not supposed to be able to be orphans. They're the ones who decided to make me join the games early and to not tell me anything about who my parents were and why I'm not with them anymore."

"They won't tell you anything?" I ask.

Anarus shakes his head. "I call myself an orphan, but I don't even know if that's true. Could be my parents saw my power and abandoned me. Enough other gods did, taking me in, thinking it wouldn't be that bad. Then, they saw my shadows when I was upset or mad and immediately told the originals to find me a new home." Shadows start to move around him and I know he feels hurt.

I get up and move from sitting with Ydum to sitting next to Anarus. Byder, seeing my intent, moved quickly to make space for me. I curl my arms through one of Anarus's. "Well, you have a family now. A permanent one."

"You couldn't get rid of us if you tried." Ydum says.

"The cave put us together." Byder reaches around me and puts a hand on Anarus's knee. "No matter how it actually works, I think it didn't just match each of us with Jinx, but each of us gods with each other too. Ydum made it seem like there was some other way this could have been, but this group? Us four? I don't think so. We were on purpose, just like this. The original gods may have decided to throw you in early, but the cave made sure you got your family out of their actions."

"If you are thinking of making me kiss each of you like we did with Jinx, I'll split your lip again, Ydum." Anarus says this gruffly, but his shadows move to only obscure part of his face. I know he isn't upset, only feeling emotional and trying to hide from it.

"Nah, we'll leave the kissing your boo boos away to Jinx." Ydum teases.

Knowing he's uncomfortable, I move the focus away from Anarus. "Should we see what the paintings are and if we can get any clue for the next game?"

Everyone agrees and we head to the hallway. The paintings are incredibly unhelpful. There are eight of them now, all in the hallway between room doors. On our side of the hallway are four paintings, all done in black. The one between rooms two and four has just one slash in black paint from the top to the bottom in the middle of a white canvas. The one between rooms four and six has two slashes. The one between rooms six and eight has three and the one in between rooms eight and ten has four. On the other side of the hallway, the paintings are exactly the same but in red.

"This is completely unhelpful." Wilros, Asteria's god, says. Someone told me he's a god of messages. If he can't figure this out, probably no one can. From time talking in the evening after the second game, I knew that Wilros had also figured out the paintings and they had purposely hoped to get snow when I took rain before they could.

I go back to our room with my gods. We aren't figuring anything out from the paintings, at least not now while everyone else is also trying to do the same thing. The only thing we can do is keep doing what we have been and work on my concentration with magic and physical agility.

I insist that all of us need to be working on these things, not just me. So, for the magical concentration, now Ydum and I fight over control of a rosebud while Anarus and Byder work together. They set up a game of basically hide and seek with each other. Anarus uses his shadows to hide himself and Byder uses his hunter senses to find where Anarus is in our rooms.

I am not so happy with them when I figure out on the second day what the prize they are playing for is. Me. They decided that whoever won got the right to go to my room that night. I absolutely call them to the carpet for that.

"Abso-fucking-lutely not. I am not a prize to be won, and it's not only your choice." I'm livid, pacing in front of the two of them sitting on the couch with their heads hung down. "What if I said no to the both of you? How would you have dealt with me denying you your prize? Huh?"

"We didn't think about that." Byder says, hanging his head down, his loose hair in his eyes.

"You didn't think at all, either of you!" I yell back. I point at them, emphasizing my point. "Disgusting. Both of you."

Lunch has already arrived and Ydum is safely hiding by the table, eating fried and salted potato slices and watching me rip the other two to shred. He's smart enough to know better than to say anything, but I have heard him cough quietly to cover a laugh.

When out of frustration, I tell them, "I'm tempted to let Ydum come sleep in my room tonight just to teach you both a lesson," his head whips up and he interrupts.

"Woah. Not the way I want that, Jinx." Ydum says. "That would make you just as bad as them."

I close my eyes and sigh. I open them again and look towards him. "You're right. I'm sorry. I shouldn't have said that. I'm just fucking mad."

Ydum comes over to the couches and takes me by the arm, leading me back to the table to talk. "I get that." He tells me quietly so the other two don't hear us. "But you just made me revenge like they made you a prize."

"I would never actually do that, Ydum." I tell him. "You know that, right? It was just a stupid thing said in the heat of the moment."

Ydum actually looks angry, which, fair. "I don't know anything, Jinx! I know you kissed me. I know what you have done with them and not me. I know what I want to do with you, but now..." Ydum stops. He takes a breath and pinches the bridge of his nose. When he's collected himself, he speaks again. "You are angry with them, rightfully so, and are lashing out in that anger. I can forgive you, but you have to understand, forgive and forget are two different things. I want, no I need you to want me for me. How do I know now that it's for me when you used me as a weapon against them in anger? How will I know, if you ever do choose me, that you aren't just angry with them again and see me as a way to get back at them? Or as just someone to fill that empty spot?"

I fucked up. I fucked up bad. Just as bad as Anarus and Byder did. Maybe worse. I lick my lips nervously and looks down, because there's nothing I can say to Ydum to make this better. There's nothing I can do to fix it. He's hurt and I did that. But he's looking at me, expecting something.

"I'm sorry." I say and mean it. "Really sorry, Ydum. I promise, if it does happen, it will never be because you are filling some empty spot. You mean too much to me for that."

Ydum just nods, but I know my words didn't help anything. Eventually, Ydum just turns back to the table, and makes himself a plate of food, saying nothing more to me. He goes into his room with the plate alone. I go into my room too, not bothering to get food. I'm too angry to eat. Angry at Anarus and Byder. Angry at myself.

We don't do any of the physical workout that day. I don't even come out of my room at dinner, but just stay in there, beating myself up for hurting Ydum. Eventually, I must have fallen asleep because, when I wake up, it's morning.

I go into the sitting room quietly. Anarus is still asleep on one couch and

Byder is asleep on the other. Ydum is up, eating breakfast at the table. He looks up at me but says nothing. I get coffee and take it into the hallway, the silence in the room oppressive. After I finish drinking my coffee, I decide to do the running I failed to do the day before. I put myself through the warmups Ydum taught me, then start the sprints.

When I stop after my second set of shuttle sprints, walking up and down the hallway with my hands clasped on top of my head to cool down, I see Ydum standing in our doorway watching. "You're still turning the wrong way half the time, Jinx. You should be able to just flip without changing which foot is in front and take off again. Try it again."

When I only look at him, Ydum shrugs, saying, "We're still teammates even if we get angry with each other."

The word teammate makes my heart clench. Yesterday morning, he called us family. Yesterday, he was calling me beautiful rather than my name. I deserve it, but it still hurts. I do what he says, ignoring the desire to cry.

When I finish my third set, Ydum nods. "Better. Cool down and come back in for the rosebud." He turns, going back into the room and lets our door close behind him.

After I cool down, and maybe cry for a minute, I go back in the room. Byder and Anarus are up and just sitting on the couches. When I come in, Ydum takes his spot on the floor and produces a rosebud. I sit and, without talking, try to focus on opening the rosebud. But all my peace is gone and with it my concentration. Anarus is simmering in shadows, hiding under them but trying not to. Byder has his elbows resting on his knees and is staring at the floor in between his feet. Ydum has the rosebud in his hands between us, but I can feel him not looking at me either. I can tell he's not trying very hard to keep it closed, just like I'm not trying very hard to open it.

I shift in my seat. "Everything's fucked up." I mutter under my breath. "Everything's ruined now."

Ydum lets out a deep sigh and closes his hand, making the dirt and rosebud disappear. "It's not ruined. We just need to fix it somehow."

"How?" I whisper.

Ydum jumps up. "We need to do something. Something to break us out of our thoughts."

I stand up with him. I'm willing to do anything for Ydum to just smile at me again. Or be a know-it-all, quoting textbooks.

"We're going to spar." Ydum finally says. This gets both Anarus's attention and Byder's. They both look up from the couches.

"Who is going to spar?" Byder asks.

"We are." Ydum says. "All of us."

"Jinx can barely do a push up. You want her to spar?" Anarus sounds incredulous.

Ydum actually starts to smile a little. "Yes. Against me."

"Are you in fact crazy?" Anarus says at the same time as Byder says, "Absolutely not!"

"Come on. It'll be fun." Ydum almost sounds normal.

"I'm game." I say. Anything. I'll do anything right now.

"You're dead in five seconds." Anarus is standing now, glaring from me to Ydum, almost angry. "No."

Ydum walks right up to him, standing incredibly close, using his height to tower over Anarus. In a challenge, he questions the younger god. "Do you think I would ever hurt Jinx? Do you think my bond to her is less than yours?"

Byder stands and butts between them, placing a hand on both of their chests. "No, but accidents happen with sparring. You know this, Ydum."

Ydum comes back over by me, standing calmly in the open area. "Open palm, one-handed hits only. No faces or groins. Or tits for Jinx. One foot on the floor at all times. Come on." Ydum waves a hand, beckoning me towards him.

"Wait." Byder groans. "Move the table first." He grabs one side of the table and stares at Anarus.

Anarus is simmering in shadows, his arms crossed over his chest. "Fuck no." He snaps. "This is not happening."

Ydum grabs the other side of the table and he and Byder move it over to the couches, pushing Anarus out of the way as they do. "This is happening, Ani. So, you can either sit there in your shadows and fume or you can come over and tell Jinx how to beat me."

Byder's immediately next to me, pulling his hair into a quick ponytail and spouting advice. "Keep your feet light, just like when you do the running drills. Keep them shoulder width apart and stay on your toes, ready to move."

Anarus groans but comes over too. "Keep your hands up and your chin tucked. He can't hit your face, but start doing it now so you don't get into bad habits."

"Don't watch his hands." Byder tells me. "Watch his shoulders and his hips."

I nod at all their advice, but feel like most of it is worthless. I've seen people fight before, of course, but never with open hands and faces off-limits. It feels like this will just be me and Ydum slapping each other's shoulders a lot.

I'm wrong, of course. Very wrong. The minute Byder tells us to start, I realize how woefully unprepared I am. Ydum doesn't hit hard, just light taps that won't even turn my skin red, but he hits often. I can't even keep up with how fast his hands move. I step back away from him to try to get space.

"Don't move back, Jinx." Byder tells me. "Go on the offensive. Hit him."

"How? He's too fast." I try anyway and end up with my right hand knocked out of the way with his left hand while Ydum taps my right side with his right hand. I try again with my left hand and Ydum grabs my wrist in his hand before I make contact. He pulls me close then sweeps my feet out from under me before I can think.

He catches me before I hit the floor, his hands a blur. One hand is behind my head and the other around my waist and he sets me on the floor, kneeling over me. I'm trapped between his knees. I try to use both hands to push on his chest, to push him off me, but he just grabs both my wrists in one of his large hands and pulls them over my head to pin them to the floor. He's now lying over me and I am very, very trapped.

Ydum smiles down at me for a fraction of a second, then he furrows his brow and jumps off me. As I get up, slower than he did, he looks at me concerned. I rub my wrists where he held them, then move back where we started. "Again." I say.

"Jinx." Ydum comes back over. "I didn't mean to trap you like that."

I pull out my hair tie and retie it in a ponytail, catching a few strands that came loose. "You're fine. Again."

Ydum just raises his eyebrows. "Alright."

Once again, before I can even figure out what's happening, Ydum is catching me as I fall and lowering me to the floor. As he straddles me, pinning me between his knees, I try to catch his hands this time. Ydum only laughs and twists his wrists, breaking my hold on him to pin my hands above my head again. He immediately lets go and moves to stand again.

I stand up as well and catch my breath. Ydum isn't even winded yet. "Again." I go back to where we started.

I try really hard to follow his hands. Anarus and Byder are both spouting out advice but none of it helps when I can't even keep track of where Ydum is going to aim next. This time, when he pins me on the floor, I try to push on his thighs to force him off before he pins me fully. Ydum's face shows surprise for one second before he falls forward. His hands slap the ground on either side of my head as he catches himself before he falls on top of me.

"Easy there, beautiful. You're really close to breaking a rule." Ydum murmurs in my ear. I realize exactly where my hands are and quickly pull them back. But he's lying almost completely on top of me and I can't help brushing against him as I move my hands from trapped between us. His eyes flutter closed and he sucks his teeth. "Shit." Ydum opens his eyes, staring at me. Some indecision flashes through his eyes, then he stands, turning away from us quickly.

He doesn't come back over, but instead sits on the couch. "Why don't one of you take a turn? See how Jinx does against someone else."

Byder moves to stand where Ydum had been each time we started sparring. I get up and go over. Byder is shorter than Ydum, but much broader and a bunch stronger. I know he'll fight differently, but I'm not sure how.

Anarus still stands close, giving advice and Ydum offers advice from the couch.

"You're tiny and he's big. Use his bulk against him, Jinx." Ydum says.

"How?" I ask.

"You're faster than him." Anarus offers.

"Ready?" Byder asks and I nod. He starts first and I see that they're right. His hands aren't a blur like Ydum's were. He's slower. I'm still on the defensive quickly, but I can move out of the way more often. Byder isn't getting a hold on me as fast as Ydum did. When he tries to trip me up like Ydum did, I can jump out of the way and stop it, even if I can't get a hit in.

"Watch his shoulders." Anarus reminds me.

I look at Byder's shoulders and, this time, I figure out what they mean. Byder's shoulders bunch before he swings. I can duck his swings in time.

Ydum is nodding at me. "Good. Now, swing for the opening he leaves with his swing."

"Are you letting me do this, Byder?" I huff, short of breath already.

"Nope." He swings again. I duck and try to swing to the right side he swung from. I miss and he catches my arm between his arm and side. "I'm not going easy on you, Jinx. Never will. You won't learn that way."

"Good." I say as I yank my arm back from his grip. I immediately push the left side of his chest before he even realizes my hand is free and am rewarded when Byder stumbles back a step. I smile and turn to look at Ydum and Anarus, proud of myself.

"Too soon." Byder says as he sweeps my feet, catching me before I hit the floor just like Ydum did. He sets me down and kneels over me. "Never celebrate until the fight is over. And never, ever take your eyes off the enemy." He gets up without pinning my arms and helps me up. "Your turn, Anarus."

Byder leans on the arm of the couch by Ydum as I shake out my hands and roll my shoulders. Anarus stretches too. "You good, little human, or do you need a break?"

"Do you just not want to fight me?" I ask, teasing. "Afraid you'll lose?"

"Never." Anarus snarls and immediately he starts. He's shorter still than Byder, but not as broad. He moves almost as fast as Ydum and is stronger than Byder. I have a hard time keeping up with him and dodging. When he takes me down, instead of catching me and depositing me directly on the floor, Anarus catches me and holds me hovering an inch above the ground.

"Think. How can you escape once you hit the ground?" He asks. "You have to be fast. What can you do?"

He gives me a moment to think, then lays me down. Immediately, I start scooting backwards, sliding on my back across the floor. I bring my knees up to do it, and Anarus is blocked from kneeling over me. He grabs my ankles as I move and pulls them tightly, forcing my legs straight on the floor. This time, he kneels before I can move.

"Good try." Anarus tells me. "Why did it fail?"

"Because you are too fast and too strong." I tell him.

"Wrong." Anarus stands but doesn't move from standing over me. He lifts me back up instead. "Try again."

He sets me down and this time, I scoot forward. When Anarus goes to kneel over me, he ends up almost sitting on my chest, his thighs pinning my arms.

Anarus shakes his head and tsks at me. "Worse. Try again." He picks me up again, positions me under him properly again then sets me down.

Immediately, I flip on my stomach and push up to my hands and knees. I'm able to move completely away while Anarus is still going down to kneeling. I stand as fast as I can.

"Good." Anarus tells me and stands up. "Always know your way out. You are never as trapped as you think you are." His words have a double meaning and I know it. He's not just teaching me about fighting, but how to feel safe by myself.

I move to the couch and stand next to Byder. "Someone else's turn. I'm beat. Literally."

Byder cocks his head at Anarus in question. Anarus nods and Byder goes over to stand where I had been. I move to sit on the arm of the couch where Byder had been, with Ydum behind me, sitting forward so he can see around me like he had done with Byder. Unlike with Byder, Ydum puts a hand on the small of my back, his fingers gently brushing me as he curls and uncurls them against the skin peeking out from the bottom of my too-tight shirt. I look down at him, hoping this means I'm forgiven. Ydum just winks at me and turns back to watch Byder and Anarus fight.

Their fight is different. But of course, it is. They both know what they're doing. When I fought each of them, we moved around the open space as I tried to evade them, but Byder and Anarus barely move around. If anything, they move closer together, invading each other's space to find openings. Their bodies are loose, movements graceful and flowing from one to the next. They knock each other's hands away before blows can land, and take advantage of each opening. Byder's bulk versus Anarus's strength and speed make them evenly matched.

I try to keep my focus on watching what they do and how they do it. Ydum points things out to me. "See how Byder, even though he's big, stays light on his feet? He's almost bouncing from one movement to the next. And Ani's arms. Watch how he strikes out, not swinging out and around, but straight out and back, keeping his sides protected. The pull back is part of the movement, not a different one. They both are leaned slightly forward, too. Not hunched over, but just leaning into their movements."

I nod at the things he points out, noticing them. Anarus and Byder are turning in circles around each other. After several minutes, and many, many blows landed by both of them. Anarus captures Byder's hand as he connects a blow to Anarus's right side. Anarus uses this to leverage Byder's weight against him, toppling him down. Byder's falls forward onto his knees with a resounding thud.

"Oof." A groan escapes Byder as he lands hard enough to rattle the walls. "I yield."

Anarus smiles and reaches out a hand to help Byder up. They are both now actually breathing hard. "Jinx needs another human to fight." Anarus announces. He heads out of the room without another word and we follow, glancing at each other with questioning looks.

Anarus goes directly to room two and knocks on the door. Esnir answers. "What's up?"

"We are teaching Jinx to fight." Anarus says with no preamble. "She needs another human to fight."

Esnir nods. "I've been working with Isis too. That's a good idea, but not her. Not now. Her arm is still healing."

Anarus shakes his head. "I didn't mean Isis in particular. I meant you. You're a war god. Instead of these stupid parties Aretha has been planning, would you plan fighting practice with all the humans?"

"You know the sixth game will have us fighting each other, right?" Esnir asks.

"I do." Anarus crosses his arms over his chest. "But I don't care if you don't. I want Jinx to survive. And enough gods and humans have died for the originals' games. If we all work together like the humans did with the witch's kits, maybe no one else dies."

Esnir stiffens, then relaxes. "After dinner, in the foyer. Let anyone else you see know and I will too."

"How is Isis?" I ask as Esnir looks about ready to close his door.

He sighs heavily. "Okay. Getting better. I have a little healing power, so I can speed things up some, but I doubt it will be completely healed in time for the next game."

I step forward. "Can I see her? I don't know that I could do anything to help, but I'm human too. Maybe I'll think of something to help you didn't."

Esnir smiles ruefully. "I'll take all the help I can get." He pulls the door open wide. I step inside and see Isis lying down on the couch, a pained expression on her face. "If I had my full mantle, maybe I could completely heal it, but." There's a tinge of guilt and worry in Esnir's voice.

I go and kneel next to Isis. "Hey. How are you doing?"

Isis grimaces. "I'm still alive."

"Can I look at your injury?" Isis holds up her arm to me, the movement hurting her. I unwrap the bandage and see a nasty cut almost down to the bone wrapping all the way around her upper bicep. The two ends of the cut don't meet but almost spiral down the top of her arm. The edges of the cut are bright pink with new skin, evidence of Esnir's attempts to heal her. "What did this?"

"Claw of a hate wraith. There was just the tiniest break in her salt circle and it reached through that small opening before we fixed it." Esnir tells me.

"What have you put on it?" When Esnir only shrugs at my question, I groan under my breath. My gods are all standing in the doorway still. I turn to them. "Calendula, echinacea, and yarrow. Go to everyone and see who has it. Oh, and anyone with any alcohol left, grab that too, but not beer."

My three gods take off and I hear them going to other rooms and knocking on their doors. I turn to Esnir. "Warm water and a clean cloth, please. And any unscented soap you have. I'll be right back." I go back to my room and grab my black string, then return to room two.

Back in the room, Anarus and Byder are already waiting. Anarus holds up a small bag in his hand. "Yarrow. Ydum is still trying doors."

Byder holds up a small bottle of an amber liquid. "Is mead good?"

Esnir has a bowl filled with water, a cloth, and square of soap in his hands. I nod at all of them and move over to Isis. "Esnir, sit at her head and hold her. This is going to hurt."

He does as I say, handing me the things in his hands. I set the bowl of water on the floor next to me as I kneel by the couch. I'm not great at this, the healing magical arts. I know what to do, and have practiced on dummies, but have never actually stitched up a person before. I start cleaning the wound with the soap and water. Isis hisses as I do it, but she doesn't pull away.

"Byder, Anarus, come help hold her still. This is going to hurt a lot." When

Byder has her feet pinned down, and Anarus is kneeling next to me, one hand braced on her stomach, I take the bottle of mead and pour some into the cut. Isis yelps and jerks, but the three males hold her down. I use the water to wash away the mead after it sits for a moment.

"Esnir, can you make a weapon from thin air like Ydum can make flowers?" I ask.

He nods at me. "What do you need?"

"Do you think a sewing needle could count? That you could make something similar to one?" I ask and he inclines his head as a yes. "I need one with very sharp point, but instead of straight, I need it to be curved."

Esnir thinks for a moment, closing his eyes and holding up a hand. After a second, a bone needle made perfectly to my description, appears in his hand. I take it and test the point, which is sharp enough to draw a prick of blood from my finger easily. I dump the mead over it then rinse it in the water bowl. I do the same with my thread, after teasing it down to the thinnest strand I can, then thread the needle.

My hands are shaking. I don't want to mess this up. It's going to hurt Isis a lot and if I do it wrong, I could make everything worse instead of better. Anarus notices and leans closer to me.

"Trust your gut, Jinx. You know what you are doing." He whispers.

I take a deep breath and blow it out slowly. I can do this. I know what I am doing. "She's going to scream." I warn them before I start. Then, at one end of the wound, I pinch the skin together and push the needle through the healthy skin just outside the wound. Isis cries out but doesn't actually scream. I work my way around the cut, doing a continuous stitch, pulling the skin together until it is just touching with even pressure. The whole time, I keep my focus on healing, using my magic to infuse the string to be both antiseptic and analgesic, as well as magically speeding her healing time.

I reach the part where the cut winds to the underside of her arm. "Anarus, can you go on the other side of the couch and hold her arm up for me?"

He stands and moves quickly to the other side of the couch, lifting Isis's arm gently. She's panting and sweating, but I hear Esnir whispering words quietly to her. Isis keeps her eyes trained on him.

Once Anarus has her arm in position, I continue my stitching and magic. Anarus easily anticipates how I need her arm positioned and moves it as I need him to. Finally, I get the whole thing stitched shut and tie off the end of my string. I sigh and sit back as Anarus gently lays her arm back down. My stitches are messy and uneven, some starting further from the edges of the skin than others, but they are holding the skin closed with proper pressure. I let myself take a small break to tame the trembling I had held off while I stitched.

While I worked, Ydum had come back in the room. Once he sees I'm done, he comes over and hands me two small satchels. "Echinacea. No one had calendula, but Saffron had chamomile and said to give it to you."

I smile a thanks at him. "Can you somehow get boiling water for tea?"

He nods and moves away, going into Esnir and Isis's washroom. While he finds that, I wrap a blanket under Isis's arm and pour the rest of the mead over the entire cut, then pour water over it. Then, I take the echinacea and yarrow in my hand and add just enough water to make it into a paste and smear it all over the wound, speaking words of healing magic over it as I coat her arm. I wrap a new strip of clean cloth over it that Esnir gives me.

Ydum returns with a cup of water that's as hot as the washroom sink could get. It's not quite boiling but close enough. I use another piece of clean cloth to wrap a little chamomile in, making a small tea ball, and set it in the cup to steep, adding more healing magic to the tea. Ydum picks it up and waits until it's steeped enough, removes the dried flower ball, then hands it to Isis after he helps her sit up.

I turn to Esnir and hand him the packets of dried flowers. "Change the bandage every morning and evening, adding more paste made from the echinacea and yarrow. Then, give her a chamomile tea while you use your healing on it. Why don't you do that now, too?"

He takes the packets from me. "Thank you, Jinx. Really, thank you."

"As Aretha said, I want to win, but I don't want to win this way. It's the least we can do. I'm sorry it took so long for me to think of it."

By the time we get back to our room, lunch has been served. We barely have a few minutes to grab food before it's whisked away.

As we sit on the couches to eat, Ydum chuckles. "Humans are so fucking creative. Fixing wounds with string?"

"What do gods do?" I ask him.

"We just heal ourselves." Byder tells me after he swallows a bite of chicken salad sandwich. "Or if we can't, are too young, we go to another god who can do it for us."

"We don't get sick either, so nothing to do with that." Ydum explains.

Byder laughs. "Drila is probably losing her shit, you know. You have a fucked-up blood test and three broken gods, but because of you, the humans are working together, sharing things and healing each other and now we are going to start all training together. You broke the games, Jinx. You destroyed the competitiveness of it, at least mostly."

We all smile at that, and the silence that follows feels tense again.

"Are we good, Jinx?" Anarus asks, his hesitance and fear evident. "Do you still hate me?"

I let out a ragged sigh. "I could never hate you, Anarus. Or you, Byder. I was very, very mad, but I don't hate you. Family gets mad sometimes, Anarus. It's going to happen. Arguments are going to happen. People say and do dumb things. Just don't do that dumb thing again."

"Never." Anarus says forcefully.

"We were complete idiots." Byder adds.

I turn to look at Ydum, holding my breath. "You weren't the only ones."

Ydum gives me a small smile. "Family does dumb things sometimes, Jinx. But family also forgives the dumb things."

I let go of the breath I was holding. The silence that follows is no longer tense, but relaxed. Not quite like it was before, but better. I don't know if it can ever be the way it was before, but we can move forward now.

That evening, after dinner, we all head out to the foyer. Esnir is already there, helping Isis sit to rest against a wall. I move to talk with her.

"How's your pain?" I say as I slide down to sit with her.

Isis gives me a grin. "Better. Thank you." She looks better, not so pale.

The other teams start trickling into the foyer and all take up positions along the walls. Esnir stands in the center of the room. Beside him, Ydum is standing as well and the two are chatting. Once everyone is settled, Esnir speaks to everyone.

"So, Anarus had the good idea that we should all work together to teach our humans fighting skills. I know I've already been working with Isis in preparation for the sixth game, and I assume all of you have been working with your humans too."

Uesis snorts. "Not me. I learned really quickly that Raven is better at fighting than me."

"That's actually good to know." Esnir says. "Wouldn't want to pair her up with someone and she hurts them because we don't expect her to be good."

Ydum takes over. "For now, the rules are open palmed, one-handed hits only. No face, no groin, and no tits for the ladies, except Iella." Everyone chuckles at Ydum removing the rule for the one female god. "Kidding Iella, don't fuck with my luck. Humans, to start, find someone about the same size as you to pair up with. Damek, you're going to work with me and Esnir. Iella, if you can find a human to pair up with that would be great. I would suggest Raven since she's already a good fighter. The rest of the gods, stay with your human and give them advice. Anarus is going to circulate to help gods who aren't necessarily the greatest at fighting."

"If someone wants to work with Isis, that would be helpful too. Her arm is still hurt, so go easy." Esnir adds. Aretha helps Isis stand up and pairs up with her.

I feel a little pride in my gods. This was their idea and they are working together, and with the other gods, to make things better for all of us. Esnir may be the war god, but Ydum and Anarus are the ones really in charge. I pair up with Asteria, who isn't the closest to my size, but looks almost scared. I know she's twenty-four, like the rest of us, but she looks and acts so much younger. Byder and Wilros stand near us to help. Anarus starts over by Raven and Uesis at first, since Uesis already admitted he's not the greatest at fighting skills.

Esnir works with Damek while Ydum calls out directions, leading all of us through motions to practice. We start out very slow, all our movements done at a slow crawl so that our gods can watch our form and correct as necessary. Occasionally, Ydum will stop us and announce something for us to watch out for as he picks up on flaws that Damek is making. Anarus does not call out like that, but lets Ydum know what he's seeing if it's a group issue or just corrects the issue with the one individual.

We work for almost an hour before Drila pops into the foyer. "This is getting ridiculous," she announces as soon as we notice her. "Why are you all helping each other? You are competing against each other. You're not supposed to work together."

For a long moment, everyone, all ten gods and eight humans, just stare at her. Then, as one, we all just go back to what we are doing as if Drila isn't even there, huffing and pouting.

"Remember to keep your elbows tucked in." Ydum calls out, drowning out Drila's words as she attempts to say something else. No one looks at her or acknowledges her.

When he stops talking, Drila tries again. "I can add points to everyone participating."

Anarus wanders over to her, stopping here and there to watch someone's skill as if she's just on his way around the room. "That would be pointless, Drila. Everyone is participating, so you would just raise all of our scores evenly. Your threat is hollow. No one cares." He continues moving around, going to Isis and Aretha, and helping Isis figure out how to stand better to protect her injured arm.

Drila is again left sputtering and red faced. She pops away and we all continue as if nothing happened. By the time we stop for the evening, all the humans are dripping sweat and ragged. Even Raven. I collapse immediately into bed after a hot shower and am asleep instantly.

For the next three days, our new pattern takes shape. In the mornings, after breakfast and a quick trip for me to check Isis's wound, Ydum and I work on rosebud concentration. Anarus and Byder go back to their hide and seek game, without the prize for winning. I'm no longer dropping exhausted after we finish, so I run before lunch instead of during it. After lunch, we do the rest of the workouts and after dinner is group fighting training with all the teams.

No one has spent the night with me in my room since the fight. Things are slowly going back to normal, but it feels like we are building the relationships up from scratch again, with slow hesitant touches and lingering looks.

The night before the fourth game, I realize we haven't discussed our plan the way we had with the other ones. After fight practice, I stop Wilros in the hallway. "Do you have any idea about the paintings?"

He shakes his head, looking down. "I would tell you if I did. Really, I would tell everyone. But I got nothing." I know he would.

Back in our room, I collapse on the couch. "We got nothing to work with. The game can be anything. The paintings are no help. And Drila is pissed we are still helping each other, so even if we did know something, the gods would probably change it to try and mess us up."

"We know it's life and death. Something to do with life and death." Ydum offers.

I snort as I lie the rest of the way down on the couch. "The whole Gods Games is life and death."

"If only one god can go, it should be me." Anarus says, pulling my feet onto his lap. "Obscurity and shadows. Death at least is something I have always felt connected to somehow."

Everyone agrees with that and it's the sum total of a plan that we can make. Frustrated, I slide down further on the couch and stare at the ceiling. Byder stands and comes over. He taps my shoulder and I sit up. He sits where my head just was and then pulls me down so my head is lying on his lap. He strokes my hair absentmindedly and I place a hand on his tattooed arm.

"We'll figure it out, Jinx." Byder tells me.

Anarus, on the other end of the couch takes off my boots. Then, he runs his hands over them with his shadows, letting the cool feeling mixed with the warmth of his hands soothe my sore feet. I turn and see Ydum sitting quietly on the other couch, watching us. I wriggle my fingers at him, gesturing for him to come over. He sits on the floor, leaning back on the couch, and I let my fingers trail through his hair.

I should feel awkward, three males sitting around me, all of us together like this. But I don't. It feels right. It feels safe. That taut tugging seems peaceful in me with all three of them around me. I close my eyes and just rest.

Chapter Ten

I MUST HAVE FALLEN asleep because I wake up in the morning still on the couch with the blanket draped over me. Anarus is asleep half on top of me, his feet scrunched up at the bottom of the couch, his head resting on my stomach with his arms wrapped around me. I turn and see Byder asleep, stretched out on the other couch. Ydum is sleeping in a ball on the floor, his head tucked in the corner made by the two couches. None of us had moved from the sitting room.

I wiggle out of Anarus's grip carefully, so I don't wake him and stand up, stretching. I step carefully around Ydum and go to the table for coffee.

"Morning, beautiful." Ydum says as he comes over to the table. He looks down into my mug and, seeing I only have taken a sip or two from it, loads a plate up with fruit and buttered toast and holds it out to me. "Eat too."

I grumble but take the plate, setting it down on the table so I can pick up a piece of toast to nibble on. Ydum doesn't look at me as he speaks, but at the table as he loads up another plate for himself. "You know you don't have to include me like you did last night. I know our relationship is different than your relationship with them."

I roll my eyes at him. "I wouldn't have asked you to come over to me if I didn't want you to, Ydum. Our relationship is different because we are different, just like how I am with Anarus is different than how I am with Byder. It has nothing to do with what you and I have or have not done."

"It's different." He retorts. "If I wanted to kiss you."

I stop him. "All you would have to do is ask."

He carefully sets the plate he was filling down and turns to face me slowly. "I want to kiss you, Jinx."

I set down my toast and coffee and turn to him. "Then kiss me, Ydum."

Ydum pulls me gently into his arms. His kiss is slow, as if he's tasting me.

He's so tall he has to bend down. I push up on my tiptoes to deepen the kiss and his hands hold my back, holding me up. There's a rush of static and Ydum groans, his hands tightening around me.

"Well, thank fuck for that, finally." Anarus grumbles behind us. "Now, move. You're blocking the coffee."

Ydum lets me go and laughs loudly. As I grab my coffee and plate of food, and move out of Anarus's way, Byder sits up on the couch, scratching at his messy hair. "Thank fuck for what?"

Anarus points at Ydum and me. Ydum smiles broadly and I blush.

"Ah." Byder nods knowingly. "So, you two finally."

"Kissed. We kissed." I correct his line of thought as I sit and eat my toast.

Byder stretches and gets up to get food. "You already did that."

"Not like that, they didn't." Anarus comes over to sit with his coffee as well.

"Can we stop talking about this?" I complain, frustrated. "Not that I am embarrassed I kissed you, Ydum. But we humans aren't so open about talking about stuff like this. And why do you all yell at me about eating breakfast and not Anarus?"

"Neither are gods, normally." Ydum tells me. "But you blush so prettily. And Anarus is a god. You're not."

"Humans need food. Gods enjoy food, mostly." Anarus says.

Ydum corrects him, pointing at him with a piece of toast he was biting. "After we get our mantle. Now, we do need it too, just not as much as humans. Even after we get our mantles, I think Anarus will still need coffee though."

"There's a reason it's called the nectar of the gods." Anarus says as he takes a long sip.

"That's mead." Byder sits down next to Ydum with a full plate and a full mouth.

I eat my fruit and leave them to their debate on if coffee or mead is the nectar of the gods. As soon as I'm done eating, I check Byder's hair then go into the guys' room and grab a shirt for each of them. They are not going bare-chested into a game, I decide. I make it back out to the sitting room, tossing them the clothes right as Anarus and Byder dissolve into a 'is not, is too' argument. Ydum doesn't put on the shirt but holds it in his hand as he launches into a diatribe about the origins of the phrase, making all of us groan. Before he can get too into it, though, the tone sounds and we have to go to the foyer.

We have no plans, beyond Anarus being my first pick. We don't even have an idea which painting to pick. I feel jittery and worried as we line up along the wall, gods behind humans, and Drila watches us, her purple dress just as sparkly as ever.

"The fourth game is life and death." Drila says when we are all in place. "The goal of this game is to wake your witches and follow their directions. Following the last direction completes the task. The amount of time you take to complete all tasks will determine standings. Instead of picking a painting, the humans will pick a color, red or black. Any questions?"

I have a hundred questions. Everyone else around me looks confused too. Wake up our witches? I am the witch for our group, but if I'm supposed to know directions to give after my gods wake me up, which I'm awake so that's confusing, I don't know them now. Drila also didn't say how many I can take with me. "How many gods am I allowed?"

"This is a group game, Jinx." She says, as if that clears everything up. "If there is nothing else, we will start the human choices."

"What do you mean wake up our witches?" Aretha asks. "We are awake. And I don't know any directions."

Drila ignores this question. "Saffron, red or black?"

I don't listen to her answer. I whisper back at my gods. "Which color?"

"Go with your gut." Byder says.

"Black." Anarus answers.

The three of us look at him. "Do you know something?" Ydum asks.

Anarus shakes his head. "Instinct. I don't know why, but pick black."

Byder shrugs. "Works for me."

Drila says my name and I pick black. "Go to the first black painting." We move to the painting between doors two and four. Saffron and Aretha are standing across the hall, at the first two red paintings, with their gods. They look as confused still as I feel. Isis goes to the black painting one door down from me. Damek and Raven fill in the other two red paintings and, with no other choices left, Wren and Asteria take the last two black paintings.

None of us look confident. None of us know the significance of the color we chose, or the number of lines on the paintings we were assigned. And the directions, wake your witches, makes no sense. But Drila ignores our confusion and just starts the game.

We pop out of the foyer and find ourselves in a flat woodland. It appears to be a beautiful, warm day. The sun is shining between the trees, and I can almost make out a clear blue sky above the tree canopy. The trees are all covered in healthy, green leaves, most of them not conifers, and the detritus on the forest floor isn't thick or wet, the dirt black and just moist enough to not be cracking, but not so damp to be soupy. I figure this means it is either late spring, early fall, or summer. All three of my gods look at me. I know they expected me to be asleep. I did too.

"Do you know anything you didn't five seconds ago?" Byder asks me.

"No." I answer. "I'm not even tired."

"Maybe you aren't the witch Drila meant." Ydum points to a spot between the trees in the distance as he finally puts on the shirt I gave him. There's something behind them, something colorful that doesn't seem like it belongs in the woods. The form is too regular for the woods, explaining how Ydum spotted it without seeing the bright colors.

We all walk through the trees and see a woman lying on a stone table. She's very old, with a wrinkled face and long white hair, wearing a bright yellow dress, homespun like mine. She's also very dead. Her skin is sagging and tinged gray. Her eyes are closed and her arms crossed over her chest, a necklace held in her hands.

"Wake the witch." Ydum shakes his head. "Not wake, but reanimate."

"Do we need to bring her back to life?" I wonder out loud.

Anarus is examining her body closely. "Doubt it. Drila said wake, not revive. And we only need directions from her. That probably will only take a few minutes."

"Okay, how do we reanimate her?" I ask. "I know I don't have anything magic-wise to do that."

"I can give life to nature, but I don't think I could give life to a human, even temporarily." Ydum says.

"I can take a life but not give it." Byder twists his mouth, thinking.

Anarus groans. "I can hide life, not give it or take either, that I know of."

We all stand around, looking at each other, thinking. Anarus is examining her necklace to see if it holds any clues. He mutters and moves on, looking the dead witch over from head to toe. His brow creases the more he looks, nothing giving him any ideas.

"If only we could borrow life from something else and put it in her for a little bit." I think out loud. "Byder, you could catch something and pull out it's lifeforce to use or something."

Byder tilts his head to the side. "You might be onto something, Jinx. I can't end a life in a way that leaves a lifeforce to capture and give to something else, but Ydum maybe could. Hunting only kills, but nature includes the whole life cycle, including probably life energy, souls, rebirth, whatnot."

We all look at Ydum. His hands move through the air, making gestures we don't understand, but I can tell by his face he's thinking through something. "If I, then I could." He mutters to himself as his hands move. Finally, he looks at us. "Maybe. Maybe, I could do it. Isolate something's lifeforce, its tie to nature and the natural cycle of life, death, rebirth. It would have to be an animal, though, not a plant, so I'm less sure of it. Have a working brain to give her a working brain, I think. But I'm not sure how I would transfer it to the dead witch."

"Could you do it, Jinx?" Anarus asks, coming back over to us. "Make the natural energy move into the witch because we need to talk to her?"

"Maybe." I tell them honestly. "It sounds plausible. It's a need, and the thing I need will already be made and here, available."

Byder stands with his hands on his hips. "So, I catch an animal. Ydum will extract its natural energy, and Jinx will put it into the witch. Anarus, I think you should focus on what she says when she wakes up. The rest of us may be preoccupied or tired from the effort and we won't get long."

Anarus nods. "Sounds like a plan." I nod too, and so does Ydum.

"Alright. I'll be right back." Byder is about to leave, but I stop him.

"Take Ydum. No one goes anywhere alone. We don't know what else might be out here."

"Good thought, Jinx." Ydum claps Byder on the back. "Ready?"

As the other two take off, Anarus looks at the witch's necklace again. "Jinx, come here. Does this look familiar to you? It feels important to me for some reason."

I join him and he doesn't touch the necklace but shifts the witch's hands gently so I can get a better look. The charm on the necklace is a small, round piece of wood with symbols burned into it. The top symbol looks like a circle with a small gap at the top, and the bottom symbol is another circle with a small gap at the bottom. In between them is a spiral going counter-clockwise.

"The top symbol looks like the symbol for life, but it's not quite right." I tell him. "The bottom one is also wrong, but looks similar to death. The spiral usually represents rebirth."

"How are the two symbols wrong? Are they wrong the same way?" Anarus asks.

"Yeah." I point to them without touching the wood. "They both should have small lines coming off the circle where the gaps are, like prongs coming from them, like two doors in the circle were opened."

"The doors are missing for both life and death." Anarus rubs his chin, messing up his goatee that he has let get a little long. "That may actually be really important."

Byder and Ydum return, and Byder is carrying a small rabbit. It's pure white and fluffy. Byder is scratching it absentmindedly between the ears like it's his pet.

"Any problems?" I ask as they come over by the witch.

"Nope." Ydum tells me. "Honestly, it was a little too easy."

"Don't jinx it." Byder says, then holds back a small snort. "Jinx. Your parents were nuts when they named you."

"Tell me about it. Twenty-four years of the jokes, and bad puns. School was awful."

"How bad are your sisters' names?" Ydum asks.

I hold out my arms, shrugging. "Completely normal. Dahlia, Samantha, Ganna, Shearah, Myrna, Ophelia, and Catarina. I think, since I was the surprise kid, they ran out of ideas."

Ydum smiles at me. "My older sister is Zimuna. We used to joke my parents were working their way through the alphabet backwards, but they stopped with me, so."

"I didn't know you have a sister." I say, then shake my head. "We're distracted. Bunny."

"Right." Ydum takes the rabbit from Byder. "We'll have to work quickly, Jinx. So, already be focusing on moving the rabbit's life energy to the witch before I try extracting it."

I take a breath and focus on the rabbit. Life, enough to speak, enough to give us directions, from the rabbit to the witch. I keep my thoughts on this need while I watch Ydum. He puts a hand on the rabbit's head and closes his eyes. At first, I am not sure anything is happening, but then the rabbit squeaks, then squeals, then twitches, yipping loudly. I bite my lip. It's in pain and I hate that we have to kill it like this. But I keep my focus. Life energy to the witch to hear what she needs to tell us.

I feel Anarus's hand slide into mine and I squeeze as the sounds from the rabbit get worse. I'm so sorry, little rabbit, please understand. We need to use your energy for the witch. We need to hear what she needs to say.

A small bit of the air above Ydum's hand on the rabbit's head starts to sparkle like gold dust. I concentrate on the sparkle, willing it to move to the witch, because we need her to be able to speak to us. The sparkle floats through the air to land on the witch's face. It settles into her skin and her eyes open.

Anarus is right there, listening. A string of unintelligible sounds come from her mouth. "Gehar bly manna fray. Nalla dodi gehar fro maka wren." Her eyes close again and she's back to being dead.

Anarus repeats the sounds. "Gehar bly manna fray. Nalla dodi gehar fro maka wren. That's not Nazean."

"Do you know what it is?" Byder asks.

When Anarus shakes his head, we all look at Ydum who's still holding the dead rabbit gently. He shakes his head too.

"Do you think it was another language?" I ask Anarus.

"I think so." He rubs his goatee again.

"Ydum flipped his power, taking life instead of giving it." I say, thinking. "Can you flip yours, maybe make something clear when it's already obscured?"

Anarus stares at a spot on the ground, his eyes unfocused. "The doors? The doors are open. No. The doors are broken open. Close the doors and put together. No. Fix the cycle." He looks up at us. "The doors are broken open. Close the doors and fix the cycle."

"The doors." Anarus looks at me and I turn back to the necklace. "Anarus, the doors."

"I knew it was important." Anarus says under his breath.

"What? What is important?" Byder asks.

Anarus actually takes the necklace out of the witch's hands. "This. Jinx said the top and bottom symbols are life and death, but they're missing a part that looks like doors."

I talk as I kneel down and look for something on the ground. "The middle symbol is rebirth, but I'm not sure how that figures in." I find a sharp stone and turn to Anarus. "Let me see the charm."

Anarus hands it to me and I use his back to lean the charm on. Using the sharp stone, I add the missing pieces to the life and death symbols. I show the others the fixed symbols and we all stand for a moment, looking around.

"Guess that would have been too easy." Byder says.

Ydum looks off in the distance. "Too easy if that was all we had to do, but it wasn't wrong. Look." He points to something.

We look the way Ydum is pointing and there's a trail of glowing bugs fluttering to the west. Ydum immediately starts trotting down the trail, the way the glowing bugs lead, and we all follow. We run through the woods, Ydum far in the lead, still carrying the dead rabbit and me following behind him, the necklace in my hand. Byder and Anarus bring up the rear.

When Ydum breaks through the trees into a clearing, he's too far ahead of us. I hear him whoop, then yell back, "There's a cabin here. The doors are open and broken and a light is shining out of them. Hurry up!"

I break through the tree line and slam to a stop. The symbols above the open and broken doors on the cabin are the same symbols as the necklace. And Ydum is running right to the glowing light coming out of the open doorway.

I scream, but it's too late. Ydum runs into the beam of light and falls to the ground in a crumpled heap. My heart feels like it's being ripped apart as the rabbit in his arms breaks loose and hops away. "No! Ydum!" I'm screaming. "Byder, catch the rabbit. Ydum!" I am running towards Ydum, who isn't moving.

Byder breaks through the trees next. "Fuck! Fuck!"

I don't look at what he's doing, my eyes only on Ydum. "Catch the rabbit! Byder! Get the rabbit." I'm almost to Ydum when an arm grabs me around the waist.

"Stop, Jinx!" Anarus is holding me back. "You can't go into the light either. Stop."

"No!" I fight his hold, crying. "Let me go. Ydum!"

Anarus lifts me off the ground and turns me in his arms to face him. "Stop. Jinx, you can't get him until we close the doors. You have to wait."

I beat my hands on Anarus, fighting for him to let me go, but he's right. If I try to get to Ydum, I'll die too. "He's dead. Ydum is dead and the rabbit is alive."

"I know." Anarus smooths his hands over my hair, his voice cracking. "I know, little human. Byder will catch the rabbit. We'll fix it. We'll get him back, but you have to wait until we shut the doors. Can you help me shut the doors?"

I still, and nod my head. "Ydum's dead." I know I should care about the games, and what his death means for us in the games, but I don't. I don't care about anything but Ydum and the feeling in me like something broke, like that taut line snapped.

"Rebirth is one of the symbols, right?" Anarus says as I cry into his shoulder. "Rebirth is one of the symbols. We can get him back. You know that. That's why you told Byder to catch the rabbit. Now, help me close the doors."

I take a deep breath and try to get control of myself. Rebirth is one of the symbols. Maybe it's not over. Maybe Ydum doesn't have to stay dead. Anarus sets me down.

"Go to the door on the left, Jinx. Don't step in the beam of light, okay?" Anarus is watching me closely and I see there are tears on his cheeks as well. I move to where he told me, avoiding the beam of light, but I can't take my eyes off of Ydum's body in a ball on the ground. The left door is broken off its hinges and lying in the dirt. I pick it up and push it against the side of the building. I try to line up the broken hinges but I can't hold the door and line them up at the same time. Plus, the pins that hinge the two parts together are gone.

"The pins are gone and I can't line it up by myself." I tell Anarus.

Anarus walks back to the trees. "The right door is the same. Hold on." He disappears into the trees for a few moments, then comes back out, coming around to my side. "Hold the door to line it up as best as you can." I struggle to hold the door up properly and Anarus shoves sticks he found in the pinholes for the hinges. As soon as he has them in place, I let go of the door slowly. It holds. We close the door and the light over Ydum's body is cut in half.

We walk in a wide arc around the light still spilling from the still open door and do the same thing on the other side. With both doors closed, the glowing light over Ydum's body is gone. I run to him and gather him into my arms.

"Ydum." I plead with him. "Please wake up. Please, Ydum."

Byder comes up at a run with the rabbit in his arms. "I got it. I got it." I'm not sure if the moisture on his face is tears, sweat, or both.

"Byder, Jinx, move." Anarus calls out from by the cabin doors. "When I open the door, drop the rabbit into the light over Ydum."

We both move back and Anarus opens the door to the cabin a small bit. As soon as there's glowing light over Ydum, Byder tosses the rabbit into the light. It falls to the ground, dead again. Anarus closes the door again and runs over to us. I am on the ground, cradling Ydum again, but he still isn't moving.

"Please, Ydum." My voice is scratchy from crying. "Please wake up."

Nothing is happening. "Why isn't it working?" Byder asks, his voice as scratchy and broken as mine.

No. No! I scream. "No!" I let Ydum's body slide back to the ground. "You don't get to die now, Ydum." I punch on Ydum's chest hard, right over his heart. "Wake up!" I scream. I punch on his chest again. "Wake up, Ydum!" I push on his chest over and over and scream. "Wake up! Wake up!" I keep doing it until I have no voice left to scream with.

Anarus pulls me away. "Stop, Jinx. Stop. It's not working." He holds me in his arms and I cry, clutching his shirt. Anarus buries his face in my shoulder as he holds me and I feel his tears wetting my shirt.

"Guys." Byder's voice cracks. "We're in the foyer."

"What?" I jerk to face him. We shouldn't be in the foyer. Ydum died. That means we failed. If Ydum is dead, we should all fail. A small cough catches my attention.

"Ydum!" I clamber out of Anarus's arms to move to him. His eyes are closed but he is grimacing. He's alive!

"Ow. Why does my chest hurt so bad?" Ydum says as he opens his eyes. He struggles to sit up and I help him, pulling him into my arms, holding him tight for one second before I start smacking his shoulders.

"You stupid, stupid god!" I yell at him, still crying. "You do not get to scare me like that ever again. Has no one ever taught you not to run through strange glowing lights before? You are so stupid, Ydum!" I hit him one more time then kiss him.

Ydum chuckles weakly. "Alright, beautiful. I'm all right." He pulls me into a hug. I squeeze him tightly then Anarus and Byder help him stand up and move over to the wall. Ydum looks weak, but otherwise unhurt by his time being dead.

"Man, you scared the shit outta me." Byder tells him.

"Yeah." Anarus glares at Ydum. "Don't do that shit. I should split your lip for terrifying me."

Once they sit him down, I claim a spot right next to him and clasp his hand in mine. I refuse to let Ydum out of my sight or touch again.

Drila sounds annoyed. "Jinx's team with the dramatic entrance again. Second place, five extra points for a temporary death."

Second place. Even with all of that, we came in second. I look around the foyer and see that Asteria and Wilros are already back. Damek and Iella appear quickly after us. Isis and Esnir come back next, fortunately in one piece this time.

Aretha is furious when she realizes that she and Zodum are back fifth. Wren and Kutar take a little longer, and we all shift uncomfortably waiting. But right behind them, before they can even fully move out of the way, Raven and Uesis return. We all wait, holding our breaths, but Drila doesn't say anything about the game being over. Eventually, Saffron and Velmos come back too.

Drila starts immediately telling us what place we're in. "Last place, Raven with two hundred and fifty points. Seventh, Wren with two hundred and forty-five. Sixth, Asteria with two hundred and twenty. Fifth, Damek with one hundred and ninety-five. Fourth, Isis with one hundred and eighty-five. Tied for second is Saffron and Jinx, with one hundred and sixty each. First place is now Aretha with one hundred and fifty points. Next game is animalism. See you all in a week." Drila pops away quickly.

"I don't think she likes her job anymore." Aretha says casually.

Damek responds. "That probably means we are doing ours right." He looks over at Ydum as we walk by, Ydum leaning on me heavily. "Dude, what happened to you? You look like death warmed over."

"About that." Ydum jokes and I give him a light tap on his stomach. "Oof. Still sore, Jinx. I actually was dead, for a bit." He smiles at Damek brightly as if this was an accomplishment and I roll my eyes.

"Dead for a little bit?" Damek laughs. "I have to hear that story." He glances at my scowl, then adds, "Later. I'll hear it later."

We make it into our room and I deposit Ydum onto the couch. I know Byder and Anarus are also sitting down, but I ignore them, and stand in front of Ydum. "Are you actually okay?"

"I'm fine, beautiful." Ydum tells me.

"Good." I say and move to sit on his lap, my legs straddling over his. I take his face into my hands and kiss him fervently. I suck his bottom lip into my mouth and bite it gently before letting him go and kissing along his jaw. The taut line feels like its back and I can't ignore it or the static anymore. I don't want to.

Ydum brings his arms around me, pulling out my hair ties and undoing my braid with his hands. "Shit, beautiful." His hands run down my sides and pull at the hem of my shirt as I kiss and nibble on his earlobe. I gasp as one of his hands travels under my shirt up to palm my breast. He takes advantage of my distraction to reclaim my mouth with his.

I move my hands to wrap my arms around him and pull him tighter to me.

"I want to taste every inch of you, Jinx." Ydum whispers in my ear before kissing my neck.

I shake my head, scrambling in an attempt to push him away so I can get off his lap, suddenly realizing myself. "No. You should rest."

He stills, leaning back to look at me. "Are you saying no because you don't want to or because you are worried about me?"

"I'm worried about you. You were dead, Ydum."

"Fuck that. I'm fine." As if to prove this, Ydum stands and grabs me, wrapping his hands under my ass as he lifts me up to hold me in his arms. "Yes or no, Jinx?"

"Gods, yes, Ydum." Ydum doesn't need to hear anything else. He carries me out of the sitting room to my room.

Once he kicks the door closed behind us, he sets me down to stand on my own. He pulls off his shirt and I see that his vine tattoos are overflowing up his left arm and across the front of his shoulder, spiraling tighter. I run my hands over them, intrigued how they respond to my touch, shivering and more leaves bursting from the vines.

"Strip for me, beautiful. I want to see you." He tells me as he pulls off his boots. I do as he says, only slightly self-conscious. When I am naked and he has only pants on, he gestures to the bed. "Lie down."

Again, I do as he says. I feel awkward and clumsy climbing onto the bed and lying down on it, but Ydum seems not to notice. He stares at me. "Shit, you're gorgeous." Ydum climbs onto the bed and lies down on my left, takes my hand in his and brings it up to his mouth, kissing my palm. Then, he kisses a trail up my arm to my shoulder. At my shoulder, he drops my left arm and grabs my right, kissing his way from my palm to shoulder again. I watch him curiously, enjoying but unsure what I should be doing.

This time, when he reaches my shoulder, he continues kissing a trail across my collarbone, then down. When he pulls one nipple into his mouth, sucking and biting, I gasp as the pleasure burns me down to my core. "Ydum!"

He looks up and smiles mischievously. "Patience, beautiful." He takes my other nipple into his mouth and sucks hard on it. I jolt from the sensation and can't help squirming. Wetness gathers between my thighs and I have a desperate need for friction.

Ydum only smiles more and continues his slow progress down my stomach touching and kissing me until he gets to my thighs. Then, he scoots down the bed, removes his pants, and stands between my legs. He leans over, taking my leg in his hands and kisses high on my thigh, making me gasp again. I wriggle in his grip. "Ydum, please."

"I told you." He kisses my knee. "I want to." He kisses my calf. "Taste every inch of you." He kisses my foot then lets go of my leg. He picks up my other foot, and kisses a trail back up to my thigh. I watch his progress, trying not to squirm more, every press of his hot lips to my skin searing me. When he gets to the juncture between my legs, I'm sure he is just going to move back up to my stomach, but he doesn't. He kisses right there, on my most sensitive spot. The feeling is such intense pleasure, I can't help but grip the blankets under me tightly as it shoots through me.

He doesn't let up. He sucks on my clit, and I moan. "Such a fucking beautiful noise. Do it again." He licks me and I moan again.

"Ydum, please." I beg him.

"This what you want?" He places his hands on either of my thighs and plunges his tongue inside me and before I can moan again, he moves his hand so that his thumb rubs over my clit. His thumb continues to rub in circles as his tongue moves inside me, making everything in me tense.

"Fuck, yes." I pant breathlessly, squeezing the fabric bunched in my fists tighter. Ydum alternates between licking and sucking, drawing his tongue between the folds of my skin and plunging it into me. He moves his mouth higher, removing his thumb to bite gently at my clit then resumes moving his mouth through the growing wetness of my need, his thumb working in tandem to make me breathless. The pleasure climbs so high, I feel as if I am about to explode. I tilt my hips to push myself into him. "Ydum. I need."

"Let me taste you come." He says, then he pushes harder with his thumb and sucks hard on my skin using his teeth and lips to rake over me.

"Oh, gods." I cry out as the pleasure takes over me. I tremble as the waves roll through me. I ride his face through my orgasm.

"Just one god right now, beautiful. Maybe later we can experiment with more than one." Ydum licks me and sucks my clit one more time, before moving away to kiss his way back up to my breasts. "You're fucking delicious, you know that?" He quickly sucks on one nipple, then the other, then moves to kiss my mouth.

I wrap my arms around his shoulders as we kiss. Ydum pushes my thighs wider with his knees and I feel him move his cock to press at my entrance.

"You ready, beautiful?" He asks, teasing me with the tip of his cock.

"Yes, Ydum!"

He pushes the head of himself inside me then pulls right back out. I groan in frustration. He does it again and desperation makes me arch against him. These edges of pleasure he is giving me is driving the need higher until I am trembling with anticipation.

"You want more?" He asks. I wrap my legs around him, pushing my heels into his ass to try to force him deeper and beg.

"Please." I rock my hips up to him and I feel his control break as he buries himself inside of me.

"Fuck, you feel good, Jinx." Ydum shudders and starts moving. I dig my nails into his back as my hips move to meet him, thrust for thrust. His teasing left me so desperate, I feel a second orgasm already building. It crashes over me and this time, it doesn't let me go, just builds again. I cry out and lock my feet together behind his back, pulling myself tighter to him.

Ydum increases his pace and reaches between us, his thumb rubbing circles on my clit as he moves. Everything in me fractures, and I can't breathe. I cry out again, but with no breath in me, the sound comes out strangled.

"Shit!" He cries out. Then, he leans over and kisses me again as he pushes even deeper in me, his release making him shudder in my arms. Again, just like with Byder and Anarus, there is something that snaps taut, that line of absolute awareness wrapping its tendrils around me as we both fight to breathe and chase the last ragged moments of ecstasy.

He keeps kissing me as we both come down, and when he pulls back, I smooth my hands over his chest, smiling as I see his tattoo of vines now covers his whole arm and chest to his stomach. I run my hand down, tracing them, fascinated by the moving tattoo and the green undertint to his skin. His eyes follow my hands.

Ydum moves off to the side and gathers me in his arms. "You're trembling, Jinx."

"I think." I'm looking at his chest, watching a leaf bloom over his right shoulder. My thoughts are scattered and all I can see is that new leaf. I kiss it gently. "Never mind, thinking's hard."

Ydum laughs and kisses the top of my head. "I should die more often if this is my reward."

I slap the leaf I just kissed and glare at him. "Don't you dare. Never be that foolish again. I thought you were gone." I shudder harder and Ydum pulls me tighter.

"No." He says firmly. "I'm never leaving you."

I move to sit up. "You said something and I, um, I'm not sure what you meant." I furrow my brow and focus still on that leaf.

"What did I say that has you looking that concerned?" Ydum sits up straighter as well, taking one of my hands in his.

"I said oh, gods, and you made a comment that we could experiment with more than one." I blush and look down at the blanket. "What did you mean?"

"Oh. That." Ydum takes a deep breath. "Well." He stops and seems to change his mind. "That's kind of a discussion we should probably have with everyone."

"Everyone?" I ask him. "Do you mean everyone, everyone?"

"The four of us everyone, Jinx." He holds back a laugh. "Brain still not firing right?"

I stand, acting indignant, but not really meaning it. "Don't make fun of me." I pick my shirt up and put it back on.

Ydum stands and grabs me by my waist. "Never. In fact, I will take it as a point of pride that you came so hard, you can't think straight." He kisses me again and I melt against him. "Fuck, yeah." He leans in to kiss me again, but then pulls back. "Wait. No. Talking to the others. That's what we're doing."

I push his shoulder playfully. "I'm not the only one who can't think straight." I grab my pants and pull them back on.

"Yeah," Ydum counters as he puts on clothes too, "the difference is I can't ever think straight around you."

"Right." I roll my eyes. "What does the Gods Games manual say about animalism?"

Ydum raises an eyebrow at me, confused at the change of topic. "Well, animalism can come in many forms. Most people think that it could be as simple as a familiar…" Ydum stops talking as I smile sweetly and bat my eyelashes at him.

"Can't ever think straight around me, huh?"

He licks his lips, smiling back at me as he opens the door to the room and walks out. "See, that's not fair. You used academic stuff to trick me."

Byder, hearing this from the couch, leans around to look at us coming out of the room. "I've heard of some weird kinks, but academic stuff? That's weird, even for you, Ydum." He points to the table where there is a plate of dinner saved for each of us.

We grab our plates and go to the couches. "Speaking of kinks, Jinx made a good point."

"I made no points. I asked a question and you said that was a discussion for everyone." I retort, settling into my seat with my food.

Anarus raises one eyebrow. "Talk of kinks reminds Ydum of a discussion we all need to have together? Why am I scared now?"

"What type of question did Jinx ask is what I want to know." Byder says.

My face is red. I know it is. I hide behind my plate of meatloaf.

"Guys, I'm actually being serious here." Ydum complains. "This is something every couple talks about, whether you think about the fact that you're doing it or not. But there are four of us, so it's more complicated, and." He takes a deep breath and looks at the ceiling for a moment then speaks in a rush. "Fine. I'm just, I'm just going to be bold here. I have not only ever been with females. Or just one on one. And I might be open to such a thing again. Just so you know. Just so we understand everyone's limits or issues."

I lower my plate and look at Ydum. I can tell he's feeling very exposed. And scared about how we'll react.

Byder reacts first. "I have never had such experiences. I've never had any desire to try anything like that. To be with other males. I can't say it ever crossed my mind. I'm not saying never, just I don't know how I would feel about it and, well, if it's something Jinx was open to, more than just one of us? I guess I'm saying that I might be willing to try, but no promises I would continue or want it again."

Byder and Ydum look at me and Anarus. Anarus's shadows are simmering, but not in an angry way. He seems more like there are feelings he's trying to hide from. He looks at me. He knows the most about the things that have happened to me in my past. He sees me struggling with this the same way he's struggling. He shakes his head, as if actively trying to dispel his shadows. He clenches his fist and speaks quietly. "Don't touch my ass. Just, don't. I'm probably on the side of wanting things more one on one, but I'm not saying no to anything else completely either. But the focus stays on her, not me."

I reach my hand out and take one of Anarus's hands in mine. At first, he seems like he will pull away, but then he sees the look on my face. I'm nervous. They are all looking at me now.

"You don't have to say more than you want to, Jinx." Byder says quietly. "This doesn't have to be a one and done type of conversation. I hope you will trust us with everything someday, but that day does not have to be today."

I look at each of them, but keep a tight grip on Anarus's hand. "I trust you. All of you. I just haven't talked with anyone but Anarus about this." When I find Anarus's eyes, he nods at me reassuringly. I take a deep breath and am brave like he was. "Anarus was my first time consensually. There are probably a lot of things I'll be uncomfortable with, at first at least. I know I won't," I train my eyes on Anarus, using him for strength, "I can't do anything beyond kissing with my mouth. It's just, I can't, not with."

My words stutter and it's hard to breathe. Until Anarus squeezes my hand and then I focus on him again as he mouths silently, "You're okay." I breathe deeply.

Byder's face is tight, a muscle in his jaw twitching. "Consensually. Is that Jacob? The touching thing? The trapped thing?"

I blink away tears that threaten my eyes and nod. "And the drinking."

Byder swears under his breath. "Shit. I am such an asshole."

"No. Jacob and his friends were assholes." I tell him. "You didn't know."

Ydum's nostrils flare wide. "And his friends? Wait, no. You don't have to answer that, Jinx. Why do I have the intense urge to take a field trip to Greenbriar? Damn, this cave magic is fucking strong."

"Desire to protect, yeah, a little strong." Anarus bites out. His shadows are not well controlled again, but he keeps his eyes on me. "One day, Ydum. I'm coming too. Fucking High Priest's son will eat my knuckles."

"Thank you, Jinx, for trusting us with this." Byder says, a lot calmer. "Ydum was right. This was definitely a conversation we needed to have. Now I know better how to take care of you so you always feel safe with us."

Anarus squeezes my hand. I turn to him. "You trusted us too. I know that was hard. Ydum, too." I turn to Ydum, and see he's sparing glances at Byder, nervously.

"Dude, if you keep looking at me weird because you think I'm going to freak out because we spent weeks sharing that bed, and you just told us you also like guys, you're sorely mistaken." Byder finally says. "I saw you and Amos when we were sixteen. You guys were not as sneaky as you thought you were. I knew already, man. And you were a perfect gentleman every night." Byder flutters his eyelashes at Ydum, and Ydum shoves him back, smiling with relief.

"Ydum, even I knew that already." Anarus says. "Why do you think I slept out here, even when Byder slept in Jinx's room? My comfort level with things, not a trusting you thing, just so you know. But yeah, Jinx was the only one who didn't know."

Ydum doesn't look at me. "And are you okay with it, Jinx?"

I analyze my feelings for a moment. I know that I don't care about who other people are with in a general sense, but want to make sure I know what I feel when it comes to the four of us. "You liking males and females doesn't matter to me, Ydum. I think. I think the four of us are a closed deal, in my mind we should be. Just like I wouldn't be with anyone else, male or female, I expect the same of you three. If you and Byder were to sneak off at some point? No biggie to me, I think, the same way it didn't bother you when it was me and Byder."

"Agreed. This is just the four of us." Ydum says and Byder and Anarus nod in agreement. Ydum sits up straight again. "Well, this has been a nice soul-bearing experiment. Unless someone else has something they think has to be said tonight, I think I'm ready to talk about literally anything else."

I finish eating my food and now feel exhausted. Anarus is still holding my hand but my grip is loose, relaxed, and I lean back on the couch to rest my eyes.

Byder clears his throat and I open my eyes again. He has that little black bag in his hand. "I'm not sure..." He pauses, looking down at the kit. "Would that classify as a hunt do you think?"

Ydum tilts his head. "You caught the same rabbit twice. I would say that is definitely a hunt."

"I agree." Anarus says, his tone serious. "A hard hunt, at that."

Sitting, Byder hands the bag to Ydum, but I stop him. "Is there a reason you are having Ydum do it?"

"No. I just know he knows how." Byder runs a hand through his hair, messing it up, then glances at me. "Do you want to, maybe, do it?"

"Will you tell me how?" I'm looking at Byder but Ydum answers.

"There's nothing magical about it. Just a poke and stick." He takes the bag from Byder and sets out the supplies. A small bottle of what I think is ink, a cloth, and a small needle. "Wipe his arm down with the cloth. Then, holding the skin taut with one hand, dip the needle in the ink. Poke the skin where you want the line to make a dot. You'll have to keep the dots very close together to make a complete line. Don't go too deep or it will blur, nor too shallow or it will fade. You'll want to re-dip the needle every five pokes or so."

Suddenly, I'm nervous. This is a big deal to Byder, I can tell. What if I do it wrong? I look up at Byder, about to suggest maybe I should just let Ydum do it. The line he did looks perfectly made. But Byder guesses what I'm going to say and shakes his head.

"My father doesn't have a line done by his witch. No hunt god I know has one done by theirs. I would take a badly done line by you as an honor, not a mistake."

Steeling myself, I take a deep breath and start doing as Ydum directed. He stays close, giving me instructions and helping me keep Byder's arm in proper position. I know I go too deep occasionally and the pokes bleed. A few times, Ydum makes me redo a poke because it wasn't deep enough. Byder sits silently, his forearm braced on me knee the whole time. Anarus watches but stays silent as well.

Eventually, I finish the circle and Ydum examines it as he cleans the excess ink away. I yawn, my jaw popping as my exhaustion settles on me again.

Byder stands up once Ydum is done. "That was perfect, baby girl. Thank you. But we all slept out here yesterday and I am far too big to sleep comfortably on this couch. Plus, you look like you're already half asleep. Ydum, take our girl to bed. I'm headed there too." He walks off to the other bedroom, yawning and looking over his new tattoo line.

"Come on, beautiful." Ydum comes over to me and pulls on my hand to stand me up but I look at Anarus for a moment, who just nods. "Kiss Ani good night and let's get some rest."

When I waver, Ydum juts his chin out at Anarus with a smile. So, I do as Ydum said and lean over, giving Anarus a quick kiss.

"Good night, little human." Anarus says, then gently pushes me to Ydum. Ydum takes the hand Anarus let go of and leads me to the bedroom, where I fall asleep tracing ivy vines on Ydum's chest.

Chapter Eleven

"I ABSOLUTELY DO NOT snore!" My morning coffee is not working enough yet for the three against one argument.

"You do." Anarus sips his coffee.

"Mhmm." Byder hums at me.

"It's cute." Ydum says as he shifts his arm that's slung around me on the couch.

"You are all awful, despicable males. I hate you all." I drink down the last dredges of my coffee and move to put the mug on the table so it can be cleaned up with the rest of the breakfast. "New rule. No one tells Jinx she snores or they sleep in the foyer."

All three of them laugh. All three of them. They are all also shirtless. Again.

Ydum breaks us away from the teasing Jinx part of our morning. "Next game, animalism."

"You started to tell me about it yesterday, Ydum, when I was teasing you, but you didn't get far. What is the animalism game?" I go back to where I was sitting and Ydum immediately drapes his arm along the back of the couch, letting his hand hang down to play with my braid. He's almost constantly doing little touches like that now. Nothing too much, just a slight letting me know he's there, as if he's making up for lost time, or just as keen to remind me he's here and alive as I am to remember it. I don't think the horror of the sight of his body crumpled on the ground will ever leave me.

Ydum straightens, becoming the academic. "Animalism magic can take a bunch of forms. Familiars is a well-known one, but isn't something the games do. The idea that a spirit inhabits an animal and guides a witch is more legend than known magical fact. Many people assign the idea of being a familiar to their pets, but it's as proven as the cat distribution system."

"Cat distribution system?" Anarus scoffs. "What's that?"

I laugh. Of course, as an orphan, Anarus has probably never had a pet of his own so doesn't know about this. "The idea that there's some cosmic force out there distributing pet cats to those in need. It's really said more in jest than anything else, but it comes from the fact that most people don't actually plan to have a pet cat. Rather, a cat will just randomly show up and decide you are its human, or god I guess, and move into your home, so you just start taking care of it."

Anarus makes an appreciative face, like that makes more sense than it doesn't.

"Anyway," Ydum draws out that word, like he's annoyed by the distraction, but I know he isn't really because he's still smiling. "While familiars are not so proven, so not a part of the games, the idea of speaking with an animal spirit is. Metamorphosis, changing an animal into a human or a different animal, or a human into an animal, is also big. There are many years that this is part of the animalism game. So is conjuring actual animals and projection, the idea that every human spirit has an animal associated with it and they can project that animal spirit outside of themselves or take on the animalistic nature without actually morphing into it."

"You said human. Was that purposeful or a slip of the tongue between the word human and people?" I ask.

Ydum smiles at me. "That's not a slip of the tongue most gods make, Jinx. I said human and meant it. A lot of different gods can change into animals as part of their power, even before gaining their mantles, but they do not become the animal. The animal shape is just part of their godhood. It's not so much metamorphosis or projection but just one part of who they are. The magic part is doing it with a human who is a type of animal, according to gods. Honestly, the way we're taught, there's no difference between a dog or a bear or a human, when it comes to what is an animal. Humans are just an animal created by the gods that we happen to be able to actually talk to, mate with, whatever. A god changing the dog into a bear is the same exercise of power that changing the human into the bear is."

I furrow my brow at that. We're just animals to the gods? Nothing more? Nothing different? "If humans are animals, then what are gods?'

Byder shifts in his seat uncomfortably. "Gods are just gods. Gods made humans, but nothing made the original gods. They just are. But you need to understand Jinx, not all gods feel that way. Many gods, my parents and me included, think that the idea that humans are just really smart animals is wrong. Humans are more of something else, a step in between animals and gods."

I turn to Ydum. "What do you think?"

Ydum's mouth twitches. "My parents taught me the animal thought, but honestly, I think that it's a bad comparison. There are gods, humans, and animals. Three separate classifications. Not a spectrum like Byder seems to think, but their own thing. Humans are no more animals than gods are."

I turn to Anarus, and he doesn't even let me ask before answering. "My thoughts are definitely different. Who made the gods? The originals say they don't just exist, but that they also made the humans and the rest of the world. I say that's bullshit. If humans are animals, so are the gods. Whatever we gods are, I think humans are the same thing. Maybe the gods made the humans, maybe not, but something made the original gods. They didn't just always exist. I think the idea of humans as animals is just a lie used as a form of control. Either we're all animals, or none of us are."

Ydum tilts his head to the side. "That's an interesting take, Anarus. What about the history we learned in school?"

"History?" Anarus snorts and leans back, draping his arm casually along the back of the couch. "You mean stories with no proof? Who's to say if it actually happened the way the originals are telling us it did? For all we can prove, the humans were here first and made the original gods and, well, all the original humans are dead so who's there but the original gods to say which way is the truth?"

Ydum looks down at the floor, his face showing confusion. He's not outright dismissing Anarus's theory, but trying to assimilate it into the things he thought he knew. When he finally does speak, he does so quietly and tentatively. "You're right. They never provided proof, just said it is and expected us to accept it. But if the original gods are lying, then all of this, the way Veirveil works, these games, everything is so much worse than we thought. This would all be just one type of being holding dominion over another when they have no right to. It's slavery, not our right to rule as gods."

"What's the difference between a god and a human?" Anarus leans forward again, watching Ydum, challenging him. He's forcing Ydum to face the dissonance between what he was taught and what Anarus thinks. "Think on that, really think on it, and see if any of this actually makes sense."

"Gods have different magic than humans. We have our powers and they just have basic magic. Beyond that, life span. Gods are immortal. We age but only for so long. We can die by injury but otherwise, we can live infinitely long lives." Byder counters.

"Is it really different, though?" I ask him back, leaning forward to debate him the way Anarus is debating with Ydum. I like that the two of them aren't dismissing our thoughts. Ydum and Byder aren't against us, fighting us, but engaging, debating, and seem willing to change their minds if they realize they are wrong. "Sure, Ydum can make dirt from thin air to grow the rosebud, but how different is that really than a beginning magic witch? When you guys explained beginning magic versus end magic to me, I really struggled to find the difference between your powers and beginning magic. If you think of the magic as a progression, from first thought to having exactly what you need completed, the gods' powers all fit nicely on that progression, just a step before beginning magic. And isn't the immortality just a form of magic too? If they can give it to human witches for being successful in the games, then it really isn't a god thing but a magic thing."

Byder opens his mouth to say something, thinks, then closes it again. "There's no difference. When you explain it that way, Jinx, there is no difference.

Not any that weren't made up and are controlled by the original gods. Everything else can be changed. We know it can because that's what the witches who succeed at the games get. We are all just a spectrum of people from the non-magical humans who fled the continent to gods with witches falling somewhere in between."

Anarus holds up his coffee mug in a mock salute. "Welcome to my point, Byder."

When the silence of my gods thinking stretches on, I put my hand on Ydum's knee. "Animalism game?"

He startles out of his reverie and shakes his head. "Yes. Animalism game. Any of these things can be the goal of the game this time, projection, metamorphosis, conjuring, or speaking with an animal. I think a trip to look at the paintings might give us something of a clue."

Agreeing, we all head out to the hallway. I stop them to ask if they are putting on shirts first, and Anarus just glares at me. "Why?"

We are one of the first groups in the hallway, looking at the paintings, but as we wander, the other groups all trickle out too. The only male with a shirt on at all is Damek. Wow. Never mind, I guess I won't ask about their shirts anymore. All of the eight paintings are different, and they each show an animal. There's a painting of a dog, a cat, a bear, a mouse, a deer, a swan, a wolf, and a horse.

Wilros is standing, his hands on his hips in front of the painting of the dog. "Well, this is easy to figure out."

Zodum comes to stand next to Wilros. "Yeah?"

Wilros gestures up and down the hallway. "We have to pick an animal and do something with it. Talk to it, make our human into it, project it, something, but we have to pick the animal we want to work with for the game."

"How do we choose?" I ask.

Wilros turns to face me and considers something for a moment. "Fuck it, we're all already helping each other more than the games ever wanted. Probably whatever animal the human is most comfortable with, Jinx. I mean, if Asteria is terrified of wolves, we wouldn't want that one but would want the swan if she loves birds."

Makes complete sense to me. With eight of us, my family didn't have pets, so my comfort level with animals is low, but not nothing. I wander around looking at the different paintings. I try to think like Wilros said, see if any of them call out to me, but nothing really does.

"Hey, beautiful." Ydum strolls up behind me as I look at the swan. "You like this one?"

"Not particularly." I tell him, sliding my hand into his. "No more than any of the others. Just looking at them all."

"Wanna head back to the room?" Ydum looks down at me, brushing his fingers through my hair. There's a heat in his eyes that makes my mouth go dry. I only nod. Ydum looks back up and over the throng of people in the hallway. He lets out a quick whistle. Everyone looks up, but when they see it's only Ydum, everyone but Anarus and Byder go back to what they were doing.

The four of us go back to our room and Ydum is talking before the door even shuts all the way. "I want to try something different, Jinx. Instead of the fight over the rosebud, I want to see if we can figure out if any of the animals has a special meaning for you."

He sits on the floor the way we always have for the rosebud and I join him.

"Do any of the animals speak to you, call to you somehow, or are any of them an absolute no for you?" Byder asks, leaning back on the couch arm near us.

I shake my head as I settle on the floor facing Ydum. "I mean, the bear and wolf are intimidating, but I think that is only if we have to control one. They are the most dangerous."

Anarus snorts softly. "You should see a swan who isn't happy with you." He shudders. "Nasty things."

Ydum purses his lips. "That's a thought, too. Any of the animals a no go for you two?" He looks at Anarus and Byder. "I'm fine with all of them."

Byder taps his chest. "Hunt god. I'm good with the prey animals. The major predators too. I think the only one I would feel odd with is the mouse. But that's only odd since I wouldn't know what to do with it."

"No swan, please." Anarus shudders again. "Home when I was five had a swan in the pond out back. That stupid thing bit me, often."

Ydum nods. "Okay, swan's out. Probably mouse, bear, and wolf too. Jinx, I want you to meditate on the animals left. Dog, cat, deer, horse. Think about them and try to call them to your mind."

I settle myself again, rolling my shoulders to release tension, and close my eyes. I take slow, deep breaths and think about a dog, cat, deer and horse, trying to clear my mind of anything else. I find my peace easily, but find focusing on the animals hard. I shift again and keep trying. My mind is blank, but it's just blank.

"Struggling?" Ydum asks. When I nod, he takes my hands in his. "Let me try something. Listen to my words and form the picture in your mind as I talk."

"Okay." I tell him, then shift once more so our hands in each other's is more comfortably resting on my knees.

Ydum speaks quietly, his voice clear but soft. "You are standing in a field of tall grass. Far away in the distance, you see trees. Everything is green and the air is warm with the sweet smell of summer. The sun is bright in a cloudless sky. Your feet are bare and you can wiggle your toes in the cool, moist earth. Do you feel the dirt, Jinx?"

I nod. The image is clear in my mind, clearer than it usually is when I do something like this by myself. I think Ydum is helping with his power.

He keeps talking. "You can hear a stream somewhere gurgling over stones. Small bugs chirp around you. A butterfly flies past. You watch it for a moment but it floats away on the gentle breeze. You're comfortable and relaxed, safe and happy. Listen closely. Can you hear a dog barking?"

I listen in my mind. I can hear the different bugs making noises around me, but no dog comes. "No?" I strain to make my mind hear a dog.

"Don't try to make it there, Jinx." Ydum tells me. "If it is, it is. If not, we move on. Can you hear the dog?"

"No." I say more confidently, understanding now.

"Okay, center yourself again in the field. Do you hear a cat meowing anywhere?"

I focus on the dirt between my toes and the sunshine on my face. There's no cat anywhere that I can tell.

"What about a horse nickering?"

I wait, giving myself time to feel it. "No."

"Okay," Ydum seems to shift his hands without letting go of me. "Look to the trees. Are there any deer there?"

I look into the distance in front of me. Shadows move in the trees. I can't make out what they are, but there's something there. "Maybe. I can't tell."

"What are you seeing, Jinx? Tell me."

"Shadows." I say. "Only shadows moving in the trees. Something but I'm not sure what."

"Okay. Try to call the shadows to you." I try. But I'm not sure how to call a shadow of an animal to me when I don't know what it is. But, Ydum had been talking about the deer, so I try that. I don't know what noise a deer makes, so I just talk in my head.

Come out, little deer. Can you come to me? I want to see how pretty you are. Something starts to step out of the woods, but it isn't the deer I called. Come out, whatever you are. Come out and let me see you. A large wolf with grey and black fur steps into the sunshine and startles me as it shakes out its fur. My eyes pop open as I pull back from Ydum with a gasp.

"What came out of the woods, Jinx?" Ydum asks.

"A wolf. A huge wolf." I swallow hard. "I called for a deer but a wolf came instead."

Byder chuckles from his spot leaning on the couch. "Well, that was effective. Now we know which painting to pick."

I frown at him. "But I said no to the wolf."

"And your magic said yes." Ydum counters. "Which one should we follow? Your magic or your mind?"

I twist my mouth to one side then the other. Ydum has a point. I may not feel comfortable with the wolf, but it was so real in my mind it had to be my magic. "What if someone else gets wolf too? There was only one of each animal."

Anarus answers from his spot relaxing on the couch. "Unless it's Aretha or Saffron, doesn't matter to us. But if you're concerned, talk to the other humans. We have all shared more than the games wanted us to, so maybe you guys can negotiate the animals and have it planned out who gets what beforehand."

I turn to look at Anarus, but the table catches my eye. Lunch is already spread out on it. "Why is lunch here so early?"

Byder chuckles at me again. "Well, you've been meditating with Ydum for hours. It's about time lunch got here."

"Hours?" I stare at Ydum then Byder. "It felt like a few minutes."

Ydum nods. "Hours. About three."

"I took a nap." Anarus says from the couch.

Ydum hums at that. "I think that may have actually been Jinx, Ani. I think your bond is still doing something through her emotion magic. Her peace made you sleep again."

"You said that was our stronger bond before. But now I'm bonded with all three of you. Did it affect you two?" I look at Byder who is making several plates of food, putting different sandwiches on each plate.

He comes over and sets a plate with a nut paste and strawberry jam sandwich and carrot sticks next to me. Then, he sets a plate with a chicken salad sandwich and celery stick next to Ydum. He heads back to the table as he answers me. "Not particularly. I felt your peace. Like, I knew you were safe and that made me feel comfortable and relaxed, like I didn't have to do anything for you right now." He grabs two more plates, both with a meat and cheese sandwiches, one with no veggies and another one with cucumber slices and walks over to Anarus, handing him the plate with no veggies. He sets his plate down then goes back to the table one more time, grabbing four cups. He brings me a cold tea and Ydum and Anarus a juice, leaving one juice for himself.

Byder has everyone's lunch preferences memorized and just served us all. I watch him with a new appreciation.

Ydum answers me as I watch Byder. "Me too. Not so much feeling your peace, but just knowing you're okay and I can relax."

"But Anarus falls asleep when I purposefully make peace in my meditation. Why?"

"I have thoughts, but no answers." Ydum tells me.

I turn to him. "What thoughts?"

"Your magic is not quite right." Ydum grabs a celery stick and waves it around almost unconsciously. "Anarus's power is strange for gods as well. His shadows acting like they do, being such an outward demonstration of his power, should be something that only happens after he gets his mantle. But as far as I know, he's been that way since birth. Maybe both of you are broken in the same way."

I nibble a carrot. "But you have an outward demonstration of your power too, Ydum. Your vine tattoos."

"Not the same." He finally eats the celery. "My vines developed slowly over time as I learned control of my power. I was not born with them, and I won't be able to physically use them, control them, until I have my mantle. Then, I may even be able to pull them out of my skin and make real vines from them."

"But Anarus can use his shadows now. Move them, control them, make them outward manifestations." Byder adds. "He can even separate them from himself completely."

"That one's hard though." Anarus remarks. "I told you, Jinx. I was moved around so much because my shadows made the other gods nervous. This is why. I shouldn't have them yet, not like this."

"So, you two," I look at Ydum then Byder, "only feel a connection to me where you can tell my emotions, but Anarus feels the full effect of them?" When they all nod, a thought strikes me that makes me blush. "Anarus, can you tell when I, can you feel when I?"

He laughs. "Can I feel when you orgasm? No."

"Thank fuck." I say under my breath.

"I second that." Byder swears. "Shit. Did not even think of that until just now."

Ydum smiles. "I didn't think it would work like that, but glad to know formally."

"It only seems to be when you meditate that I get the full weight of what you are projecting, Jinx." Anarus continues. "Otherwise, I feel the same as Byder and Ydum. I know if you are stressed or worried or happy, and feel motivated to do something to fix a problem or relaxed when you are okay."

"Why do you guys feel that but I don't about you? Is that a cave magic thing only for the gods?"

"I think," Ydum offers slowly, looking at me from the corner of his eyes, "that if you thought about it, you'd feel it too, Jinx. But there are three of us and your own emotions in there. We just have ourselves and you. If it isn't my emotion, it must be yours. It's not nearly as confusing for us as it would be for you."

I try to focus on each of them and determine if I can feel their emotions, but all I feel as I look at them is desire. Desire strong enough to make my throat dry and start a small fire deep in me. I blush under it, wondering why I'm feeling this way so much.

Byder laughs again. "I think all three of us are probably feeling the same thing and Jinx is blushing from it."

It's them, not me. They are all three feeling desire for me, and it felt like it was my own. I try to push it away and talk. It takes a couple of tries for my voice not to come out husky. "That, that's intense."

Ydum smiles. "It's not as bad for us. You felt four people's desire all at once. I only feel yours and mine."

"That is not fair." I mutter.

"Wait until we all feel different things. Then, you're in for it, I'd bet. Try to tease out which one of us is pissed off and which one is happy and what you actually feel yourself. That'll be the real test." Byder takes a bite of his sandwich as he holds back a chuckle because I glared at him playfully for that comment.

Anarus is sitting up on the couch, an odd expression on his face. I struggle up from the floor. After sitting so long without moving, pins and needles run up and down my legs as I move. Ydum stands easily and helps me up. Once I am steady on my feet, I go sit next to Anarus. "What are you thinking?"

"Can I try something?" He asks me.

"Yeah. What?" At my agreement, Anarus turns to me. I turn to face him how he did me and he takes my hands into his.

"Move my shadows?"

"I don't know how to."

"The same way you called the wolf." He tells me. "Concentrate on them and need them to do something, come to you, hide in me, something."

I close my eyes and focus again. I can feel Anarus's shadows, the coolness floating just above the warmth of his skin where he's holding my hands. Can I borrow you for a moment? I ask them. Just a moment. I feel resistance. It almost feels like Anarus is pulling his hands away from mine, but at the same time, I can tell he hasn't physically moved at all. I let go of one of his hands and move it to rest on his chest. Please? Just for a moment, then you can go right back. I have no need except curiosity, but can you please come to me? I feel a cold tickle on my skin.

"Fuck." Byder whispers and I open my eyes. Anarus is as clear of shadows as I have ever seen him. They are still there, at the edges of my vision, but his face is visible in a way I have hardly ever seen.

"That should definitely not be able to happen." Ydum intones.

"What?" I turn to Ydum and realize the shadows that were on the edges of my vision are still there. "Shit, they're on me, aren't they?"

Ydum nods. "And not on Ani."

"This is the strangest sensation." Anarus says. "I can't even feel them. I didn't know what not feeling them felt like."

Ydum is pacing thoughtfully, one hand scratching his chin. "Jinx, hold the shadows. Ani, can you still command them? Even though they are on Jinx?"

Anarus closes his eyes, and I feel something prickle at my skin. I can't help but giggle as the sensation moves across me as if Anarus had tickled me. I close my eyes and see myself in my mind. I'm seeing myself through Anarus's shadows that he's controlling even though they are with me.

"Can you control them, Jinx?" Ydum asks.

The tickling sensation goes away, as well as the vision of myself, as Anarus stops controlling the shadows. I keep my eyes closed and try to ask the shadows to look at Anarus. Suddenly, I feel warmer and almost empty. I open my eyes again and all the shadows are back with Anarus. I shake my head. "Maybe if I hadn't thought of Anarus, it would have worked better."

"This is big." Byder says from his spot leaning against the couch. "This is really huge. Anarus's power should not be creating shadows yet, and even if it was, you should not be able to control his power like that, Jinx. Can you do the same thing with Ydum's vines?"

I let go of Anarus's hands and stand to move over to Ydum. As soon as I do, the world spins and I fall to the floor. All three gods dart to me, hands helping me up.

"Woah, there. You good, Jinx?" Byder asks as he steadies me.

I shake my head to clear it. "Just got dizzy for a second."

Ydum pulls me over to sit on the couch next to him. "Too much power, I think. You're not designed to handle a god's power like that. Maybe we shouldn't try mine right now."

"No." I put a hand on Ydum's leg. "I'm fine now. I want to try it. This is important. I feel like it's really important."

Ydum doesn't seem sure, but he holds out his arm anyway. "Okay. Try to make them move. I have less control over them than Anarus. It might be harder."

I place my hand on Ydum's shoulder where the vines are bunched together. Can you come to me? I just need to borrow you for a moment for an experiment. I will give you right back.

Nothing happens. I keep trying. Just a little leaf? Please? Can you grow? Or shrink for me? Move at all?

"Nothing's happening." I slouch, frustrated.

Ydum has his thoughtful, academic look. "There could be so many explanations for that. My vines aren't external like Anarus's shadows yet. You may be too tired right now. It may be something with your magic, like it's closer linked to Ani's. We haven't been as connected for as long. Many possible explanations."

"I think we should just tuck this in the back of our minds as another puzzle piece in the Jinx's magic is weird file, and move on." Byder declares. "She called a wolf in her meditation. I would have said that, with the game this week animalism, I am the best god if she's limited to only one of us, but I think I'm going to change my mind. All the possibilities require an external manifestation of some kind. Anarus would be better with that since he's the only one who has experience with it."

Ydum agrees. "And Anarus should take over meditation and magic practice."

"Sounds logical." Anarus wavers. "If you're okay with that, Jinx."

I shrug. "If it sounds right to Ydum, then it's fine by me."

"We have a plan much easier than we ever have." Byder smiles broadly. "We know what painting, what to work with Jinx on, and which god if she has to choose."

"And with that out of the way," Ydum says with a mischievous glint in his eyes, "do you know what you need to do now, beautiful?"

I groan. "Run?"

"Run."

I glare at Ydum. "I hate you."

Our personal group workout and the after dinner fight club continues like they always have. I feel like I'm getting better at the physical things. Anarus isn't helping me with the planks anymore and I've graduated to actual attempts at pushups. And Ydum doesn't correct me near as much in my running technique. I'm still out of breath and sweaty far sooner than any of them are and I can't win in a race against them, but that's to be expected. They've been doing this for years and I've only been doing it for weeks.

The fight club with the other teams is going well. Oddly, Ydum seems to be leading them more than Esnir is, even though Esnir is the war god. I try to ask about that as we go back to our room but Ydum doesn't answer. He just tells me that Esnir will take over more when it comes to the actual fighting rather than just learning to move.

The next morning, after breakfast, Anarus sits where Ydum usually does when we work on the rosebud meditation. When I take my spot, he tells me, "Rebuild the scene Ydum had you construct yesterday. Do you need him to walk you through it again?"

I shake my head and close my eyes, finding my peace and rebuild the scene. Tall grass, sunny summer day, trees in the grass, dirt under my toes, bugs chirping. I find it easily.

"Call for the wolf." Anarus instructs me. "You know who it is now, and where it comes from. Call for it." _____

I need to see the wolf again. Can you come out of the trees, please? I look at the trees and see the shadow moving. Because I know it's a wolf now, I wonder how I ever mistook it for anything else. Come here, please. Come see me.

The large gray and black wolf steps into the sunlight in the field and shakes out its fur. It looks right at me. I try not to be scared of it and notice more details. Its eyes are yellow and it has a black nose. It has short ears that are standing up, alert. Its fur looks like it might be soft under my fingers.

I hear Anarus's voice, but keep my real eyes closed so I can keep my internal eyes on the wolf. "Start small. Can you get the wolf to come close enough to touch it?"

Can you come closer? I ask it.

The wolf takes a tentative step towards me, ducking its head as it watches me.

I promise I won't hurt you. Please, a little closer?

It takes a few more steps, then stops again. I move a step or two towards the wolf, slowly so I don't scare it away. Step by step, I move closer, then the wolf does. Soon, we are close enough to see each other fully. Without thinking about why, I sit down in the grass cross-legged and keep still, watching the wolf the whole time. The wolf, in response, stretches its neck and sniffs the air around me. Timidly, I hold up one hand. I don't touch the wolf, but let the wolf approach my hand.

The wolf steps close enough for me to touch. It ducks its head under my hand and slowly lifts up until my hand grazes its neck. With that touch initiated by the wolf, I bury my fingers in its fur. The top fur is coarse, but under that is another layer that's as soft as I thought it would be. I scratch its neck and the wolf turns into my hand. Staring into the wolf's eyes, I realize there is knowledge there. Knowledge it's giving me.

"Her name is Kinshra and she's really soft." I say out loud.

"Is she talking to you?" Anarus asks.

"No." I say. "She's letting me pet her, but I just know. I don't know how, but I know."

I feel Anarus nod. "Trust that. However she chooses to communicate with you, go with that. Share with her too."

My name is Jinx, I tell the wolf with my eyes. But she already knew that. She knows Anarus too.

Kinshra turns suddenly and looks back to the woods. Do you need to go? The wolf turns and bounds away, back to the woods.

I open my eyes and look at Anarus. "That felt so real."

"It was real." He tells me. "Not physical, but still real."

"She said she already knows you, Anarus."

Ydum crouches down next to me. "Wait, so you touched the wolf and talked to her?"

"Not talked so much, but it was like, I looked in her eyes and knew what she wanted to say." I look at Ydum and his mouth is hanging open. He looks back at Byder who is leaning against the couch like normal.

Byder shrugs. "I dunno, man. That's beyond me."

"What?" I ask, looking between the two of them. "What is it?"

"You just did in one morning what most people take years to do." Anarus tells me. "I would highly doubt that any other witch here could do that yet, even if they have known an animalistic connection for a long time."

Ydum tilts his head, thoughtfully. "Then again, you made it rain in a week. I'm not sure we should be so surprised. It seems like, anytime Jinx needs her magic to do something, she just asks for it and whatever it is just does what she asks. That's not how end magic should work, but Drila already told us your end magic isn't really end magic."

Byder comes to sit by us as well. "The more you trust you can do a thing, the quicker you are at doing it. And a point we should not gloss over, the wolf knows Anarus. That's interesting."

"Part of me just thinks I made it up." I rub my forehead. "Ydum made up the field. He gave me that. How do we know that the wolf wasn't just my imagination?"

Anarus pushes me on this point. "Does it feel like your imagination, Jinx? When you don't doubt yourself, and believe that it could be your magic, does it feel like you made it up?"

I take a deep breath. "No. How would I know that a wolf coat is coarse on the top but soft when I dig my fingers deeper in it? The little details all make it feel real."

"Then, trust that." Ydum tells me. "But I wouldn't exactly broadcast to the other teams you can do this. I know we're all working together more than normal, but like Anarus said, you doing this much this fast? We're still in a competition. They don't need to know."

On the third day, after building the field and coaxing Kinshra out of the woods, which is much easier this time, she lies down at my feet, allowing me to stroke her fur. Where did you go yesterday? I ask her.

The alpha was calling her back. She has to go when he calls. She's young, not a pup but still too young to have any pups herself. She's curious where I go when I leave too.

I try to figure out how to explain it to her. That this is all in my mind and I don't go anywhere. Before I can, she lets me know that it's the same for her. It's the last day of September, not summer anymore. She sees this all in her head. Part of her knows that she's curled in the dirt near her pack, probably asleep. But that when I need her, I call and she comes.

I'm meditating, I tell Kinshra. I'm purposely doing this to learn more about how to connect with her. I ask her if there's a better time to do this for her, and she tells me no. That right now, the later morning, is perfect. She and the pack hunt later in the evening, twilight and dusk, and sometimes hunt or move around during dawn, but by the time I come every day, she's usually resting.

Kinshra asks why I want to learn this, and I give her the vaguest ideas of a competition about magic. Anarus, Ydum, Byder and I are a team, competing together, and that in four more days, we'll have to do something with her and magic to win the game for this week.

Kinshra laughs, or it feels like she laughs. Why didn't I just tell her that?

175

What will we need her to do? And will Anarus be there too? She wants to actually meet him. He smells good on me, with the darkness all over him, and she's curious what he looks like.

I tell her I don't know exactly what we'll have to do for the game, and won't until I'm in it. But, yes, Anarus will be there, maybe Ydum and Byder too.

Kinshra stands then, and stretches very much like I have seen dogs stretch, then tells me that the alpha needs her again. I open my eyes and look at Anarus, who's watching me curiously.

"You were smiling a whole lot, little human."

"Kinshra's sweet. And she wants to meet you, Anarus." I tell him the whole conversation, forcing myself not to blush about the wolf saying he smells good on me.

"A whole fucking conversation with the wolf, who's sitting at your feet letting you pet her?" Byder shakes his head while making everyone's lunch plates. "Freaking ridiculous, Jinx. Absolutely ridiculously amazing."

The next day, Anarus tells me he wants to try something. He holds my hand as I find the field and Kinshra. Once the wolf and I are settled, he has me squeeze his hand.

I feel Anarus move his hands to cup my face. "Let me see you, Kinshra."

In my mind, Kinshra perks her head up, asking me what's happening. I tell her that Anarus is trying something. She wants to know if she has to do anything.

Without opening my eyes or breaking my concentration, I ask Anarus. "Kinshra wants to know if you need her to do anything."

"Did you tell her what I was doing?"

I shake my head. "Not until after she felt it and wanted to know what was going on."

Anarus hums. "Can you ask her to look at you if she isn't already, and both of you concentrate on understanding each other, being one with each other?"

I let Kinshra know what he said and she stands, shaking out her fur again. She turns and faces me, and we look into each other's eyes. I know that, without meaning to, I opened my eyes in the real world, the ones looking at Anarus, but I can only still see Kinshra.

I smile. "She likes your tattoo."

"Fuck." Byder breathes and my concentration breaks.

I shake my head to clear it and glare at Byder. I hope that the wolf isn't upset I just left her without saying anything, but I want to know why Byder spoke before I try to call her back. "Why did you interrupt me?"

"Sorry." He says repentantly. "But your eyes were yellow."

"What?" I gulp.

Anarus interrupts my minor freak out that my eyes turned yellow. "Did you tell Kinshra about my tattoo?"

"No." I look down at his chest. Anarus is actually wearing a shirt today. "How did she see that?"

"The better question is why did Anarus get that tattoo?" Ydum asks. "And does the wolf on his chest bear any resemblance to Kinshra?"

Anarus pulls off his shirt and looks down at himself. "I just felt drawn to it."

"When?" Ydum pushes. "When did you get it?"

Anarus's mouth falls open and he sputters. "A year ago, after they told me I was going to the games this year."

"What about your other tattoos?" Byder asks.

Suddenly, I'm taking stock of all of Anarus's tattoos. I circle him, running my hands over his skin, moving to touch each tattoo as I mention it. "A wolf. Flowers. They make sense. Flowers and Ydum. And that wolf does look eerily like Kinshra. The moon and stars, barbed wire and lines, and all the symbols don't match anything though."

"The flowers were black and white before." Anarus looks at his own body. "I got them colored in for my twenty-first birthday. I don't know why. I just wanted more color since everything is shades of gray. I got the barbed wire sleeve when I was sixteen. Added the symbols on that arm at seventeen. The symbols on the flower arm at eighteen. The flowers added at nineteen. The stars at nineteen and moon phases added at twenty. They were birthday presents to myself since no one else gets me one."

"What are the symbols?" I ask him, taking a moment to look myself and see if I know, trailing my finger over them as I figure each one out. "I can see the ones in the flowers are fire, water, earth, and air. The ones in the barbed wire are the symbol for salt, there's gold, I don't know this one." My fingers stop at an arrow with two dots on either side of it.

"Iron." Anarus's eyes are on me, not the tattoos. "Below that is stone."

"Salt, metals, and stone. Sounds like more nature stuff." Byder comments.

"The four disciplines too." Ydum adds. "Byder, you know better than us the hunt god connection to that."

"What's the connection?" I ask.

Byder moves over by us as well, abandoning making lunch plates in favor of running his fingers over Anarus's tattoos as he mentions each one. "Air carries the scent. Water washes it away. Earth feeds the animals. Fire feeds the animals to us. I was considering a tattoo of those same symbols, just wanted to wait until after I got my mantle in case I got something like my dad and wanted to work the one tattoo around the power one."

"And the phases of the moon are huge to witches. We base so much on the phases of the moon." I run my fingers down Anarus's spine following the moons there. He can't look at me with me behind him, but I feel his muscles tense as I touch him. I pull my hand away and he twists, looking at me intensely. I can't look away.

"Could this all be coincidence?" Ydum doesn't sound like he's talking to us anymore, but just thinking out loud. "A wolf in gray scale is going to look like any wolf, but the timing is so strange." Ydum wanders to the couch and sits, lost in thought.

Byder goes back to making lunch plates and handing them out, not that any of us are paying any attention. Ydum is thinking too hard to notice and Anarus is still looking at me.

"The wolf in your mind could see my tattoo." Anarus whispers. "Your eyes were yellow and she saw my tattoo through my shirt."

"Did she see it because I've seen it and she knew it from me?"

"I don't know." Anarus's face contorts and he finally looks away. Shadows play at the edges of his face.

"Hey." I sit back down, take his face in my hands, and pull him to look back at me. "What's going on in that head of yours?"

"Nothing." I feel Anarus start to close off, his shadows deepen.

"Mm, no. Not doing that." I keep looking at him, keep making him look at me. "Your shadows are all over the place. Talk to me, Anarus."

He groans. "I can't. What if Ydum is right?" He sighs and rubs his hands down his face. "That would mean I matter. I matter somehow, my tattoos matter somehow. I've never mattered to anyone before and this? This feels like it matters. But it could all just be coincidence. We could be seeing things, making connections because we want to find connections. What if Ydum is right? What if we think he's right and he's wrong?"

"So, couple of things here." I pull myself into Anarus's lap, wrapping my legs around his waist, and he moves his hands to let me, surprised by the movement. "First, all this stuff with the tattoos, let Ydum think about that. He's the brain guy with too much book knowledge. It's fun for him to rattle out puzzles like this. Your tattoos and choices with them either are coincidence or not. I don't think it is just coincidence, just so you know. It's too much to be coincidence. You get a wolf when you are told you will be going to the Gods Games and now, I talk to a wolf in my head who says she knows who you are already? You get symbols that are important to hunt gods when you aren't one and are teamed up with a hunt god? You get flowers, then get them colored in and are teamed up with a colorblind nature god? Nope, that's a whole lot to brush off as coincidence."

I shift and Anarus's hands instinctively go to hold my waist. "Second, it's too late for you to worry about mattering to people. You already matter. You matter to me. A lot." I lean in and kiss him, a lingering, slow kiss. Then I lean in to whisper in his ear. "I love you, Anarus."

Anarus tenses, the entire room going darker as his shadows escape his control completely. His hands at my waist grip me tight enough to bruise. He pulls back to look at me, his eyes dark and a muscle jumping in his jaw. Suddenly, his arms are around me, pulling me tight to him, his face buried in my shoulder.

I have an awareness that Byder and Ydum have come closer to us, concerned by the room getting darker, but I ignore them for the moment. I trail my hands down Anarus's back, stroking him soothingly. I drop my head down to keep whispering in his ear. "You beautiful man, didn't you know that already? I love you, Anarus." I keep holding him as I feel him shudder under my fingers.

When he finally looks up, his face is contorted. "No one's ever told me that before. No one has ever said they love me before. The parents where I stayed, they would tuck in their own children, give them kisses and hugs and tell them, then just tell me good night. No hug, no tucking me in." He takes in a deep shuddering breath. "No I love you. Just goodnight and gone. I thought no one ever would say that to me."

I bite my lip, trying to fight back the pricks of tears at his pain. It feels like my heart is ripping open for him, and I know I am actually feeling Anarus in pain.

Ydum crouches down behind Anarus and places a hand on his back. "I know it's not the same as our girl here, but you know I love you too, man."

Byder doesn't touch him, but does also sit on the floor right next to us. "I love you too, Anarus. All three of us love you."

Anarus buries his face back in my shoulder, still holding me tightly. "I love you, Jinx. I never thought you would love me back. I love you so much it hurts, and I thought you would never love me back."

I kiss the top of his head over and over. "I love you so much, Anarus."

"Someone want to tell me what happened to the lights?" Kutar is yelling from the hallway.

"I don't fucking know either, but I was reading. This is bullshit, the games can't even keep the lights on now?" Zodum is yelling too.

"Um, listen, I know we're having a moment here," Ydum says, "but you think you can reign in those shadows, Ani, before the other gods come for our heads?"

I try to suppress a laugh. But Byder makes it worse. "Yeah. Do you want a witch hunt on our hands? Shadows, man, control the shadows, then be emotional."

The snort escapes before I can stop it. I look over Anarus's head and glare at them but it's entirely ineffective while I am fighting laughter. The room brightens just before Anarus lifts his head from my shoulder. His umber skin is shiny from tears.

"Assholes." Anarus grumbles as I wipe his face.

"You made the whole place dark." I am trying really hard not to smile.

Anarus is trying to regain some sort of sense of himself, the aloofness he usually carries. "Not the first time."

I raise an eyebrow at him. "That's a lot of shadows you carry, to make at least eight suites of rooms, the hallway, and foyer all darker."

"I made a whole house pitch black in the middle of the day before."

My other eyebrow meets the first one high on my forehead. "What happened?"

Anarus puts his face back in the crook of my neck, not hiding this time but nuzzling against me. His facial hair tickles my skin as he talks. "The male I was staying with said that I was like a rabid dog and my pureness was too broken to let live. He said the originals should just put me down and save everyone the effort of dealing with me."

My heart clenches again and I know it isn't from Anarus's pain this time but my own anger. "How old were you?"

"Ten." Anarus says this with no feeling. But I feel things. A whole lot of things. I'm enraged.

My arms tighten around him. "You were a child. A fucking child." A rumble builds in my chest and I feel myself snarling. A wave of fury crashes over me. He was a child. So young. When I turned ten, Dahlia was getting ready to go to the testing center in two months. My parents were worried and stressed over their oldest child going to the center and maybe the games, but they were still kind and loving to all of us. But when Anarus was ten, people were threatening to put him down like a rabid dog. I want to kill them, rip out their throats, make them all feel every ounce of the pain they caused him—

"Jinx." Ydum says my name cautiously, distracting me from my thoughts. "Hey, beautiful, what're you thinking about there, honey? You're eyes are a little yellow and you're growling."

I look at him and blink a few times. The sudden rush of fury settles. I'm still mad but not devastatingly so. I close my eyes and try to focus on peace. Why did I get so angry so quickly? Inside my head, I don't rebuild the scene from Ydum, but I find Kinshra anyway, or her letting me know things at least. I don't actually see her but know she is incensed.

Anarus is her pack. Hers! How dare anyone harm him!

Your pack, Kinshra?

Mine! She yells in my head. I feel her shake her fur out. *Where are they? The ones who hurt my guide. Where are they? I will ruin them!*

Long gone, Kinshra. I let her know it was a memory from when he was a child, not something happening now.

She settles at this. *Well then, something that can be dealt with later. The ones that hurt him will suffer, but I can do that later. Comfort first, then hunt the ones who hurt him as a pup.*

"Okay, that was different." I tentatively pull back some from Anarus. "Anarus, not to interrupt your snuggling me, which is very nice, but Kinshra said something and I think we may have an issue."

Anarus's head snaps up. "You weren't meditating."

Byder snickers. "No, but she was channeling."

"Channeling?" I look at Byder, my brow furrowed.

He takes a deep breath and blows it out. "I felt your intense anger, so strong I wanted to hunt and kill something. Yellowing eyes, growling, and I'm pretty sure you had a few claws instead of fingernails."

"All because what Anarus said made you mad and go all protective over him." Ydum adds. "Although, I'm not sure we can completely discount the protectiveness as yours versus your wolf's."

"What did Kinshra say?" Anarus asks quietly.

"Well," I fidget a little with his braid, giving my hands something to do. I channeled the wolf and that makes me nervous. "She said you were her pack and then called you her guide. But she also went from just knowledge in my head to actual sentences to me."

"What do you mean knowledge to sentences?" Ydum is squarely back in academic mode.

I twist my mouth, thinking how to explain this. "Um, before I just knew things. Like the thought would come to me. She needs to go to her alpha. Her name is Kinshra. Like that, like I was thinking about her as I looked at her. But this time, I didn't actually see her, just heard her in my head. It was her actually saying things in my head, her voice. Her saying I will hunt the ones who hurt Anarus. The thoughts in my head went from third person to first person, without me actually having to go to her, if that makes sense."

"Makes complete sense." Ydum says. He leans over and places his hand on Anarus's shoulder. "Do you feel up to a little experiment? I have thoughts."

Anarus groans. "Why is it whenever you have thoughts, I end up in an experiment, Ydum?" He sighs. "Fine. What do you want me to do?"

Ydum smiles broadly. "Nothing. This one is for Jinx. Touch the wolf on his chest, and try to talk to Kinshra again. Byder come around so that you can see Ani's tattoo clearly. I will too, but I want both of us watching."

Ydum moves and once he and Byder are settled, I pull back more from Anarus, enough to see his wolf tattoo clearly but still sitting mostly in his lap. His hands are still on my waist, but they have loosened their punishing grip. I place two fingers on the wolf tattoo, caressing it as I did Kinshra's fur.

I close my eyes. Hey, Kinshra? You still there?

Always here now. I'm up and hunting but I can hear you.

Hunting? I thought you hunt at dusk? Never mind. Doesn't matter. We are just trying an experiment. There was nothing I specifically needed.

What are you trying?

I'm talking with you while touching Anarus's tattoo of a wolf. I'm not sure what Ydum expects to happen, but he's the one that suggested it.

Oh. He wants to see the guide bond. Why didn't he just tell you to ask me that?

I don't think he knew to ask that, Kinshra. What is the guide bond? I've never heard of that before.

Me either, but I told my alpha about you. He told me it happens between witches, gods, and animals sometimes. I'm your wolf. I come to you, we can do things together, but Anarus is my guide to you. His tattoo of me is over the link in his heart, so became the representation of it. We can do so much more than normal familiars can because he links us physically, mentally, and magically.

Wait. Familiar? Ydum said there's no evidence that type of bond is real.

Kinshra huffs. *Humans and gods.* She shakes out her head. *They use the word wrong. Familiars are just animals a witch has a bond with. That can share attributes with their human. We don't come live with you. I mean, some do but I'm a wolf. I'm not doing that. We don't teach humans or increase their magic by our presence or anything. Just are bonded and can share things, like you having my yellow eyes and claws when you need them. And I get your human understanding. Alpha says it's been a long time since he's seen a true familiar bond and he never actually saw one with a god guide before.*

Did this happen because I meditated to find a connection to an animal?

Hang on. Kinshra is silent for a bit and I wait. I know when she's back. *I asked alpha. He said no. That you, me, and Anarus were always connected. We just all realized it now. He also said to tell you that the bond is only between you and me, Anarus is just the string between the two of us. His tattoo became the anchor of that string that had always been there. But I have to go. I scented a deer.*

"Shit." I breathe out and open my eyes. I expect the males to be looking at me expectantly, waiting, but they aren't. They must have been talking while I talked to Kinshra and I didn't hear them.

"No shit, I know that, Anarus. But it happened all the same." Ydum is saying.

Byder shakes his head. "It happened. I saw it too."

"What happened?" When I speak up, they seem startled, as if they hadn't realized I was present enough to hear them.

"They're trying to say the wolf turned and looked at them, but it's a regular tattoo. I even got it at a human-owned tattoo shop." Anarus looks frustrated. "It can't do that."

"Well," I draw out the word and look down at the wolf tattoo. It looks the same to me now. "Kinshra may have said that it actually isn't a normal tattoo."

"What did she say?" Ydum is excited.

I give them the rundown of what Kinshra told me.

Ydum stands and paces the room. "I have so many questions." He looks around, then shakes his head. "No time now. We have fight club."

Now, I'm really confused. "Fight club is after dinner."

"It is after dinner, Jinx." Byder tells me. "Something to work on, every time you meditate with Kinshra, or talk to her, you lose time. We need to find a way for you to talk to your wolf and still be aware of what's going on around you and how long it's been. You missed lunch and dinner today."

Byder and Ydum both putt around, getting ready for fight club, but I stay where I am with Anarus. I cup his cheek in one of my hands. "Hey. You okay?"

"You love me." Anarus attempts to still sound gruff but I can tell his heart isn't in it. "I'm fucking perfect, little human."

Fight club is delayed as everyone wants to talk about the brown out and what it means. The four of us play dumb and act like we have no idea why it happened either. The looks Aretha is giving me makes me think we weren't quite convincing. But eventually, everyone lets it go with frustrated ideas that the originals are probably angry with us about working together so much and the dimming lights was probably meant to distract us and make us turn on each other.

Chapter Twelve

AS SOON AS WE return to the room, Anarus pulls me into his arms. His grip on the back of my neck is firm but doesn't hurt. He kisses me hard. "I want to be inside you."

"Make love to me, Anarus." I tell him. And he does. Sweet, gentle, and loving, with a soft tenderness I didn't expect from him. When we come, together at the same time, he clings to me and we stay that way, falling asleep still in each other's arms. We wake up twice more in the night and do it again. I expect that I would be tired in the morning, but I'm not.

We are still holding each other when dawn comes.

"Hi." I say with a smile when I see Anarus's eyes are open.

"Good morning, little human." Anarus brushes a hand up and down my arm. "You okay?"

I smile bigger. "I'm perfect. I don't even know that I need coffee."

"Don't get ahead of yourself." Anarus teases. "Last night was great, but no coffee? I think you're pushing it."

I laugh at him playfully.

In the sitting room, Ydum and Byder are already awake and more grumbly than normal.

"I retract my prior statement about not knowing what you are doing, Jinx." Ydum tells us as I come to sit down with my coffee. With no shirt on, I can see his vine tattoo is very active, twirling around his arm and growing lots of tiny leaves. He takes the mug out of my hand, steals a sip, and grimaces before handing it back to me. "Disgusting. How do you drink that every day? Anyway. Yeah. I think the bond got deeper or something, more tangible. Did you guys sleep at all last night?"

I feel the blush heat my face. "Oh my gods. You felt me feel all that?"

"You need a different swear, Jinx." Byder gripes. "It wasn't like that. Just more of a feeling that you were very happy, very satisfied, and feeling pleasure. It was distracting and just obvious what would cause that level of those feelings for you even if I didn't outright know what was happening."

I try very hard not to think about that. This idea of us knowing how each other is feeling, at least me knowing all three of them and each of them knowing me, has a lot of potential to be helpful for us, so I want to forget about the ways it can make things very awkward.

Anarus distracts me from those thoughts by making me work hard. Instead of sitting on the floor cross-legged to meditate and talk to Kinshra, he makes me do other things. First, he makes me do my running workout with Ydum.

It's easy to call her to my mind as I run back and forth in the hallway. We aren't the only ones out there, so we are careful how we talk. Raven and Uesis are doing running practice as well, so Byder and Anarus stay in our doorway as Ydum stays at the end of the hallway between rooms nine and ten. I stick to one side of the hallway and Raven sticks to the other.

"Keep your focus on Kinshra, on talking with her, while still maintaining your form running and knowing where you are going." Ydum whispers to me before I start to run.

As soon as I have her attention, I let Kinshra know what we're doing. She seems eager to join our practice.

It's fun, she tells me. *You're always doing something new.*

Yeah, we are working hard to be ready for the game in two days.

What happens if you don't win the game?

Depends how we don't win. If we do what is needed but just not as fast as other people, we get points and just aren't the winner. If we fail to do what the game wants us to at all, I will probably die and the gods will either die too or be stripped of being a god.

Kinshra shakes her fur out. *That sounds harsh, but at the same time, the alpha will only put up with so much from wolves that can't keep up. Our elderly are revered and protected, but if a young pup can't learn to hunt or help the pack somehow, they get left behind and probably die without a pack. You smell strongly like Anarus. Did you mate with him?*

I trip over my feet running at that, but I catch myself. I keep running, though. Um, yeah.

Are you going to have pups now?

This time, I actually fall to my knees as I trip over my own feet. Gods, I hope not.

"What happened?" Ydum is by me, helping me back up.

I glance over at Raven. She's down by the foyer and we are closer to our room. I whisper anyway. "She could tell what Anarus and I did and asked if I was going to have pups now."

Ydum's laughter booms off the walls. Even though I'm blushing, I can't help but laugh too.

Byder and Anarus are looking on from our door, confused. Ydum walks over and whispers with them. Anarus goes pale but Byder laughs as hard as

Ydum did.

Did I say something funny? Kinshra seems confused.

Humans and gods don't do that just to make pups, I tell her. I think you freaked Anarus out a little.

Well, don't you want pups with him?

That is a loaded question, Kinshra. Not one I'm ready to think about.

"You gonna pass out, beautiful?" Ydum asks me. "You're looking kind of pale."

I shake my head and just point to my head. Raven and Uesis are too close now for me to say it out loud. Ydum nods, his chest twitching with the laughter he's holding in.

I push him and go back to my running. Once I finish my drills, we move on to the other workouts and I talk with Kinshra. For the most part, our conversations are bland. She tells me about their hunt last night and I tell her about my sisters. She's not as impressed with the fact that I have seven sisters until I explain that we were all separate litters.

Several times, what I'm doing distracts me from Kinshra or she distracts me. Each time, either she or one of my gods calls me back. After a while, though, Kinshra tells me she's tired and wants to rest so I leave her be.

"This didn't tire me out like making rain or the rosebud did." I tell them when she leaves to sleep. We are sitting on the couches, having just finished lunch and I cleaned up, at Anarus's insistence, so I can keep busy while concentrating on my wolf.

Ydum leans forward, resting his elbows on his knees. "It wouldn't. Not any more than a conversation with me would. Well, maybe a little more for most people, but you seem to be better at things quicker than most people, Jinx. You're just having a long-distance conversation in your head."

That night, I decide it's time to talk to the other humans about the paintings. We all need time to adjust our plans if we don't want to step on each other's toes over which painting we want. Before we start fight club, Ydum calls a meeting.

"So, here's the thing." I start, nervous how everyone will respond. "The original gods, and Drila, are not happy with us and the way we are cooperating. I have a sneaking suspicion they are changing the way things work to try to stop us from working together like this, which, honestly, just makes me want to work together with you all more."

People murmur their agreement, even the gods. Several comment on the light issue and I don't correct them about that maybe being the original gods.

"So, here's my thought." I continue. "I think we should actually talk about what painting we want. They are all different and I know which one I want. Maybe a lot of you do too. If we discuss it now, we have time to fix any issues of two of us wanting the same one. Or stop someone from choosing one at random that someone else really wants. Then, in two days, we will all know what we need and no one is at risk as much for failing just because they didn't prepare right."

"What's to stop one of you using this knowledge against someone else?" Uesis asks. They are in last place. His question is understandable. If they really want one painting, it would be too <u>easy for</u> one of us to take it to spite them and keep them from bumping one of us down.

"Standards." Saffron says. "The original gods may want to make this about winning and losing, and expect us to be the same way. But if that's the way we felt, why would we be teaching each other to fight and sharing witch's kits? I honestly don't care if I win, I just want to survive."

I nod. "Same." All the other humans are nodding as well.

"None of us chose to have to do this." Damek looks at everyone. "Not you gods or us humans. This thing, the Gods Games, none of us chose for it to work like this. None of us are the ones breaking the rules of it, either. For fuck's sake, Anarus isn't even old enough to be here. They broke the rules before the games even started. I say we do everything we can to make sure as few of us are lost to these games as possible."

"Why don't we all just go stand in front of the painting we want, like Drila will make us do?" I offer. "Then, we can see if there are any issues and find a way to solve them. If you don't know yet, just don't move. If you're uncomfortable telling the rest of us, you can choose not to move either, but know that if someone higher on the list chooses the painting you want because they only kind of like it, you may lose out on what you need because you didn't speak up."

Everyone moves except for Saffron and Asteria. Wren and Aretha both go to the swan.

"Do you have a real connection with the swan?" Aretha asks.

Wren shakes her head. "No. My name is a bird so I thought bird. You?"

"There were swans in a lake outside my home my whole life." Aretha explains. "They weren't actually my pets, but sometimes I felt like they were. I love swans."

Ydum wanders to them casually. Kutar and Zodum are both already there, so he's cautious. "Sounds like neither of you have a calling for the swan, but just affection." He looks at the gods. "Did either of you do a led meditation with them?"

Zodum shakes his head no. Kutar shrugs. "I tried but Aretha didn't see anything."

"Do you mind if I try?" Ydum offers. When all four of them just shrug, he leads them away from the painting and to the foyer. They find a quiet corner and he settles on the floor with Aretha and Wren.

I turn my attention to Saffron and Asteria. "Are you choosing not to tell us or do you not know where to go?"

"I don't know." Asteria chews on her thumbnail. "Wilros tried the meditation thing with me a bunch of times, but nothing ever happened. I couldn't even see the field in my mind."

Saffron bites her lips. "I saw the field but nothing ever came, no matter how many ways Velmos tried."

I gesture for them to follow me and lead them over to Ydum, Aretha, and Wren. I place my hand gently on Ydum's shoulder. Fortunately, he hadn't actually started yet. "Two more?" I tell him and he immediately backs up, making space in the circle for them. Zodum and Uesis are standing a few steps away and are joined by Wilros and Velmos.

I realize suddenly that I never moved to a painting, but focused on everyone else. I go look down the hallway and see Anarus and Byder standing by the wolf painting. Isis is standing at the dog painting next to them and chatting with them. They claimed my painting for me, leaving me to help the others, and the other humans just accepted that.

I move to talk to the four gods watching Ydum work with their humans. "How is everyone okay with Ydum doing things like this? Leading a meditation with your humans for you? Leading the fight club when Esnir is the war god?" I keep my voice low so as not to disrupt the meditation.

"Ydum never told you?" Zodum sounds surprised.

"Never told me what?"

All four of them snicker quietly. Velmos is the one that actually tells me. "Your god is a genius. Really, a legitimate, tested genius. Never missed a question on a test, never got less than perfect in a class. His mom was super overprotective, but he was always the first to get something, understand it, and always helped the rest of us once he did. This?" Velmos gestures at the five people meditating. "This is nothing new for him. He even was recruited often to help older gods that were struggling before going to the games. The professors for the games classes started pulling him out of class to help someone or another who was headed to the games soon and struggling when we were sixteen. Fuck, Ydum taught me more about what to do in these games than those professors ever did."

I look at the other three gods and see they're nodding. "Ydum was always the one to tutor Byder when the games professors wouldn't." With the way Ydum had taunted Byder at the beginning of all this, Wilros's comment actually surprises me, but he doesn't stop there. "Ydum was always the one to tutor any of us when we needed it. He also was the only one who got away with arguing with our professors because he knew just as much, if not more, than they did. Remember science class when we were nineteen?"

All four gods start quietly chuckling. Uesis shakes his head, saying, "Oh yeah. Two weeks. We didn't have homework for two weeks because Ydum and Professor Naughtly spent all class debating the meaning of the word 'natural' when it came to god created things. Is gravity natural or god made? Does god made have to mean not natural? I lost money in the betting pool once it lasted longer than two days. Everyone lost money in that pool because none of us thought Ydum could keep the debate up longer than a week."

I look over at my god. The idea that his mom was overprotective isn't unexpected. She was actually hiding his secret of being colorblind. But that he was the genius in his class? That he was seen as the go-to for help because he was that good at everything? Debating professors? I knew he was smart, but with everything else, I'm surprised. I shake my head at myself. I shouldn't be. He may have started out the games as somewhat of a bully, but really Ydum is sweet and caring as much as he is goofy and teasing. The bullying was just him trying to hide his fear over our reaction to what he saw as a lack. Pride swells in me. Ydum is amazing and he is mine.

———

Byder comes over to me. "What'cha thinking there?"

"Ydum is amazing." I beam at him.

Byder raises his eyebrows and glances at the other gods. "They tell you about him?"

I nod and Byder shakes his head, smiling. "He didn't want to tell you. Thought it would be braggy or something. Like you would think differently about him. He says he had to be that good to hide his issue. But I know it's more than that. He really is just that damn smart."

"He really is." I lean on Byder as I watch Ydum help a struggling Asteria build a vision in her mind patiently and calmly. "Kind and fucking smart."

Eventually, one by one, the humans leave the circle with Ydum. Aretha hops up first. "Thought so." She says as she moves to the swan. Damek is already at the mouse and Raven at the horse. With Isis at the dog and Anarus holding the wolf for me, so far there are no complications. Saffron gets up next and moves to the cat. Wren claims the deer soon after.

For the longest time, Ydum and Asteria still sit on the floor together. Eventually, Ydum looks up and waves over Wilros. Asteria stays sitting as Ydum gets up to talk to Wilros. "How close are you two?"

"Pretty close." Wilros looks down. "Not that close, but definitely really good friends, maybe a little more."

Ydum nods. "She trusts you?"

Wilros shrugs. "I think so."

"Keep working with her. I think she's holding back, scared of something. It's there. She's there, but she keeps panicking out of it. What painting is left?" Ydum looks at me.

"Bear." I tell him.

Ydum seems thoughtful for a moment. "That could be the problem. Bears can be pretty intimidating. But whatever it is, keep building her trust with you, and herself, Wilros."

Wilros claps Ydum's shoulder. "Thanks, man."

Ydum only smiles. "Of course." He moves to walk away, and I stop him.

"Nuh uh, come here." I pull him over to me and wrap him in a hug.

"Not that I'm complaining, beautiful, but what is this?" Ydum asks, with a slight chuckle in his voice as he wraps his arms around me.

I look up him. "I'm proud of you. I'm proud you're mine."

He raises his eyebrows. "Oh? How proud?"

I lean up on my tiptoes and kiss his cheek. "Very."

A huge grin breaks across Ydum's face. "Proud enough to…"

"Later. Maybe later." I tell him, grinning. "Right now, you have a fight club to run."

"Whatever I did, remind me to do it much more often." Ydum teases and kisses my nose. Then, he lets me go and starts calling everyone back together as Wilros talks quietly to Asteria.

I hang back. I hear Asteria softly crying and Wilros trying to convince her everything will be okay.

"No, Wilros. We'll fail because I'm not good enough."

"No, we won't, Aster. I trust you. We'll get it, I promise."

Wilros sees me waiting for them. He gives me a pained, desperate look. I move over and take Asteria's arm in mine and wander away from the group with her, Wilros behind us but leaving space for us to talk privately.

"How are things with Wilros?" I ask her, trusting my own gut on what she needs.

"Good." Asteria tells me. "He's sweet."

I raise an eyebrow at her. "How is it really?"

We stop by the doors to our rooms. Asteria is in room six, so her door is next to mine. She sighs heavily. "Honestly?" I nod at her. "I think I might love him. But he's so. I don't know how to explain it. It's like we're just friends and I'm scared that if I say something, he'll not feel the same way. I would rather things stay like this than say something and regret it because it ruins everything."

"Do you know the point of the Gods Games, Asteria?" I ask her. When she nods, I turn her to face me. "Then, tell him. Tell him how you feel. Trust him. The cave knows what it's doing."

"The cave gave you three gods, Jinx." She laments. "How can I trust the cave when you have to choose between three... Oh." Asteria takes in the look I'm giving her. "You aren't choosing, are you?"

"The cave knows what it is doing." I reiterate. "Trust me, I didn't think it did either, but it does. Tell him. Let Wilros in. You won't regret it." I look at Wilros a few feet away from us and nod to him as I move back to the foyer, giving them space to be alone.

I have to practice fighting with Anarus because Wilros and Asteria never come back out to the foyer.

When we get back to the room, Ydum pulls me into a hug like I had him in the foyer. "You know, you said you were proud of me, but I didn't tell you how proud I am of you."

"What have I done for you to be proud of?" I smile at him, letting him hold me.

"I saw you with Asteria." Ydum smiles conspiratorially. "And all of this, all the defying the original gods, teams working together stuff, it's all because of you." Ydum suddenly lifts me into his arms, bringing me up to him so he can kiss me. When I instinctively wrap my legs around him, he puts a hand under my bottom, his long fingers wrapping through my legs to tease at my center as he kisses me and walks across the room.

When he kneels on the ground with me, his speaks softly. "Don't overthink this, beautiful. Just lean back on Byder. I want to kiss you."

"You were kissing me." But I lean back anyway and find my head cradled in Byder's arms.

"Not on your mouth." Ydum lets go of me and settles me so that my lower half is on the floor. He pulls down my pants and moves between my knees, his mouth going to kiss my clit. As Byder lifts my head to kiss me, Ydum wraps his arms around my thighs to hold my bottom half still as he licks me and bites me gently.

"Fuck." I pant out as Byder's hand pushes my shirt up and over my head, then claims my breast. Part of me realizes how trapped I am between them. But before I can think about it too much, Anarus is taking my hand in his.

"You good with this, little human?" His touch, holding my hand in one of his, centers me. His other hand is gently running up and down my arm. "Do you feel safe?"

"Yes. With you three, always." I say. Then, I moan as Ydum pushes his tongue inside me and brings his thumb up to rub where his tongue had been. Byder kisses me again, capturing the moan in his mouth as his tongue moves in my mouth in tandem with Ydum's between my thighs.

"Do you want to touch me?" Anarus asks me.

Byder stops kissing me so I can answer, but his hand does not stop, rolling and pinching my nipple between his fingers. "Gods, yes." I answer Anarus. Byder returns to kissing me as Anarus guides my hand to his shaft.

One of Anarus's hands is guiding me to stroke him while his other hand is on my breast. Byder is kissing me and rubbing my other breast, and Ydum is moving his mouth and hands between my legs. The overwhelmingness of all the sensations burns pleasure through me. I cry out as I feel tension coil and fracture in me.

"Fuck. Make that sound again." Anarus groans. He lets go of me for a moment to grab my shirt from the floor, then his hand is back over mine on his cock, tightening his grip so that my hand tightens around him as I stroke up and down on him.

Ydum moves his mouth to lick me from front to back of my slit and I cry out again, arching my back at the fire running through me. I move my free hand to Ydum's hair, gripping it to pull him closer. "I need. Oh, fuck. I need."

Ydum slides a finger inside me, his mouth sucking and licking my clit, and I moan again.

Anarus groans and his hand over mine stills as he drops my shirt over himself, catching his seed as it spills out of him. He lets go of my hand, but his fingers still run up and down my arm as he leans back. "Fucking beautiful, little human."

Byder sucks my bottom lip into his mouth and bites down at the same time as Ydum bites my clit and my world explodes. I scream and arch my back again, my hand in Ydum's hair pulling him tighter and my other hand circling around to latch onto the back of Byder's neck, gripping him tightly as well. I tremble as the waves ride over me and I gasp for breath.

Ydum sounds frantic as he pulls away from me. "I want to come inside you. Can I come inside you, beautiful?"

"Yes." I pant out between Byder's kisses. I expect Byder to leave or Ydum to take me back to the bedroom but that doesn't happen. Instead, Ydum lifts me so I am sitting up on my knees and Byder moves behind me, letting me lean back against his chest. He kisses along my neck, his hands trailing up and down my sides, as Ydum moves my hips so that I am almost sitting on him, his knees between mine as we both kneel on the floor.

"Shit." Ydum moans as he fills me. He moves, his hands holding my hips as he rocks himself inside me and the waves of pleasure that had just started to calm down build in me again. I moan against the rising sensations and move my hips to meet his thrusts.

"You keep making those pretty sounds and this will be over quickly, beautiful." Ydum quickens his pace, his thumb tracing circles over my sensitized clit, making me moan again. Every nerve in me sizzles as my muscles contract around him.

He tries to pace us, but the amount of need and desire between the four of us is overwhelming. I feel it all, just like Byder had said, pleasure that isn't all mine making every sensation in my body stronger. Ydum must feel it as well, because quickly, he's swearing and lost all control.

"Shit!" He yells as he breaks. "That's intense. It's too intense. I need. Oh, fuck." He roughly grinds his pelvis into mine, his hands squeezing my hips tighter. Stars dance behind my eyes as he hits the deepest, most sensitive parts of me over and over. Ydum groans loudly, and holds me close as he comes. Then, he sits back, still holding me as he slides out of me gently, panting.

"Do you want me too, Jinx?" Byder whispers in my ear. "You want one more, baby girl?"

I can't speak so I only nod.

"I need you to say it, Jinx." Byder orders.

"I want you, Byder." I lay my head back on his shoulder.

Ydum lets go of me and Byder pulls me towards him until I am kneeling again, my back braced against his chest. He wraps one arm around me, low on my stomach, his fingers brushing against the top of my clit, and the other arm wraps around my chest, his fingers teasing my nipple. He continues to kiss along my shoulder as he plunges inside me, his movements quick and possessive.

"Fuck!" I cry out. "I can't." My eyes squeeze shut and my hands move, needing to grip something but finding nowhere to land. I know by feel alone that it's Anarus's arms my hands find to grab hold of.

"I got you, little human." His voice is rough and I grip his forearms tightly.

"Come for me, Jinx. Come one more time for me." Byder breathes into my ear and the orgasm that started with Ydum regains strength. I dig my nails into Anarus's arms and my legs shake as the pleasure spins through me so intensely I shout myself hoarse. I'm overrun by it, my whole body a blaze, at the same time Byder moans and buries himself deep in me with his release.

As he pulls out and sits back, Anarus pulls me forward to him, gathering me in his arms. As he leans back against the couch to cradle me, he uses my shirt to clean between my legs. "Such a mess we made of you, little human."

My entire body is liquid with spent pleasure and I can't focus on one single thought. I bring my fingers up to trace Anarus's mustache and goatee. His dark, coarse, curly hair feels rough on the pads of my fingers. "I wonder what you look like without this."

Ydum chuckles. "I think we broke our Jinx."

"Did we break you, little human?" Anarus asks, my fingers tracing his lips as they move.

My mind doesn't focus on their words but on Anarus's mouth. "You're so fucking beautiful."

"Yup." Byder laughs. "We broke her. Take her to bed, Ydum."

I think it's Anarus who actually carries me to my bed, but I know Ydum tucks me in, curling against me and stroking my hair.

When I wake up, no one is in the bed with me. I think about what happened the night before and try to find the guilt I feel like I should feel about it, but there is none. This is right for us and no one else matters. I get up and head out to the sitting room, where Byder and Ydum are already waiting. I look at the table for coffee and find nothing on it.

"We let you sleep in." Byder points to a plate of fruit and toast on my spot on the couch and a cup of coffee sitting on the floor near it.

Ydum's eyes glitter wickedly. "You were very tired. You snored—"

"Do you want to sleep in the foyer?" I raise an eyebrow at him.

"No ma'am. I didn't say nothing about you snoring." Ydum teases.

Anarus comes out of the bathroom, obviously fresh from a shower. I notice but disregard the fact that he's only wearing a towel wrapped around his waist because he has no hair on his face.

"What did you do?" I say, shocked.

Anarus shrugs. "You asked what I look like without it last night."

"Fuck no." I say. Anarus looks so young without the facial hair. "Abso-fucking-lutely no. You look like a baby face. Grow that back out and don't shave it again."

Anarus runs his hands over his clean cheeks, scratching them. "I dunno. I kinda like this."

I scowl and shake my head. "If you actually like it better, I won't say anything more, but I am letting you know now, I hate it."

Anarus leans over me. "Don't you want to try it out before you write it off?" He kisses me, taking his time to explore my lips.

When he stands back up, I tell him. "That was nice, but no. Facial hair. You don't look right without it."

"I don't know." Ydum pretends to inspect Anarus. "I haven't seen you clean shaven since you were first able to grow facial hair when you were what, twelve?"

"Fourteen." Anarus corrects him.

Ydum waggles his eyebrows. "Same difference. It might be time for a new look. Maybe trim the braid and…"

"Touch that braid and you sleep outside, Ydum." I growl.

"We can't go outside." He counters.

I glare. "I'll pitch you through a window. Do not touch that braid."

Anarus shrugs at Ydum. "Jinx has spoken. The braid stays and the goatee comes back."

Byder scratches his chin. "Maybe I should grow a beard if she's so fond of them."

"You tried that once." Ydum says. "It came in so patchy and thin, it looked like your face was just dirty. And mine is so blonde, you can't see it's there anyway. Jinx will just have to live with one hairy male."

"Jinx likes all of you just as you are." I say. "Well, as soon as Anarus grows back his beard."

"Finish your coffee, beautiful." Ydum kisses me quickly. "You're so upset, you're speaking in third person and threatened me bodily harm three times already."

I roll my eyes. "It was only once. The other two were just commentary on where you will sleep if you keep annoying me."

Ydum smiles, holding his arms wide. "You love me. But you also need to run and talk to your wolf." Before I can speak, Ydum holds up a hand to stop me. "I know, I know. You hate me. Run anyway."

I groan. "You're lucky you're cute."

My run and talking with Kinshra goes well and I get no questions about how I smell or making pups this time. I find myself losing the thread of my talk with her and what I am doing less than I did the day before. The only thing that hampers how well I do in the personal workout is how sore my body feels, which is a whole different issue that all three of my gods laugh about as I glower at them.

At fight club, after everyone has minor panic attacks about Anarus's clean shaven face, Asteria lets me know that she took my advice and she and Wilros are "Great!" and she saw her bear. Now, we know that every human definitively will choose a different painting without tripping each other up. I feel a small sense of satisfaction that we may have just messed up the original gods' plan to cause chaos and disputes between us.

The next day, Anarus and I spend most of the day working with Kinshra, preparing her for what may happen in the fifth game. She communicates what we tell her to her alpha, who is surprisingly accommodating about it all. Apparently, Kinshra tells us, her alpha believes that a familiar bond is sacred and needs to be respected. He even offers to move the pack closer to us, but I let her know that I don't exactly know where we really are and the gods use paintings to magically transport us to somewhere else for the games. Since the painting I will choose is one of a wolf, I hope that, instead of her coming to us, we will be transported closer to her.

With that understood, Kinshra's alpha tells her that the pack will just stay put until after the game is over. They'll hunt in the evening, but Kinshra will be exempt from a dawn hunt if they do one so she can rest and be ready for whatever I need. I make sure she thanks him for being so understanding, but Kinshra says that the alpha says that this is just his duty and familiar bonds need to be protected. Especially ones with a god guide.

Everyone agrees to skip fight club in lieu of resting before the next game. Anarus and I go to bed early, just to sleep, knowing that we are going to do the most work in the fifth game, maybe all of it. It takes several minutes of him whispering peace into my hair before I calm my anxieties enough to actually doze off.

Chapter Thirteen

WE ARE ALL IN the foyer before the tone even sounds the next morning, all anxious and jittery. Anarus is more grumbly than normal because I forced him into a shirt for the game. When Drila pops in, in orange this time, she's startled to see us all already in position, lined up along that back wall, gods behind humans. The fact that she's rattled by us doing this does not escape anyone's notice.

"Well," Drila smiles her fake smile, "isn't this nice? Ahead of the game, aren't you?"

We all ignore the bait and wait patiently for Drila to get on with it. She furrows her brow. This isn't going the way she had thought it would at all. Drila looks down at the papers on a board in her hand and seems to try to gather herself. Our obvious disdain for the games may backfire on us later, but for now, it feels good to see her flustered.

She finally speaks again, attempting to still seem as if she's in control and nothing is wrong. "The fifth game deals with animalism magic. This game will be only one god and one human. Jinx?"

"Anarus." I say flatly.

"Well, that was easy." Drila attempts a laugh but it comes out strangled. "You will have a choice of actions for this game. The god can perform metamorphosis, conjuring, or projection with their human. Now, so everyone understands, the power must be channeled through the god, not the human, although the human can be the end result of the magic but does not have to be. For instance, a human cannot conjure a familiar and call that good. The god must do the work and the human must only help or be who the magic is worked on.

"The painting choice determines what animal the god must work with, no matter which action you choose to perform. Now, to pick the paintings, we would normally go in order from first place to last place. But due to the nature of this magic, we will be doing something different. All the humans will choose their paintings at the same time and tie breakers will be used if two or more humans choose the same painting."

A slow smile starts to creep over my face, but I smother it. Drila is expecting chaos. Instead, when she gives us the go ahead, all the humans calmly walk to their pre-chosen paintings and there are no disputes or issues. The only problem that happens at all is Isis and Aretha accidentally bumping into each other on their way to their paintings and that's solved easily with apologies on both sides.

Once again, Drila is left confused and out of sorts as she watches this. Glancing up and down the hallway, I think all the other humans and gods are feeling the same as me. They are just as satisfied by her consternation as I am. When Anarus comes and stands next to me, his shadows are simmering just below the surface but he has a vindictive look on his face, so I know it's not anger but pride in what we've done.

"Well, it seems this may be the smoothest game five in history. Let's see if it is so smooth in its completion." Drila finally gives up. "Off you go."

Anarus and I find ourselves very close to a village. It's similar to mine, with the same mud and daub huts and muddy roads that don't seem too soupy right now, but it's not actually mine. It seems as if it's a beautiful day with a slight nip in the air. In reality, it's October and the weather seems to match that.

"We can't call Kinshra here. The humans will panic." Anarus says.

"Plus, it has to be you, Anarus." I remind him. "Drila said the god has to do the magic."

"I know." He starts to walk away from the village and gestures for me to follow. "You live someplace like this. Where do you suggest we go to not have wolves worry the humans?"

I stop and look around. We're already on the western edge of the village. I try to look down the roads into it and only see small amounts of activity. If there are people living in this village, it's only a handful or most of them are already gone. Whether the gods made them leave for the games or if they left for some other reason, I can't tell.

Beyond the village, on all sides, is large farm fields. To the north, the farm fields go for as far as I can see. To the east, the fields seem to move up slowly growing hills that I can't see beyond. In the south, there's a large river that has a stone bridge over it. The road we are on runs north and south and the bridge takes it over the river, blocking my view of anything else. The fields may continue on the other side of the river, but I'm not sure. Far past the river is trees and the road runs into the trees. The only option that goes away from the road and the village is west, towards what looks to be a breakline of trees between one farm field and the next.

"There." I point to the breakline. "As long as there's not more village past those trees, it'd be the best bet."

Anarus nods and we walk that way. We try to skirt the edges of the farm fields, so as to not damage any crops, but occasionally we're forced to walk between rows of low green leafy plants. I'm not sure if these plants are onions or some type potato, not being a farming girl myself, but we try hard not to step on the plants in any case.

At the line of trees, we walk through them and discover that the breakline is only three or four trees deep. On the other side is another field that's growing corn. I tell Anarus that this will do. With the low activity in the village and our distance away from it and any humans, no one should be concerned, especially if the wolves come quietly and stay hidden as much as possible.

He leads me to what looks like a comfortable opening between several trees that keeps us in the shadows and less visible to the village, but has enough space for us to move around well, even if several wolves join us. We sit and Anarus removes his shirt.

"Call Kinshra." He tells me.

"But you have to do it."

"I have a plan."

"Want to share it with me?"

Anarus looks at me and shakes his head. "Sorry, yeah. I think if you can actually call Kinshra here, and she can come, I can bridge the gap between the two of you and maybe either make you morph fully into a wolf or cause you to project one."

"Me morph into a wolf?" I ask surprised.

Anarus shrugs. "Your eyes have gone yellow and you've gotten claws. Doesn't sound so far-fetched to have you change all the way. I thought about morphing Kinshra, but when she was talking about familiars, she said the wolf only gets the human understanding and said nothing about wolves morphing like humans."

I consider this. "Sounds reasonable. Well, actually it sounds insane, but reasonable considering my life right now."

I close my eyes and try to call Kinshra. I feel her perk up immediately.

Are you doing the game?

Yes, Kinshra. Do you have any way to tell where I am?

Hold on. Kinshra vanishes from my thoughts for a moment, then returns. *I can't smell you or Anarus. Not in the real world. Can you tell me where you are?*

I give her the basic directions, what I can see around us. I'm not sure it will be helpful, though.

Actually, that is a lot for us to go on. Water south, hills north, humans and food gardens everywhere in between. Wait again, I'll ask alpha.

While I wait, I tell Anarus what's happening. "Kinshra can't scent us in the air but she's asking the alpha if my description of this place sounds familiar."

Kinshra comes back before he can say anything. *Alpha says he thinks he knows. He'll bring me, and we'll keep trying to scent you as we go to know if we are going the right way. The rest of the pack will stay here so we don't scare the humans.*

Tell him there doesn't seem to be many humans in the village. I don't know if there normally is and they're all gone or if it's always this empty.

I'll tell him. I'll let you know when we scent you.

"Now, we wait." I tell Anarus.

"Just wait?"

"They're headed here, or think they are if the alpha is right about where we are."

For a while, Anarus and I just sit and enjoy the quiet. Eventually, I get restless. "This feels weird after the rushing of all the other games. Just sitting like this."

"Yeah." Anarus agrees. "Do you want to try something?"

"What?"

Anarus trails a finger in the dirt, drawing absentmindedly. "Maybe we don't need Kinshra to actually be here to make you project. We could try it until she gets here, and if it works, great. If not, we wait."

"Sounds better than doing nothing."

Anarus directs me to place one hand on his wolf tattoo and close my eyes. "Think of Kinshra, what she looks like. What she feels like."

I do what he says and Kinshra perks up in my mind.

I don't need anything, sweetie, just trying something.

She huffs. *You're always trying something.*

I smile. I thought you said it was interesting.

That was when I wasn't trying to look good in front of alpha. Now shush, I'm trying to scent you and make alpha proud of me.

Okay. I'm going to be thinking about you, but I don't need anything.

"Jinx?" Anarus gets my attention.

I open my eyes. "Sorry, Kinshra thought I needed her. Let me try again now that she knows what I'm doing."

Anarus mutters. "Of course, we would get the chatty wolf."

I settle my hand on his chest where I know the wolf tattoo is and think about Kinshra. Her black and gray fur, wet nose and yellow eyes. How her fur has a coarse outer layer but soft underlayer. How she likes to curl up at my feet as we talk. Her ears that twitch when she is thinking or listening to something. How she shakes her fur when she is upset or confused.

I can smell you now. Anarus too.

Is it because you are close or because of what I'm doing?

I think we are close.

"Kinshra says she thinks they're close." I tell Anarus, but he just points in the distance. I look to the east, where he's pointing and can see two small figures trotting by the river, following it.

I think I can see you, Kinshra. Are you following the river?

Yes. And I can definitely smell you.

The two figures near the river cut through the fields, not being nearly as careful as Anarus and I were. I'm quickly able to see one very large wolf and one smaller one. The large wolf stops some distance away while the smaller one trots right into the trees by us.

I called her smaller, but Kinshra, the real Kinshra, is a large wolf. Since I'm sitting, she towers over me. She even towers over Anarus. When she sits on her haunches near us, panting with her tongue lolling, her head could comfortably rest on top of ours.

Can I come over to you? I ask her.

Sure.

I glance at Anarus, who's just staring at her. Slowly, I stand up and take tentative steps towards the wolf.

"Jinx, be careful." Anarus doesn't move, just keeps watching her. "I should have brought one of Byder's knives, just in case."

"It'll be fine." I say more to myself than to him. I take slow steps towards the wolf, who is so much bigger than she was in my mind. She could destroy me with one leap. And her alpha a few yards away is even bigger. Step by step, I creep closer.

Oh, for goodness's sake. Kinshra says. The wolf stands and comes right over to me, butting her head against my shoulder. My shoulder. Her head is at my shoulder when we both stand. *There, you touched me. Are you still scared?*

"No, I'm not scared anymore, Kinshra." I talk out loud for Anarus's benefit. "Anarus, on the other hand, still is."

Kinshra huffs. Out loud, she huffs out loud and moves a step to butt her head against Anarus's head, knocking him over. *Still nervous?*

"No. I'm not nervous anymore." Anarus tells her. "Can you let me sit up?"

"Anarus. Did you hear her?" I ask.

"No, you told me…" Anarus sits up now that Kinshra moves off him. "You didn't tell me what she said? That wasn't you talking?"

I shake my head slowly.

Don't we have a game to win?

"Right." I say, but now Anarus is looking at me, confused.

"Did she talk again?"

He can only hear when I am touching him. Guide not familiar.

"You can only hear her when she's touching you." I tell him. "You're only the guide."

"Of course." Anarus huffs, very similarly to how Kinshra huffed. "Because that's totally rational and makes complete sense."

I laugh. "Anarus, we're talking to a wolf and you want something to make rational sense?"

"Good point."

Kinshra headbutts Anarus again. *Game.*

"Right, the game." Anarus sits up again after being knocked over by the wolf. "Kinshra and Jinx, sit close together enough to touch. Jinx, also touch my wolf tattoo. I'm going to touch both of you as well. I'm not really sure about this power, so I want to cover all the bases."

We all move to do as he says. I place one hand on Kinshra's scruff and love how her fur feels just like it did in my mind. Then, I place my other hand on Anarus's tattoo. He grips my arm that's touching his tattoo and the other side of Kinshra's scruff.

What should we do?

"Nothing, Kinshra." Anarus says. "At least, not yet. Let me try conjuring first. So you know, if it works, Jinx and I may just disappear."

We sit quietly for a long time, Anarus has his eyes closed and he's concentrating hard. But nothing happens. He opens his eyes and rolls his shoulders. "Let me try projection."

Again, we sit for what feels like a long time before Anarus opens his eyes. "Nothing. Okay, Jinx, try to think on Kinshra. Meditate on her the way you were before, but look at her as you do it rather than seeing her in your mind."

I nod and look at Kinshra. She looks at me and I can see her bright eyes, intelligence shining in them. She's still panting slightly, her red tongue just visible past her sharp teeth. I can smell her hot breath. It doesn't smell bad, just earthy.

Do you normally glow like that?

"Which one of us?" I ask.

You. Anarus, she's glowing.

"I know." He says without opening his eyes. "I'm concentrating. You keep concentrating too."

I keep my focus on Kinshra. Beautiful fur. So soft. She's so big. I look down at her paws. She has black claws on her toes and the whole thing is the size of my head.

"Well, fuck." Anarus says softly, awe in his voice.

I don't want to look away from the wolf in case it breaks the concentration of his power and whatever he's doing. "What?"

"Your wolf is silver and white." He tells me.

"No, Kinshra is black and gray. I thought Ydum was the colorblind one."

"No, Jinx. Kinshra is black and gray. Your wolf is silver and white."

Your wolf is very pretty.

"Do you think it will mess something up if I look?" I ask.

"I don't think you can, Jinx, but that has to be animalistic projection." Anarus says. "The wolf is standing over you. Kind of shining around you. Not sure if we have long until the game decides we are done. If not, I don't know what else to do."

As if his words provoked it, we're back in the foyer and Kinshra is gone.

"That is so cool." Ydum says.

"Wild." Byder agrees with him.

"You guys can still see it?" I ask. "Why can everyone see it but me? That's not fair."

"Because it is you, Jinx." Anarus tells me. "That's like asking why everyone else can see your face when you can't."

"Well, this is great." Drila comments dryly. "Jinx's team finally has a quiet entrance and there's no one else here to see it."

"We're first?" I ask.

"Yup! You guys did it first, and fast too." Ydum tells me proudly.

Anarus and I move over to the wall next to Byder and Ydum and wait for the others to start coming back. It takes a long time. Long enough for me to start getting nervous.

"What happens if no one else comes back?" I finally ask my gods quietly.

Ydum puts a hand on my knee and pats it comfortingly. "They will. Give it time. You and Anarus did that in record time."

"It felt so easy." I tell him. "Too easy. Half the time, I was bored waiting for Kinshra to show up."

By the time even Ydum starts looking nervous, Raven and Uesis appear in the foyer. Raven's nose looks a little long and she's standing oddly, with her hands and feet on the ground and her butt in the air. She shakes her head and her nose goes back to normal.

"I will be perfectly happy to never do that again." Raven shivers as she and Uesis move to sit next to the wall. "I was a horse. A horse!"

Quickly after them, Saffron and Velmos appear. Or we assume it's Saffron with Velmos because what actually appears is a black and white cat held in Velmos's arms. After a moment, the cat becomes Saffron and Velmos almost falls over from the weight change. He sets her down quickly and they move to the wall.

"You kept licking me." Velmos complains.

"So?" Saffron grumbles.

Velmos groans. "So, I told you I'm allergic to cats. I'm going to have a rash, I swear."

I do not even try to hide my laughter. No one else does either, not even Velmos.

When Damek comes back with Iella next, I get to see what the projection looks like. Or kind of. It's hard to see the shimmery brown mouse around Damek's toes on one foot. "It tickles." He says as they move to the wall.

Aretha and Zodum follow right behind Damek and Iella, and Anarus grips my arm until their conjuring of a swan shimmers away.

"Scared, Anarus?" Aretha teases and I shoot her a look.

"Not nice, Aretha." Zodum tells her.

Wren and Kutar and Isis and Esnir come so close to each other that Drila has to take a moment to figure out which group came first. Wren's projection of a deer and Isis's conjure of a dog both disappear at the same time. Drila eventually decides to give them both sixth place because we really couldn't tell who was first.

Again, we wait a long time. With everyone here, chatting and talking about how they did what they did, the time doesn't seem as long. But I know it has been quite a long time since the last two teams came. I listen to the others but none of us offer up how Anarus and I completed the task. It's apparent none of them actually called an animal to them to work with.

"You're awfully quiet there, Jinx." Wren says. "Not gonna share what you did?"

"We projected a wolf." I say.

"Wow, the details are killing me. Such vivid descriptions, Jinx. You should be a writer." Aretha rolls her eyes.

Ydum leans over and whispers in my ear. "Should we have Ani throw his shadows over her and make her think she went blind?"

"No, bad Ydum." I tap on his arm, trying not to laugh. "We do not threaten the other contestants. Not unless they threaten us first."

"Aww." He moans at me, inspiring me to laugh again.

I am spared by Asteria and Wilros finally returning. "Never again." Asteria is clinging to Wilros and shaking. "Never a-fucking-gain."

Once they've moved out of the way, Drila takes over. "Well, with that rather anticlimactic game over, the standings are Wren in last place with three hundred and five points, Asteria in seventh with three hundred points, Raven in sixth with two hundred and seventy points, Isis in fifth with two hundred and forty-five points, Damek in fourth with two hundred and thirty-five points, Aretha in third with two hundred points, Saffron in second with one hundred and ninety points, and finally, Jinx in first with one hundred and seventy points. But next week is the combat game and that can really shake things up. Hope you're all ready!"

With that Drila pops away and we all start to file back to our room.

"We're in first." I say, slightly awed.

"We are." Ydum agrees. "But Drila's right. Combat always changes things. More humans die in the combat game than any other game. I think we need to spend a lot of time on physical training and fight training over the next week, Jinx."

I look at all three of my gods and see them each hiding a worried look in their own way. "How bad is it? How bad is it really?"

Byder closes his eyes and takes a deep breath. "Remember how we said that two or three gods die in the games usually?"

"Yeah?"

Byder opens his eyes and looks at me again. "They're almost always in the combat game. We joked about Bokysus probably being the one who died in the first game, but more than likely it wasn't him. Gods die in the combat game. Lots of gods die in the combat game."

Ydum sits down on the couch heavily. "It's usually some form of all-out war between the teams. They give it some sort of accomplishable goal, like retrieve something or make it to some mark, but in reality, the goal is to beat the shit out of the other teams."

I cross my arms over my chest. "But look at what we've done here. We're all friends. All the teams. What happens if we won't senselessly fight? What if we just refuse? Fight only as much as we have to so we complete the task, but refuse to kill just to kill?"

"I don't think we can trust the other teams to be that way when it comes down to it." Anarus says. "Or even if they are, for the original gods to allow it. I wouldn't put it past them to do something that makes us forget we don't want to hurt each other."

Ydum nods. "That could be too. The combat game always seemed excessively bloody to me. The only thing we do know for a certainty is that only one of us can go. There has never been a game where teams with more than one god were allowed to bring more than one to the combat game."

"So, whose going with me?" I look at all of them, unsure who it should be.

But it must not be confusing for them. Anarus and Byder both say, "Ydum," at the same time Ydum says, "me."

"Well, at least that was easy." I snort.

As much as I feel like we should be happy at how easy the fifth game was, and that we are actually in first place, a black cloud descends over us. Anarus actually develops a small black cloud of shadows around him.

"So, we work on fighting. Ydum and I will work on it together." I try to be

201

optimistic. "I'll be fine. Ydum will be fine. Everything will be fine."

"You're going against a war god, Jinx." Byder sighs. "A war god. No one is coming out of this unscathed."

"Esnir is nice. He wouldn't hurt anyone." I try again, pacing the sitting room.

"Esnir is a war god." Anarus reminds me. "It won't matter that you helped heal his mate or that he's been helping everyone learn to fight, once he gets in the game, he will feel it. He'll feel his power in a way he never has before. Even without his mantle, it'll be intense for him. You cannot forget that. He's a war god, Jinx, and he will be very, very dangerous."

Ydum leans forward on the couch. "Think about it like this, Jinx. What if the thing you loved most in this world was something you only had ever had a taste of doing before, but that taste was enough to tell you that you would do anything, sacrifice anything, to get more? Then, someone put you in a room with that favorite thing and told you that you could have as much of it as you want? Would you be able to have any restraint? Would you be able to stop yourself? That's going to be Esnir in the next game. A fist fight between guys at school is nothing, a taste to him, and they are serving him up real war on a platter and you and I will be that platter. And that's only one person out of the fourteen we will have to worry about."

I collapse on the couch next to Ydum. "It's really hard to stay positive when even Ydum thinks we are fucked."

"I don't think we're fucked." Ydum pulls me close, his hand around my waist in a side hug. "I think it's going to be fucking hard and really dangerous. If it was just me, I wouldn't even worry. I've kicked Esnir's ass before and I can do it again. It's you I'm worried about."

"We're back to me being the weak link?"

Ydum squeezes me tight for a moment. "Not a weak link. But human. And important. You could be a badass and I would still worry about you in this game." He holds up one finger. "Correction. You are a badass and I'm still worried about you."

"We all will." Byder sits next to me, on the other side than Ydum. "Just like we will worry about Ydum. Man, I don't think the sight of your body hitting the ground like that will ever not haunt my dreams. The idea that I won't be there, able to help you two, is driving me nuts. I know you will both be amazing, but I'm still worried."

"Same." Anarus says from his dark cloud on the other couch. "It's weird how much I feel connected to you two as well as Jinx."

We eat dinner when it appears, setting aside the alcohol to give to another team like we normally do, and all of us keep our conversation casual after that. The feeling of worry and anticipation never goes away, but we try to ignore it. I go to bed early and, without much discussion, Ydum joins me. It's almost as if everyone decides that, if Ydum is going with me in the sixth game, we need our relationship to be a strong as possible and sharing a bed is one way we can make sure it is.

The next day, we change the training plan again. Kinshra and I do talk for a little bit and I tell her what the next game will be. She lets me know that alpha thinks it's a good idea that, every time I'm in a game, she's waiting for me, available if I need her for anything even if the game isn't specifically geared towards working with an animal. I agree. Her claws could help me if I need to fight.

The entire day becomes one long workout session. Running and stretches in the morning. After lunch is sparring which actually isn't sparring but just mock fights between me and either Byder or Anarus with Ydum running commentary on my form and movements. He often makes me start over a movement I did instinctively in the mock fight to adjust the way I held my arm or made a fist.

Then, after dinner is fight club, but with a whole new attitude. Everyone is grim and focused. There's no more chatter or laughing, but humans and gods alike giving rapt attention to everything they are being taught. Esnir takes over teaching now as we move to actually attempting to fight each other. Ydum works with me now, instead of Damek. Esnir has us constantly shifting partners, fighting someone smaller or bigger to get used to the feel of it.

Not that any of us are actually fighting. It's still open-handed and gentle hits. More often than not, we are focusing on avoiding getting hit rather than actually hitting each other. As Saffron and I face off, Ydum and Velmos stop us often to make us think about how we can escape the other's hit but never really worry about how that hit is being delivered.

After fight club, Ydum is thoughtful, pacing the sitting room and constantly fiddling with the cuffs on his long sleeves. "Jinx, there is something I think we need to work on, but it may be hard for you."

I give him my attention and Byder and Anarus also look at him, curious.

"Don't hate me, but," Ydum grimaces, "we have to work on you being trapped. It's a problem for you. If anyone makes you trapped in the game, it could be devastating if you panic."

Anarus's face twitches. "And how were you thinking of working on this?"

Ydum closes his eyes and licks his lips, sighing. "We have to trap her. We have to make her panic and then help her move past it to survive."

My heart stutters and I feel a hitch in my breath. "Fuck." I say, barely above a whisper.

"That. What you're feeling right now, Jinx. That's a problem in the game." Ydum kneels in front of me as I am sitting on the couch, and takes my hands into his. "I don't want to do it. I don't want to make you feel this way. But I sure as fuck would rather I do it now than any of them do it in the game and you have no preparation to defend yourself."

"I know." I fight to keep my breathing even. Ydum is right. Feeling this way in the game would get me killed. "I'm safe with you three. I know this. I really know this, but still, I'm having to fight down the panic at the idea of being trapped. Which means I really do need to work on it."

"We'll start small, okay?" Ydum stands back up, his hands on his hips, pacing. "Anarus, don't help us. Be the safe space for Jinx. If things get too bad, she can trust you because you aren't involved."

"Good idea." Anarus scratches the scruff regrowing on his chin and drinks the juice in his hand as he contemplates this. "Also, we need some sort of full stop. A way for Jinx to tell us when it's far too much and she can't take anymore."

Byder nods at this and looks around. "A safe word. Butterfly. You say butterfly and we stop everything, Jinx. Okay? If it gets too bad, you say butterfly and we stop."

"Butterfly." I repeat the word to memorize it. "Butterfly."

Ydum turns his attention to Byder. "You good to do this?"

"I do not like it." Byder is sitting on the other couch, his hands clenched and his body taut. "I can already feel her panic building and I feel like I want to throw up at the idea of making worse on purpose. But, yeah. We need to do this or she could die because she panics."

Ydum takes my hands and pulls up me to stand. His voice is ragged at the edges. "Before anything else, I love you, Jinx. Just, I love you. Please remember I don't want to hurt you." He kisses me gently.

Byder walks stiffly to me and kisses me as well. "I love you, Jinx. Use the safe word, if you need to."

"I love you both and know this is to help." My heart is racing already with anticipation of what they will do.

"Try to tune out how Byder and I feel. It will confuse this." Ydum says as he immediately pushes on me, forcing me backwards to the corner of the room behind the table. At first, the thoughts from them, Ydum directly in front of me and Byder right behind him, are so strong, I can tell they won't hurt me, so I don't panic.

Then, Byder slides between me and the corner of the walls Ydum is pushing me into and grabs my wrists, pinning them behind me. Ydum pushes me back into Byder, pinning my hands further between his body and mine. Part of me knows that this is only Ydum and Byder and I'm fine, but I feel the edges of panic starting. I'm breathing fast and gritting my teeth.

"Fight back, Jinx." Byder says in my ear. "You can get away."

I pull on my wrists, trying to unpin my hands, but Byder tightens his grip. Ydum pushes my shoulders back with a harsh shove. Then he moves his feet so mine are trapped between his.

He pushes his whole body against mine, pressing against my chest. "You can't go anywhere, Jinx. You can't get away from us. What do you do?"

I pull at my wrists again. Byder's holding them so tight, I think they might bruise. My mind forgets this is practice. He has me pinned. I can't move. I can't do anything. I'm trapped between them and I can't do anything to stop them from doing whatever they want to me.

"Fight, Jinx." Byder says again. "Fight us."

Ydum puts one hand around my neck and squeezes gently. "You're stuck. You can't get away. I could squeeze tighter and you won't be able to breathe. What do you do? Think. What do you do?"

I already can't breathe, I think to myself. Ydum's face is very close to mine. I turn away from him, shutting my eyes. I'm trapped. I'm trapped. I can't get away.

"Fight, Jinx." Byder pulls my wrists down so that my elbows lock straight. It hurts my shoulders. I try to pull away from his grip but I can't. Ydum has a grip on my neck.

The edges of my vision go gray. I don't think I am breathing at all. But not from Ydum's hand. It just won't come. "Ani!" I scream.

"Good." Byder pushes his knee into my hip. "Scream, Jinx. Fight."

I can feel Anarus is angry but he isn't stopping this. He isn't coming to help me. I start crying and my mind is frantically thinking of how to escape. My eyes wildly look for something, anything, to break away from them.

"Pinch, bite, kick." Byder tells me. "Use anything you can to fight back. Don't just think about hitting us or pushing us away. Cause pain. However you can, cause us pain back."

I twist my wrists in his hands, my skin burning from rubbing against his callouses. "No! Ani!" I shake my head, trying to use it to hit either of them. My vision is distorted from hyperventilating and tears. "Please. Please stop. Let me go. Please."

"Get free, Jinx. You can get free." Byder encourages me, but I barely hear it over the pounding of my heart.

"ANARUS!!" I scream. "Help me, please. Please! Why won't you help me?" Why isn't he coming? Why isn't he stopping this?

"Fuck!" Anarus yells. "Butterfly. Fucking butterfly."

Ydum and Byder immediately drop their grips on me and move away. I fall to the floor and curl into a ball, still crying and screaming. My breath is ragged and I'm shaking as I wrap my arms around my knees that are drawn up to my chest.

Anarus is by my side, trying to pull me into his arms. But I push him away. "Don't touch me!" I scream, not seeing him. "Don't touch me! You didn't come. I called and you didn't come!"

"I'm right here, Jinx." Anarus says, but he backs up a few steps, giving me space.

"That's what you said." I pant out, my mind confused. "That's what you said but you never came. I screamed and screamed and screamed, but you never came. You never came. You never came. You won't come. You didn't stop them. You heard me, Sam, I know you heard me but you didn't come." I curl up tighter, hiding my face and crying. I scream wordlessly into my knees, overwhelmed and scared. I don't know how long I hide, curling my body around itself to be small and hidden and safe, screaming and crying and hoping someone notices me, someone helps me.

"Sweetie, can you look at me?" Isis asks me quietly. "Look at me, Jinx. Look where you are."

I look up, surprised to hear Isis. She's crouched next to me, close enough to touch, but not actually touching me. Isis wasn't there. She's at the games, not there. "Isis?"

"Yeah, Jinx. Come here." Isis waves her hands at me to move towards her. I lean over and she collects me in her arms, stroking my back and whispering in my ear. "You're safe. You're okay. No one will hurt you."

"He didn't come." I cry into her shoulder.

"Anarus is right here, sweetie." Isis tells me as she soothes me. "He's right here. He was here the whole time. Do you want Anarus?"

I shake my head. "He didn't come. He didn't stop them."

"He did stop them. He was right here the whole time." Isis tells me again.

"I don't think she is talking about Anarus." Byder says. "She said a different name earlier."

My brain starts to come down from the terror and I look around. Anarus is on his knees behind Isis, a pained expression on his face and his shadows arcing from him. Byder is standing behind him, his arms crossed over his chest and his knee bouncing as he stands. Ydum is far back, on the couch, his head in his hands as he leans over, looking at the floor. Esnir is sitting next to Ydum, naked from the waist up, hair tousled and his pants haphazard as if he just threw them on carelessly. There's a sword in his hand. It's the sword that brings me back to myself.

"Why does Esnir have a sword?" I ask.

"We heard you screaming." Isis tells me, her hand still rubbing my back. "He thought that one of the guys was hurting you. He was coming to stop them."

I look further and see the door to our room is open. There are a bunch of people milling around in the hallway. "Oh, gods. Did everyone hear me?" I say this softly, just to Isis.

"Yeah. Everyone came to defend you."

"I'm sorry." I look at the floor, ashamed.

Isis shakes her head. "Nope. Don't apologize. Ydum explained it. You were working on something you struggle with and it got out of hand. Happens to the best of us."

I lean back against the wall and put my hand over my face. My breathing feels more normal and I stop crying, but my legs and arms are still trembling.

"Do you want Anarus now, Jinx?" Isis asks.

I shake my head again. My brain is still warring with the difference between what happened a long time ago and what happened today. In my head, I know that Anarus was right there the whole time and was the one to say the safe word I forgot, but I can't convince the rest of me. Byder kept telling me to fight even as he held my wrists, and Ydum was telling me I wasn't going to get away.

"Byder." I say very quietly, almost feeling like a traitor. They expected Anarus to be able to comfort me, but my mind will not accept it. He didn't come when I called.

Isis moves away from me and Byder takes her place. "What do you need, baby girl?"

I climb into his arms and he pulls me tightly to him. "Jacob's not here. Randy and Devon aren't here. Sam's not here." I whisper.

Byder smooths a hand over my hair. "No, baby girl. Jacob's not here. Sam's not here. Only Ydum, Anarus, and I are here. And we will always come for you."

"Sam never came. He was there. He said he loved me but he never came." I shudder in Byder's arms and he squeezes me tighter, making sure his hands are far apart so I can get out of them if I want. "I screamed so loud, but he never came. He didn't care. He didn't stop them."

"We'll always come, Jinx." Byder tells me again. "We'll always come."

I have an awareness of Isis and Esnir leaving, closing our door as they go.

Anarus yells. "We are never fucking doing that again. Never!"

"I was wrong. I'm so sorry, Jinx. I was wrong. We should never have tried that." Ydum's voice is shaking.

"Do you want to move to the couch, Jinx?" Byder asks me. When I nod, he helps me up and we walk to the couch. As we sit, I see a red stain on the carpet.

"What happened?" I gesture to the stain.

"Anarus shattered the glass cup in his hand." Byder tells me. "He's fine now."

I look at Anarus and see he hasn't moved from kneeling on the ground. "Anarus?"

Anarus doesn't moved from his spot on the floor. "I should have stopped them sooner. I thought you would tell them, but you didn't and I should have stopped them sooner."

"Anarus, please come here." When he shakes his head, I ask again. "Please come here."

Anarus groans and comes to stand by me.

"Let me see your hand."

Anarus holds out the hand he broke the glass with. There are long cuts crisscrossing the palm and fingertips. They are bleeding sluggishly.

"You're hurt." I look up at him but he turns his face away.

"I didn't protect you." He shudders. "I didn't protect you, and now you hate me."

I reach out to take his uninjured hand. "I hate Sam. I may have confused you two for a moment in my panic, but I don't hate you. I hate Sam for not coming."

"Can you tell us who Sam was, baby girl?" Byder asks.

I close my eyes. "He was my boyfriend. He was drunk at the party and told me he loved me. Everyone was drunk and doing things. When he told me he loved me, he said he wanted to find a quiet place and be with me. I told him no, that I wasn't ready for that, and that I wanted to go home. He got mad and we argued. I stormed off with him yelling at my back that he would always come for me, not to walk away from him because he would just come for me. But, he didn't. He didn't follow me and I was leaving when Jacob and his friends found me."

"When they," I take a deep breath, the memories hard to talk about, "they made me do all those things, I screamed and fought them. For a long time, I screamed for Sam, but he didn't come. No one came. No one cared. The High Priest was home and even he didn't do anything. So, I stopped fighting. I stopped screaming. I let them do it. Just use my body how Jacob told them to while I just cried and let them. Then, they held me down. Jacob sat on my chest. I couldn't breathe but they didn't care. They just laughed as I struggled to breathe and they made me. They used my mouth to. They used everything. They..."

I choke up, just remembering it, and shake my head. "Afterwards, I went home. The next day, Sam came over like nothing had happened. He wanted to talk to me and my family couldn't figure out why I wouldn't talk to him. We had been so close, and now I couldn't even look at him, and they didn't understand what changed. I finally talked to him, just to make them happy, but he laughed and said it was all just good fun and everyone was doing it. He didn't care that they hurt me. That I was bleeding and in pain, bruises all over me. I never spoke to him again. I never talked to Jacob or his friends again. I planned to never talk to the High Priest again but had to when I was at the testing center because my test was messed up."

When I finish talking, the three of them don't say anything, but I feel an oppressive guilt coming from all three of them.

"I am such an idiot to have suggested we try this." Ydum's guilt is the strongest. "I am so, so sorry, Jinx. I shouldn't have. I thought it would help but I think we made it worse. Can you ever trust me, trust us, again?"

I sigh heavily. "I do trust you. All three of you. Now. With the panic gone, I can tell the difference between what happened then and what happened now. But when you were doing that, I couldn't. I felt like I was there again, in Jacob's basement."

We don't say anything for a long time. Their guilt doesn't wane. The calmer I feel, the more exhausted I become. Eventually, all I want is to go to bed. I tell them and they all nod at me, but don't move from their seats on the couch, and Anarus on the floor. Once I climb into bed, I feel like there's no way I'll be able to sleep, but I do, a restless sleep that leaves me still exhausted in the morning.

When I come into the sitting room, none of them have moved. Ydum is sleeping in the same spot he was sitting last night, still sitting up with his head hanging over the back of the couch. Byder's awake, sitting on the couch next to Ydum, staring at the spot on the floor he always stares when he's upset. I'm not sure if he's slept or not. Anarus is also awake, but he has shifted some to lean on the couch. I know he hasn't slept. He has dark circles under his eyes that stare out straight ahead, unfocused. He is rubbing the hand that he cut with the broken glass.

I make two coffees and bring one over to Anarus. He looks surprised when I hand it to him and sit on the couch, curling my legs under me, drinking the other cup.

Ydum grunts, then wakes up. He rubs his eyes, then his neck, twisting it to crack it. "When did everyone else wake up?"

"Just now." I say.

"Never slept." Byder answers.

Anarus points lazily at Byder. "That."

There's still guilt coming off them in waves. I take a long sip. "Okay, yesterday sucked. But we are not going to accomplish anything sitting here feeling guilty and upset. I'm sorry that I'm broken and have baggage that makes me panic, but you should not feel sorry for trying to help me."

Byder doesn't change where his focus is. "If anyone has no reason to feel sorry, it's you, Jinx. I bruised your wrists. Ydum made you terrified. Anarus didn't really do anything, but in your head, that was the problem. We should be sorry. Jacob, Sam, the High Priest, and everyone else at that party should be sorry. You survived the best way you could. You do not need to be sorry for surviving."

"And you all don't need to be sorry for trying to help me continue surviving." I retort. "I didn't tell you. You couldn't know how bad it really is. You only knew bits and pieces. I should have made you understand before we did that so you knew what to expect."

I take a breath and drink my coffee for a moment. "But we have a bigger problem now. Now, everyone knows this is my weakness. If they somehow get us to fight against each other, the other teams may try to use this against me. It's more important than before that I figure out how to not panic when I feel trapped and be able to fight back."

Anarus looks up at me, his shadows loose and moving. "We are not doing that again."

"No." I agree. "Definitely not. But teaching me self-defense and how to break out of holds is something we definitely need to do."

"Do you think we can do that without tripping your panic again?" Ydum asks.

"We have to figure out how. If we don't, I die in the next game." I frown into the cup, not sure how we do both, teach me to escape being trapped while I panic and not letting me panic because I am trapped.

Byder nods. "You're right. We have to do it somehow. But the safe word idea didn't work. You panicked and forgot it. One of us needs to be the safe word, constantly monitoring how you feel and the moment you start panicking, call it off. I say Anarus since he's the most sensitive to your emotions. Unless you aren't sure about trusting him now, Jinx."

I look at Anarus. I wait a long time until he looks at me. "I trust you, Anarus. I still trust you."

"Why?" There's a pleading look in his eyes.

I move down on the floor next to him. "You came."

"Not quick enough."

"But you did come."

"Let's do this before I lose my nerve." Ydum stands up, rolling up his shirt sleeves to his elbows. He tries to put on the academic airs he wears when teaching things but only gets about halfway there. "Byder, I want to demonstrate with you, then we'll have Jinx try it."

"Sounds good to me." Byder says, standing with him. He takes out his hair tie and redoes the bun. It looks awful and he missed a few strands of hair, but I don't say anything.

Ydum sets Byder up gripping his wrist like Byder had done with me the day before, except in front of him. "If someone grabs your wrists, you want to make your wrists limp. Don't tense, Jinx. Then, twist your wrists towards their thumbs and pull your arms to cross your wrists as you pull back towards you." Ydum then demonstrates a few times.

"Come try it." Byder tells me. I stand up and hold out my wrists. Byder grimaces slightly when he sees the bruises already there peeking out of my shirt sleeves, but he takes my wrists in his hands. I try what Ydum did, but I can't break out.

"Don't stop trying." Ydum tells me. "If it doesn't work the first time, keep doing it over and over. Use your meditation skills to stay calm and keep your body loose, especially your wrists. If you tense, you can't move as well. The force should come from your shoulders, not your hands."

I try again and manage to twist my wrists in Byder's hands. "Good. Keep going. If you get movement, that means their grip is weaker. That gives you more leverage."

I keep twisting my wrists and, when Byder shifts his grip, I break free. "You loosened your grip."

"I did." Byder acknowledges. "But so would someone who wants to harm you. You move your wrists that much, they'll eventually need to adjust and, if you never stop trying, you can take advantage of that opening."

Ydum nods. "Take advantage of every opening, Jinx. You doing okay? Do you need a break or do you want to try again?"

"Try again." I tell him.

Ydum glances down at Anarus, who only says, "Determined, not scared."

"Okay. Do it again." Ydum instructs us. Byder takes my wrists again and it still takes several tries, but I break out faster. We try it a few more times until I have the motion down.

Ydum takes my place with Byder again to demonstrate. "Now, for when they put your wrists behind your back. Most of the time, when someone has your hands trapped behind your back, they will naturally cross the wrists, or at least hold them close together. Pull the wrists together and up your back." Ydum demonstrates again, letting me see it a few times, then has me take over and try it.

I try it several times before Anarus calls out. "Pain."

Both Byder and Ydum look at me. "My wrists hurt a little. I'm fine." I think they see the lie. My wrists are burning from the bruises and friction.

Byder drops my wrists immediately. "Okay. Moving on. We don't want you to hurt, Jinx."

"Next part." Ydum says. "Just because your wrists are caught, or not, doesn't stop you from using other parts of yourself to get away. Males are particularly vulnerable. I won't actually demonstrate because I like Byder, but if you can, connect something, anything with their groin. Pretty much any male will drop whatever part of you they have a hold on if you hit their balls. Come stand next to Byder and show me, without actually hitting, what you think you could do from each position."

I stand next to Byder and he holds me loosely from behind, then from the front and the side. Each time, I raise my knee or foot to show how I could move to hit Byder's most sensitive spot. Ydum approves the moves, then switches with Byder.

"I'm much taller." He says. "How would you do it now?"

We run through it again, and Byder helps me figure out different ways to move because Ydum is too tall for what I did to Byder.

"If they are short enough, like Byder," Ydum moves on, "remember your head. Your skull is hard. Their nose isn't. A quick head toss backwards, or forwards with your forehead, will give them a bloody nose and a huge burst of pain. But make sure you can reach with the hard parts of your head before you do it. If they are tall like me, you'll just aggravate them and give yourself a headache."

"For taller people, like Ydum, I would suggest dropping." Byder says. "Especially if you are facing away from them. Fall on your butt on purpose, then turn either right or left quickly. Do it fast because they may fall down too and you don't want them to land on you, pinning you to the ground. If you are facing them, it won't work as well, but dead weight is harder to hold up."

Ydum continues, the two males bouncing back and forth between them to either be the teacher or the practice, while Anarus continues just rubbing his hand and sensing my mood. "Teeth. Don't forget your teeth. Bite anything you can reach. If it's close to your mouth, bite and do not let go. Draw blood and keep biting. You only stop when their skin is in pieces in your mouth. Then, you spit out the skin and bite again."

"Whatever you do, make sure you know your next move before you do it." Byder says. "Know exactly, if you are successful of breaking their hold, how and where you are moving to so that you are away from their reach. Don't focus on where you can hit or fight them, but on getting away as fast as you can."

Once I feel comfortable with the basics, Ydum changes things up. He takes me through methods for if I'm pinned to the ground. He tells me how to pull my arms down, hitting their knees with my elbows while jerking up my hips to throw an attacker off balance. Then, he demonstrates how I flip them using their own weight to topple us until I am on top of the attacker. Then, again, he emphasizes that the goal is get away not fight.

He has me try with him a couple of times, then with Byder to know how to work the techniques differently depending on the attacker's height. I struggle a little with the way Byder's leather pants are slicker than Ydum's cotton ones. Ydum checks in with both me and Anarus often.

After having me try to escape Byder's pin unsuccessfully several times, Ydum asks Anarus how I feel, still worried I won't recognize my own limits before panic sets in.

Anarus chuckles. "She's not complaining about being under Byder like that."

"Anarus!" I yelp as I blush.

Anarus only smiles. "They said to say how you were feeling. Horny is a feeling."

"Oh, my gods." I blush.

"We told you, Jinx." Ydum says. "Get a new swear. That one is not appropriate anymore when you actually have gods." He laughs and tells us we should take a break because lunch is here.

After lunch, Byder brings out one of his knives and, with the sheath still on, we work on what to do with an armed attacker and how it changes things. Then, we work on how I hold and use the knife as well. We learned about how to punch, hitting with the right knuckles, in fight club but they review it with me and talk about when to try to punch and when not to.

After dinner, we head out to fight club. Ydum goes to stand with Esnir to lead it like normal, but there are murmurs moving through the group. Several people glare at him. I don't know who said it, but I hear someone whisper, "he attacked Jinx, why is he still here?"

Ydum looks at the ground, biting the inside of his lip and looks like he is going to leave.

I can't take it and growl loudly. "Alright. I'm going to clear this up, so listen. Ydum did not attack me. Byder did not attack me. No one attacked me. We were working on fighting skills and I had a panic attack about something that happened in my past. In the past. Long before I ever came to the games. It was not their fault and they all feel guilty enough about scaring me. You don't get to make it worse."

"There are bruises on your wrists, Jinx." Aretha says. "They hurt you."

"And sparring is dangerous." I repeat Anarus's words. "Accidents happen when you spar. Especially when one of you isn't completely honest about your limits, like I wasn't. That one is on me, not any of them. Tell me, none of you have accidentally hurt each other practicing fighting techniques? I get to decide if I trust them, not you. I know I scared a lot of you when I was screaming, but that was me, not them. They did nothing wrong."

When mostly everyone seems unconvinced, I grumble. "Fuck it." I walk over and take Ydum's hand. I take him back to our room, with Anarus and Byder following behind us. "Fuck them."

I can feel Ydum's warring emotions. Guilt, fear, despondency, self-hate and I'm seething. "Stop. You did nothing wrong."

Ydum shakes his head, not looking at me. I have never seen him look as heartbroken as he does now. "It was my idea, and I should have stopped."

"There is only one person who gets to decide if your actions were wrong or bad, Ydum, and it isn't any of them." I poke a finger in the middle of his chest. "And it isn't you either. It's me, and I say you did nothing wrong. Are you going to take my control away from me and tell me what I should think now?"

This makes him look at me. His face is a bundle of confusion.

I nod, crossing my arms over my chest. "That's right. Saying you did something wrong is telling me how I should feel about something that happened to me. It happened to me. Me. That means I get to say how I feel about it, not you, not them. Trying to say otherwise is taking away my control again."

Our door creaks open slowly and Damek pokes his head in. "So, can we practice with you guys or do you need to have some time alone?"

"Absolutely!" I smile, knowing it probably comes off slightly feral, and move away from Ydum. "We are definitely still practicing, because I am fine," I shoot a look at Ydum, "and you are more than welcome, Damek. As long as you don't believe Ydum did anything wrong."

Damek holds the door wider. Iella, Isis and Esnir are all with him. "I'm not gonna say he didn't maybe make mistakes in how he attempted to train you, but that's a whole lot different than doing something wrong."

Iella nods. "Plus, we don't know the whole story, and don't need to, but without knowing everything, we don't have the right to comment."

"We came in at the middle of the crisis." Esnir says. "You can't judge off the middle of the crisis. I know Ydum felt awful and Byder and Anarus were beside themselves with worry. Whatever happened was not on purpose."

"Whose training the others if you are here, Esnir?" Byder asks.

"Don't know." Esnir shrugs. "Don't care. Now, are we getting to work or not? We have four days."

Ydum holds my eyes, his still showing pain. I go over to him and pull him away from the others, who are moving the table and creating space for the eight of us to work. I put a hand on his cheek. "I love you. I trust you."

Ydum's mouth twitches. "You hate me when I make you run."

"Then, and only then, do I hate you." I smile. "The rest of the time, I love you."

Ydum grabs me and pulls me close, burying his face in my hair. "I love you, Jinx."

"Hey, you two wanna stop canoodling and get over here?" Esnir yells out.

The next three days pass quickly in a flurry of fight training. Running and stretching first thing in the morning. Byder and Ydum working on my ability to escape being trapped with Anarus guarding my moods in the afternoon. After dinner, Esnir, Isis, Damek and Iella come to our room and Esnir puts us through our paces, pairing us up in different groups to gauge our techniques on different sized opponents.

I hold a slight bit of anger against Saffron, Aretha, Wren and Asteria. They never move to join our group and never try to even talk to me about what happened. Even though Ydum helped them so much with the fifth game, they still bear a grudge against him for something they think happened that never did. Raven is also not on our side of this divide between the teams, but she has had less contact with us, so I don't feel as bad about her. Plus, even if I'm angry with them, I don't want them to fail or die in the sixth game so Raven staying with the other group to teach them fighting skills is understandable.

On the fifth night, as I'm trying to break out of Damek's hold, we realize that none of us ever bothered to look at the paintings for this week. Damek is tall like Ydum, but bulky like Byder, so my normal techniques aren't working. He also has picked up on the male gods' habit of going shirtless now. He has me pinned against him, my back to his front, my arms crossed in front of me and his hands holding my wrists pulled back towards him. We had a discussion with the entire group that, if Anarus says stop while they are fighting with me, they are to stop and let go, backing away from me immediately, so Damek is glancing every so often at Anarus as he basically just stands there and I struggle to find a way to escape.

I'm not worried at all, just more frustrated I can't figure anything out. Especially since Damek keeps looking down at me with a curious expression and doesn't even seem to be trying, while I'm sweating and cursing. He's literally carrying on a conversation with Ydum and Esnir while I struggle. Without a shirt on, I can tell he's not even sweating. His chest at my back is completely dry.

"The sixth game is a free for all fight." He says. "Whatever game part there is, doesn't usually factor in to the planning as much, so it never occurred to me to think about the paintings. We know we'll all be going to the same place."

Ydum hums. "Sometimes the choice for six dictates what weapon you get. Or where you start in the game. It can have an impact, just not as much if you train right."

Finally frustrated enough to try anything, I lean forward so that I am hanging over my own arms, my full body weight pushing down on them to make Damek's grip loosen. But I lean too far over and end up losing my footing. My back legs lift from the ground and come up between his legs. I swing them wildly, trying to regain traction or tilt back and my foot swings up to hit Damek in the groin.

"Oof." Damek lets go of my wrists as he drops to his knees, clutching his groin. Because he let go while I was hanging half upside down, I can't catch myself and I slam to the ground on my shoulder and side, screaming as I jar hard enough to clack my teeth together and bite my tongue and lip.

Iella is by Damek's side in a flash and I am surrounded by Byder, Ydum, and Anarus.

"Ow!" I groan as Damek moans out a "Fuck!"

"Are you okay?" Iella asks both of us.

"I'll live. I hope you never wanted kids, Iella." Damek pants, his voice an octave higher than it normally is. "Jinx?"

I sit up and groan again, rubbing my right shoulder. I wipe my mouth and pull back my hand to find blood. "I'm bleeding."

"Let me see." Anarus makes me look at him. "You split your lip. Open." I open my mouth. "And bit the side of your tongue. Not too bad, but it'll hurt like shit."

"Split lips are Ydum's thing." I try to joke.

Ydum raises an eyebrow. "Did you hit your head, too?"

"No." As I try to talk, my teeth rub against my tongue and it hurts. "Ow, shit. It hurts to talk."

"Then, don't Jinx." Anarus grumbles. He has moved to inspecting my shoulder, trying to lift my arm and make me rotate it. "Shoulder is dislocated."

"That hurts." I tell him, sweat from the pain forming on my brow.

He glares at me. "You're talking."

"Well, how am I supposed to tell you it… Fuck!" I yank my arm from him as he pulls on my wrist and pain shoots up my arm, but that just makes my shoulder hurt worse. I hold my wrist against my chest, still swearing. "Fuck, that hurts."

Anarus sits back. "I think she broke her wrist too."

"Shit." Ydum looks over at Esnir. "Can you help?"

"Why Esnir?" I ask.

"War god, remember?" Isis says. "Soldiers need to be fixed quickly on a battlefield, so he can heal some. He helped me after you stitched me shut."

"Oh. Right." I shake my head then groan again as the movement jiggles my wrist and shoulder.

Esnir checks over Damek, helping him get to one of the couches. Once Damek is settled, and Esnir assured himself Damek's injuries are minor, he comes over and focuses to me. "Maybe we should check for a concussion too. Just in case." He looks in my eyes and tells me to follow his finger with my eyes. Then asks me to stand.

Anarus helps me by holding my left, uninjured arm and Ydum tries to help on my right, but brushes my injuries. "Fuck, shit, damn, balls, crap!"

Esnir laughs. "Yeah, that's broken. Come sit on the couch."

I make my way to the couch, realizing as I walk that my hip is probably bruised too. Once I sit, Esnir takes my wrist into his hands as gently as possible.

"It stings." Isis warns me before he starts.

I'm not sure if it felt differently for Isis because it was a cut instead of a broken bone, or if I'm a wimp, but Esnir's magic did not sting. It felt like a thousand hot knives being shoved into my already tender wrist. Anarus sits on my left and I bury my face into his shoulder, masking my screaming as I dig my nails from my good hand into his arm. I can feel the bones grinding together and want to throw up.

"Sorry. Sorry. I know it hurts. Almost done." Esnir keeps saying. After what feels like far too long, Esnir says he's done what he can. "I would still splint it for a bit, but the bone is fused now."

Iella comes over with two small wooden boards and, as I cling to Anarus again, uses strips of fabric to tie the boards on either side of my wrist, immobilizing it.

"Now that that's done, we can fix the shoulder." Esnir says. He looks at Anarus who nods at him.

"Look at me, Jinx." Anarus says. I do and he turns me sideways on the couch to face him completely. I feel Esnir stand to my right side and take my injured arm into his hands carefully. There is burning and pain as he moves it slightly, but I look at Anarus. Anarus takes my good hand in his and says, "Squeeze hard."

"Alright, Jinx. I'm going to pull on three." Esnir says. "One. Two." He yanks on my arm, hard.

"FUUCCKK!" I scream as the shoulder pops back into place. "You fucking liar. You said three."

"Works every time." Esnir laughs. I want to glower at him, but the shoulder pain is simmering down to just a burning ache, so I can't complain.

"I'm so sorry, Jinx." Damek is sitting on the other couch and is looking better. "I should have paid attention better."

I give him a weak chuckle. "I'm sorry too. Maybe I should have been more careful not to kick you in the balls while you were literally holding me up."

Ydum quips. "Well, it was an effective technique to get free. Not sure you could run away or fight after that, but you weren't trapped anymore."

"Can we go look at the paintings, now, please?" I ask the group. "Anything to distract me from how fucking bad this hurts."

We all walk to the hallway. Well, I slightly limp. Yeah, that hip hurts a lot now too. I'm a mess and we only have one more day until the game. In the hallway, the other teams are all breaking up after their fight club. I hear Aretha whisper as she passes me. "Oh look. Jinx has more bruises. I wonder which of her gods did it this time."

"It was Damek!" I yell after without stopping to consider that saying this helps the situation not at all. "Sparring!" I add as an afterthought.

Anarus comes over, his eyebrows raised at me.

"To think I used to like her." I grumble out, feeling all sorts of pissed off.

He just chuckles darkly. "Such a vicious little human."

The paintings, it turns out, are different weapons. There's two of a dagger, two of a sword, two bows and arrows, and two whips. It doesn't take long for me to become completely disinterested and remember the pain. I go back to our room and Ydum follows me.

"How hurt are you really?" He asks me once we're inside.

I tell him honestly. "I'm bad. I'm sorry. We're screwed, aren't we?"

"Depends what the game is, and how bad is bad." Ydum walks to the washroom and gestures for me to follow him. "Esnir said heat or ice on the sore muscles. Heat from a shower would be the easiest way."

I follow him into the washroom and, after stripping down to just his pants, Ydum helps me strip completely.

"Fuck." He says, looking over my body. There's a huge black and purple mark on my right hip. My right shoulder blade is definitely bruised, or so he tells me. And there's a long yellowing mark running down my right side by my ribs, evidence of an injury I didn't even feel. Add to that the semi-healed broken wrist, split lip and cut tongue and I'm a right mess.

"I'd say the floor won that fight." I try to make him smile. "I don't think I'll demand a rematch, though."

Ydum laughs despite himself. "Are you sure you didn't hit your head? You're never this silly."

"If I don't laugh, I'll cry, Ydum. We have to fight for our lives in two days and I'm already half broken because I was an idiot."

"Not an idiot." He turns on the hot water and as soon as it's warm, ushers me into the shower. "Keep the wrist dry. You did what we said to do. It just worked a lot better than you expected."

I step into the stream of water and groan immediately at how good it feels. Ydum comes into the shower with me and, as he tries to find a good way to help hold me up without touching my bruises, I drape my bad arm over his shoulder to keep the wrist dry. It hurts my shoulder to have my arm up like this, but I let the water beat on the muscles and it only throbs a little.

"How are you not on the floor in a puddle of tears, Jinx?" Ydum murmurs. "Everything must hurt."

"Me? Hurt?" I lay my head on his bare shoulder over the vines growing there. "I forgot I was. There's a very beautiful male holding me right now and it's a rather good distraction."

"Shit, Jinx." Ydum runs his fingers up and down my spine, sending shivers of desire running through me. "I'm trying to be good here and remember you're injured."

"You're failing miserably." I press my body against his and his wet pants cling to him, letting me feel exactly how badly he's failing. "Why don't you just forget being good and I'll forget anything hurts?"

I pull myself up on my tiptoes to kiss him and he groans.

"Do you know how many times I thought about fucking you in this shower that first week when we were all in here all the time?" Ydum asks me. He backs me up carefully until I am leaning against the back wall of the shower. "Tell me the first second it hurts."

"I promise to absolutely not tell you if anything hurts."

He groans. "Jinx, I'm serious."

I huff at him. "Why is it the one time I'm not serious, you are? Fine. I'll tell you. Just fuck me, Ydum." I press myself against him harder and he groans again.

"Shit." With one hand Ydum undoes the ties of his pants and pushes them down around his ankles, then sinks himself slowly inside me. "Fuck, you feel good."

He stays still, waiting, not moving and my body rebels against this, trying to move to make friction. "Gods, fuck. Move. Please, Ydum. Move, please."

"Begging, are you?" Ydum kisses me but still doesn't move inside me.

Tension builds inside me in anticipation. He's filling me but not moving and it's driving the need higher. "Yes. I'm begging. Please."

Ydum twitches inside me and I groan in frustration. I try to move but I am already standing on my toes in a slick shower with water running over both of us. I have no purchase to move with. Ydum has a wicked smile on his face and I groan again, my body trembling with need.

"If you're sure." He says slowly.

"I'm sure. I'm sure. Please." I wrap my arms tighter around his neck, clinging to him, but careful of my wrist.

"Okay, then, beautiful." Finally, finally, he moves. He goes from nothing to a hectic pace so fast, I nearly break apart from the start.

My breath is gone and I moan into his chest as my body reacts with fire everywhere. My entire being is pleasure instantly from the anticipation and swiftness of it all. As he moves, my insides tighten, pleasure twisting in me. He reaches a hand in between us and uses his thumb to trace circles on my clit, driving me even higher.

"Don't, don't stop." I groan as I feel myself fracture apart. I ride the waves of my orgasm over the edge but Ydum doesn't stop and before I can catch my breath, it starts building again.

He moves his hand down to pull up on my right hip and, for one second, pain rips through me. I yelp and he immediately drops my leg. "Fuck, sorry." But he doesn't stop the relentless pounding and the pain is forgotten almost immediately to be replaced with desperate need.

A second orgasm crashes through me, leaving me a trembling ball in his arms, moaning as all I can feel is the pulsing pleasure that won't let me down from its high. I feel Ydum tense as he spills inside me, gasping and out of breath as well.

"Shit, beautiful." He leans down and kisses me deeply.

When he pulls back, his green eyes are all I can see. "I love you, Ydum."

He smiles and pushes wet hair off my face. "I love you, Jinx. Can you stand?"

"I think so." Ydum slowly lets go of me and, once my legs prove they will support me, he steps out of his saturated pants, leaving them on the floor of the shower stall, turns off the water, and helps me out of the shower.

Then, he takes a huge towel and dries me off carefully before drying himself. He wraps me in the towel and cautiously lifts me into his arms to carry me to the bedroom. Ydum deposits me on my bed with a swift kiss. "I'll be right back."

I snuggle into the bed and wait, the pain from my multiple injuries far from my mind. I know they will hurt tomorrow but right now I don't care.

Ydum comes back and climbs in the bed with me, taking care as he wraps his arms around me.

"Where'd you go?" I ask him, sleepily.

"Clean up the bathroom. Sleep, Jinx." Ydum runs his fingers through my hair, but I roll over, groaning only slightly when it hurts, and trace his vines.

"I love these things, you know that?" I tell him. "I could spend days just tracing their movement."

Ydum just chuckles. "Sleep, Jinx."

In the morning, I regret nothing, but I'm a bundle of pain and it takes me multiple tries to get out of bed. I eventually relent and let Ydum help me up after he asks to help the fourth time. I struggle on clothes after examining my bruises, which all look far too colorful to be healthy.

"Face and back of shoulder are just as bad." Ydum tells me. I lift my bad arm slowly and see that the shoulder bruise has spread down my arm and groan.

"We are so screwed tomorrow." I mutter after taking another break while pulling up my pants.

When I finally make it to the sitting room, Ydum steers me right to the couch.

"But coffee." I whine.

"No coffee today." Byder tells me, handing me a mug of something. "Lemon and peppermint tea with rosehip, courtesy of Isis. She said it'll help the pain and swelling."

"How bad is it really?" Anarus asks me.

Ydum answers. "She's basically one solid bruise from shoulder to hip down her right side."

"Fuck." Anarus grumbles.

Esnir shows up, offering to try to heal me more. I argue, saying he needs to save his own strength for tomorrow, but it becomes five against one when Isis, Anarus, Ydum, and Byder all tell me to let him help me.

After he spends time applying the healing to my wrist and shoulder, which does only burn now, I try to be done with it, but Ydum tells him about the other injuries. Esnir insists I lift my shirt to show him my side, worried that I might have injured something internally. Once he's satisfied that it's just a bruise, he continues applying a healing on my side down to my hip.

I have to admit that the healing helps and the amount of pain I feel when I move gets dramatically less.

"I'm not going to be able to get you perfect before tomorrow, but at least we can take off the edge." Esnir tells me when he's done.

"I appreciate it, Esnir." I know he didn't have to do any of this and he could be wasting energy he needs for tomorrow. My gods don't let me move beyond that, telling me I need to rest and let them worry over me.

At lunch, Damek brings me another tea, made from his grandmother's special blend that's supposedly a cure-all.

"I am so sorry, Jinx." He tells me. "You look like shit and it's sort of my fault."

"We are equally to blame. How are you?" I say.

"Walking a little crooked but I'll be fine." He says teasingly. "You got a good kick in there."

Damek's grandmother's tea makes me fall asleep on the couch, and when I wake up for dinner, I do feel significantly better. After dinner, Esnir comes again, and I don't fight it. When four gods and a witch glare at you, you do what they say.

As I try to relax from the burn of the healing, I talk to my gods. "We know it will be me and Ydum, but we still never decided on a painting."

Byder answers. "Probably dagger. I don't know if the painting decides what weapon you can bring or what weapon the game will give you, but you are both strapping up with my daggers either way. More won't hurt, but if it's just what you're allowed to bring, you're covered."

"Is there anything else we've ignored about this game that could matter?" I ask. "It's called strength and combat, but we have mostly focused on the combat part. Could we be missing anything?"

Ydum shakes his head. "I don't think so. Not really. Anything the game throws in there beyond the fighting is stuff that there's no way to prepare for. Stuff like getting a flag from the top of a bunch of steps or running to a certain point."

Anarus agrees. "Even going further back than the traditional manuals go, the sixth game has always been about taking out as many of the other teams as possible. Injury and death are the purpose."

I'm confused. "How do they convince us to fight if the game is so simple?"

Ydum sighs. "That's what confuses me. I asked my parents and they said you just do. You just fight. They tell you to and you do, and don't even realize you didn't actually need to until after it's all said and done."

"That's what mine said too." Byder adds. "You just will fight and will know you need to fight."

I sit listening and find myself frustrated by this explanation. We can't have been the first group of teams to get along like this. Even if the other years didn't do as much to help each other, they knew each other, or at least the gods did, for years before the games. They were friends or friendly. How are the games able to just convince everyone to want to harm people they have known for years, or been through so much with?

As I think about this, it occurs to me that it's odd that, right before the combat game, Aretha suddenly chooses not to work against the original gods and the games. We were fine. We were all fine. Sure, I screamed and cried and scared them all. But why does me telling them what happened, what actually happened, not seem to change how they feel? Why are they still blaming Ydum? And it isn't even just the other humans, but their gods too. Gods who, just a week ago, loved Ydum and thought he was great for helping them.

I go to sleep worrying over this and wake to feeling better. My bruises are still there but much further on the healing path than they would be naturally. As I get out of the bed, I roll my shoulder and flex my wrist. Sore, a little tender, but not too bad if I'm careful. Today is the sixth game, the combat game. and chances are we are not all coming home. These games the gods are making us play have been dangerous, but none as dangerous as today. I take a deep breath and steel my spine. Today we fight, not the gods we want to, but the gods we are being forced to. And I have no idea how I will stop myself from having to kill my friends.

Acknowledgements

There are so many people who help an author writing their book. I want to start with the most important person. My husband/muse, Brent. Thank you for reminding me to eat, for making me gallons and gallons of coffee, for listening to me ramble on and on about people who only live inside my head, and well, now on paper. Thanks for lunch. Had you not refused to take me to get food until I finally screwed up my courage and actually applied to college, I don't know that any of this would have happened. I know the dream changed a lot during those years studying for my bachelor's, then my master's, but you stuck by me through it all, spent Valentine's Day going over flashcards to help me study for a big test, and cooked a million dinners after working all day because I really, really just needed to get done that one scene. You also never teased me when I blushed and laughed my way through reading you those fun spicy scenes, so thank you. I love you more than words. Maybe more than Anarus loves Jinx.

To my friends, and friends of friends, who helped by reading this and telling me what was good, bad, and ugly, I cannot express how much I appreciate you. Shoshana Kronfeld, you are the best big sister ever. Not many people would be down to read spicy scenes written by their baby sister. Especially when said sister is, in your words, "the queen of cliff-hangers." Sorry, not sorry.

Heather Douglas, every single "Unsolicited Editing Comment" was great. It made me feel good every time you put one of those "this was funny" comments in too. Also, the fact that this is a trilogy instead of a duology is entirely your fault. Thanks!

To all the others who read this for me, you know who you are and I appreciate all of the advice and support.

To my children, who will never read this because, in Daniel's words, "Ew, I cannot read... that stuff... when my mom wrote it," thank you for being so understanding and supportive. I am proud of each and every one of you, every single day. I hope I have made you proud I am your mother. Even if I do write... that stuff...

Mom, who also will never read this, I love you. I know you said this would be one of my books you buy, display on your shelf, but never read, because you knew to stop at the trigger warning page like I suggested. But just in case you get really bored one day, I just want to say it. I'm glad you're my mom.

Finally, thank you to everyone taking a chance on a new author and reading this. I hope you enjoyed it as much as I do. The 375th Gods Games will finish in the next book, *When the Gods Learn Lies*, where our favorite foursome will battle for their mantles, survival, and the truth. Then, we will see what happens when they learn that truth in *When the Gods Wage War*. See you then!

About the Author

Kefira Zink is an author from a little town in Michigan. She has a bachelor's degree in Sociology from Arizona State University and a master's degree in Sociology, with a specialty in Religion and Deviance from American Public University. She loves buying books, especially rescuing old books and giving them a loving home as well as reading books (which any reader will tell you, buying books and reading them are two very different hobbies). She is married to her wonderful husband/muse and together they have six grown children, two cats, a dog that thinks it is a cat, and a lizard that thinks it is a dinosaur.

Connect With The Author

Website: https://sites.google.com/view/kefira-zink-author
Email: kefirazinkauthor@gmail.com
Facebook: Kefira Zink Author
TikTok: kefira_zink_author

www.ingramcontent.com/pod-product-compliance
Lightning Source LLC
Chambersburg PA
CBHW030139180626
46812CB00002B/766